$\mathcal{V}$OICES OF THE $\mathcal{S}$OUTH

Where the Dreams Cross

Where
the Dreams Cross

ELLEN DOUGLAS

LOUISIANA STATE UNIVERSITY PRESS
BATON ROUGE

Originally published by Houghton Miffin Company
LSU Press edition published 2000 by arrangement with the author
Manufactured in the United States of America

09 08 07 06 05 04 03 02 01 00
5 4 3 2 1

Library of Congress Cataloging-in-Publication Data

Douglas, Ellen, 1921–
    Where the dreams cross / Ellen Douglas.
        p.   cm. — (Voices of the South)
    Originally published: Houghton Mifflin, 1968.
    ISBN 0-8071-2639-X (paper)
      1. Women—Southern States—Fiction. 2. Southern States—Fiction. I Title.
    II. Series.
    PS3554.O825 W48 2000
    813'.54—dc21
                                                                00-058169

The paper in this book meets the guidelines for permanence and durability of
the Committee on Production Guidelines for Book Longevity of the Council on
Library Resources. ∞

For Kenneth

"All of us, among the ruins, are preparing
a renaissance beyond the limits of nihilism.
But few of us know it."

— Camus, *The Rebel*

Where the Dreams Cross

1

OCCASIONALLY — sometimes twice in a year, sometimes not for two or three years — Nat Stonebridge (Nat Hunter, she was before she married.) comes home to Philippi for a visit. No one ever knows how long she will stay. She may be in town overnight or for a week or a month. Once she rented an apartment, entered her son, Hunter, in school, and stayed all winter. As it turned out, she was establishing residence for a divorce. But she changed her mind before the year was out and went back to her husband, at least for a time. Eventually she did get a divorce — but not in Philippi.

Very few people in Philippi know or care when Nat comes or when she goes. There are some, it's true, who remember the years when she was the talk of the Mississippi Delta and her reputation was known in certain circles from Vanderbilt and Sewanee all the way down the college circuit to Tulane; but even these have probably not thought of her for a long time. As for the rest, they may never have heard of her. Many of them are new to the Delta; they have come from other parts of Mississippi (or even from faraway places like New York and California) since the Consolidated Paper Company and International Screw and Valve put in their plants in the late forties. They know next to nothing of the small and placid river town that Nat left early in 1946.

It is true, too, that Nat might not be remembered even by some people who have always lived in Philippi — girls and boys who were a class or two behind or ahead of her all the way through grammar school. (She did not go to public high school, but boarded at Miss Howell's Episcopal Academy in Port Wilson, where her aunt, Miss Louise Hunter, felt she would benefit from what the school catalog called the "strict moral climate," as well as the "congenial companionship of other young ladies, and the atmosphere of intellectual stimulation.") The schoolmates that Nat left behind in Philippi were, many of them, from families that Miss Louise would have referred to as "plain people." (The Hunters feel that it is "common" to call people "common.") A great many of them, now, can no longer be called plain by anybody. They have been alert to opportunity and, taking advantage of the convulsion in community life caused by the Second World War and the years of prosperity afterwards, have climbed out of poverty and obscurity into middle-class affluence. In the late forties they began to build sprawling ranch houses with family rooms and conversation pits; they joined the Yacht Club, the Rotary Club, the Country Club, and, in many cases, as a last step in the right direction, the Episcopal Church. Now they associate absentmindedly, if at all, with people like the Hunters who no longer have much money and who cherish the old-fashioned notion that it is vulgar to have one's parties written up in the local newspaper.

Take, for example, the lady who is president of Philippi's exclusive new study club, "Les Pensées," organized in 1946. Of her Miss Louise Hunter says, "Why, I can remember when her mama ran off with a circus clown. That's why she named her

Marigold, you know." (Not that Miss Louise would say this to any except female members of her own family. She is sure such subjects are better ignored, except as horrible examples; and it is only with difficulty that even a female relative can extract from her the connection between running off with a circus clown and naming a child Marigold.) "Well," she finally says, lowering her voice to a confidential whisper, "they *say* it was a year when the circus came early and the marigolds were still blooming, you know, and, well, they *say* she was conceived among the marigolds. I mean, outdoors. In the *backyard*. Anyhow, she never did marry him. The clown, I mean. And she came back to Philippi and brought Marigold and never made any explanation regarding what had happened. But," she adds, "Marigold has done well for herself. She was always a clever girl and she made a good marriage. There's nothing wrong with the Shotwell family. Old county stock. And Morris, of course, is quite well-to-do. I must say, though, that the clown pops out sometimes. Her face powder is entirely too white. And when she puts on one of those ridiculous, tall, twisted hats of hers and paints her mouth with that wide grin — really!"

Miss Louise is not a member of "Les Pensées." She belongs to another study club, "Blue Stockings," of which there are now only nine surviving members, all from pioneer county families, and all ladies in their sixties or older. This group had a series of programs a few years ago on British and Scottish royalty. One of the best talks, on Mary, Queen of Scots, was made by a lady who claims descent from Charlemagne by way of Robert the Bruce, and thus a collateral connection with Mary herself. Miss Louise suggested that, since there was a blood tie with an old Mississippi family, they submit this paper for publication in the *Journal of the Mississippi Historical Society*; but, as she afterwards wrote Nat, it was turned down by an ignorant editor (not even a native Mississippian), who then devoted practically the entire winter issue to a notorious carpetbagger from Yazoo City named Charles Morgan — a man who was married to a Negro!

When one of Nat's visits to Philippi lasts longer than a few days, it sometimes happens that a young matron — a girl with whom Nat grew up, to whose birthday parties she was once dragged, bored and sullen, in white silk socks, Roman sandals, and smocked voile party dress — would see her on the street, recognize her, and report at the next meeting of the Thursday Bridge Club, "Nat Stonebridge is in town."

"Who?" one of the newcomers to Philippi asks.

"Nat Stonebridge — Hunter, she was."

"Who's that?"

"You mean you never heard of Nat Hunter? But she must have been at Ole Miss at the same time you were at Newcomb. Surely you remember . . . !"

"Oh. Nat *Hunter*. Of course I've heard of her. I even met her once — at an Ole Miss-Tulane game in, let's see, forty? Forty-one? We were all at Pat O'Brien's and . . . Well, that's a long story, but anyhow, I didn't know she was from Philippi."

"Yes, she's *from* here, all right."

"What does that mean?" another of the women will say. "Sounds like a scandal."

"No. Just that she's a wanderer, I reckon. And goodness knows how she'd fare if she ever came back for good. She . . ."

Then: "Nat Hunter! Isn't she the girl who fell off the bluff at Natchez?"

"That's Nat all right."

"Well, I've heard about her all my life from my brothers, but I thought she was a myth."

"I never understood why everyone used to go on so about Nat." The woman who spoke was a motherly-looking mouse-blonde with pale blue eyes. "If nobody paid any attention to people like Nat," she said, "they wouldn't always be flaunting themselves. I saw her, too, as a matter of fact — in the A & P — but I pretended not to. The children were with me and I didn't want them thinking I knew anybody who dressed like that. She had on a pair of boy's blue jeans that looked like she'd been poured into them, and a bare midriff shirt — at her age!"

"Then she hasn't lost her figure? I heard last year she'd been drinking. It runs in that family, you know."

At this point, if Sunny Griffith is present, she will break in and bring the conversation to an end. "I was at Ole Miss with Nat and I liked her. I don't mean I knew her very well then. She was a senior and I was a freshman. But there was something about her . . . Maybe, in a way, her girlhood *is* a myth — a myth of what it was like around here when we were young and poor and carefree and — irresistible."

"Well, really, Sunny. She's not my ideal, and never was," the mouse-blonde says. "You can have her."

"I didn't say anything about ideal. I just said what it was like. Anyhow, she's Wilburn's cousin and I know her better now. And I still like her."

"What it was like for Nat has nothing to do with what it was like . . ."

"Come on, girls, let poor Nat alone. After all, in some ways she's had a rough time. She's divorced now, you know, and I heard she lost custody of the child on account of her reputation. And they say her ex-husband isn't exactly a model of charm and virtue."

"I *said* she's Wilburn's *cousin*," Sunny repeats.

"Let's play cards. The afternoon is half over."

"Whose bid is it?"

"Two spades."

"Partner! You're opening! *Two?*"

"That's what I said."

It would not occur to any of these women, even the one or two who once knew her well, to have a tea or a luncheon at the country club for Nat — although they plan parties for other women who have married and moved away from Philippi and who occasionally come home for a visit. Not that Nat appears to notice. She may call one or two old friends (male) when she comes to town, and sometimes, if she stays long enough, she meets new and surprising people; but usually she makes no effort to see anyone other than her family — reduced now to the aunt and uncle who raised her, a sister in nearby Moss Ridge, her cousin, Wilburn Griffith, and a few elderly connections on whom her aunt insists she call.

. . .

To Miss Louise Hunter, Nat's visits, like those of everyone else in the family, are always resolved into terms of food. Even in the lowest days of the Depression, when she sometimes couldn't pay the cook, Miss Louise set a lavish table. One might say, in a paraphrase of the Sunday school song, that to her Food is Love. On a spring Sunday, sitting down after church to a dinner of fresh green peas, buttered rice, boiled spring chicken, hot biscuits with scuppernong jelly, and strawberry shortcake, one can scarcely believe there is better food anywhere. Miss Louise's Lady Baltimore cakes and dewberry cobblers are famous throughout the Delta; and she is one of the few people left in Mississippi who still know where the wild muscadines grow and how to prepare the tiny delicate river shrimp that run in June and July. She has a recipe for oysters Rockefeller as good as Galatoire's, and everybody in Philippi follows her directions for making okra gumbo and jambalaya.

Miss Louise's husband, Aubrey, a wiry little old man with a tiny beaked nose and round eyes like a screech owl's, eats voraciously of all this plenty; but he looks, all the same, as if he has never had enough to eat in his life.

"My metabolic rate is unusually high," he says, speaking of himself with proprietary pride, as one might of a powerful and finely tuned engine that burns a great deal of fuel and produces a mighty thrust.

Anne Farish, Nat's sister, is an eater, too, and gains at least five pounds every time she comes to visit the Hunters. But Nat has always watched her figure. Miss Louise can never reconcile herself to Nat's diets. It's possible she thinks that all Nat's problems would be solved if she would put on some weight and quit wearing her belts so tight.

"At any rate," she says to Anne Farish or Aubrey or anyone who will listen, "she would certainly be less nervous, if she ate more and put a little meat on her bones."

Whenever she hears that Nat is coming for a visit, Miss Louise goes to the kitchen to talk things over with Clakey Morrison, who has been cooking for the Hunters since 1925. "It's not too late to get a turkey," she'll say. "If we order one this afternoon and leave it out overnight, it'll be thawed in time to stuff in the morning. And . . ."

Miss Louise toddles with ladylike steps through the kitchen and into the pantry, while Clakey sits at the kitchen table, a weary-looking Negro woman whose dark face is pitted with smallpox scars and whose wide mouth, held firmly closed, has on it a habitual expression of austere reserve. In the presence of her composure, Miss Louise looks by contrast like an oversized but still timid white mouse.

"Look, Clakey." She comes out of the pantry. "Here's a jar of last summer's fig preserves. I believe they're the prettiest we've ever made." She holds them up to the light from the kitchen window, and together she and Clakey admire the perfectly-shaped, amber figs, the thin wheels of yellow lemon and brown cinnamon sticks suspended in a clear amber syrup. "Yes, I believe they're our

very best. And they're Nat's favorites, aren't they, Clakey? Do
you remember? Or is it Anne Farish? Anyhow, we gave Anne
Farish half a dozen jars when we put them up last summer, so
let's open these for Nat. And, let's see. We can't live on fig preserves and turkey, after all. You can bake a squash casserole. Isn't
that one of Nat's favorites?"

"No'm. She don't care for squash casserole. Never did. And
you know she never did have no sweet tooth. You might as well
not waste fig preserves on Nat. Grits. Mustard greens and corn
bread." Clakey allows herself a smile. "Nat eats like us niggers,"
she says. "Collard greens — she loves 'em. Sweet potatoes, if she
ain't dieting. That's what she likes. Fresh dewberries — coming
in this week. Old Man Carter passed the house yesterday, says
he'll bring you some Friday."

"*Miss* Nat," Miss Louise says. "She never ate collard greens at
my table. They're too coarse for me. And you know she likes
squash casserole. Everybody likes *your* squash casserole. And a
caramel cake. Tomorrow afternoon I'll make her one. I know
very well that caramel is Nat's favorite."

"Yes'm. You fix her a cake, Miss Louise. Mr. Aubrey'll like
that."

It's true that Nat used to like caramel cake when she was a
little girl. It was one of the few sweets she would eat. "I may not
remember some things," Miss Louise says, "but I certainly remember that."

And so, year after year, on the day of Nat's expected arrival,
while Clakey on one side of the kitchen table chops celery and
onions and pecans and oysters for the corn bread dressing, Miss
Louise on the other stirs the batter for her cake, folding in the
glossy, stiffly-beaten egg whites with skillful caution, sliding the
pans gently into the oven, taking them out when the cake is exactly the right shade of brown and springs back to the touch; and

at the last moment, after just the right amount of beating, spreading the golden icing in decorative swirls on the top and sides.

At dinner, after the plates are cleared away, Clakey brings it to the table and sets it in front of her, and she says in her reedy little southern voice, "Here it is, Nat. You see, I haven't forgotten. I still know exactly what you like." And she cuts the first slice and passes it to her niece, holding the dessert plate out with both hands, as if for a blessing. It might be a kind of familial host which will effect some miraculous purification and restoration of innocence in them all.

2

Miss Louise was in the kitchen baking her cake the afternoon of Nat's expected arrival one September day in the middle 1950's.

"Well, Clakey, she ought to be here any minute now," she said. "It's past two o'clock, and she said on the phone last night . . . It was after nine when she called, and it put me in a pinch for supper tonight. If Aubrey hadn't happened to stop by the Shotwells' — you know, this year Morris has a garden, so he gave Aubrey the most beautiful tomatoes, the last ones of the season, I reckon (I never knew Morris Shotwell to be so open-handed; it was like a gift from heaven.), and some nice greens, little bitty new ones — you saw them on the back porch. You can wash them and put them in the icebox for tomorrow. I'm just going to have a cheese soufflé tonight, and salad. Stuffed tomatoes. I suppose she may have stopped in Meridian to see Charley Boy Winter and his wife. And if they're having a good time, Nat may stay overnight. It doesn't really . . ."

She broke off and, with her tongue caught between her teeth, carried the cake tins one at a time across the kitchen and put them in the oven.

"I'll be glad to see Nat," Clakey said. "It's been a long time since she's been here." She sighed. "I naturally miss her," she said. "She does liven things up."

"Step lightly, Clakey," Miss Louise said. "Modify that heavy tread of yours, or my cake will fall."

"Yes'm," Clakey said.

"It doesn't matter, really, if she stays overnight," Miss Louise said. "She always says the icing is better the second day." She sat down at the kitchen table, brushed a strand of fine yellowish-white hair back from her face, and began to break pecans into a measuring cup.

"Mr. Aubrey'll be glad to see that cake," Clakey said.

"It's for *Nat*," Miss Louise said. She looked sternly at Clakey, as if daring her to contradict. Her square, slightly dished face with its determined jutting chin should have been strong and threatening, but some flaw — perhaps the childishness of the deep-set, pale blue eyes, perhaps a shadow of uncertainty around the thin mouth — marred its force.

Clakey's dark pocked face was intent on her work, as she trussed the turkey's legs with a strong jerk. When she had finished, she glanced contemptuously at Miss Louise. Then, with one shoulder raised and her chin tucked down, she made the parody of a cringe and said, "Yes'm, but I *know* Nat . . ."

The telephone rang.

"There she is," Miss Louise said. "I'm not surprised. She's probably staying in Meridian."

Clakey picked up the phone from its hook on the wall beside her. "Mrs. Hunter's residence . . . It's for you, Miss Louise. Long distance."

"I told you. What did I say? Is it Nat?"

"Is that Miss Nat Stonebridge calling?" Clakey said into the phone. And then, "The operator says nemmine who it is. Are you at home?"

Miss Louise went to the telephone. "Well . . . Yes, I'm Mrs. Aubrey Hunter . . . Yes, I suppose so, Operator, if she hasn't any money. Doesn't she have any money . . . *Well*, you needn't be so snippy about it. All right, put her on . . . Nat . . . What in the world, Nat, dear? You're supposed to be here right now. Where are you? I'm baking a cake for you."

. . .

At the other end of the line, Nat sat beside the desk in the office of the sheriff of Catalpa County, Alabama. Ten feet or more above her head, hanging from the vaulted ceiling, a fan turned slowly and stirred the warm September air, blowing her dark hair across her face and rustling the papers on the desk. Behind her, pigeons walked in and out through an open window and kept up a dreamlike watery cooing and gurgling. A broken screen leaned against the wall by the window, and along the opposite wall stood a row of rusty filing cases. Except for the desk and two straight-backed chairs, the office was empty — a huge, bare, echoing chamber that might once have been an auditorium or a court-room. One long wall was covered with a peeling mural — Doric columns, tapestries, and smoking censers in the style of David, from among which the stiff figures of Roman senators stared fixedly out into the room. One was pointing at Nat — or perhaps at the sheriff, since he usually sat at the desk.

Three men stood in the high double doorway that opened from the sheriff's office into a smaller anteroom where his secretary had her desk: one in the uniform of a highway patrolman; one in a rumpled seersucker suit with a star on the pocket; the third, a deputy, in khaki pants and a sweat-stained khaki shirt. All three were looking at Nat. A tiny bubble of saliva trembled and glowed like an opal in the corner of the deputy's mouth. He licked it away and rubbed his hands absently up and down the legs of his pants. The patrolman said something to the sheriff in a low voice and the sheriff nodded his head slowly without taking his eyes off Nat. She smiled uncertainly but reassuringly at them all, as if to say, "I don't know what you think of me, but wait, you'll see — I'm harmless." Then she crossed her legs at the ankles, braced the telephone receiver between cheek and shoulder, and rummaged through her purse for a cigarette. A visible tremor shook her hands as she put the cigarette into her mouth and looked at the three men with an expectant smile. All three responded, but the deputy got there first and lit her cigarette with a kitchen match, while the sheriff had to put away his gold-plated cigarette lighter. The men continued to stare at her while she talked.

And no wonder. She was a sight such as seldom appears in the office of the sheriff of Catalpa County. At thirty-six she still had the figure that had made her a legend at seventeen (when the math professor at Miss Howell's Episcopal Academy had tried to persuade her to run away with him to South America) — long tanned legs with small elegant knees and ankles, small high breasts above a flat stomach, tiny waist, and round hips. ("Not a brick out of place," had been the caption under a picture of her in a college humor magazine back in 1940.) Today, to drive all day through the heat of late summer, she had on a pair of brief white shorts, a boy's white shirt with the sleeves rolled up and the tail tied around her waist, and brown thong sandals on slender, scarlet-tipped, bare feet. Her fine thick hair, dyed a shining black, hung loose almost to her shoulders, curving under smoothly at the tips. Her green-flecked hazel eyes (She had always thought they were too small.) were carefully made up with too much eye shadow and mascara. From her figure, she might have been twenty-five, but her face, haggard, netted with sun wrinkles from too many hours on too many beaches, with puffs of dissipation under the eyes and downward lines from the strong hawk nose to the wide mouth, gave her age away. Striking, she was, in a sexy, but at the same time almost ugly way — any man could see that. But she was no spring chicken. That was what the highway patrolman had whispered to the sheriff.

"Well, that's nice, Aunt Louise," Nat said. The hair rose along the deputy's forearms. He was an emotional man and Nat's voice was low and gentle. "A cake!" She paused. "Caramel! Well, don't eat it up before I get there. . . . No. No, I'll be there tonight. I just called to tell you — I was afraid you might be worried about me." Another pause. "Yes, but listen to me, Aunt Louise; that's what I'm trying to tell you — I'm in jail." Nat giggled. "*Jail.* Don't get excited now. It's all right. I didn't do anything bad . . . No, *listen.* I was just riding along the highway drinking a can of beer and . . . Yes, beer. And this nice patrolman . . ." Here Nat looked over at the patrolman and nodded kindly at him again. ". . . drove up and made me pull over to the side of the road, and, can you imagine! You can't drink even *one* can of beer if you're driving a car in Alabama. Is that true in Mississippi, too? And they have to take you away to the nearest county seat and even if you're not drunk, you have to stay in jail for six hours. Isn't that ridiculous? And they have this charge called Driving While Drinking, so of course I'll have to pay a fine, and I didn't have all that much money with me, and that's why I had to call you collect . . . It's Catalpa County." Nat took the receiver away from her ear. "Please," she said, "could you tell me the name of this town? I probably ought to know, but not being on the main highway and all, I don't believe I've ever been through here before . . . It's Greensboro, Aunt Louise, and it's a nice

little old town. *Old.* Kind of like Woodville, you know, with lots
of trees and . . . No, I don't know anybody here, and besides, I
couldn't look them up, anyway. I'm in *jail* . . . They do?
Well, yes, I remember when they used to visit their grandmother, but . . . No, I can't; I just called because you were expecting me around one or two, and it's already two, and I can't possibly get to Philippi before eleven tonight, and I knew you would
think I had had a wreck or something . . . What? Well, I've
got on shorts, naturally. What else would I be wearing in this
kind of weather? Now, don't cry, Aunt Louise. Be sensible. Nobody is going to think *anything* about it. Who cares whether I'm
in jail or not, or what I have on? Besides, it's a nice jail. You ought
to see this old courthouse. It's prettier than the one in Philippi.
Like in a picture show or something. It has white columns across
the front and back, and a cupola on top; and you ought to see the
pigeons — flocks of them!" She smiled at the sheriff and covered
the mouthpiece with her hand. "My *aunt*," she said. "She's worried about me. Maybe you could tell her how nice it is here and
how good you've been to me. Listen, Aunt Louise, the sheriff wants
to talk to you."

The sheriff cautiously took the telephone from Nat and held
it an inch or so from his ear. He was a short, swarthy, heavy-set
man with a roached mane of white hair, and he had the uncertain
look in his eyes of a henpecked husband. "M'am," he said into
the telephone, "this is Jo Sam Ventura, sheriff of Catalpa County,
Alabama. Your dau —— your niece is sitting right here in my
office, m'am, and she wants me to tell you she's all right."

At this point two Negro men came through the door and walked
noiselessly across the room; they were dressed in the striped uniforms of convicts and each one carried a case of whiskey.

"My goodness," Nat said to the deputy, "you all must be planning to have a party."

"Stack it in the corner, Newsy," the deputy said. "No, m'am. This is a dry county, and that's confiscated whiskey."

"Yes, m'am," the sheriff was saying into the telephone. "We'll take good care of her. Don't you worry about her for a minute."

The Negroes went out and came in with two more cases.

"My goodness," Nat said. "Virginia Gentleman! And Jack Daniels! But I really don't like a sour mash whiskey, do you?"

The deputy stayed where he was at the opposite end of the room from Nat. He raised his voice slightly and gave her a serious look. "I like it better than regular bourbon, myself," he said. "I've noticed that men are more partial to a sour mash whiskey than women." He was a thin, sandy-haired, middle-aged man with the leathery skin of a farmer and hunter.

The patrolman crossed the room to the sheriff's desk. "Jo Sam," he said, "I got to get back on the road. I can't stay here all afternoon."

"M'am," the sheriff said, "I got some people here in my office. If you'll excuse me . . ."

"Are you going to put me in a cell?" Nat said to the deputy. "I wish you wouldn't, if you don't mind. I kind of have a slight case of claustrophobia."

"If you're sick, miss, we can call a doctor," the deputy said, "but I reckon we'll have to put you in the cell. The law says we got to lock you up for a while. You ought not to been drinking that beer."

"I just feel kind of queer," Nat said. "I don't think I need a doctor. But there's this other thing, too, like, well, little bitty places scare me. You know how some people don't like to ride on an elevator?"

"Yeah," the deputy said. "I got a cousin like that. A elevator fell two floors with him one time in Birmingham and broke both his ankles."

Nat shifted in her chair, uncrossed her legs, crossed them again at the knee, and swung her foot nervously until, as if conscious of inviting sympathy, she abruptly stopped and put the offending foot flat on the floor. She put out the cigarette she had been smoking and got another from her purse. The deputy crossed the room and lit it for her; she held it between trembling fingers and took a long drag. "I'm not really scared or anything," she said. "My hands just tremble, that's all. It runs in our family."

"How about a cup of coffee, miss?" the deputy said.

"That would be nice," Nat said.

"Yes, lady," the sheriff said into the telephone, "I know Judge Wright. But this case ain't going to come up in federal court."

"Aunt Louise is just ridiculous," Nat said to the patrolman who was still standing by the door and had begun to swing his key chain impatiently. "Maybe I can get her to hang up." She smiled at the sheriff. "Thank you so much, Mr. Ventura," she said. "I know my aunt feels better now." She took the telephone. "Aunt Louise? The sheriff just had to go arrest somebody. He said tell you to excuse the interruption. Now you've got to hang up. You're paying for the call, you know. Just don't worry about me. Wasn't the sheriff nice? And I'll be home about twelve or twelve-thirty. I don't want to drive too fast. I might get arrested again.

". . . Go to bed. Don't stay up for me. Leave the front door open . . . It doesn't make any difference to me *what* you tell Uncle Aubrey. You can make something up, if it'll make you feel any better . . . Well, all right, tell him the truth, if you don't want to lie . . . Aunt Louise, I'm *thirty-six years old.* Remember? Relax! Good-bye . . . I said, good-bye, dear. Good-bye." She sighed and hung up. "I could have talked a long time and put off going to that cell, but she *is* paying for it," she said to the sheriff.

"It's none of my business, lady," the sheriff said, "but why did you tell her you were in jail? Why didn't you say your car had broken down?"

Nat looked startled. "I never thought of that," she said. "I reckon I was excited about being in jail for the first time and all, and I thought she'd be interested."

The deputy came in with Nat's coffee; the patrolman finished his business with the sheriff and left; the trusties came in and out with more whiskey; and Nat sat quietly by the sheriff's desk, looking at the Roman senators and drinking her coffee.

The sheriff left the office for a few minutes, came back, sat down behind his desk, and began looking through a stack of papers.

"I was telling your assistant that I have . . . I have this kind of *thing* that makes me scared of being shut up in little bitty places," Nat said.

"Yes'm," the sheriff said. "Dwight, how many cases whiskey you all get out at Old Man Cartwright's?"

"Not much. Eight cases bourbon, two cases Scotch, five of gin, five of Mogen David. Half a case of Southern Comfort and ten gallons of Dago red. He's been keeping most of his stuff loaded in that old hearse parked back of his place. Drives off as soon as he hears we're coming — *somebody's* tipping him off, if you ask me."

"Yes, I know all that, Dwight, but it looks to me like you're short a case of bourbon here, and . . ."

"I better put this lady in her cell, if you want to talk business," the deputy said. "Come on, lady. I'll stay with you a few minutes until you get used to it."

Nat stood up, hitched her shirt a little higher and tighter around her waist, so that a band of tanned skin showed between shorts and shirt, and walked slowly across the room. She was tall, at least five-eight, and she moved with the easy, loose-jointed stride of a country girl. The sheriff stood up, too, started to follow her, and then stopped, his eyes moving tenderly from Nat's round bottom in the crisp white shorts to the expanse of curving thigh and calf. At the door Nat turned. "Maybe you could leave the cell door open just a teeny weeny bit," she said. "I promise not to try to escape."

"I don't know about that," the deputy said. "That ain't exactly according to the rules. What do you think, Jo Sam?"

"Do you play gin rummy?" Nat said. "Or bourrée? I've got some cards in my purse. We could play gin rummy for a little while. I'll bet you all get awfully bored sitting out here with nothing to do all day. Or we could talk. Do you . . ."

"I'm a poker man, myself," the deputy said. "But . . ."

"Blackjack!" Nat said. "The three of us could play blackjack. Y'all got any chips?"

One of the trusties came up to them where they stood in the doorway and peered around at the sheriff. "That's all, Mr. Jo Sam. You through with us, we'll go back to raking."

"All right, boys. Go ahead. Now, Dwight, you take this lady and settle her down, will you? We got work to do here. It's entirely too much going on here at one time. I can't keep track of it."

"I didn't mean to be inconsiderate, Sheriff," Nat said. "I really didn't. I'm just as sorry as I can be. It was just that that funny feeling I told you about got on my mind, and I forgot how much you must have on *your* mind."

"Dwight," the sheriff said, "you stay with this lady until she feels comfortable, will you?" He sighed. "And you don't need to lock the cell door, if she don't want it locked. It's OK. And as far as I'm concerned, you can play gin rummy, or anything else she wants to play. I mean *cards*. I'll be up there in a little while to see how you all are getting along."

"I'll put you in the bullpen, lady," the deputy said, as he followed Nat out the door. "It's a pretty good-sized room, and we never got enough folks in jail these days to use it. This county's gone down bad the past few years. Niggers all moving to Chicago, Detroit — and some white people, too. We got so we hardly ever have anybody in jail anymore." He sighed. "Times change."

"Look," Nat said. "Another picture. You all certainly have an unusual courthouse, don't you?" They were climbing the stairs now, and one wall of the stairwell was decorated with a gigantic mural of Cornelia and the Gracchi, the figures looming upward toward the second story.

"Crazy, ain't it?" the deputy said. "I've heard folks say the fella built this courthouse was a picture painter. He done all these funny-looking people dressed up in sheets and such. Ku Kluxers, probably. But, my Lord, that was before my time. This courthouse was built before my grandpa's day. If anybody was to consult me, I'd say cover 'em up with some good-looking Weldwood paneling. But I ain't consulted."

Nat was staring eye to eye now at the ten-foot figure of Cornelia. Fly specks marred the pale bluish-white surface of the huge cornea, and an irregular brown stain, marking a leak in the wall behind the mural, mottled the flesh tones on neck and arm. Nat shivered. "You'd still know they were underneath," she said. "That would be worse."

· · ·

In his office, the sheriff sat at his desk for a few minutes, and then he picked up the telephone and dialed a number. "Johnnie?" he said. "Honey, I'll be late tonight. We're pretty busy down here . . . I know it, but we're waiting on a load of whiskey, and I ought to be here to check it in. They're not going to raid until suppertime. Waiting for him to get in a new shipment. And be-

sides that, I got a office full of people here . . . That's OK. It
don't matter, honey. I'll get my supper at the jail. We're having
fatback and greens, and you know how I love . . . I got to hang
up now. I got three people waiting on me."

The sheriff gently laid the telephone in its cradle, got up from
his desk, went over to a filing case, opened it, got out a rack of
poker chips, and left his office, locking the door behind him. In
his secretary's office he stopped a moment. "I'm going up to in-
spect the jail," he said. "Anybody calls, tell them to call back after
six o'clock."

3

THE "HOME" toward which Nat set out, when she got out of jail that September evening, after a pleasant game of blackjack and an excellent supper of greens, sweet potatoes, and fatback, was a modestly-scrolled, late-Victorian cottage shaded by two ancient water oaks — the house which Aubrey Hunter had bought for his bride, Louise, more than forty years earlier, and to which Nat and Anne Farish had come as little girls when their father had been killed. Set back on a deep narrow lot in a row of half a dozen similar houses on one of the side streets of Philippi, the cottage was a very different place from the home on Hunters' Refuge plantation where Aubrey had spent *his* childhood.

There, in the middle of a thousand acres of flat Delta fields and rough pastureland, he had lived in a neoclassical mansion of the type common to the lower Mississippi valley, gracefully proportioned, but somewhat vulgar in its size and pretentiousness. Ornate pier mirrors on the drawing room walls reflected rooms crowded with carved rosewood furniture, Meissen vases, and crystal-hung girandoles; the ceilings were covered with fantastically ornate stucco duro relief. Not that Aubrey, as a boy, had ever noticed the mirrors or the ceilings. As long as he was reasonably comfortable, he paid little attention to his surroundings. Louise, on the other hand, his cousin and later his wife, although she had visited the house only once or twice as a young child, remembered it quite well and often described it in loving detail to friends and relatives who had never been there. The Hunter family, she would explain, had lived there ever since they received the land grant on which the house was built — and that had been early in the 1830's after the Treaty of Dancing Rabbit Creek opened up the Choctaw reservations. She spoke as if the house had materialized in the wilderness, as soon as the first Hunter appeared; but Aubrey's grandfather had, in fact, lived for twenty years in a log cabin near the spot where Hunters' Refuge was finally built. He had not built the big house until the late 1850's.

Louise would have liked more than anything in the world to live at Hunters' Refuge; but the house had been sold some years before she married Aubrey and had burned to the ground in a spectacular fire one icy January night a few years later. By that time, Aubrey, who never liked the country, had almost forgotten that he had ever lived there. If he had kept the place, he sometimes said, he would certainly have rented it out. He honestly preferred living on a side street in Philippi and working in a hardware store — though, of course, the *money*, the income from renting out a thousand acres of the finest sandy loam in the Delta, would have come in handy. "But that's all water under the bridge," he would say, and "No use crying over spilt milk." For his father, in his old age, had gambled and drunk and frittered the estate away.

Senility was Louise's explanation of what had happened, when she could bring herself to speak of Aubrey's loss. She even said to Nat and Anne Farish that Aubrey *might* have saved the place.

"If only your uncle had been a little bit older, if he had asserted himself," or, "It's a hard thing to face, but in justice to us all Aubrey should have had the old gentleman declared incompetent the day he got married. (I mean the day your *grandfather* got married.) And if your grandfather had been sane, he would have said the same thing himself."

Judge Hunter (The title was a courtesy one dating from a term as justice of the peace.) had been all his life a man of wealth and probity, a pillar of the church and the county — his worst fault, his neighbors would have said, a certain cold penuriousness that kept his family from living as grandly as they might have, and that made people feel sorry for Aubrey, particularly after his mother and older brother died in the last big yellow fever epidemic in 1886.

The judge had married late. He was a man of weak passions, it was said, who could get along well enough without women. Later he said of himself that he was a slow starter — didn't marry until 1866, didn't beget a child until 1870, and didn't have any fun until 1897.

At any rate, Aubrey, born late of a late marriage, only six years old when his mother died, was a lonely little boy with an old man for a father, left most of the time to his own devices — to play with the Negro children on the place or alone. Unlike most boys of his time and circumstances, he cared nothing for hunting or fishing; and he ignored the Negro boys who might have been his companions, preferring to putter around in the barn with scraps of iron, discarded cogs, nuts and bolts, chains, and plow-points, from which he constructed strange machines, the uses of which were known only to himself.

Nobody ever asked, "What are you making, son? How does it work?" Probably he never expected anyone to.

He had a tutor for a time; but this gentleman proved to be a drunkard, and the judge dismissed him. He spent two or three years at the Jefferson Military Academy near Natchez. At sixteen he matriculated at the state agricultural and mechanical college and told his father that he intended to be an engineer.

It was during Aubrey's second year at State that his father bought an automobile — the first one in the county and probably the first in the state. Of course, by that time — 1898 — people had *heard* of cars. Those who traveled were used to seeing them in the East, and those who went to Memphis for the circus had, the preceding year, seen one driven around the ring as part of the entertainment.

But Judge Hunter, that cold, penurious old man, was the first person in the county to *own* one. Ironically, as it may seem, considering the consequences, Aubrey, without knowing it, aroused his father's interest in automobiles. He brought home at the Christmas vacation a stack of pamphlets, magazine articles, and advertisements of all kinds of machinery and mechanical devices. Judge Hunter (who had begun to grow increasingly restless and unlike himself that winter, pacing the huge silent house and muttering continuously to himself; or calling for his horse and riding out for no reason at all, sometimes in the middle of the night) wandered one day into Aubrey's room and looked through these things — possibly out of boredom. An article on motor cars caught his attention.

Two months later his Winton arrived by train, a trim compact little buggy with the motor in a box behind the seat. It was accompanied by several drums of gasoline and a mechanic who stayed long enough to teach him how to drive and service it.

From the day Judge Hunter cranked up his car and drove out onto the streets of Philippi — hand on the tiller, head high, mouth open, beard flying — until his death, he was a changed man. He took to drink and gambling with the most mysterious enthusiasm, drove into town in a cloud of dust and noise that frightened the horses and sent the chickens flapping and squawking into the ditches, and left the car to sputter itself cold in front of the Elks' Club, while he spent long afternoons and evenings playing an abominable game of poker with men who had played hard for high stakes all their lives. No one in Philippi seemed to mind taking his money, even if he was an old man.

On the days that he did not play poker, Judge Hunter parked the Winton in front of Mr. Kelly's saloon, next door to the Douglas Hotel, and went in for a drink or two. The judge was a distinguished-looking old gentleman — sixty-seven when he bought his car — tall and stooped, with pale blue eyes, a high-bridged "Roman" nose, and a silky white beard that hung in splendor almost to his waist. He wore a black frock coat, a heavy gold watch chain across his vest to his watch pocket, and an onyx seal ring on his right hand. (He had certainly inherited the watch chain and the ring, and probably the coat, which was greenish with age and shiny at the elbows.) When he dressed to drive his automobile, he put on a wide-brimmed Panama, a duster to protect his clothes, and a pair of goggles; his beard, he carefully deposited in a brown paper sack which he secured to his chin with a long ribbon threaded through holes in the sack and tied in a bow on top of his hat. He was an unusual sight, climbing down from his car in front of Mr. Kelly's saloon, and he attracted considerable attention from the townspeople — and from Mr. Kelly's daughter, Joyce, who sometimes helped her father tend bar.

When he got inside Kelly's, the judge untied the paper sack, removed it from his chin, folded it carefully, and put it in the pocket of his duster. Then he took off his goggles and hat and duster and hung them on the hat tree. By the time he finished,

Joyce would have had time to rearrange her long black hair, pinch her cheeks, bite her lips, tighten her belt, and lean forward over the bar with a happy smile. The judge paid no attention.

Now at this time Joyce's situation had already caused comment among the ladies of Philippi, who considered it improper for a woman to enter a barber shop and who blanched at the mere thought of a female bartender. It may be, on the other hand, that Mr. Kelly and Joyce thought a saloon the best possible place for a young woman to meet eligible men. They appeared to be oblivious to the gossip of the matrons — as oblivious, in fact, as Judge Hunter was to Joyce's charms — until one day when he came in and laid a dead guinea hen on the bar. The bird's scrawny head, with its ridiculous fuzz of hair around a knoblike topknot, flopped against the counter at an angle to the plump speckled body.

"I ran over this damn hen," the judge said.

Joyce looked at the bird. Then she raised a hand to her hair and patted it. *"Did* you?" she said.

"Got caught in my spokes," he said. "Had to stop the car to pull her out."

Joyce may have been annoyed because the judge had never before paid any attention to her. "Well, *I* don't care," she said coolly.

"Can you cook?" he said, looking directly at her for the first time.

"Of course I can cook, old man. I'm a woman."

"I see you are," said the judge, and then, "There's no sense wasting a good guinea hen. Here, haven't you got a nigger around can pluck and draw her?"

"No," she said.

"Well, I'll do it myself, if you'll invite me to dinner."

Joyce smiled at him then. "All right," she said. "Come on back to the kitchen."

Within a month of this conversation Judge Hunter was married to Joyce. Within less than a year she bore him a son, Edward.

During her pregnancy there was considerable speculation among the men of the county regarding the judge's capacity to "plow his own field." (The ladies put their doubts in the form of uncompleted questions: "Who do you suppose . . . ?" or "Do you really think . . . ?" to be answered by, "Let's not even discuss it!" or "What do you expect? After all, she's a bartender's daughter.")

But from the day Edward was born, he was so unquestionably a Hunter, with his father's pale blue eyes, silky hair, and high-bridged nose, that all jokes and questions abruptly ceased.

· · ·

Shortly after the judge married, and before his new stepmother's pregnancy was evident, Aubrey moved away from Hunters' Refuge. The year was 1899, and he was not yet nineteen years old. The servants at Hunters' Refuge told the servants at other places around the county and these servants told their masters that Mr. Aubrey had come home at the end of the school year (His train got into Philippi in the early morning and the old man sent a buggy into town to meet him.), had put his suitcases in his room, and gone to knock on his father's bedroom door. He entered at the old man's "Come in," and found him in bed with his new wife. "Excuse me, Papa," he said. "I thought you said, 'Come in.'"

"I did," Judge Hunter said. "I want to introduce you to your new mama. We got married day before yesterday. Ain't she pretty?"

According to the houseboy, who had just brought morning coffee to the bride and groom and was still in the room drawing back the curtains, the old man's beard was spread out on the blanket, as smooth and shining as if he had just brushed it, and his teeth were in a glass on the washstand. Being black, the house-boy edited (at least for his white acquaintances) his remarks about the bride. All he said was, ". . . and there she was, laying up beside of him."

At the time Aubrey confided his emotions at this confrontation to no one. He unpacked his clothes, put them away, and immediately went to work for his father, supervising cotton choppers and repairing farm equipment. It was a busy time of the year.

Some weeks later his father told him that he was through sending him to school.

"But Papa," Aubrey said, "I want to be an engineer."

"I can't waste any more money on colleges," the judge said. "I need every cent I can scrape together to take care of my own affairs." (He had not stopped drinking and gambling and roaring around the county in his Winton just because he was married.)

"But Papa," Aubrey said, "you're acting like you're crazy."

"I was a slow starter, my boy," the judge said.

"Yes, I know," Aubrey said. "You told me that last week."

"Well, I intend to make up for lost time."

"What am *I* going to do?" Aubrey said.

"You can stay here, if you want to, and help me farm," the old man said. "I'll give you your board." He leered at the boy. "But see to it that you keep away from your mother," he said, and hee-hawed as if he had made a great joke.

Aubrey stayed on until mid-July, but he had no real interest in farming, and he certainly had no interest in his "mother."

One Saturday he happened to be in the hardware store in Philippi buying trace chains and plowpoints, when the clerk who was helping him collapsed with a heart attack and was taken away to the hospital. Aubrey waited until the owner came back from the hospital and approached him. "How about a job?" he said.

"What?"

"You've got to have somebody to take that fella's place, don't you?" Aubrey said. "He looked pretty sick to me."

"Yeah," the owner said. "I'll have to get somebody. Are you laid by?"

"Yes," Aubrey said. "I could work for a couple of months, anyway."

That was how he started to work in Philippi. He drove out to Hunters' Refuge, packed his clothes, collected a few tools that belonged to him and his books, pamphlets, and advertisements, and moved into town without even mentioning that he was going. He took a room at the local boardinghouse and went to work. The following Monday his father came into town for the trace chains and plowpoints that Aubrey had forgotten and found the boy behind the counter.

"What became of *you?*" the old man said.

"Well, I decided I would work in town awhile," Aubrey said. He had no desire to fall out with his father. "It'll be good experience for me," he said. He hesitated and then glanced away from the old man, out the window at the automobile where his stepmother sat. "You can get along all right without me," he said. "We're all laid by."

Judge Hunter shrugged. "Suit yourself," he said.

. . .

Aubrey worked three years at the hardware store before he got a raise, and even then he did not ask for one. He was content, it appeared, with things as they were. He liked his room. The food at the boardinghouse was plentiful and excellent. At the store he was free for long hours to do as he pleased, coming to the front only when the bell on the door jangled to signal the entrance of a customer. The owner of the store was an elderly bachelor who shared Aubrey's passion for tinkering and who already had a little shop set up in the stockroom at the back. Here Aubrey spent not only a part of every day, but evenings as well, working at such projects as an improved post-hole digger or a new design for a plowpoint. As the years passed, he sometimes undertook more complicated projects. One winter he built a small gasoline-powered engine and attached it to a kind of tricycle which he rode back and forth to work in good weather.

Now and then Aubrey was pressed into service by one of the matrons of Philippi to take a visiting young lady to a picnic or dance; even less frequently he made an engagement on his own initiative, but he was not much interested in women.

In 1911, when his father died suddenly of a stroke, Aubrey took his share of the money left from the sale of the last remnant of Hunters' Refuge (The old man had sold it off piece by piece over the preceding ten years.) and bought a half interest in the hardware business. At about the same time, the owner of the boardinghouse where he had been so comfortable and well-fed died. Aubrey moved to another boardinghouse, but the food was poor and the house had about it a smell of damp walls, dirty dishwater, and urine. Aubrey was uncomfortable. He was also thirty-one years old, and it occurred to him that perhaps he should marry. After some thought, he settled on a distant cousin, Miss Louise Griffith, a young woman of twenty-eight whose matrimonial prospects were getting dimmer by the year. The courtship was brief. One Sunday afternoon after a particularly delicious dinner at the Griffith house, Aubrey proposed and was accepted.

· · ·

No one in Philippi knew where Edward Hunter and his mother went after the judge's death. As soon as the will was probated and the estate sold, they took their share of the money and left town. Edward was eleven. The next time Aubrey heard from him was in 1920, when he happened to be passing through Philippi and stopped in at the hardware store. He was a grown man by then, twenty years old and already married. He had been working in Texas on a cattle ranch, he said. Aubrey invited him home for supper. After that visit, he wrote an occasional postcard to Aubrey and Louise and the following year sent an announcement of the birth of a daughter.

In the fall of 1927, when Aubrey and Louise, along with everybody else in the Mississippi Delta, were clawing their way out from under the debris left by the flood, they received a telegram from Edward's wife saying that he had been killed in an automobile accident and that she wished to bring him back to Philippi to be buried — she would not wait for a reply.

She arrived on the 1:44 train from Memphis and brought with her not only Edward's body, but also his two children, Natalie and Anne Farish. She explained immediately, on the way from the railroad station to the cottage on Muscadine Street, that she was Edward's second wife, that the first wife had deserted him and the children, that she had been married to Edward for less than a year, and that she had no interest in assuming responsibility for her two stepchildren. "Why, I hardly know the poor little things," she said, patting Nat on the shoulder.

Nat sat very straight and looked at no one. She was not pretty. At six she already had her grandfather's hawk nose, and her face lacked the childish softness that appeals to grown people. She pressed her lips together. No one noticed or knew her well enough to say if it was to keep from crying. Anne Farish, who was only four, not old enough to know exactly what had happened, looked up wide-eyed at Louise. "I'm hung'y," she said.

"Let's not make any hasty decisions about the future, my dear," Louise said to Edward's widow. "We know you must be beside yourself with grief and shock."

The following night, after the funeral, the grieving widow brought up the subject again. It began to sink in upon Aubrey and Louise that they might have no choice in the matter — she was resolute in her determination to give them the children.

"We can't," Louise said positively. "We're too old. And we don't know anything about children. It would be an injustice to them. Of course, my dear, I don't mean that we won't help you in any way we can."

"We'll have plenty of time to work things out," Aubrey said. "Everybody is too tired and distracted tonight. And Edward's not cold in his grave." He went outside, as he always did before going to bed, for a look at the outdoor thermometer and barometer on the side gallery. "Eighty-one degrees and steady," he said. "It'll be fair and hot tomorrow." Then, "Maybe we can find their *real* mother." No one replied to this and he went back to his room and closed the door.

But they did not work things out the next day. The widow had other plans. She got up early in the morning (even earlier than Aubrey, who liked to drink his coffee alone and go downtown an hour or two before his hardware store opened), packed her flimsy blackish suitcase, laid a few papers that had to do with the children (their birth certificates, an insurance policy, and a copy of Edward's will) on the table by her bed, quietly unlocked the front door, walked four blocks to the train station, and got on the early morning train to Memphis.

Aubrey and Louise were left with three alternatives. They could keep Nat and Anne Farish, they could try to find the real mother, or they could send them to the Episcopal orphanage in Port Wilson. (And the orphanage might not have taken them, since Aubrey was an uncle and able to support them.) At the time no one in Philippi except Clakey Morrison knew whether the last two alternatives were tried.

But in the privacy of her kitchen one day, after a series of mysterious telephone calls to and from Memphis, New Orleans, and Austin, Texas, Miss Louise, who had been for some minutes absorbed in the intricacies of beaten biscuit making, slammed down the biscuit brake in a fit of frustration "We're going to *have* to keep them," she said. "We can't find her."

"M'am?"

"Oh dear, Clakey, if the Lord had intended me to be a mother, He would have blessed me with children."

"Sometimes both you all act to me like you don't know where people git 'em," Clakey muttered.

"What did you say? Speak up."

"I say I'm glad we got 'em, Miss Louise. I like children in the house. And the big one, 'specially. She's a spunky little thing."

"Here. You take over this biscuit brake, Clakey. I'm on the verge of nervous exhaustion."

"You just relax and quit worrying, Miss Louise," Clakey said. "I'm going to see to them kids."

Later Miss Louise told the ladies in the Episcopal Guild that the two little girls were like two little rays of sunshine, and that the opportunity to take care of them was a God-sent privilege as well as a sacred duty and responsibility. To the ladies of the Blue Stockings Club she added that Nat and Anne Farish were as skinny as jaybirds and that she couldn't wait to fatten them up.

"Why," she said, "the first words those poor children said to me were, 'We're hungry.' "

4

"HE'S ACTING like a bastard," Nat said. "Just his usual hateful peck self. Did you know he broke my jaw before I finally left him?"

"Nat, you know I don't hear anything about you except from Cousin Louise, and she's not going to tell me Jeff broke your jaw." Wilburn Griffith looked skeptically at Nat and began doodling on the pad on his desk. They were in the small back office of the Hunters' Refuge commissary, Wilburn at a battered rolltop desk piled with dusty letters, old seed tickets, and account books; Nat opposite him in a straight-backed oak office chair surrounded by piles of plantation debris — cotton samples in twists of brown paper, stacks of ancient daybooks, low bookcases with more account books on the shelves and, on top, tin pie plates full of nails, screws, shotgun shells, .22 bullets, broken pencil stubs, pennies, nuts and bolts, and broken small machine parts. Outside the open door into Wilburn's office, Negroes came and went in the commissary, and there was a constant sound of voices raised above the clack and rattle of machinery in the cotton gin across the road.

Occasionally someone — a tractor driver or one of the gin operators — put his head through the door to ask Wilburn a question or to give him some information.

Nat sat swinging one long brown leg nervously, the other doubled under her. Her dress, a narrow brown and orange print shift, was hitched up above her knees. The bright dusty September sunlight streamed in at the commissary window and picked out blue lights in her black hair.

"And now he hasn't sent my money for four months," she said, "and it looks as if I'm going to have to get a lawyer to get it, and in the meantime I've got to *live*, Wilburn. You're going to have to help me find a job. Oh, it's enough to make you . . . !" She broke off. "He's just doing it because he hates me," she said.

Wilburn looked up from his pad. A thin dark man in his late thirties with a faint brownish smear of birthmark along one cheek and temple, he had delicate regular features, a shade too fine for a man, without, however, any suggestion of effeminacy. His eyes were gray. "I'm glad you're not my wife, Nat," he said, grinning at her. "I might break your jaw one day."

"Wilburn, I'm not *kidding*. He did. He came home drunk one night and snatched me out of bed, out of a sound sleep, and I hit my chin on the marble-topped washstand by the side of the bed and broke my jaw. And I still don't know what he was mad at me about. And he doesn't either."

"Did you ask him?"

She shrugged. "Ask who?" she said in the slow gentle voice that could bring tears to a strong man's eyes. "Ask *who*? Jeff drunk or Jeff sober? One doesn't make sense, and the other either doesn't remember or is too stupid to figure it out."

"Nat! Don't sell Jeff short. He's a good, steady, sensible fellow. He may not be the sort of husband *you* need — I told you that when you married him, if you remember. But don't make him out to be a stupid scoundrel just because you can't get along with him."

"You haven't seen him for *years*," she said. "All you know about him is what he seemed like when we got married — and the few times he's come home with me for a weekend. Do you think he's still a courageous young paratrooper cutting a figure in his jump boots? With his chest covered with campaign ribbons?"

"Nat!" He shook his head. "You're too ferocious for me," he said.

"He's a pot-bellied, middle-aged, semi-alcoholic fool," she said. "And you never had to sleep with him. Or, even worse, *live* with him."

"I'm sorry you've had a rough time, Nat."

"I'm not. It took a broken jaw to make me leave him. I was a coward, Wilburn." The low voice filled Wilburn's dingy little office with suggestions of helplessness, abuse, outrage. "I'm not going to make that mistake again," Nat said. "Being a coward, I mean." She picked a wisp of cotton fluff from her dress and laid it gently on the ashtray on Wilburn's desk. When she moved her hand away from the ashtray, the swirl of air sent the cotton up into the motey sunlight, and in a moment it settled in her hair. "Give me a cigarette, Wilburn; I just smoked my last one," she said, and then, without changing her tone, "You know I told you three years ago I'd been trying to leave him for four solid years. I already hated him then — so much I got gooseflesh just when he walked through the door." She took the cigarette and bent forward for a light. "If it wasn't for money . . ." she said. "That's what I mean about being a coward. You know how it's always scared me thinking about being poor and leading a dull life. That was the problem. I told Jeff when we got married that

I was marrying him for his money. I *told* him. I never tried to fool him, did I, Wilburn?"

"My Lord, Nat, don't be frivolous. Just looking at you is enough to fool a man."

"But he said he didn't care, and I believed him. If I didn't mind, after all, why should he? And then he said I'd learn to love him. Isn't that picturesque? At the time I thought he was kidding. Anyhow, that wasn't what I was going to tell you. It was money that kept me with him so long. I thought I just couldn't possibly *stand* to work for a living. And where would I work and what would I do now, at my age? Fifteen, even ten years ago, I could have gotten a job modeling. That's what I did that winter I was in New York during the war. I stood around for months while two little pansies with pointed toes made clothes on me, and then, when the actual modeling started (for buyers, you know), they *fired* me. I couldn't learn how to walk. You know, Aunt Louise always said I walked like I was stepping over cotton rows. And I tried and tried, but . . ."

Wilburn laughed and Nat frowned at him severely. "I'm talking about insecurity," she said, "and it isn't funny."

"What about the year you worked at Camp McNaughton? You managed to hold down a job there."

"Yes," she said, "I was Campus Queen at Camp McNaughton. But do you know how much money I was making? About a hundred and twenty dollars a month. I was stenographer for a funny little old National Guard colonel who had been a hospital orderly in civilian life. He was too dumb to get his own outfit and go overseas — even the U.S. Army couldn't make such a blunder as to send *him* overseas. And I was as dumb as he was. I could only type twenty-five words a minute — not counting errors. There was a curly-haired blond sergeant with the most beautiful green eyes in the office, and he used to do my typing.

My Lord, what eyelashes he had! I haven't thought about them in years. He should have been a woman." She sighed. "But things were different then, Wilburn. That kind of job doesn't turn up in peacetime. In a way, it was just another kind of modeling — modeling for the army. That's all I can do, really, you know — look like me. I mean that's all I can get *paid* for doing. I knew it then. I was sure I'd be facing hardship for the rest of my life if the army ever got rid of me. And you know, on VJ-Day when they came in the office with the glorious news, and everybody was hugging everybody else and shouting and laughing, I went over to the post library and hid in the stacks and *cried*. The war had been one long party for me, and I couldn't bear for it to be over."

Nat took a long drag on her cigarette, half-closed her eyes, and blew out a cloud of smoke. "Maybe I could be a *librarian*," she said. "I hadn't thought of that. Can librarians smoke in the library? I wonder if it would be much trouble to learn the Dewey Decimal System again. Remember in the seventh grade when Miss Tovey taught us to find books? I could do as well as she did. And I could get some of those little, round, steel-rimmed glasses like she used to wear. And indigestion! We had library right after lunch and she always had indigestion; I *know* I could get that, if it's required, the state my nervous system is in. What kind of clothes did she use to wear?"

Wilburn tilted back in his chair. "Nothing like that," he said, pointing to Nat's flowered dress. "And besides, you haven't the figure for a school librarian."

"You see? Nobody takes me seriously, even when I'm trying my best to be sensible. Year before last, when I was in Puerto Rico, right after I left Jeff, I tried to get a job teaching. Actually there's not a reason in the world why I shouldn't be able to teach. I *did* graduate from college. But the superintendent of schools was a native, and he discriminated against me because I'm white and from Mississippi."

"Oh, God, Nat!"

"Well, he did. He listened to me talk for about five minutes, and then instead of me he hired a Yankee dike with only two years of college. As it turned out, she drank. And she had an affair with the girls' gym teacher and caused a terrible scandal. Served him right. Racist! The superintendent, I mean."

She sat up straight and pulled the loose shift tight around her waist. "My figure does look good, doesn't it, Wilburn? To be thirty-six years old. Waist twenty-four inches, and I still don't have to wear a girdle — or even a bra. And I'm brown all over. Of course, my face looks a thousand. I can't help that. But what I was getting ready to say before I got off the track, and what you've got to help me with — I have to do something, at least until I can get my money from Jeff. What do you think? It has to be in Philippi, because I can't afford to live anywhere but at home, and I'm just baffled trying to decide where to start trying. Can you see me working in a bank, for example? Wearing a navy blue shirtwaist dress and sensible shoes, counting stacks and stacks of other people's money? Wouldn't that be torment! And I can't even make change — that's another drawback to that idea, even if I had enough pull with a bank president to get a job. The year I had to make change at the Junior League Bazaar in Concordia, our booth came out in such a mess we had to hire a CPA to straighten us out."

"Maybe if you got a job in a bank, you could marry the president," Wilburn said.

"I wouldn't," Nat said. "It would be immoral for me to marry again, and that's the truth. I wouldn't mind being his mistress, if he was nice and didn't bother me too often, and if his wife didn't make any trouble; but I certainly wouldn't marry him.

Besides, bank presidents already have wives. Nobody lets bachelors get to be bank presidents. It's not acceptable."

"You can't type and you can't make change. About the only job you could manage would be something like receptionist, answering the telephone and so forth. Maybe you could get something like that — with a doctor or a lawyer."

"Don't you need somebody like me to answer your telephone?"

"Farmers answer their own phones," Wilburn said, and then, "Nat, did Jeff really break your jaw?"

"Yes, thank God. I swear he did. It was like a nightmare, Wilburn; really a *real* nightmare. And I knew I mightn't ever wake up or might wake up inside another dream. That's the worst thing with me, thinking . . ." She broke off and bent attentively over the ashtray, putting out her cigarette so thoroughly that the stub broke open and scattered tobacco on the desk. Then the slender brown hands lay still, flat on the desk on either side of the ashtray, the tremor for a moment frozen, as it were.

"Nat," Wilburn said, "What do you suppose makes your hands shake all the time?"

"It's in*herited*," Nat said. "Aunt Louise says my father's hands shook." She looked down. "Maybe I'm vibrating to the music of the spheres."

Wilburn laughed.

"But anyhow," she said, "about that peasant, Jeff — he snatched me out of bed like I told you, and I felt this awful pain in my face; and then I was lying on the floor in the dark and he was standing over me. I kept wanting to say: Who . . . ? What . . . ? because at first I didn't even know it was Jeff. I tried to open my mouth — just once. It hurt too bad; I didn't try again. And besides, I realized almost right away who it was. I *smelled* him. He always smelled cold and rusty and cindery, like old railroad tracks; even right after he had a bath and used some fancy after-shave lotion, he smelled that way underneath, because of being around them all day long. It was all through him, soaked through him. And then, too, he was muttering to himself — something that I couldn't understand — and I recognized his voice."

"What was he saying?" Wilburn asked in a dispassionate but interested voice. "Did you ever understand him?"

"After a while I did. He was saying, 'Where are you?' and then, 'I *love* you,' and 'Sweetheart!' and 'Nat, baby,' and dreadful things like that; and I almost laughed out loud right there on the floor (only I couldn't), because I halfway expected him to say, 'I'm yours forever,' or something else out of TV or a movie — with me on the floor half dead and my jaw broken.

"But I was scared, too, because it was dark, and I couldn't talk, and he was stumbling around the room and feeling all over the bed and grunting and moaning like some kind of monstrous pig.

"I thought: Maybe I can scream. I'll try to scream. But I didn't. I held my mouth still and crawled under the bed and out the other side and got up off the floor; and then I could see enough light from the living room to get through the door; and I went straight out — out of my room and out of the house, with my jaw like somebody had run a red-hot wire through it. I was standing in the yard in my nightgown almost before I had waked up. It was a clear, beautiful night. I even saw a falling star, Wilburn. And of course I thought: I'm dreaming.

"But I had that other feeling, too, that I get when I'm dreaming. I'm asleep and something is happening — some terrible thing, like drowning, maybe, and I think: I have to wake up. And then I think: How can I be sure that if I wake up I may not really be waking into another dream, and maybe it'll be worse than this one? And when it's very bad, Wilburn, I do wake up. I wake from dream to dream, and after a while I know that that's the way it's going to be — I'm going to go on waking from dream to dream all the rest of my life, never, *never* to be sure again that I'm awake, and it scares me so — oh, I can't describe how it feels — so that when I finally do wake up out of it, I sit straight up in the dark, soaking wet and *sick*, and I have to get up and smoke and have a drink and watch TV. And maybe I won't go to bed again that whole night, for fear I'll go to sleep — especially if there is anything at all good on the late, late show."

Nat stopped talking and held her hands together in her lap for a moment. "Even talking about it scares me," she said. " 'Specially in a place like this, a good dream place." She pointed out the commissary window at the gin vibrating in the midst of snowy fields to its own raucous music, its roof and the trees along the road and the road itself, white with blown cotton. "Look at the cotton on the gin roof," she said. "Like a play snowstorm. That's the kind of thing that sets you off." She drew a deep breath, touched her hair, picked out the web of cotton trembling there, and flicked it away. "See, I'm getting snowed on," she said.

"Is that why you always tell the truth?" Wilburn said.

"What? Yes! Lies scare me too much. You can't make them stay still. I never, never tell them except for practical reasons, you know, when it's absolutely unavoidable. But anyhow, what I was telling you about, with the broken jaw there was the advantage of its hurting so bad. I said to myself that I'd better import a doctor into that dream or else get out of it myself — and I got out. If he hadn't done it, I might never have gotten up the nerve. It was a matter of: Nothing can be worse than this.

"So I left him stumbling and roaring in the dark and walked half a mile in my nightgown to Jimmy Wilcox's house. That's one of my few friends in Concordia. I wrote on a piece of paper that my jaw was broken, and they took me to a hospital."

"And Hunter?" Wilburn said. "Did he know anything about it?"

"Not that night. He slept through it all. And then later Jeff got mad because I told him what had happened."

"What about Hunter now?" Wilburn said. "How did Jeff get custody? You were so careful — you know, that winter you started to establish residence over here — not to give him anything he could use against you."

"There wasn't any question of custody," Nat said. "I changed my mind and let Hunter decide for himself who he wanted to live with and he chose Jeff."

Wilburn said nothing.

"Well, it was natural," she said. "A boy that age. Jeff promised him a swimming pool or something, and besides, he would have had to leave his horse if he'd come with me. I would have done the same thing, if I'd been in his place. Have you any coffee, Wilburn? Did you know I'm kind of on the wagon?"

Wilburn got up from his desk and went over to a little two-burner stove standing on a table against the wall. "Already made," he said. "Do you like chicory?"

"Any kind. Just coffee."

He lit the stove and with precise careful movements began to get the coffee ready — pouring cold milk from a thermos into a clean saucepan on one burner and setting the coffeepot to heat in a pan of water on the other.

"Isn't it going to take a long time to heat that way?" Nat asked.

"Coffee's no good if it boils," he said. He stood a few minutes watching the milk until it began to steam and then cut the burner down low.

"You're like a woman in the kitchen, aren't you, Wilburn?"

Nat said. "Did you ever think that deep down you might be a latent homosexual?"

"I don't think about it, and I don't give a damn."

"Well, you know, you're so — *precise*," she said. "And you don't like to hunt."

He picked up the coffeepot in one hand and the saucepan in the other and poured two cups of café au lait, mingling streams of milk and coffee in the cups. "Who have you been lying on the beach with?" he said. "A psychiatrist?"

"There! You see? Look at the way you pour coffee."

"I like it this way," he said. "The milk doesn't get a skin on it. If you'll forgive my mother fixation, this is the way Mama used to make it." He put a cup in front of her and sat down behind his desk again. "To go back to what you were saying before you started analyzing me," he said, "I did hear you were hitting the bottle too hard before you left Concordia."

"It's true," she said. "It was such a challenge over there. I mean, people *cared* whether you drank or not. Just like home. You could bug them a little bit. I was so immature, Wilburn, that that actually gave me a kick. But that isn't all there is to it, either. You can't let those people box you in — the Stonebridges and their *associates*. And if you turn the maturity bit around, you realize that *they're* the ones who decide what is and what isn't mature. So I take back what I just said. I won't let them trick me into accusing myself of immaturity. I just drank, that's all. Mainly, I was bored."

"How about now? Why are you on the wagon?"

"Well, when I went down to the Islands, it was so *different*. Whiskey isn't even expensive down there. Everybody drinks, morning, afternoon, and night. So why bother? And there was the beach. I spent so much time on the beach, and you always get sand in your drink. In Mexico, too. Of course, good whiskey isn't cheap in Mexico, but the native stuff is, if you've got a strong enough stomach to take it. Actually, you know, when I quit, I realized I'd had a hangover for ten years. It was marvelous! And still, every morning, I wake up and think: What's the matter with me? Why do I feel so good? And then I realize: I don't have a hangover!"

She grinned at him. "I'm healthy," she said. "You can't imagine how disappointed everybody in Concordia was when I went back this fall — sober, sunburned, and healthy. They'd expected to learn a spectacular lesson from me on the wages of sin. After all, I'd deserted my child. And worse than that, I had once been asked to leave the Concordia Country Club golf course because my shorts were too short."

"You may be over-estimating yourself," Wilburn said. "They probably hadn't any of them except the Stonebridges given you a thought."

"Don't kid yourself," she said. "They hated me enough to stay interested. And besides, people kept bringing home these grand rumors about me, keeping my memory alive — or so I heard afterwards. Like, for example, that I was hustling for drinks. Naturally, you know, people in Concordia assume that any woman living by herself in Mexico or the Islands, or maybe any place outside the States and not working at something respectable must be a prostitute. Isn't that logical? Anyhow, when I got back, that was the first thing Jeff asked me — if they were true, the stories that had been going around Concordia. It seems one woman said she'd seen me tending bar in a nightclub in Acapulco. (She did, too. I was helping out this very good friend of mine who is a bartender.) She reported back with that tidbit, plus the well-known fact that I was a whore. Afterwards, Jeff said, he heard that I'd been asked to leave the hotel where I was staying for soliciting in the lobby.

I was sweet as could be. 'Why, Jeff,' I said, 'I knew that story got in the New York *Times*, but I never *dreamed* the Georgia papers had picked it up.' And he began to cry. And *moan*. Actually. 'Oh, how could you possibly do such a thing to your only son,' and all that. It was so boring, I finally said, 'Shut up, Jeff. Shut *up*. Relax! I am *not* a prostitute. I swear. On my Tri Omega honor.' So he was satisfied and told all our old friends that it absolutely was not true.

"But he didn't pay me my back alimony. He owes me eight hundred dollars. Four months he hasn't paid me a cent of that piddling little allowance. And he could, if he wanted to. His bill at the country club is more than that every month. He's just harassing me. So that's the other thing you have to advise me about. I've got to get a lawyer."

"All right, Nat. Don't worry about it. I'll think about who's the best person to get, and we'll go see him."

"You're *sweet*," Nat said. "Do you know you're practically one of the only people in the world I would let be my pallbearer?"

"I'm overwhelmed," Wilburn said.

"Well, I mean it. You're just about the only person in Philippi who cares a thing about me or even wants to be seen with me (not to mention Concordia, Georgia) except Aunt Louise and Uncle Aubrey, and he's too old for a pallbearer, besides being a close relative. And here, I've been talking to you a mile a minute about me, because so much has happened to me in the past three years (and I haven't even begun to tell you everything), and I haven't asked you about Sunny and the children, or if you're making a lot of money, or anything. You look kind of pigeon-breasted to me. Have you been sick?"

Wilburn got up, took their coffee cups back to the stove and lit it again. He carried himself like a man who has recently had a major operation — carefully, with his shoulders high, as if to ward off pain; but at the same time erect, his chest out, almost offering himself to the knife.

He stood waiting for the coffee to heat. "In the order asked," he said, "Sunny is not well. She has gallstones or something. And diverticulitis. Probably going to have to be cut on, if she can ever get up the nerve to face it. The children are thriving. The cotton crop was lousy last year, but it looks as if we're going to make baskets of money this year (Here he rapped the table with his knuckles.) if the rains hold off three, even two more weeks. I could be ninety percent picked out in a little over two weeks. Did you look at the fields on your way out here? My God, it's almost unbelievable! Prettiest crop I've ever seen. Some fields I've got more than three bales to the acre. I want to drive you over the place and show it to you." He filled their cups again and came back to the desk. "As for me," he said, "I'm fine — even if I do look pigeon-breasted. But I've been lonesome. You know — old friends move away, and it takes a while to make new ones." He smiled at her. "Stay awhile, Nat," he said. "It's like old times. Things get dull around here, especially after the cotton is picked, when there's nothing to do again until March. I'm *really* glad to see you."

"I'm certainly going to stay until I get this alimony mess straightened out. I haven't got the bus fare to go to Itta Bena."

"Well, God knows Cousin Louise will see that you get enough to eat. And we can keep you in whiskey. Have you got cigarette money?"

"I told you I'm on the wagon for now — not that I intend to make a *thing* of it, if I want to get drunk. But I didn't mean I was that poor, Wilburn. You know, I get a little bitty check from Daddy's estate every now and then — bonds or something. I've got one due in a few days. I might even buy you and Sunny a bottle."

"Sunny's not supposed to drink," Wilburn said. "Gallstones. But I'll take you up on it."

The commissary clerk, a balding white man in seersucker pants and a tieless striped shirt, strolled into the office.

"What is it, Doy?" Wilburn said.

"Sarah Henry is out here to see you, Mr. Griffith."

"All right," Wilburn said. He turned to Nat. "You remember Sarah, don't you? She worked for you when you were here five years ago."

Nat nodded.

"Come on, Sarah," the clerk called. He leaned against the wall just inside the office door. "She's got payment troubles, Mr. Griffith," he said. "About to get her washing machine repossessed."

A tall, lanky, light-skinned Negro woman came into the office and strode up to Wilburn's desk. Nat got up. The Negro woman looked at her for a moment without speaking, and then Nat said, "Hi, Sarah. Don't you know me?"

"Lord, Miss Nat! I thought for a minute you was some kind of Indian, honey."

Nat laughed. "I'm not," she said. "Don't you like my tan?"

"You're darker-complected than I, Miss Nat. Too dark. And your hair has got blacker."

"That's better than getting gray," Nat said.

"Is that a Indian outfit you got on?" She pointed to Nat's brilliantly flowered dress.

"Kind of," Nat said.

"Honey, I'm glad to see you. Haven't laid my eyes on you since God knows when. You look fine, if you is dark. Did you bring Hunter with you? Who's nursing him?"

"He's too old to need a nurse now," Nat said. "He's almost eleven."

"Hmm-m-ph. I can't realize it. Time passes fast out here in

the country. You forget altogether about clocks and calendars. You go to town for something and, looka here, a couple of months have gone by. How's your auntie and Mr. Aubrey? And Miss Clakey? I know she's pleased to have you home."

"All fine," Nat said.

"Sit down, Sarah," Wilburn said, indicating another straight-backed chair beside his desk. Sarah and Nat both sat down, while the clerk continued to stand by the door.

"Pass my regards along to Miss Clakey," Sarah said to Nat, "and tell her I'm coming to see her next time I catch a ride to town."

"I didn't know you had moved to Hunters' Refuge," Nat said. "When did you come out here?"

"Come the year Mr. Wilburn bought the place. Let's see. Fifty-four. I was cooking for him in town, and I just moved on out here. Didn't you know it? Nothing to hold me in town. I was glad to come to the country again. You know, my people lived here in your daddy's day. Raised on this place. My daddy was your grand-daddy's hostler."

"Was he? I didn't know that."

"He was. I know everybody in this part of the county, black and white. Every good fishing hole. Every borrow pit and bayou and grudge ditch." She sighed. "But that don't necessarily make me smart," she said. She turned to Wilburn who had gotten up and was sitting on the edge of his desk. "I got trouble right now," she said, "and it's out of my own stupid self."

"That's the truth," the clerk said. "Let herself get took." He shook his head. "Damn fool niggers," he said.

Sarah looked coldly at him. "No more damn fool than some others," she said.

"They're having trouble with old Morris Shotwell, Mr. Griffith," the clerk said. "Two of 'em on the place bought washing machines from Grossi's appliances, and now Shotwell has bought Grossi out and they got payment trouble."

"The man says he can't find no record of me making the last three payments," Sarah said. "He looked me right straight in the head and told me I ain't paid. And he's coming out here today and going to take my machine, if I don't pay up all the back payments — and this month, too. And I don't have the money to do it, Mr. Wilburn, even if I owed it to him. Miss Sunny says come tell you about it."

"When's he coming?"

"Supposed to be at my house this afternoon around four. So I come up here to talk to you before he gets there."

"Don't you have any record of your payments?"

"No, sir. Mr. Grossi's salesman give us a receipt every time we made a payment, but he never asked to see 'em again, and I been trading with him twenty years and never had no trouble with him. So I didn't think I'd need 'em. I didn't exactly throw 'em away, but I can't find the last three."

A car drew up outside the commissary and the clerk looked out. "Here he comes now," he said. "Floyd. The old man sends him to do the dirty work."

Nat walked over to the office door and looked out, too. "Who are the Shotwells?" she said. "This one drives *some* car."

"You know who they are, Nat. Marigold Truitt, she was, and married well. She's a friend of your Aunt Louise's — or at least they did church and garden club work together. Morris used to be in the real estate business, but he's branched out. Owns half the east side of the county and a big chunk of the Farmers' Bank. This is Floyd — the son. Strange fella. I've never gotten three words out of him; but I've heard he knows more about the stock market than anyone else in the county."

"Married?"

"No," Wilburn said.

Floyd Shotwell had gotten out of his pale blue Cadillac after carefully locking the doors, and now he came up the plank steps onto the broad porch that ran the length of the commissary. Three Negro men standing and talking on the porch lowered their voices and did not look up as he walked past them and came in at the commissary door.

Wilburn, Nat, Sarah, and the clerk had moved out of the office and into the commissary. The clerk went behind a back counter and began to examine his stock.

Floyd stood in the doorway, looking first at Wilburn and then for a longer moment at Nat — a great, long-armed man, wearing his khaki pants low on his hips and under an incipient bay window in the style of country people in the South, his khaki shirt blousing out above the pants in wrinkled folds. His head, balding noticeably, although he appeared to be in his early thirties, was markedly too small for the powerful, fleshy body. His small round chin seemed no indication of weakness, in part perhaps because of the powerful body, but even more because everything about him gave the impression of a withdrawal so deep that weakness could have no place in it. The face was closed, with an expression of dread around the small rosy mouth and in the black eyes shadowed by jutting brows and deep circles. He looked as if the necessity of meeting and talking with other people were more than he could bear. One could imagine him as a taciturn child, standing alone on the edge of a schoolyard crowded with playing children. His fists would have been clenched and his eyes filled with baffled pain.

After a long pause, he ducked his head, as if he had made up his mind not to speak to any of them, and half-turned to go out again. Then he saw Sarah and hesitated.

"That outfit and a *Cadillac?*" Nat said in a low voice to Sarah.

"Hush," Wilburn murmured, and then, "Hello, Floyd. Come on in." He started across the room with his hand outstretched.

"Ummmmm . . ."

"How have you been? Haven't seen you in a long time."

"Fine." Shotwell made no response to the offered hand.

"Nat," Wilburn said, "you remember Floyd Shotwell, don't you? Floyd, my cousin, Nat Stonebridge."

Nat moved out into the commissary. "Of course we remember each other," she said. "How are you?" She, too, held out her hand cordially. Shotwell looked at it for a moment as if it might pinch him, but this time he stepped forward, took the hand, and gave it a hasty shake.

"My goodness!" Nat said. "Floyd Shotwell! I don't reckon I've seen you since long before the war. Since we used to be in Sunday school together."

"I was three years behind you," Floyd said.

"Well, now, you don't need to remind me of that!"

"I hear you've had a little misunderstanding with Sarah here," Wilburn said. "Maybe I can help you straighten it out."

"No misunderstanding," Shotwell said. "She's three months behind. If she doesn't pay today, we've got to repossess."

"Well, she tells me she was paid up with Grossi — but it seems she's lost her receipts."

"We go by what we've got," Shotwell said. He shrugged. "Grossi kept lousy records. Piddling little two-bit operation."

"And you're trying to straighten these poor folks out," Nat said. "My, isn't that nice! Sarah, I know you're not going to have a minute's worry about your machine."

"Maybe if we talk to Grossi's salesman, he can remember — or maybe he even has duplicates of the receipts," Wilburn said. "I know him right well — the Roselli kid."

Shotwell did not answer. He was staring at Nat.

"Why don't we go back to your office and have a cup of coffee, Wilburn?" Nat said. She turned to Shotwell. "Wilburn makes the best coffee north of New Orleans." She moved toward the back of the commissary, and the men followed. As she passed Sarah, Nat brushed against her, glanced at her, and gave an almost imperceptible shrug.

When the office door had closed behind them, Sarah turned to the clerk. "Miss Nat thinks time she finishes with him, I'll have two washing machines," she said. "But she don't know them Shotwells."

"Why you reckon the old man's got him out collecting from you people?" the clerk said. "Looka there — in a Coupe de Ville! Picking up ten bucks here and ten bucks down the road. Man, that's crazy."

"Teaching him how to get rich," Sarah said.

"He don't need to learn how. He's already got all he can use."

"Got to learn how to keep it," Sarah said. "Gimme five pounds of sugar, please, and a ten pound sack of meal. Two pounds of salt meat. And a Eskimo Pie. I got to get on home."

Floyd Shotwell sat for perhaps ten minutes in Wilburn's office stirring a cup of coffee and listening to Nat chatter. During that time he said scarcely a word; but before he left, he asked if he could take her back to town, and she explained that she had her own car.

When he was gone, Wilburn looked at Nat with amusement and exasperation. "Well, you snowed him," he said. "I'll bet he hasn't offered anybody else a ride in that sky-blue Cadillac — not even his mother. Was all that for Sarah's benefit, or do you have plans of your own?"

"A little of both," Nat said. "Now, don't be a bore."

"But what do you want with him?"

"He's probably a nice fellow, once you get to know him," Nat said. "He just seems to be a little bit shy. He's not an alcoholic, is he?"

Wilburn said nothing.

"Look, sweetie, be realistic," Nat said. "I'm stuck here — maybe for months. I'm broke. There's not an unattached man over thirty between here and Memphis. And all of a sudden Floyd Shotwell drives up in a Cadillac convertible. Yes, he's ugly. (Did you notice he doesn't have any hair at all on the backs of his hands?) But Uncle Aubrey is ugly, too, and if I have to choose between spending my evenings with Uncle Aubrey or with Floyd, I'm delighted to have the unexpected choice."

"You have us," Wilburn said. "Me. You can spend your evenings with us." He reached across the desk and laid his hand on hers for an instant. "Let him alone, Nat," he said. He shrugged and, tilting back in his chair, put his hands in his pockets. "Maybe I'm jealous," he said. "I sit here looking at you and talking with you (And I ought to be over at the gin working.), and I hear the old fire bell ringing for a conflagration. It's automatic! And the corollary to that is, 'She may not be for me, but she's too good for that clod.' "

"You know you can't be like that, darling," Nat said. "What a mess that would be."

Wilburn grinned. "All in the family," he said. But then he shrugged. "Don't worry," he said. "I'm not going to 'be like that.' But I'm not going to sit by and watch you cook up a romance with Floyd Shotwell, and say nothing."

Nat got up. "I've got to go, Wilburn," she said. "Aunt Louise's car is in the shop, and I promised I'd come back by five and take her to somebody's tea."

Wilburn rose and went with her into the commissary, pausing at the counter where the clerk was weighing nails for a waiting Negro.

"Who else on the place bought a machine from Grossi, Doy? Besides Sarah?"

"Bishop Tillman's wife. What's her name? Clara."

"You all don't need to worry about that," Nat said. "I fixed it."

"Well, to be on the safe side, I think I'll call Roselli and see what he's got to say about it," Wilburn said.

" 'Bye Wilburn. I've just *got* to go."

"I'll tell Sunny you're here and she'll call you." He followed her out to the car and opened the door. "Let me think about the job problem," he said. "We'll come up with something. As for a lawyer, I believe Coleman and Coleman are probably your best bet. The old man is your cousin, you know — fifth or sixth — and he'll take an interest in you for Cousin Louise's sake. Call him, and be sure he knows who you are. And for God's sake, don't wear that Mardi Gras dress. Have you got a suit — like, say, gray or black? No, not black. You manage to make black sensational. Dirty brown."

"I can dress myself to go to a lawyer, Wilburn Griffith," Nat said. "I'm not feebleminded."

5

THE GIN AND COMMISSARY on Hunters' Refuge are only a mile from the comfortable, two-story, clapboard farmhouse, built in the late twenties on the site of the old Hunter mansion, where Wilburn Griffith and his family live. Quite often, in all kinds of weather, Wilburn leaves his car at the commissary when the day is over and walks home. He is a man who takes pleasure in the weather — bad or good — and in the smell and sound of the fields spread out around him under the huge Delta sky. Even in February, at the nadir of the year, he sees in this gray and barren landscape under a cold, dripping sky an austere beauty like the beauty of the desert or the winter sea. The fog smoking up from pond and drainage ditch, the gray sky and bare cypress trees, even the rows of dead stalks rattling in the wind that sweeps the unturned fields — these are as lovely to him as the drifts of white locust blossoms that perfume the April air, the greening willows along the creek bank, or the pale, pencil-thin rows of germinating cotton.

Most afternoons Wilburn scarcely thinks at all as he walks, but listens to and watches the moving creatures and the changing foliage in his fields and woods — in winter, the stiff-legged bouncing flight of a cottontail startled out of its hiding place by the roadside, or the sudden descent of a flock of cedar waxwings into the swamp holly thicket; in spring, the first green-gold flaming of the trees, when all the woods catch fire with life and the ditches are awash with primrose seashells tumbled on a strand of oats as coppery gold as an island beach under the bright sunlight; in summer, the flash of a red-winged blackbird out of the briars in the ditch, the trumpet vines, heavy with orange flowers in the throbbing heat of July, the first modest pink blossoms on the cotton plants, and everywhere the proliferating life of the earth: dragonflies poised over the pond waters, wood ducks and coots and kingfishers and orchard orioles, doves and mockingbirds and field larks calling and answering from woods and fields and water and, in his garden, staked tomato vines heavy with fruit, eggplants shining, as purple as the night sky, and okra and corn and Johnson grass and wild strawberry vines; and, in every season, the downward plunge of the red sun behind the sweep of levee, the long shrill of locusts, the distant barking of dogs, and, at last, the night, vast and mysterious above the silent earth.

If his two children are at home when he gets there, Wilburn will sometimes take them out with him, down the road toward the commissary to see what he has seen: The dewberries in the thicket on the ditchbank are ripe; there is a pair of ivory-billed woodpeckers (rarest of birds!) in the sycamore tree by the pond; or a flock of grosbeaks flying like blue flowers above the flowery blue vetch. "Come quick! If we go right now, they may still be there."

On the afternoon of Nat's visit to his office, however, Wilburn walked in an abstracted mood. He had been moved by Nat out of the ordinary rut of his life, and he knew it. He was a man with few illusions about himself, one who looked curiously at his own emotions and motives, and tried, as a matter of principle, to call them by name. Impatiently he shrugged off the anarchic impulse toward an affair with Nat. "No, that won't do," he said aloud. "Out of the question." He had felt in himself during the months of his wife's vague and intermittent ill-health the pressure of his passions — and had stayed baffled and miserable. He was not a man who could sleep happily with strange women, and besides, he took his responsibility toward his wife seriously. It's not so much *sexual* responsibility, he said to himself. He knew well enough what happened to that kind of morality confronted with desire. No, it's more than that. But, heavily, at the bottom of his mind, glimmering clearly in the darkness of his thoughts, lay the conviction that his wife did not want him, might never want him again, regardless of whether she was ill or well — that she would be glad, so long as she did not have to know about it, if he took his urgencies elsewhere. We can still have the patience to arrange our lives so that things work, he said. But he did not know how to begin.

It was not that she rebuffed him. If there had been anything so clear-cut as that to begin with, he would have spoken out. But it was only a feeling that he had — a feeling about their nights together, of duty performed, a silent compliance that turned him cold and left him with a crippled sense of himself. Still (He continued to reason calmly.), nothing is so important as the children. *Nothing.* To keep everything steady for them. And Nat . . . ? He shook himself again. Nat didn't want him either. That was evident.

Another curious thing, he said to himself, is why we don't talk about it — don't ever bring it out into the open. Why doesn't Sunny want to *tell* me — something — *anything?* But we can't, he said. Would be disastrous — everything cracked wide open.

No place to put ourselves anymore; no way to protect each other. Better to let it be.

It had not once crossed Wilburn's mind during the months of this dilemma, of wondering what Sunny wanted and how to bring their life together into some tolerable shape, that he might get a divorce. Such a ruthless cutting of ties for the sake of "happiness" was entirely outside the range of alternatives that seemed possible to him. And when he told himself that nothing was so important as the children, it was not with the intention of shoring up a crumbling conviction, but simply a statement of the central fact of his life — a way of looking at and doing things that only an almost unimaginable upheaval could change.

And yet, he did not carry over into his thoughts about Nat — or about anyone else for that matter, even his wife — the rocky limitations that governed his own life, but regarded every person he knew as if he might have come from another planet — as a creature with standards and traits and necessities that he could not presume to judge. His habit was always to say about a judgment on someone's behavior, "But on the other hand . . ." So much so that his mother, a somewhat straitlaced Presbyterian, had once said to him in exasperation, "Nothing is black and white to you, Wilburn — *nothing!* You see everything in varying shades of gray." And he had said with a grin, "I suppose that's true, Mama, *to a degree*." But she didn't take it as a joke. "For some things people do," she said, "there are *no* mitigating circumstances."

He thought of her now and of what her reaction would have been this afternoon if she had heard Nat say of her son, "He would have had to leave his horse," and "Jeff promised him a swimming pool." But how can you know what Nat means, he thought — how much of her ruthlessness is real and how much a pose, or a shield against sympathy, or even a genuine concern at some level of her thoughts for the boy's welfare? No way to know with Nat. He had seen her take the least probing at her motives and turn it into an accusation of sentimentality — "Are you talking about Mother Love?" — had seen this quality operate again and again, and had said to himself about it for years that if anything could modify it, surely a child could. But that's *my* point of view, not hers, he thought. I dreamed it up with reference to myself, or at best to some woman I imagined into Nat's shoes. As for Nat, she *never* wanted a child.

He remembered quite well a conversation he had had with her a few months before she first filed for a divorce, the time she had intended to fight for custody of Hunter. "If it weren't for Hunter . . ." she had said. "He makes things so difficult."

And Wilburn had supplied the easy platitude. "Yes, the child always suffers most in a divorce."

"Oh, Wilburn," she had said, *"really!"* And then, detached and inquiring, as she often was regarding her own circumstances: "I never should have had him. Damn Jeff Stonebridge! He kept telling me that a baby would change our lives. I knew it wouldn't change me — except for my figure, maybe — but I thought it might make Jeff easier to handle. And then he *talked* about it so much. Finally I said all right just to shut him up.

"But I was right, after all. Hunter didn't change anything except to tie me down when I couldn't find a sitter. And now he's probably going to be the bone of contention in this divorce (if I ever get the nerve to ask for it). He *says* he wants to come with me. And of course that means I can get more money out of Jeff. But suppose we get into a hassle about whether I'm a fit mother? You see how complicated it all is? It's scary. I might end up a *pauper*, Wilburn!

"Those damn Stonebridges," she had said. "The old woman wants Hunter, even if Jeff doesn't. And she wants to make me pay. *Peasant*." She had grinned at him. "You know I'm a true aristocrat, Wilburn," she had said, "even if my grandmother *was* an Irish barmaid. And a true aristocrat should be able to associate with anybody. But Mrs. Stonebridge! Did you know their name used to be Steinbrude? He would never have thought of changing it — Jeff's father; but she made him do it when they got married. Isn't that contemptible?"

"You're a terrible snob, you know, Nat," Wilburn had said.

"No, I'm not. But, Wilburn, they're the kind of people who talk about *current events* at the dinner table. And have the whole family over for Sunday dinner. Everybody brings a 'covered dish.' And she says things like, 'We're a *close, loving* family. Is your family like that, Nat?' First time she said something like that to me, I said, 'No, thank God. We *hate* each other.' Now, *really*, should I let Hunter grow up in an environment like that?"

That had been during the first round, when she had intended to keep Hunter with her. He had been seven at the time.

"How much does Hunter know about what's going on?" Wilburn had asked.

"As much as anybody else. That is, I talk to him like I do to you. After all, he's got a lot at stake."

"You mean he knows you're going to ask Jeff for a divorce?"

"And he knows how to keep his mouth shut, too," she had said.

Walking through the dusty October afternoon, Wilburn thought of Hunter and then of his own son. He quickened his step and took two or three deep breaths to get rid of the constriction in his chest. Something so terrible — so moving — about the lives of children, he thought, that one can scarcely bear to think of them. He was inclined to poke fun at himself regarding this queer feeling of his, but it was real enough. He could go, unhappily, to a grammar school program to see his nine-year-old play the part of a pirate chief in the fourth grade operetta and, watching a couple of hundred small children — runny noses, mismatched socks, snaggled teeth — march to their places in the auditorium, be brought close to tears at the evidence of their gallantry, day after day to return with unquenchable optimism to battle this frightful incomprehensible world. I reckon Hunter has that kind of guts, he thought. God knows Nat had when she was a kid.

He thought of her as she had looked at eight or nine, dressed in one of those high-necked, starched guimpes and jumpers that little girls wore in the twenties, knee socks sagging, heavy shoes laced above her ankles, climbing up into the topmost branches of the elm tree in his yard, the waist-length black hair that Miss Louise kept in long corkscrews swinging behind her and sometimes catching in the branches, so that she would have to hang on with one hand and untangle her hair with the other. Oh, the weight and length and symmetry of those shining curls! The hours that Miss Louise forced Clakey and Nat to spend brushing and training them! And then . . . yes . . . there she was, standing in the middle of the living room (Had he put her up to it?) with a pair of scissors in her hand and a handful of the heavy ringlets lifted away from her head. And Miss Louise, in the doorway, her face a mask of horrified shock, saying in her sweet piping voice, "No! Nat, *dear!* No!" Someone else was there, too, he thought. Who? Yes, it was Clakey. Somewhere in the background behind Miss Louise was Clakey's dark pockmarked face with its grim infrequent smile, filled now with passionate complicity. "Let that child alone, Miss Louise. She *due* to cut off her hair." And Nat, with a smile, gave a great whack and let the ringlets fall to the floor. Ridiculous to call that courage, I suppose, he thought. Even then, she was barbering and molding herself to conform to some mysterious notion of a woman that she had in her own head. He sighed. And I suppose even then she heard hollow echoes behind every wall she knocked on. To her,

from the beginning, something was wrong, unacceptable, false
. . . Maybe it's that she is an artist — he smiled to himself at this
conceit — obsessed with imposing order on chaos and transform-
ing false reality into real make-believe. Only instead of using ordinary materials like clay or paint or words, she uses time and action,
and the work she creates is herself. She makes flesh and blood into
a work of art, and then it's as if the Naked Maja were hanging in
Miss Louise's parlor. Slightly embarrassing. Nobody knows quite
what to do with her — lying there on the parlor sofa, crossing her
legs and showing her brown thighs. You can't put a live picture
in the attic or paint a respectable dress on it.

Poor Cousin Louise, he thought. After all, maybe she's the courageous one. It's a marvel, really, that she survived Nat's childhood.
But then, of course, she had Anne Farish. That made it easier for
her — Anne Farish was a little lady from the time she took her
first step; she knew how to make it. Here Wilburn admonished
himself: charity, boy, charity. You needn't be so quick to judge
Anne Farish's motives. Whatever goes on inside that fat head,
she's managed to give Cousin Louise her money's worth. Come to
terms, come to terms. At thirty-seven are you still looking for pu-
rity? And in Anne Farish?

The trees that marked the location of his house loomed up ahead
— an open-ended square with rows of ancient dark green cedars
on the east and south and a windbreak of white locusts along the
ditchbank on the north. Wilburn unlatched the gate in the fence
on the west side of his yard and went in. He passed an elm tree with
an automobile tire swing and a rickety tree house in it, avoided
toys scattered on the walk and porch, opened his front door, and
went inside.

Half an hour later he was lying on the living room sofa with the
evening paper draped over his legs and a highball on the coffee
table at his elbow.

It was a comfortable room, put together out of the odds and ends of furniture that he and Sunny had gathered from their families or picked up themselves over the past twelve years. The sofa and chairs were covered with a rough linen print material, and sunny yellow curtains of the same material hung at the windows. Wilburn had built the shelves that lined one wall and were filled with a worn collection of modern fiction, old textbooks, gardening books, children's books, technical books on farming, and the sets of classics that Wilburn had inherited from his father — Dickens, Scott, Thackeray, Balzac, *The Arabian Nights*, and *The Library of Southern Literature*. On the wall over the fireplace hung a portrait of Sunny's great-great-grandfather, an odd-looking little Dickensian clerk of a man to whom Wilburn, in his cups, sometimes addressed silent speeches on the subject of traits that Sunny might possibly have inherited from him.

Wilburn picked up his drink from the battered coffee table, took a swallow, put it down, and for a few minutes absently watched his son Billy who was sitting on the floor beside him picking at the tangled line in a fishing reel. He reached down and ruffled the child's hair. "How's it coming, son?"

"I'm going to throw this damn reel in the creek, Daddy. It's *never* going to get untangled."

"Don't do that," Wilburn said. "Wait'll I finish my drink, and I'll help you."

Sunny, sitting on the other side of the table from them, pulled a long fuzzy thread through the piece of canvas on which she was working. "Don't say 'damn,' Billy," she said in an even voice.

Wilburn looked up at his wife. "Nat's in town again, Sunny," he said. "Jeff is behind on his alimony and she's broke."

"Last time she came, I was sweeping beer cans out from under the beds for weeks afterwards," Sunny said.

Wilburn continued to watch her without expression. Beginning to get old, he thought. Aloud he said, "She's on the wagon."

Sunny glanced at him and, as if she read his thought, touched her own cheek. "I'm not really up to Nat, on or off the wagon," she said. She brushed back a strand of pinkish hair and went on with her work.

Curious how strange she is to me, Wilburn thought. Fifteen years of marriage and still — no hold, no loving familiarity . . . He cut himself off and surreptitiously waggled his foot, watching it as intently as he had Sunny. For that matter, he said to himself, my own foot is as strange to me as she is, except that I hardly ever get irritated with my foot.

"Where has she been?" Sunny asked.

"Beachcombing, I suppose. She was in Mexico for a while, and then Puerto Rico."

"Working?"

"I don't think Nat will ever be troubled by the immorality of loafing," Wilburn said. It's mainly fat, he thought. If she lost fifteen or twenty pounds . . . "Sunny?" he said.

"Yes?" Absorbed, she continued to look sternly at the piece of canvas in her hands. She was a large woman — a considerable presence sitting there in a wing chair with her feet planted firmly on the floor and her back straight. She sat, very calm and erect, pulling threads in and out of her handwork with unhurried skill. Her hair was the odd shade of faded pinkish amber streaked with gray that one sometimes sees in an aging strawberry blonde. It was wavy at the temples and she wore it in a long braid wrapped twice around her head. The big, slightly equine face had been handsome when she was younger, but now, as Wilburn had observed, she was too heavy, and the delicacy of line that had marked her straight nose and high cheekbones was obscured by flesh. Her arms and shoulders and bosom had none of the shadowy hollows that had made them lovely, but were a convex expanse of very soft white flesh, flecked here and there with reddish-brown freckles.

"We won't have to go to any trouble for her," Wilburn said, "but I'd like to give her a little moral support."

"All right. I'll call her tomorrow," she said. "I didn't mean to sound grumpy. How long is she going to be here?"

He shrugged. "Until she gets hold of enough money to leave, I suppose."

"I'll ask her to dinner," Sunny said.

"You know there isn't anybody else in Philippi she cares about. Just us."

"That's true," she said. "And Nat's not dull, you can say that for her. Once I make the effort, I always enjoy her." She said nothing for a few minutes, then, "It's time for her to marry again. Maybe we can find her a man."

"One seems to have found *her*," Wilburn said. "Floyd Shotwell came in while she was at the commissary this afternoon, and he was obviously smitten."

"Floyd Shotwell? I don't believe it. He never goes out with anybody."

He nodded. "It's not so surprising as all that," he said. "Nat makes an impression — even on somebody like Floyd. But he's not my notion of good company. Why don't you see if you can scare up somebody a little bit more prepossessing?"

"He's got money," Sunny said.

"Do you think Nat's as simple as that? Jeff had money, too."

Sunny spread her work on her lap and regarded it with a serious and satisfied look. "You're always trying to make things more complex than they are," she said. "Billy, go find your sister, please. Supper'll be ready in a little while, and I think she's gone down by the pond."

"What are you making?" Wilburn said. "Something new?"

She held out the rectangle of canvas for him to see. The threads were drawn through it in an intricate pattern of scrolls and leaves. "Table mats," she said. "Aren't they going to be pretty? I was thinking if I made three or four sets, they would be grand Christmas presents."

Things will be different, once she has this operation, Wilburn thought. I make a mistake to think of things as they are as permanent. Right *now* — always so immediate, so consuming, that over and over again I haven't the imagination to see how different the future will be (maybe even in ten minutes) or to remember how different the past was, much less to pull together all the threads that turned last week and last year into now. And he tried to think concretely of what his life had been like five years ago — ten years ago — in the early days of his marriage. He sometimes said to himself when he lapsed into this kind of reverie that he had been unfair to Sunny when he married her. He had come home on leave from the army in the early days of 1943, already determined to marry; and he had taken one look at Sunny — nineteen, grown-up while he had been gone — and had begun to court her. What had gone into it? Like a great many men, and some who were right, he had had a strong premonition of death. He felt, even then, at twenty-two, not the least conviction of his own immortality. He wanted a lovely girl to sleep with as many nights as he could have her and, as much as he wanted that, he wanted a child and a home — to squeeze into a few months all that could be squeezed in.

As for the reasons why she had married him — he supposed that she, too, had been caught up in the ambience of that particular time and place. He had been a soldier, and besides having about him, like all soldiers, the irresistible glamour of threatening death, he had been a reasonably attractive and handsome young man. It was quite simply almost impossible for a girl to stay unmarried in 1943. What else could she give for her country except herself?

The time of bliss that was to stay him for his death had lasted
a month. He had gone overseas and left her pregnant.

But Sunny was not made for childbearing. The big healthy
body rejected a child — not once, but after he came back from the
war, again, and then a year later, again. He had wanted to adopt
children, but Sunny had refused. "How can you be sure how they
would turn out?" she said, and, "How can you be sure about your
own?" he replied. "Exactly," she said. "If you run a risk with your
own, think how much more chancy it is to take on someone else's."
Finally, in 1948, she managed to carry his son seven months. (She
stayed in bed most of the time.) And two years later they had a
daughter.

But now, in 1957, in the concrete excitement and reality of
harvest time (or planting time or poisoning time) with two children under his roof, an ailing wife to persuade toward a frighten-
ing operation, and Floyd Shotwell trying to cheat his tenants, all
that time in the past — the end of the war, the early years of his
marriage, the inevitable fate of romance — seemed unimportant
to Wilburn. He thought occasionally with detached interest about
the behavior of the man he had been then and particularly, if
he was in a mood to generalize, he dwelled on how very little he
knew about that man — what had motivated him, what had
brought him step by step to any one point in time, any one act,
that he could now remember. And yet, he would say to himself, I
know more about him, know him more intimately, than it is possible to know anyone else in the world. The darkness that he felt
in himself, layer upon layer, beneath his slightest action, would
fill him with dismay. It's *there*, he would say to himself. I take it
into account. But now, *today*, the gin has broken down again.

6

"WE USUALLY SIT on the gallery this time of the year," Miss Louise said to Wilburn as she led him into her parlor, "or the back sitting room, if the weather is cool. But I'm painting." She smiled dimly and apologetically at him. "This is the only dry room in the house. You see," — she gestured at walls which were papered with bright bouquets of red roses and wandering tendrils of vine — "I put wallpaper in here (and in my own room) in spite of the bayou. I know it won't last more than two years before it begins splitting, but I couldn't resist it."

"The bayou?" Wilburn said.

"Yes. Aubrey says we're on the old filled-in bed of Carney's bayou. It ran into the river just south of here. And you should hear it at night, dear. The house, I mean. Creaking and cracking like it's getting ready to fall down. Some days I get up and the walls have actually shifted enough to split the paper. But I just don't worry about it. It's been moving all over this lot for at least fifty years, and there's nothing to expect but that it will keep right on moving." She shook her head and frowned. "Still," she said, "I don't understand how the water could be running under all that dirt. You would think . . ." Her voice trailed away.

"Probably he doesn't mean that the water is actually still running under there," Wilburn said. "Just that the land is not very stable."

"Whatever it is," she said, "I couldn't resist this wallpaper. How have you been, dear?"

"Fine," Wilburn said. "I . . ."

"Besides, I like to sit in this room. It's my favorite room in the house. But Aubrey says there isn't a comfortable chair for him. That's why we use the back sitting room most of the time. Why can't he sit a little more lightly? That's what I'd like to know. If he had more *feeling* for furniture . . . It came from Grandmama, you know. I think your mother got some of her things, too, didn't she, Wilburn? You remember her, don't you? She was your great-great-aunt Caroline."

"Yes'm," Wilburn said. "I've heard Mother speak of her. I was wondering, Cousin Louise, is Nat . . . ?"

"How is that lovely wife of yours?" Miss Louise said. "I haven't seen her at church lately, and I've been concerned about her. She's not sick, is she, Wilburn?"

"She hasn't been very well this fall," Wilburn said, "but . . ."

"You were a lucky boy to land Sunny, Wilburn. I suppose you know that. But I always like to tell a man how lucky he is. Some men just don't realize . . . Sunny had half a dozen others dangling from her string (including James Carstairs, who owns three-fourths of the town of Lexington), but she chose *you*. Sit right there, dear. That's the sturdiest chair in the room, I believe. We so seldom entertain a young man, you know . . ." She chattered on in a thin, reedy voice without giving Wilburn a chance to reply, and he began to look at her with interest.

I wonder what she's got on her mind, he thought.

After a few minutes, he tried again. "Cousin Louise," he said in a clear firm voice, "is Nat here? She asked me to get some information for her and . . ."

"Yes, I'm going to tell her you're here, but . . ." She faltered and looked at him uncertainly. "I wanted to tell you before you saw her," she said, "did you know Nat has a beau? Such a . . ."

"A beau!" Wilburn said. "A *beau*, Cousin Louise?"

"Yes, she has. A perfectly lovely boy — and from a lovely family, too. Floyd Shotwell. I want you to encourage her to take him seriously. It would be such a good match for her. You know, Morris is in business with Aubrey now, and . . ."

"Cousin Louise, you know I couldn't encourage Nat to marry somebody, even if I wanted to. She goes her own way."

"Oh, I know, dear. I know. I really meant, don't *dis*courage. It's so easy to blow the cold breath of discouragement on romance. After all," she glanced at him and then looked uneasily away, "Nat has *nothing*," she said. "She just threw away that nice Jeff Stonebridge — a lovely home, servants, position in the community — a *perfect* marriage."

Wilburn did not reply.

"Well," she said, "I'll go tell Nat you're here. Why don't you look at my hens while I'm gone, dear? Right over there in the étagère." She led Wilburn to a corner of the parlor, and he found himself confronting an elaborately-carved Victorian cabinet filled with a collection of small china baskets in the shape of setting hens.

"Just examine them, dear," Miss Louise said. "You'll find quite a variety — even including one very early example in pottery — Austrian, I believe. I've been gathering them for years. Now . . ." she took one from the shelf, handed it to him, and left the room.

Wilburn put the hen down, stared at the shelves for a moment ("Chickens!" he muttered. "I'm standing here looking at china chickens!"), then turned and began to examine the parlor. No wonder Aubrey doesn't like to sit in here, he thought, as he looked at the collection of fragile and uncomfortable chairs and sofas and graceless marble-topped tables. He sat down carefully in the chair that Miss Louise had pointed out as the sturdiest and continued his inspection. The long narrow windows were hung with green velvet, fringed in gold, drawn back with gold-tasseled ties, and finished with curving, velvet-covered cornices. Opposite Wilburn on the interior walls were three or four photographs of members of the family hung at odd heights and with no apparent plan. On either side of the étagère were small reproductions of paintings — on the left "Madame Lebrun and her Daughter," the round white arm and shoulder of the woman painted without a trace of thought for the muscles that lie beneath the skin of a human body, the expression on the mother's face a simper of affection, on the child's one of lunatic innocence; on the right, Reynolds' "Age of Innocence," the distillation of idealized, unsuffering childhood.

I wonder where Paul and Virginia are, Wilburn thought. And Jenny Lind. Then he corrected himself. No, there's a nice distinction between the kind of old lady's house that has Madame Lebrun and Sir Joshua Reynolds, and the kind that has Jenny Lind. And a Paul and Virginia house is somewhere between.

At this moment Miss Louise wandered back in and sat down on the love seat opposite Wilburn. "Nat will be along in a minute, dear," she said. "I'm sorry the house smells so painty, but everything had gotten dingy. Can you stand it? When the paint begins to yellow, you know, you can scarcely tell if anything is clean or not, can you? And I always say, 'Cleanliness is next to Godliness.' Don't you? So fortunate Aubrey is in the hardware business and we can get paint wholesale. Although I must say he acted this time as if he hadn't already paid for all that paint he's got down there on his shelves. He didn't want me to paint. But I just *have* to stay clean. I can't *bear* dirt." She pointed to the deeply-carved legs of a marble-topped table. "Look at those acanthus leaves," she said. "You won't find a speck of dust in there, and that's the acid test. And incidentally, that's one thing that makes it so fortunate about the washing machine. The way I feel about dirt, I mean. I suppose I've worn out half a dozen washwomen as well as three washing machines in my lifetime. Have I told you about Aubrey's wonderful washing machine?"

"No, m'am," Wilburn said.

"I have the greatest difficulty understanding exactly how it works, but it is certainly going to revolutionize washing, and it will be so cheap to manufacture, too. It's the first one of Aubrey's inventions I've ever been able to take an interest in. My goodness, Wilburn! From what Aubrey says, it's entirely possible we're going to be rich. Isn't that exciting? Morris Shotwell has gotten interested in it, and . . . But I've gotten off the subject, dear, and besides it's all supposed to be a secret. I was telling you, before I went out, you know, about Nat and Floyd. He comes to see her almost every day. He's just been rushing her off her *feet*, and (Of course, I wouldn't mention it to *her*.) I'm so hoping she'll consider him. She listens to you, Wilburn . . ."

"Cousin Louise, do you mean to say that Floyd Shotwell has asked Nat to marry him?"

"Oh, *asked!* I'm not worried about that. He would ask her, if she wanted him to. Nat has the most mysterious power over men, Wilburn. (I'm speaking very frankly to you, dear; after all, you *are* a cousin.) It's something I've never really been able to understand. Of course, she's my niece and a dear child; I don't mean *I* don't love her. But if I were a man, I don't think she would be my type."

"No," Wilburn murmured. "I suppose not."

"She's an abominable cook," Miss Louise said. She shook her head at the mysteries of human behavior and, getting up, wandered over to the étagère again and picked up a small hen made of hobnailed glass. "Did you see this, dear?" she said.

"It may be that Nat is going to be better off single," Wilburn said.

Abruptly Miss Louise turned on him, and the uncertainty in her manner dropped away. "No!" she said, shaking the hen at him. "Don't say that. Nat's been a trial to me all my life, Wilburn — you're just in no position to know! She — sometimes I think she has no moral sense at *all*. It's as if she's bent on turning the accepted way, the *right* way, of doing things upside down. And *now* — now she has a second chance to make a decent life. So don't say she ought to stay single — and especially not to her."

"Floyd is a very strange man, Cousin Louise," Wilburn said. "I don't think you have any idea — maybe none of us have — what kind of man he really is. He might not be a good husband — to Nat or anybody else."

"When you come to that, all men are strange, aren't they? To women, that is." She turned away, put the hen back in its place on the shelf and picked up another. "But after all," she said, "you have to have them around. I mean, I'm a realist, dear."

Nat came in as Miss Louise was saying this. "Did you know Aunt Louise was a realist, Wilburn?" she said. "Doesn't that surprise you a teeny weeny bit?"

"Hey, now, you two let me off the hook," Wilburn said. "I'm a very simple fellow."

"Of course, I like things to be nice," Miss Louise said. "But there's nothing unrealistic in that. And I try to see the best in people. That's just plain, ordinary Christianity. But I'm practical. All I was saying was that a woman needs a man around the house."

"Not me," Nat said.

"She does. I mean to — to open jars, and — and reach things on the top shelf. Isn't that true?"

"Yes'm," Wilburn said. "I reckon so. Although I hadn't thought of my indispensability in quite that light."

"And besides," Miss Louise was off on another wandering, almost incomprehensible dissertation. Her voice, reedy and insistent, broken into now and then by Nat's softer lower one, continued to impinge vaguely on Wilburn's consciousness, but he was no longer trying to follow the sense of the conversation. He was thinking, instead, of Floyd and of the possibility that Nat, out of boredom or the fear of poverty, might trick herself into marrying him.

What is it I dislike so much about him, he wondered, except that he's courting Nat? I hardly know him. And then: I reckon Miss Louise is right in a way. All men and women are strange to each other (except maybe for the first little while when they're in love, and, of course, that's illusion). So why should the notion that he and Nat are alien to each other make me . . . ? You know very well why, old buddy, he thought. It's the brutal and saddening fact that *you* want her. And she's not interested in you, but she may actually be planning to marry Floyd Shotwell.

He thought of Floyd as he had seen him, over and over during the past ten years, walking the streets of Philippi; the cold withdrawn face and the hulking body; the eyes, like the eyes of a man who has been tortured. And again, driving his car — the sky-blue Cadillac convertible — too fast down a country road, smothering the tenant houses and the little front yard flower gardens — the marigolds and zinnias and scarlet coxcomb — with suffocating gray dust. That's all I know about him, Wilburn thought —nothing else. But suddenly he remembered an evening in the early fifties when he had seen Floyd under other circumstances. Driving home late from a party, he had found himself without cigarettes, had stopped at the first roadhouse he passed, and leaving Sunny in the car, had gone in. Floyd had been sprawled at the bar, drunk, and, when Wilburn had come up to get change for the cigarette machine, had spoken to him as confidently as a man might speak to an old friend — almost, in fact, as if he had been expecting Wilburn to join him. He looked up from the study of a puddle on the vinyl counter top and said, "I'm here."

"Hello, Floyd," Wilburn said. "How've you been?"

"Drunk."

The bartender handed Wilburn his change and Wilburn nodded and turned to the cigarette machine. He was tired and a little bit drunk himself; and he was in a hurry to get home and go to bed. Christ, I've got to take the sitter home, he thought.

Floyd followed him to the cigarette machine. "Damn whores in here," he said. "Goddamn whores everywhere. You know it?"

Wilburn looked quickly around to see if there were any women near enough to have heard Floyd, but the few in the room were sitting with their dates in booths around the walls. No one appeared to have paid any attention to him.

"All whores," Floyd said. He stood swaying beside Wilburn, giving off the reek of a long, uninterrupted drunk, his skin illuminated by a greenish pallor that might have been illness or a reflection from the fluorescent lights glaring out above the mirrors behind the bar. "Some of 'em don't know how to make any money at it," he said. "Tha's only difference."

Without answering, Wilburn put his money in the machine, pressed the button, and pocketed his cigarettes.

"I asked girl to marry me tonight," Floyd said. "No. Not girl. Woman. Divorced. Offered her five . . . five hundred dollars to marry me. She wouldn't do it."

"I'm sorry," Wilburn said.

"Why should she?" Floyd said. "Didn't even know me."

The bartender was leaning on the counter watching them and listening to the conversation with a half-hopeful smile, as if it had occurred to him that Wilburn might take a troublesome customer off his hands.

"Look, Floyd," Wilburn said, "I hate to rush off, but I've got Sunny waiting in the car."

Floyd put out his hand to the cigarette machine and steadied himself. "You ever read about Haiti?" he said. "Zombis?"

"I gotta go, fella. Sleep it off. It won't be so bad tomorrow." He tried to start for the door, but Floyd reached out and caught him by the shoulder.

"Can they make love?" he said. "You think they can get a hard on?"

"Who?"

"Zombis. *Zombis.* You think . . . ? Int'restin' spec . . . speculation. Looked it up in *Encyclopaedia Britannica,* but no reference to zombis — in nineteen-forty-seven edition, that is."

"I've really got to go, fella. Sunny'll skin me." He had broken away and left Floyd swaying by the cigarette machine.

"My God," he had said to Sunny in the car. "My God."

"*Wilburn,*" Nat was saying, "wake up. What have you got on your mind? Aunt Louise was talking to you."

"It was nothing, dear," Miss Louise said. "I just said I have to go now. Look in on the painters. So if you young folks will excuse me . . ." She rose from the love seat and put the glass hen, which she had been holding and admiring all through the conversation, back in the étagère. "No telling what'll happen if I don't keep my eye on them. No *telling.* They're Cajuns. I can't imagine how they happened to settle in Philippi."

"M'am?"

"*Frenchmen,*" she said. "And you know even normal house

painters are inclined to drink too much, so what can you expect with Frenchmen? But they owe Aubrey some money, so here I am stuck with them."

. . .

"So you have a suitor, Nat," Wilburn said as soon as Miss Louise had left the room. "Is it true that you're going to marry Floyd Shotwell?"

"Aunt Louise dreamed that up out of next to nothing," Nat said. "He's been to see me a few times, that's all. Didn't I tell you two weeks ago it would be immoral for me to marry *anybody?*"

"OK," he said. "I just wondered if all that Shotwell money had changed your mind."

"It is tempting, isn't it?" she said. "Maybe I can figure out some other way to get some of it."

"What I stopped to tell you," Wilburn said, "I heard this morning that Francis Parsons (Do you remember him? He's a radiologist now.) needs a receptionist. His is pregnant and quitting right away. I told him you were looking for a job for a few months, and he said to tell you to come to see him. There wouldn't be very much to it. No typing or shorthand required."

Nat sat down in a Victorian armchair upholstered in green brocade, immediately got a cigarette from her shirt pocket, and began to smoke. "All right," she said. "I'll call him."

"You don't sound very enthusiastic. I thought you were desperate for a job."

"I told you I'm working on some way to get my hands on a little Shotwell money," Nat said in an exaggerated drawl. "It takes all my attention." She sighed. "But I still haven't done any good with Jeff," she said. "Mr. Coleman says it's just a matter of time, but meanwhile I'm broke. All this propaganda about the woman get-

ting the best of it in a divorce is ridiculous, Wilburn. I put up with
Jeff for ten long years, and I have to fight like a tiger to get my
two hundred a month out of him."

"I reckon it's easy only where the woman is taking care of the
kids," Wilburn said.

"Don't tell me! Judges and lawyers don't like my figure. That's
what the root of the trouble is. But I'm not going to bore you with
that sad tale again." She frowned severely at him and went on.
"I *know* I ought to have a job," she said. "It looks better when
you're trying to get your alimony, if you're working your fingers
to the bone and barely surviving. Besides, I have to have something to fall back on, in case I don't manage to get anything out of
him. Who knows, he may be about to go broke or something. He
never was much of a businessman, and now that his father is dead
and he doesn't have anybody to tell him what to do . . . But
working is so dull, Wilburn. You can't expect me to be enthusiastic. Anyhow, I'm glad you came by this morning — I was getting
ready to call you. Why don't you and Sunny have dinner with
Floyd and me on Thursday night. Anne Farish and Mr. McGregor
are coming over from Moss Ridge to spend the night, and I thought
I might get Floyd to take us all out to Sarelli's."

"Mr. McGregor?"

"You know — Charles Taliaferro. Anne Farish's husband."

Wilburn laughed.

"Well, his feet are so big," Nat said. "Do you remember in the
illustrations how Peter Rabbit always saw Mr. McGregor's huge
foot coming down, and the hoe? And his fingernails are dirty, too.
I wouldn't be surprised to see him coming in from the cabbage
patch in a pair of blue overalls. Will you go with us to Sarelli's?"

"Lord, Nat, we haven't been out there in ten years or more."

"I know, but they have a new cook and everyone says the food
has improved. Good pasta. Floyd goes out there all the time. He

says they've put in a real gambling room in the back on account of the new sheriff. Have you ever played roulette or anything like that?"

"What do you mean, on account of the new sheriff?"

"I mean, he doesn't mind, you know, as long as he gets his cut. He's supposed to be a reasonable sheriff. And as long as the syndicate stays out. The bootleggers are crazy about him. The General says . . ."

"The general?"

"General *Pershing* Pruitt. Don't tell me you don't know him, Wilburn. He's a very interesting character — a friend of Floyd's. You just *have* to meet him."

"Oh. *That* general. Yes, I know him," Wilburn said. "And he's probably an authority on the syndicate. You're moving in strange circles, sweetie."

"Well, I think criminals are interesting, Wilburn, don't you? I just can't help it. And the only difference between The General and Morris Shotwell . . ." She broke off.

"Morris is a hypocrite," Wilburn said. "Is that what you were going to say?"

"Maybe I was," Nat said. "But it's really a lot more complicated than that, isn't it? I don't believe I think Morris is a hypocrite at all. He and Marigold strike me as *sincere*. All I know for sure is he's dull, and that's worse than being hypocritical. I met them the other night and I couldn't pry a word out of him, but she talked very sincerely about what kind of drapes she was going to get for her living room. As for The General, he isn't a *real* criminal. He's more like that nice fellow in Tommy Trotter's band, the one who fell in love with me our last year at Ole Miss. Do you remember him, Wilburn? The one who saw me at a dance on the Peabody Roof and followed me to Oxford and took an apartment for the winter?"

Wilburn laughed. "How could I forget him? I rescued you from him that night he got hopped up on marijuana and wouldn't let you go back to the dormitory. I thought I was going to get shot."

"He was *sweet*," Nat said. "He composed a song just for me. It started out, 'Natalie, you're all the world to me.' " She sighed. "I wonder what ever became of him," she said. "People just drop out of your life and don't leave a trace. When he left Oxford — you know, after I wouldn't help him push dope . . . (I just couldn't, Wilburn, although he said it would be profitable. I was too chicken. And I felt bad about it, too, because he'd been so *devoted*. But I didn't really like him all that much. I never intended to be his mistress or anything, and it turned out that was kind of included in the deal.) Anyhow, when he left, he gave me an address in Chicago — not his own, because he didn't really have one, but of somebody who would always be able to find him — and he told me if I ever wanted any money, if I was ever in a jam, or if I ever needed anybody bumped off, just to write to that address and they would let him know." She giggled. "You see how sweet he was? I started two or three times to write him and see if he wouldn't have Jeff bumped off for me. But I'm a coward."

"The General probably knows him, if you're still interested," Wilburn said.

"There wouldn't be any point in it now, silly," she said. "But anyhow, how about Thursday night? Will you go? It's really civilized out at Sarelli's now. You can order a drink and have it brought to the table instead of having to take your bottle and hide it underneath. And they have a little band on Thursday, Friday, and Saturday nights, if anybody wants to dance. So come on. It's my turn to entertain you all, you know. I've had supper with you three times since I got home."

"I reckon I'd better check with Sunny first," Wilburn said. "I don't know what her plans are."

"I've already talked to her this morning, and she said she would ask you," Nat said. "You all certainly are *punctilious* with each other, aren't you, Wilburn? I think that's nice. So come on — we might have a good time. You know, you don't have to stay out in the country listening to the birds sing all the time. Besides, I just absolutely *have* to do something on Thursday night. It gives me the jimmies to sit home with Aunt Louise when Anne Farish is here. All they talk about is preachers and preserves."

"All right, Nat," Wilburn said. "We accept with pleasure. Matter of fact, I'm curious to see how Delta night life has changed in the last ten years." He rose. "I've got to get home," he said. "I have a couple of picker parts in the car."

"Thursday night, then," Nat said. "Seven-thirty all right with you? Shall we pick you up?"

"We'll meet you at Sarelli's," Wilburn said. "No point in your driving out in the country to get us." They walked out onto the gallery that ran the length of the front of the house. "Fall," Wilburn said. "The blackbirds are here." Big grackles with iridescent greenish and purple heads uttered their dry and rusty calls as they walked and pecked in the grass in front of the cottage. Along the border of the lawn, clumps of red spider lilies starred the flower bed, and at the corner a bearded sumac tree was beginning to flame. "Sometimes I think this is my favorite time of year," Wilburn said.

Nat shivered. "I don't like blackbirds," she said.

A long black Lincoln Continental swung around the corner into Muscadine and passed the Hunter cottage. The driver, a small round-faced man with deeply sunken black eyes and a small mouth with the lips pursed as if he'd just eaten a green persimmon, was hunched over the wheel of the car as if he were driving in a race. He glanced once at the Hunter house and, seeing Nat on the gallery, nodded curtly.

"There he goes," Nat said. "Morris. I wonder what he's doing on Muscadine Street."

Wilburn touched her affectionately on the shoulder. "How have things been going with you, *really*, Nat?" he said. "I've been so tied up trying to get the cotton out, I've hardly had time to breathe. And incidentally, I'm sorry I had to abandon you and Sunny the other night. Damn gin breaks down out there every day. I'm ready to scrap it and build a new one."

"I've been having a real interesting time," Nat said. "As soon as your crop is in, I want to sit down and have a nice long talk with you."

"Good."

"Wilburn, did you know Uncle Aubrey is in business with the Shotwells?"

"Your Aunt Louise was talking about it before you came in, but I couldn't make much sense out of what she said."

"He's got this invention," Nat said. "You know how Uncle Aubrey is always working on an invention? Of course, nobody pays any attention to them — he does it mostly for fun. But did you ever hear about the plowpoint he designed?"

Wilburn shook his head.

"It was supposed to be revolutionary — for a while he was having them made here and selling them at the store — he even took out a patent on them. But then — this was long before I was married — people quit using mules and plows and began to use tractors instead. And since then he's made all kinds of things, Wilburn. Like, he designed a record changer. That was after he began repairing small appliances in the back of the store and got interested in working with radios and record players. It would pick records up and turn them over instead of dropping them like an automatic changer. Do you remember the old Capehart record players? This did the same thing, but it was much simpler and cheaper to manufacture. He was going to take out a patent on that, but then the record people brought out long-playing records, and of course afterwards nobody was interested in it.

"Anyhow, now he's designed something else — it has something to do with washing machines, and he is awfully excited about it. He told Morris Shotwell about it, and Morris is going into business with him, and they're going to make a whole lot of money together. That's what Floyd told me. But it's supposed to be a secret. Aubrey and Louise made me swear not to mention it, so don't tell anybody."

"This interesting time you've been having," Wilburn said. "You've been going out with Floyd?"

"He's not like you think he is, Wilburn. At least I don't think he's like I thought he was. I mean, he's different. He doesn't *care*. That's kind of refreshing."

"I don't know what I think he's like," Wilburn said. "Besides, honey, it's none of my business. But I can't help being curious. You two . . ." He broke off and smiled. "You know," he said, "a man never can understand what an attractive woman — one who moves him — sees in another man."

"I think he's intelligent," Nat said. "I mean, he's even read people like Camus and — Plato — and — and — " (She giggled.) "Henry Miller."

"Oh, come off it, Nat," Wilburn said.

"He has. At least when he says something about them, it sounds like he knows what he's talking about — I mean, not phony. But I'm not saying he is an *intellectual*. He doesn't talk much about anything. I might as well admit he's not the most fascinating company in the world. If I wasn't desperate . . . But you know I can't bear to be alone very much, Wilburn. I hate to admit that my *resources* are *limited*, but — there it is. And at least he's shy. That has certain advantages I really appreciate. He never bothers me — like most men do. I mean, you know, he never pesters me to jump in the sack. He's a *gentleman*. It's such a relief! Why, I can relax with him just as safely as if he were a fag. Although fags are usually better conversationalists. So, as long as he continues to behave . . . I mean, he could take me down to Jackson or New Orleans for football weekends, and I might meet some really interesting people. Besides, there's all that money. I can't get it out of my head. Somebody ought to be doing something constructive with it."

"I've heard he doesn't get his hands on much of it," Wilburn said.

"Really? Well, he hasn't spent much on me, it's true. I'd thought it was because there isn't much to spend money on around here."

"Champagne and caviar," Wilburn said. "Furs. Diamonds. Automobiles. You've got to think big."

"I know it," Nat said. "Give me time. I still have to decide exactly what I'm going to think about."

7

IN A NIGHTCLUB the first thing Wilburn usually paid attention to was the music. He had his generation's nostalgia for the style of bands like Glenn Miller's or Hal Kemp's; he enjoyed dancing, and he always hoped to hear a good dance band. Tonight, however, the blare (clearly audible in the parking lot outside Sarelli's) of a rock and roll combo — electric guitars, drums, and bass fiddle backing a singer who was shouting out the lyrics to "All Shook Up" in the style of Elvis Presley — told him that he was not going to do much dancing. Inside, he looked around in astonishment, as a waiter led them to the table Nat had reserved.

A collection of balls, ranging in size from baseball to basketball, hung like Christmas tree ornaments from lengths of chain attached to a slowly-turning circular frame in the ceiling of the room. The balls were covered with tiny octagonal bits of mirrored glass; and four colored spotlights — rose, lavender, green and blue — shone on them from the corners of the room. The room was shadowy, and the spots of light reflected from the mirrored balls moved in swarms like hypnotized fireflies across the floor, the walls, in which panels of mirrored glass were set, and the faces of people sitting at tables around the edges of the room or dancing in the cleared spaces in the center.

"My," Sunny said. "This is quite a spot."

Wilburn looked down at her as they walked across the room. Flecks of light drifted slowly across her pinkish hair and white face. "What do you reckon we're doing here?" he said in a low voice. "I must be losing my grip to have let us in for this."

"It wasn't just you," she said. "I wanted to come."

At the table they found the other two couples waiting for them, Charles Taliaferro and Anne Farish on one side and Floyd at the end with Nat on his right. Sunny sat down beside Nat and Wilburn next to her; they ordered drinks. The others were already drinking.

Two drinks later, despite Nat's efforts at conversation, they were still a group of uncomfortable strangers. Wilburn drummed soundlessly on the table, and Sunny leaned close to him and said in his ear, "Don't panic, darling. After all, it's a *change*. And the food is going to be good."

He touched her affectionately on the arm. "Country life has made a recluse of me," he said. "I wasn't prepared — I'd forgotten what nightclub conversation was like. To say nothing of the decorations. And Shotwell! If he doesn't loosen up and make it a little easier on all of us, I'm going to get drunk."

Floyd sat at the end of the table, a drink gripped in both hands and held directly in front of him. From his expression, he might have been holding on to a life preserver in the middle of a whirlpool. His eyes were fixed and blank, the pupils contracted, his small mouth set in its habitual expression of panic. Nat leaned toward him and said something, and he took one hand away from his drink, raised it, and drank it down. Then he nodded distantly to her and signaled to a waiter. "Bourbon and water," he said. "Two."

"Anybody else need a patch?" Nat said.

The men shook their heads and then Wilburn spoke to Anne Farish's husband. "How's your crop, Charles? About in?"

The other man nodded. "Early over our way," he said. "I was already defoliating in the middle of August. How about you?"

"We're in good shape," Wilburn said. "This is going to be my best year since we bought Refuge."

"Been hunting yet?"

Wilburn shook his head.

"Man, we've been getting some dove around Moss Ridge. Plenty of quail, too, if you want to come over when the season opens. I put out a few pair three or four years ago, broke up the coveys last year, and man, they're all over the place — if you can just get 'em up. I've got a section now where they've got enough cover to thrive, you know, and still not too much. Best quail hunting in the Delta.

"And wild turkeys — you're not going to believe it, but they're really coming back in the woods along the creek over there."

"I wish Wilburn would go quail hunting," Sunny said. "I love quail. We haven't had any since Daddy died."

"I'm not much of a hunter," Wilburn said.

"You're kidding! Somebody told me you were a good shot."

"I used to be fair," Wilburn said. "I just don't like to hunt."

Charles tilted back in his chair, put his thumbs in his pants pockets, and shook his head sadly. A big, broad-shouldered man with mouse-brown hair and yellowish skin, he was not heavy, but had the kind of round, doughy face that made one remember him as fat. He looked at Wilburn with an expression of intense dedication on his face. "You owe it to your boy," he said.

You ought to be able to take your bare hands and punch that

face into some kind of shape, Wilburn thought; and then, but doubtless the passage of time will do something for it — bad or good. "What's that?" he said. "My boy?"

"A man ought to teach his son to *hunt*," Charles said. "You know, I'm teaching the men's Bible class in my church this year, and I said exactly the same thing to them last week. When we begin to talk about family relations and teaching our children values, I take a practical approach. Hunting! The great outdoors! The beautiful sight of doves coming into the water at dusk and the thrill of a good shot! Nothing like it to establish companionship — communication — with a boy, to teach him . . ." Here Charles brought his chair down on all four legs and leaned forward, as if carried away by the intensity of his feeling. "Mind you," he said, "you'll find plenty of justification in the Bible itself for the use of hunting in the way I'm talking about. Just to take one example, doesn't it say in Genesis that Nimrod is a mighty hunter before the Lord?"

"Yeah, I reckon it does," Wilburn said.

"Charles is a *serious* student of the Bible," Anne Farish said proudly.

"There's no end to what a boy learns from hunting," Charles said. "Respect for your skill, love of nature (And of course that means God, doesn't it? I bring that out in class.), obedience to the rules of good sportsmanship. That kind of thing will stick with him through life. And," (Here he lowered his voice and went on only after observing that Anne Farish was talking to Nat and not listening to him.) "he learns that there's a whole great big world where women can't follow you, where you can be *free*. Be a *man*. Of course, I don't say that in Sunday school."

"Well, I reckon Billy is going to have to get along without all that knowledge," Wilburn said, "or acquire it elsewhere."

"Wilburn is hard-headed," Sunny said. "I know he and Billy

would love hunting together, if he would just take him."

"Oh, those beautiful birds coming in at dusk!" Charles said, and with his hands imitated the rising and falling flight of a pair of doves, and then aimed an imaginary shotgun. "Blam," he said.

Wilburn gave Sunny an angry look. "I thought it was against the law to shoot them when they're coming in to water," he said.

"I didn't say anything about shooting, I said it was a beautiful *sight.*" Charles turned to Floyd. "What about you, Shotwell?" he said. "Be glad to have you come over and hunt with us this fall. We've got a nice lodge fixed up on the creek. Plenty of niggers to cook and clean the birds. You'd have a good time."

"Don't say 'nigger,' Charles," Anne Farish said. "You know how I hate that word. Say *nigra.*"

"Jesus," Wilburn said under his breath.

"I don't have time," Floyd muttered.

"Floyd's a good shot with a pistol," Nat said hastily. "He took me out the other day and we shot at tin cans."

"What do you folks do over here when your crop's in, if you don't hunt?" Charles asked.

"Most people do hunt," Wilburn said. Nat was looking anxiously at him, and besides, he was ashamed of having been angry at Sunny's effort to enter into the conversation. "I'm looked on by most of my friends as a freak," he said. "And, of course, Shotwell isn't a farmer. He can't loaf all winter like we can. He's a working man. That right, Floyd?"

"Gamble," Floyd said.

"Yeah, we do some gambling around Moss Ridge, too," Charles said. "Those who can afford it."

"And if you're like us, plenty who can't," Wilburn said.

"There's a card room in the back here," Floyd said. "Pretty nice. Craps. Blackjack. Poker. They did have a roulette wheel, but most people around here can't play roulette and won't learn how. We could go back, if you want to." It was more than he had said all evening.

"We'll have to give it a whirl after dinner," Charles said. "Not that I'm much of an expert at cards. If I'm going to gamble, I'd rather go over to Hot Springs and play the horses. Now, that's real excitement."

"Don't let Charles kid you," Anne Farish said. "He wouldn't dare bet more than two dollars at the races or get into a poker game with more than a three-cent limit. I'd make his life miserable. Wouldn't I, darling?"

"You know I'll bet on whatever I want to bet on, Anne Farish," Charles said. "But as a matter of fact, it's the *races* that are exciting. The horses. That's what I meant."

Anne Farish cocked her head to one side and looked at him with bright, unblinking eyes. She was a puffy little woman, addicted to Miss Louise's hot biscuits and grits soufflé; but her round bosom and ample hips were firmly controlled by a girdle. The hawklike profile that marked her as Nat's sister was blurred by fat and reduced in scale, so that she reminded one, particularly in her greenish, shot-silk cocktail dress, more of a plump corseted parakeet than of a bird of prey. Now she moved her head as if preparing to preen her ruffled feathers. "I didn't mean you didn't have the *money*," she said.

"Excuse me," Floyd said. "I see a friend of mine." He got up and left the table.

The swarms of colored lights continued to drift around and around the room, each separate swarm moving at its own speed, depending on the size of the ball that reflected the spotlights and the speed at which it was turning. A small pattern of intense blue moved across the table, climbed up onto Nat's bosom and across her face, and jumped to the wall behind her.

"Nat, you've got blue freckles," Wilburn said. "It's quite striking."

"You're kind of lavender, yourself," she said. "I don't believe lavender is your color."

"Come on, everybody, let's have another drink," Wilburn said. He beckoned to the waiter. "Nat?"

"All right, honey," she said. "I believe I *will* have just one more little patch."

Floyd was gone for ten minutes or so, and when he came back he was visibly more cheerful. There was a cautious smile on his rosy little mouth. He had brought a friend with him and he presented him to the group with a flourish, as if to say, "Look, everybody! He's mine."

"This is General Pershing Pruitt," he said. "General, you know Nat. This is Mrs. Griffith. Mrs. Taliaferro. Do you know Wilburn Griffith? Charles Taliaferro?"

The General looked at Anne Farish. "Yes, my name is actually *General* Pershing," he said. "Most folks around here refer to me as The General. And I always tell acquaintances about my name right off, so as to avoid confusion. General is *not* a nickname. On the other hand, in a way, it *is* a nickname — in so far as I live up to it. Take it either way you like. My mother's uncle served on General Pershing's staff during the First World War, and he passed on to the family a great admiration for the old gentleman. Tell you the truth, I'm proud of the name. I think it gives a man high standards and ambition to be named after a great man. Don't you?"

Anne Farish nodded uncertainly. "I'm awfully glad to meet you," she said.

Wilburn and Charles who had been standing during this speech shook hands with The General.

"The General and I are old friends," Wilburn said. "We were

in the National Guard together. How are you, Pruitt?"

In a moment everyone was settled again, The General, now apparently a part of the party, with a bottle of Orange Crush in his hand. "I don't drink hard liquor," he said to Sunny. "I have to keep my head clear at all times."

"My!" she said.

The General put his bottle down, leaned forward, put both hands palms down on the table in front of him, and looked around at them all. "Well!" he said in an expansive, almost proprietary way that seemed to mean, "Relax, everybody. I'm here to tell you what to do next." He was a tall man, solidly fat, and his presence made the table seem crowded, although it was long enough to seat eight. Anne Farish and Charles both eased their chairs back, as if preparing, if necessary, to escape. Wilburn smiled; he might just have remembered a funny story.

"You're looking well, General," he said.

Pruitt looked down with interest at his own body, which was encased in a curving sheath of fat that rounded him off like a huge capsule with arms and legs and a head, and nodded in comfortable agreement. He had a small beaky nose and an ill-fitting set of false teeth that let his mouth cave in, exaggerated the curving sharpness of his profile, and occasionally made a clicking sound when he talked. He was dressed in black with a black bow tie on his white shirt bosom and wore a pair of round-lensed, black-framed glasses behind which his small eyes moved restlessly. Sitting there, leaning forward, his agile gambler's hands like nervous claws on the table, he looked, Wilburn thought, very much like a huge black beetle ready to skitter out of his corner and seize one of them in his mandibles — or, if not that, perhaps to spread his wings and go buzzing around the glittering balls in the ceiling, like a big stag beetle around a streetlight, bumping at the balls in a trance of ecstasy until he fell exhausted among the dancers, to lie on his back, legs waving in the air, unable to turn himself over.

"How've you been getting along, General?" Wilburn said. "I haven't seen you in — let's see — it's been a couple of years since you went out of the bootlegging business, hasn't it?"

"Oh, I'm in and out, in and out," Pruitt said. "I wholesaled for a while after I closed out my last retail place. But I've mainly settled down to serious gambling. It's a more stable life. You know, I've got my kids to think about. I've had two more since the last time I saw you, and I'll tell you, five youngsters to educate is no light matter. And in this county, God knows who'll get elected sheriff next time. I might find myself out in the cold. That was one thing made me give up wholesaling. Last sheriff we had hijacked a truckload of my whiskey, and I never got a *dime* from him. And we had an *agreement*. Of course, I was insured." He paused. "Lloyd's of London, that's who I'm insured with. But it was the principle of the thing. I just quit."

"Are you running the tables here?" Wilburn said.

"No. This kind of thing is as chancy as bootlegging. Depends too much on the sheriff. I've got a private club out on the old Bogue Road. Low overhead. Rented building. I can always move without any trouble — even over into Arkansas, if necessary."

"My, that sounds like fun," Nat said. "Maybe we could all go out there and play poker one night."

"Men only, honey. Like to have you, but that's the rule. We've got a fine, serious group of men playing cards out there. Best men in the county. I mean, *real* gamblers."

"I wouldn't be in your way," Nat said. "I'd be like the lady gamblers on the TV Westerns — you know, the ones all the men accept as equals. I could dress up in a tight black crepe dress and win all the money and talk in a deep but feminine voice, and they would *respect* me."

"I just don't think we could work that out, honey," The General said seriously, "although you would certainly be an addition."

"Nat, you wouldn't!" Anne Farish said. "Aunt Louise would just die of shock."

"Don't worry, Anne Farish, I think Nat is joking," Sunny said.

"I believe we've got two or three fellas over in Moss Ridge who play in your game," Charles Taliaferro said. "Bob Tuttle, Williford — those boys."

"Why those men are *gamblers*, Charles!" Anne Farish said. Her plump shoulders quivered under the tight sheath of iridescent silk. "I'd be terrified if you ever played cards for the kind of stakes I've heard they play for."

"I'll tell you, Mrs. Taliaferro," Pruitt said, "the way a man plays cards — that's a matter of principle. Nothing to be scared of, if you understand it." He smiled reassuringly at Anne Farish. "The fact is, the point of view of a serious gambler is somewhat different from an ordinary man's," he said. "A man who gambles has to make up his mind at the beginning exactly what kind of game he's going to play, and then *stick* to it. If he sticks to it, his life ain't any more dangerous than the fellow's who plays the market. If he don't have sense enough to be consistent, he's gonna find himself in trouble. And worse than that, he's gonna lose the *respect* of his *associates*. He won't find a serious game he can get in." The General drew a deep quick breath and hurried on. "It's like my father told me years ago, when I went off to the army. 'Son,' he said, 'I want you to remember two things. First: Quit when you're losing and play a winning streak to the limit. Second: Don't ever get in a five dollar limit game. A man who'll play that kind of poker is either playing for fun or he's lost his nerve. He ain't a serious person.' "

"Oh," Anne Farish said, "was your . . . ?"

The General ignored the interruption. He continued to talk rapidly and loudly without keeping still for a moment, moving his hands restlessly along the table, passing them over his thin black hair, and picking at his tie, while he turned this way and that in his chair and looked from one to another of his astonished listeners. "Yes, my father was a wise man," he said. "I've never gone wrong by listening to him. That's one thing we could learn from the Chinese and Japanese, you know it? Respect for our parents. We wouldn't regret it. From time to time mine has given me advice that has gotten me out of some tight spots. Why, I don't reckon I'll ever forget the day he told me I was a gambler. I was about ten years old at the time and we were sitting out on the back steps at home one day, just sitting there together, and he was reminiscing about his youth, and he began to rub the back of my head; and then he took my hand and put it on the spot he was rubbing and said, 'Son, you feel that lump?' And I felt it all right. A funny little knot right on the crown of my head. 'Yessir,' I said. 'That's the Pruitt Gambling Knot,' he said. 'We've all got it. All the Pruitt men. You're a born gambler, boy, and you've got to learn to live with it. Don't expect it to go away. *Use* it.' And then he said, 'My father told me the same thing when I was your age, and I've never forgotten it.' "

Sunny leaned close to Wilburn. "I believe The General has seen too many 'Mavericks,' " she said in a low voice.

The General sighed. "I loved the old bastard," he said. "I *respected* him. You'll note that I called him 'Father' and not 'Daddy' or any other light-weight name. And as for my grandfather! There was a gentleman of the old school. A real Delta aristocrat. They don't make 'em like him these days. What a magnificent figure of a man he was, Mrs. Taliaferro! *Dignified. Big.* He was over six feet three inches tall, stiff as a ramrod and dark and hairy. He had such a mat of black hair on his chest and shoulders — even when he was an old man — you could see it through his shirts — he always wore a white silk shirt."

"White silk!" Nat said.

"It was the style then, if you had money enough," The General said. "And he wasn't just magnificent to look at, either; it wasn't just skin deep — or shirt deep." He laughed, a dry shrillish chuckle. "He owned thirteen thousand acres of Delta land, and he got it all for himself. Hacked it out of the canebrake when the Delta was still half wilderness. But he didn't believe in leaving his children on easy street, so he sold the land and gave it away toward the end of his life — and spent the money. Just kept enough so that each kid got a couple of hundred acres. 'I made my own way,' he said, 'and I want them to have the satisfaction of making theirs.'"

"Your grandfather sounds kind of like mine," Nat said. "He threw all his money away, too."

"Yes, Grandfather was *smart*," The General said. "And my father did the same thing. Saw to it that I had a chance to make it on my own. And I intend to do the same thing for my kids. That's family tradition for you. If you ask me, that's one of the finest things about the South — the strength of family tradition."

"That's certainly true," Anne Farish said. "I've always said . . ."

"Ask Wilburn here," The General said. "He came back from the service same time I did — on the same boat — didn't you, Wilburn? I parlayed my pay into ten thousand dollars crossing the Pacific Ocean on a troopship. When I got off that boat in San Francisco, nobody on it had any money but me. That is, me, and a few like Wilburn who didn't get into the game. Wilburn was an *observer;* he was interested, but he didn't participate. Well, as I was saying, when I got off the boat, I sat down and looked around me.

Took a long, cool look. Went to the Gulf Coast and to Hot Springs and even out to Vegas. I saw that Okatukla County, Mississippi was as fine a place for a gambler to settle as any in the country. A stable community. Not run by crooks (or not by dangerous crooks, anyway). No major gamblers already established. And most folks in a line of work that leaves them idle from the middle of November until March, just the time of year when the crop's in and they've got plenty of money. So I came home. There were plenty of people in the county who wondered how I'd turn out. Some even thought I might be a crook. People like you." Here The General at last relaxed, leaned back in his chair, and folded his arms across his chest with an air of honest pride. "But I've made my place in the community by myself. I'm an established man; I've never stolen a dime in my life; my word is my bond; and I drive a nineteen-fifty-seven Oldsmobile. Ain't that right, Floyd?"

"Yeah," Floyd said. "The General is the biggest gambler in the county."

"Satisfaction," The General said. "Self-confidence. That's what comes of making your own way."

"You certainly are a philosopher, General," Nat said.

The General acknowledged this compliment with a modest smile. "Well, now," he said, "I didn't mean to bore you ladies with all this moralizing. I just got carried away. And I know you ladies would rather dance than talk, wouldn't you? I never saw a lady in my life that didn't want to dance if she had on a pretty dress and was out with a man." He turned to Sunny and held out his hand. "Mrs. Griffith," he said, "may I have the pleasure?" And on the way out onto the dance floor, "You don't mind if I call you Sunny, do you? Wilburn and I are such old friends."

Wilburn and Charles got up and asked the other two women to dance. Floyd was left alone at the long table. For a few minutes he watched Nat dancing with Charles; then he beckoned to the waiter and ordered a double bourbon. He sat stiffly erect, still watching Nat, and drank it down. There was in his attitude, in the tension of his posture, the unmistakable appearance of waiting — as if he had an important appointment. He even looked at his watch.

"I'm an old-fashioned waltzer," The General said. "I don't ordinarily do much dancing. I reckon you can tell it." But as he said this, he was guiding Sunny about the floor with assurance, holding her so firmly against his broad chest and curving belly that her feet were sometimes lifted off the floor. "Especially these new dances," he said. "I don't say I don't admire this fellow, Presley. He's parlayed a very small piece of capital into something big, and I always admire that. But I ain't cut out for the rock and roll. The truth is when I'm in a place like this, it's usually on business. As I told you earlier, I don't drink. I'm a serious man. And I usually don't have time to dance, either."

"Don't worry about it," Sunny said. "I'd rather waltz. I haven't learned rock and roll."

He danced her from one end of the room to the other without the least regard for the beat of the music, all the while looking restlessly here and there and continuing to talk. "You know, Sunny, those are mighty fine kids," he said. "Fine. I get all the pleasure in the world out of watching them together."

"Your children?"

"No, no. Not *my* kids. They're with their mothers. I'm talking about Floyd there and that lovely girl he's in love with. Nat. Ain't she a sensation?"

"Yes, Nat is attractive," Sunny said. She tried to shift in his arms and loosen his hold on her, but he whirled her around like a dervish, and she was almost swept off her feet again.

"That's what I mean," The General said, "and he never takes his eyes off of her. You notice that? Makes me want to *help* those kids. I can't stop myself. I see people in love and I want to do everything in the world I can to help them. I'm built that way."

"That's mighty fine," Sunny said.

"Why, you can see they're made for each other," he said. "Look at him over there mooning. They just need somebody to light a fire under 'em. You agree?"

"I reckon they can find out for themselves if they are made for each other," Sunny said. Her voice had slowed to an exaggerated drawl, as it did when she was angry or upset.

"No, no. That's exactly what I'm getting at. They can't. Floyd is slow. (By that I mean slow about himself and slow to act. Nothing actually wrong with his *brain*.) He'll never find out anything about himself without somebody telling him. And then, say you tell him, you've still got to find a way to help him act on it."

"Really," Sunny said, "I don't think it's any of my business, Mr. Pruitt."

"But you can encourage Nat like I'm encouraging Floyd."

"Or yours either," Sunny said.

For the first time since they had walked out on the floor, The General paused in his restless searching of the faces of the dancers and looked directly at her. "You don't know me, dear lady," he said. "I can see you don't know my reputation. I haven't got anything to gain from helping these kids. I just like to help people. Why, I'll tell you — just to give you an example of the kind of man I am — I was looking over my books a few days ago, checking out my income tax deductions, and I ran up some totals and, Sunny, I found out that I'd spent seven hundred and fifty-three dollars on flowers last year — on *flowers* — for sick friends and funerals. Now there ain't many people in Philippi, I don't care how rich they are or what kind of car they drive, who spend that kind of money just to give other people pleasure. I don't take too much credit — it's selfish in a way. It gives *me* pleasure. Yes, that's the absolute truth. I'm being honest with you. You're no fool — you were probably getting ready to make that observation yourself. But you can't tell me even a *saint* don't get a certain amount of personal pleasure out of his good deeds. Even *Jesus.* Well, I was looking at these bills and I saw one for thirty-nine fifty, and I said to myself, 'My God, who the hell were these for?' And then I remembered they were for old Smooth Mouth Davidson's funeral. I doubt if you knew him, Sunny, although he was an important man in the county (I've seen him win or lose twenty thousand dollars in a night and hardly even notice it.) and a good friend of mine. Well, when he died, I made up my mind to do the right thing by him. I sent a blanket of red carnations for the casket — beautiful! It had eight dozen carnations in it, Sunny, *eight dozen.* Old Smooth Mouth always liked red — used to wear a red bow tie to give him luck when he gambled — and I knew his wife would appreciate my remembering that. I was thinking of *her.* And of him, too. I can just see the old bastard looking down at the funeral and saying to Saint Peter, 'Looka there, will you? The General really give me a red-assed send-off.' "

At this point the band wound up its playing with a sudden flourish and The General let Sunny go so abruptly that she staggered.

"In spite of that," he said, "they didn't allow it."

"What?"

"The Internal Revenue people. That kind of charity ain't deductible."

"I'm a little bit dizzy," Sunny said. "I believe I'd better sit down."

"Well, it was a pleasure," The General said. "I hope we can do this right often. You don't realize until you get out with the ladies how much you miss by keeping your mind on business all the time."

At the table Sunny sat silent for a few minutes. Her face was the thin bluish-white color of skimmed milk, and her hands trembled slightly.

Anne Farish leaned across the table. "Are you all right?" she asked. "You don't look very well."

Sunny nodded. "The General is a little bit strenuous for me," she said.

"Who *is* that fantastic man?" Anne Farish said. "I'm certainly glad there's nobody here tonight from Moss Ridge. I'd hate to be seen with him by anybody I know. Did he say he was a bootlegger?"

"Now, Anne Farish, you know bootlegging is a perfectly respectable occupation in Mississippi," Wilburn said. "Besides, he isn't one at the moment."

"He did say he was a wholesaler, didn't he?" Anne Farish said. "That's not quite so bad."

"Oh?" Wilburn said.

"Well, I mean, you know, you don't actually stand behind the counter and wait on everybody. Nigras and all."

"Oh," Wilburn said.

"You mean like Uncle Aubrey does at the store?" Nat said.

"That's entirely different," Anne Farish said. She moved restlessly to the left and then to the right on her chair, almost as if she were sidling along a perch. She looked brightly at Wilburn. "At least the food is good here — or so they say — even if the company is a bit strange. Why don't you go bring the others back to the table, Wilburn, so we can order dinner?"

"All right," Wilburn said. He turned to his wife. "We ought to go on and have dinner, Sunny," he said. "You look as if you need to go home and go to bed." She nodded and he got up from the table. "You all excuse me. I'll see what they want to do."

In a few minutes he came back. "They're coming, honey," he said. "Floyd invited The General to have dinner with us." He grinned at Anne Farish. "You'll be delighted to hear he declined. And Floyd appears to be a little bit drunk."

At this point The General and Nat came up to the table. "Miss Nat here and I are going to have one dance before I go," The General said.

Nat put her purse down on the table. "You order for me, Wilburn," she said. "Will you? I like most anything."

"Come on, you pretty thing," The General said. He seized her hand and swept her out onto the floor. As soon as they were dancing, he held her away from him and began to talk with manic intensity, not so much to as *at* her. "You know, Nat," he said, "I'm going to be frank with you. I'm a man who believes in being honest with a woman. Honest! I came out here tonight because Floyd said you and he would be here and I needed to talk to you. That's the only reason."

Nat looked vaguely up at him. "I declare," she said, "I can't take my eyes off those spots. You know how it is sometimes on the beach at night — when you see schools of little bitty phosphorescent shrimp and fish — all transparent and shining? That's what they remind me of. Or fireflies, maybe. Do they remind you of fireflies? Especially the greenish ones, if they just went on and off."

"Fireflies?" The General said. "You don't ever see a firefly in the Delta anymore. Cotton dusting killed 'em all."

"My goodness, I didn't realize that," Nat said. "Isn't that terrible! But I didn't mean real ones, you know — just the lights. Nightclub fireflies."

"Honey," The General said, "I want to talk to you about a serious matter. Now you forget about fishes and fireflies and listen to The General."

Nat's attention was as diffuse as a dreamer's who persists in following the vague peripheral shapes that float at the edges of his vision, while in the center, sharp-edged as a silhouette, some curious action is taking place.

"*Nat!*" The General said.

She looked directly at him.

"This is the situation, honey. Floyd wants you to go with him down to Jackson for the Ole Miss-Tulane game."

"I know," she said. "He mentioned it the other day. I think that's nice. Are you going?"

"No," The General said. "I have some commitments that weekend. But I want to talk to you about Floyd, honey."

"Yes?"

The General drew her away from the center of the floor. "Come over here," he said. "We can't dance and talk at the same time." For the first time since he had joined Floyd's party, The General faltered, and his speech and gestures lost a part of their compulsive quality. It was as if he had suddenly realized that he was playing with a gambler whose idiosyncrasies were unfamiliar to him. "Floyd is an unusual boy," he said.

"Yes, I reckon he is." Nat was listening now and watching him with interest.

"Intelligent," The General said. "Most people don't realize that. But shy."

She nodded.

"You've got to encourage him to come out of himself," The General said. "That's been my experience." He looked at her for a reaction to this statement, but she continued to listen with polite interest. "I mean you're the woman who can do it when nobody else can," he said. "You've got no idea how crazy he is about you. And when I think what you could *do* for him! Why, it's entirely possible you could change his life. Now wouldn't that be a great thing for you to do!"

"It does sound inspiring," Nat said. "You mean I could kind of be the power behind the throne? Like — like Lady Hamilton was with Lord Nelson, or, let's see, maybe Madame de Pompadour?"

"That's what I'm talking about," The General said. "You just look back in history. All those old lords had women behind them. But, like I said, Floyd is shy. Left on his own, he'd never . . ." He hesitated. Then, "With a woman like you and a friend like me — you see what I mean?"

"Why you're propositioning me for Floyd, aren't you?" Nat said. "Just like John Alden and Myles Standish — well, almost like them. I think that's sweet."

The General cleared his throat.

"You needn't be embarrassed," Nat said. "I'm just fascinated."

"I got nothing to be embarrassed about, little lady," he said. "To tell you the truth, I just wanted to make sure I didn't shock you. But I can see you're a woman who believes in being *sincere*. Besides, it's not exactly a proposition. He doesn't know, at least I don't think he really knows what he wants, much less that I'm talking to you about it. He wouldn't like that, I don't think. You see, you and I can talk. We know the world is really a simple place. But Floyd — he sees all kinds of complications."

"I suppose whether it's simple or not depends on whether you're asleep or awake," Nat said.

"Huh?"

"I mean, if you're asleep, look at all the adventures you have without even moving — that's certainly simple."

"I don't think you're following me exactly," The General said. He was in command again now. "I'm gonna lay my cards on the table," he said. "Play my hand and put my money behind it, so to speak. And I mean, I got my money behind Floyd. Ha. Ha."

"Oh, I understand you, General," Nat said. "You want me to have an affair with Floyd. For some reason you think it would be good for him, and for — us. And you think he's too shy to start things himself, so I've got to kind of lure him into bed. Is that right?"

"Well," The General said, "in a way it is. But . . ."

"I don't know that it would be worth it to me," Nat said. "I'm not real crazy about hopping in the sack. I mean, most men just honestly don't interest me."

"Floyd *said* that," The General said, "but you know, I don't believe it. A woman like you . . . ! You just need the right man, honey." He stepped away as if to give her the opportunity to get a better look at him. "I could show you . . ." he said.

"Well thanks," Nat said. "You're *sweet*, you know. I said that. But maybe we'd better stick to Floyd. What I was going to say was, I don't believe I'd be interested in having an affair right now."

"Well, that brings me to the heart of the matter," The General said. "Actually, I think it's possible things could be managed in another way."

"Oh?"

"I mean, if we really want to *help* Floyd, we got to take certain possibilities — even *probabilities* — into consideration. Like for example: Have you ever wondered why he ain't married?"

"No," Nat said. "It seems sensible to me."

"But I mean he ain't *ever* been married. And you're bound to see, too, that he's not pushing you to go to bed with him. There's got to be something behind that. See what I mean? Well, I think I've got it figured out. *I* believe he's got a problem. With women. He never has talked to me about it — he's a sensitive boy — but . . ."

"I don't see what's in it for you," Nat said. "I'm kind of confused."

"Now, don't *talk* like that," The General said. "That's not my point of view. Let me tell you something, Nat. You try to make things work for other people, and pretty soon you'll see they're beginning to work for you. There don't have to be something in it for anybody."

"You mean like casting your bread upon the waters?" Nat said.

"I mean Floyd needs somebody to help him get out from under his daddy's thumb and in control of what ought to be his own money, and you and I are the ones who can do it.

"And furthermore, it's entirely possible you can manage your part of it without actually going to bed with him, if you don't want to. Something's taken the starch out of that boy. (Ha, ha! That's a kind of appropriate way to put it, if you see what I mean.) He'll chicken out."

"Are you sure?" Nat said.

"I mean, honey, I think he's im*p*otent."

"I'll declare," Nat said. "Isn't that interesting! I said you were a philosopher, General, but I believe you're a psychologist, too."

"Besides," The General said, "if push comes to shove, so to speak, you ought to be able to put up with him. Ha, ha. Just think how good for him it would be. And like I said, sooner or later it would turn out to be good for you, too."

8

THE CONVERSATION between Floyd Shotwell and The General which produced this curious proxy courtship had taken place the preceding week and was the result, not simply of Floyd's having gotten drunk, although that was a contributory factor, but of a tangle of apparently irrelevant circumstances that gave Pruitt what he called a "piece" of Floyd, as well as a hint of the means by which he might make a profit on his investment.

The two men had known each other slightly — as people who move in the limited world of a small town know each other — since childhood. But it had been only recently, since Floyd had begun to gamble, that The General had taken a serious interest in him.

Floyd, as Wilburn had told Nat, was known in the county as a successful investor, his reputation based on two or three shrewd (and lucky) moves in the stock market and on the fact that he often sat for hours in the local stockbroker's office, motionless and attentive, watching the changes on the board and the ticker tape and saying nothing to anyone. But it was true, too, that his father kept him on a short rein. He drew a meager salary; and the shares in various businesses that his father had for tax purposes put in his name were administered by men whom Morris controlled. As often as not, Floyd never heard of their existence. The only reason he had money to invest at all was that he spent none — or almost none. Whether out of conviction or indifference, he saved his money. He cared nothing for clothes or travel or show, he slept and ate at home, and his sole indulgence was an occasional two- or three-day spree of drunkenness.

He came by his penury naturally. Neither Morris nor Marigold were spenders, although each had a private passion which he indulged — Morris to the hilt and Marigold — well, Marigold's passion was respectability, and one can scarcely think of indulging a passion for respectability. The clown father of whom Miss Louise sometimes spoke in a ladylike whisper may have vanished before Marigold was born; but somewhere in the back of her mind he still cavorted and grimaced; and she drew curtain after curtain to close him off from public view. Floyd, as it might have seemed to a disinterested observer, was simply another screen to be interposed between the world and the curious circumstances of her birth.

She had forced him, at the age of eight, a dark, silent, solitary little boy, to take part as crown bearer in the annual charity ball. "It is an honor to be invited," she had said when he wept, "and it's your duty to accept. Besides," she had added, "if you don't do things like this, you won't be invited to join the Bachelors' Club when you grow up." But Floyd already knew that he would never want to join the Bachelors' Club. The night of the ball he slipped away from his mother in the confusion of the court's entry into the country club ballroom and hid in a locker in the men's room. He took the crown with him. The ceremony of crowning the king and queen was ruined. Not only that. Floyd sat on the crown and broke off the rhinestone-encrusted papier-mâché points and the Ladies' League had to buy a new one the following year.

It was at about this time that some of Marigold's friends suggested to her that a psychiatrist might be able to help Floyd. Marigold was outraged. No one in the family, she said, had ever had any mental trouble. As for Morris, when she told him about the suggestion, he looked up from his paper only long enough to say snappishly that psychiatrists were all quacks who were interested solely in parting you from your money.

For money was Morris's passion: the amassing and manipulation of money. A dark, tight, little man, inches shorter than his big-boned bovine wife, he never, except at Marigold's prodding, spent money in any way except to make more money. It had been because she had insisted that he had bought the Lincoln Continental which he drove from his house to his office, always a few miles above the speed limit, as if he could not bear to waste the time it took to get there. He leaned forward with fists clenched on the steering wheel and looked out at the world with burning eyes. When Marigold was beside him on the front seat, he glanced at her appraisingly from time to time, as if estimating her weight. He might have acquired her by the pound.

Marigold smiled and took his glances as the due of a successful wife from an admiring husband. "Everybody knows Morris and I have an unusually happy marriage," she said one day when marital relations were the subject of conversation at a garden club meeting. "We almost never quarrel. And the secret of that is, he goes his way and I go mine."

If it seemed sometimes as if Marigold slipped like a clumsy skater over the surface of her life, Morris might have been caught in a frozen cave beneath her, silent, vibrating to imagined triumphs, his calculations lit by a phosphorous, cold, subterranean fire.

As for Floyd, by the time he was grown perhaps he too wandered in that frozen cave, although as far as anyone could tell, he never noticed Morris's presence there. He lived in the house with his mother and father like a quiet but slightly hostile stranger, shutting himself in his room to avoid them, sitting through meals with a paperback book in his hand, speaking, when he had to speak, in a voice a little too low to be heard. Periodically he burst loose in a brief orgy of drinking and fighting that ended in a brawl with Marigold and Morris. That was his method of communicating with them. They were terrified of him when he was drunk. Usually, if they had the least warning that one of his "spells" was coming on, they left town.

But then, in his thirty-first year, after two or three small ventures in the stock market, Floyd began to play cards at The General's club. Perhaps, encouraged by his success in the market and anxious for more room to maneuver, he intended only to run up his capital a bit and then quit. Certainly he must have found cards interesting out of the same turn of mind that had drawn him into the market to begin with. And — who knows — there may have been more obscure motives involved. At any rate, he took to cards with the single-minded absorption of a potential addict. At first he won. He bought his blue Cadillac and a diamond ring. It was after he bought the car that his father, almost as if he wanted Floyd to appear ridiculous, took him out of the office at Grossi's Appliance Mart and turned over to him the collection of accounts. But Floyd did not seem to care. He went right on playing cards. He won and lost the diamond ring two or three times; then he lost his little nest egg of stock. Now he was in debt to Pruitt for several thousand dollars. Except for the salary his father paid him, all he had left was the Cadillac. That he would not throw into the game. "It's only partly paid for," he would say. And if someone suggested that he put up his equity, he would shake his head.

"No," he would say coldly, "I'm not a gambler." No one was sure what he meant by that.

Pruitt put very little pressure on Floyd to pay his debt. Instead, he continued to advance him enough money to play a few hands every night. As he said with earnest sincerity to anyone who would listen, "I *like* the boy. I ain't interested in his money."

Apparently the admiration was mutual. Floyd tolerated The General's company as he did no one else's, listened to his lectures with attention, and talked to him at great length, not only when he was drunk, but even when he was sober. They talked mostly about percentages and odds, about the technicalities of gambling and the psychology of gamblers.

But they did not move on to the discussion of more personal matters until one night when The General for the first time suggested that there must be ways Floyd could lay his hands on some money.

They had spent the evening playing cards with a group at The General's poker club, a ramshackle building that stood in the middle of a pasture on a graveled road half a mile back from the nearest highway. The lights in the house were not visible from the highway, and no one would have guessed that it was anything but what it appeared to be — a dilapidated Negro cabin. The General had put it together out of two shotgun tenant houses shoved against each other and tied together with a few planks. He had done as little as possible to improve it — had put in wiring, patched up the fireplaces, cut doors between the two sections, and installed a stove, refrigerator, and sink in one of the back rooms, and a chemical toilet in the other. Each of the two front rooms held a poker table and seven or eight chairs. The walls, finished with a single coat of whitewash slapped haphazardly over rough unplaned planks ("Picturesque," The General would explain to his guests. "Like an old-fashioned darky's cabin."), were decorated with a dozen or more pictures in dime-store frames of men leaning on guns or standing, surrounded by dogs and ragged Negroes, beside the bodies of dead animals or fish. Ready-made Sears, Roebuck curtains of printed cotton hung limply at the windows. Over the fireplace was a large calendar with a naked girl on it, and opposite, staring out of the autumn landscape on another calendar, a pointer dog examined the girl with mournful eyes. Outside in the darkness a cow lowed now and then; or a calf bawled for its mother.

Floyd and The General sat opposite each other at one of the poker tables talking. The game had broken up and everyone else had gone home. From the kitchen came the sound of water running, as the Negro cook and handyman cleared up the debris of the evening's card game. Occasionally he drifted through the card rooms, gathering up ashtrays or throwing a log on the fire, a thin, dark wisp of a man, so noiseless as to seem invisible, with dark eyes shining in a shadowy face. "He's so quiet he can put a log on the fire without making a sound," The General would say about him. "He just *ain't here*. That's the kind of nigger you need in an establishment like mine — where nobody wants to have the flow of his thoughts disrupted, so to speak." And he would shout for the benefit of his guests, "Come here, Kilroy. Ain't you the quietest nigger south of Memphis? Huh?" And when Kilroy nodded, he would add, "That's my nickname for him. Appropriate, eh?"

The General leaned across the table toward Floyd with his usual air of intense but restless concentration. "I'm not trying to push you, Floyd," he said. "I *trust* you. To tell the truth, I don't play cards with a man I can't trust. You know that. And I've found I can trust a *real* gambler every time. He'll mortgage his house, sell his clothes — *anything* — to pay his gambling debts. And when I size a man up — well, I'm not fooled very often or I wouldn't stay in business. *But* — I've got a lot of capital tied up in you, and some nights I need my funds to be a little bit more liquid. See?" He hesitated. "Besides," he said, "I want to see you assert yourself. You've got rights, you know. It ain't decent what he pays you — you a thirty-three-year-old man, and him as rich as he is. It's no more than he pays any starting clerk or bill collector."

The General had a bottle of Orange Crush in his hand and Floyd had a drink in front of him. He was already beginning to be drunk, and before he was very much drunker, he told Pruitt about his father's interest in Aubrey Hunter's washing machine.

"It's gonna be big," he kept muttering, "I mean, really big. Make all kinds of money. All kinds. I can smell it. Yes. We're gonna make more money than . . . You just can't even begin to imagine how much."

Pruitt listened and sometimes asked a question. His manner was open and businesslike, his questions directly to the point. As for Floyd, it would probably not be true to say that he told The General about the invention because he was drunk and in debt. In the case of complex people, simple explanations are usually at least partly false, and Floyd's motives may have been both better and worse than simple drunken desperation.

"It's got a little thing in the side like a boomerang," he said. "*Simple.* Unbelievably simple. Even if we just sold the plans to some place like GE — didn't attempt to manufacture it ourselves — we'd make — God knows how much we'd make."

"You mean your *daddy* is going to make all that money," The General said. "And this other fellow."

"Oh, Aubrey," Floyd said. "He hasn't got any sense. He's a crazy man. Inventor. He doesn't even care about money. At least, maybe sometimes he thinks he does, but then he gets interested in something else. Forgets about it."

"What about his wife?" Pruitt said. "Does she know what's going on?"

"Miss Louise? She's a lady. Doesn't think about sordid things like money."

"It sounds fishy to me," The General said. "You mean this fellow — the owly-looking old man who's been puttering around down in the Mid-South Hardware Store for the last fifty years — has invented something that's actually worth . . ." He broke off and ran his hand restlessly over his thin hair. Then he said thoughtfully, "he's probably stringing your daddy along. He must have something *he's* parlaying. Now wouldn't that be a joke?"

"*Aubrey?*" Floyd laughed, his stiff face cracking and the laugh coming out almost soundlessly as a slight snorting heave. "No, it's the real thing, all right," he said. "The old man explained it to a fellow he knows — a man who has retired to Philippi — used to be one of those planned-obsolescence engineers. You know what I'm talking about — one of those fellows who design washing machines or whatever so they'll wear out right after the warranty expires. He says . . ."

"You mean your daddy actually showed the plans . . . ?"

"Yes. He controls this fellow. They've been in on a couple of deals before, and I suppose he's going to cut him in on this one. So it won't pay him to try anything. Besides, it's already patented."

"Well, if old man Hunter already has the thing patented, how do you figure your daddy can make anything out of it?"

"That's the question," Floyd said. "What's he doing? Why is he so damned excited about it that he's practically drooling? He's bound to have figured some way he can get control."

"I say your daddy's crazy. It don't make sense to me, if Hunter has invented something so good, that GE or Westinghouse or some-body else hasn't invented it already."

Floyd shrugged. "Everything gets invented the first time," he said.

"But not by people anymore," Pruitt said. "By companies. Laboratories. Experiment stations."

Floyd drank the remainder of his drink in one long gulp.

"Hey, Kilroy," Pruitt called, "fix Mr. Shotwell a drink. How'd your daddy get onto this, anyway?" he began again, as the Negro slipped in and took Floyd's glass.

"Hunter owes him money. Mortgaged his house to him, and stock, and the building the store is in. The business never has made much money and now, since Hunter's gotten so obsessed with the washing machine, it doesn't make any. Half the time, the past year or so, he's kept the store closed up while he puttered around in the back all day. God knows what he does back there. So the old man told him he was going to foreclose, and Hunter told him about this invention and offered him an interest in it, in return for tearing up the notes."

"A controlling interest?"

Floyd shook his head. "Just a piece."

The Negro brought Floyd a fresh drink and then retreated toward the kitchen where he stood in the doorway, leaning against the lintel, eyes closed.

"Anyhow," The General said, "I don't see what this proposition has got to do with us. What are you telling me about it for? You don't even own a piece of it. I want you to put your attention on something practical. We got to work out ways for you to get hold of some money for yourself and to get even with me, too. I *like* you, boy. I want to see you independent. Your own man."

There was a tiny noise from the doorway, and The General looked around. "What you doing standing there?" he said. "Go on and finish up, so we can get home."

"I'm through, Mr. Pruitt," the Negro said.

"Well, you're making me nervous. Wait for us in the kitchen."

"There's bound to be some way I can get in on *this*," Floyd said. "I've got a feeling this is what we ought to concentrate on." For a moment he appeared to be entirely sober. His small, deeply circled black eyes focused in shrewd thoughtfulness on Pruitt, and he spoke in a cold measured voice. "I think the old man will overstep himself," he said. "He's too excited. If I'm patient and watch him every minute, I think I can trip him up some way. I can get the upper hand."

"You courting Nat for the information you can get out of her?" The General said.

But Floyd appeared not to hear him. "My *father*," he said in a venomous voice and, rising, tipped an imaginary hat and bowed to the space in front of him. Then, "Planning to squeeze Aubrey out. Bound to be. That's where somebody — can — trip — him — up." He articulated his words slowly and carefully, as if it hurt his throat to speak.

"What about Nat?" The General said. "Where does she come in?"

"She hasn't got anything to do with it," Floyd said. He slumped back in his chair and gulped down nearly half of the drink at his elbow. Immediately, as if the drink had gone directly to his brain, he lapsed into the drawling slurred speech of drunkenness. "Beau'-ful — woman," he said. "My God." He picked up the drink and finished it. Without comment, The General got up and refilled the empty glass. He brought the bottle back to the table with him.

"If I had some money, I could show her a good time," Floyd said. "You not the only reason I need money." He put his head down on his hands and said into his drink, "You know how much one weekend in New Orleans costs? I mean, if you eat at the right places and go to the right places? And she's a woman who ought to go to the right places. She has a good *time*," he said. "Even with somebody like me. And she's . . ." He groped for the right word. "She's *clear*," he said. "I've never been around a woman like her before in my life."

The General sat opposite him, silent, his round eyes behind the round black glasses frames fixed on the wall behind Floyd's head.

"Why don't you say something?" Floyd said. "Say something! You know tha's what I like about you, don't you? You — you talk a lot. I like that."

"I'm thinking," The General said. "Possibilities. But you got to level with me, boy."

Floyd looked up. "Thinking!" he said. "Who told you you could think, General? Never had thought in your life. You got a machine in there — record playing machine — and — and *computer*. Add. Subtract. Multiply . . ."

"Ne' mind, boy," The General said. "I can add up how much you owe me. But do I push you for it?" He picked up the bottle and added whiskey to Floyd's drink.

Floyd was following his metaphor. "You know 'bout computers, don't you, General? 'Mazing things. All they can be is off and on — off and on." He snapped an imaginary switch in the air. "Every single thing comes out of 'em result of combinations of off and on. Can you believe it?"

Abruptly The General said, "So you're crazy about her. You might as well admit she's mixed up in this washing machine business, too. After all, she is Hunter's niece."

Floyd groaned.

"How does she feel about you?" The General said.

"I don't talk to her about it."

"Well, why don't you? How you ever going to get anywhere with her?"

"No," Floyd said. "She wouldn't want me."

"Man, you're nuts," The General said. "Listen. I can size a woman up about as well as I can a man. That's a hot little number, if I ever saw one. She likes *men*. She wants a man around all the time. Look at that body. And the way she walks. The clothes she wears. *Jesus*."

Floyd crossed his arms on his chest and pressed them tightly against his body, as if he might be using them as a tourniquet on a bleeding wound. He was very drunk by now, wavering slightly in his chair, his lids drooping. "She's — cold," he said. "Iceberg. One thing I like . . ." He squeezed his arms until his knuckles whitened, crushing his pain into himself, embracing the iceberg and grinding it to powder against his breast.

"And furthermore," Pruitt said, "you're nuts in general — I mean as far as women are concerned. You want a woman to appreciate you. You ain't supposed to like 'em cold."

Floyd shook his head. "You — don't — know — anything — 'bout — me," he muttered. "Nobody — knows . . ."

"What have you got to lose?" The General said. "Nothing. If you was to give it a try, I bet you'd find that . . . that . . ." He paused, as if trying, in deference to Floyd's feelings, to find a delicate way to speak of seduction. Then, as if the thought had just struck him, "Say, you don't want to marry her, do you?"

"*Marry?*" Floyd came out of his stupor enough to repeat this word as if it had some cruel and exotic meaning for him. "No. *No.*"

"Well, then. I don't see why you and she can't work things out so that — so . . . Seems to me a happy arrangement can be made, if you approach this situation in a subtle way. Yes. That's what I mean. Taking in considerations of the washing machine, as well as everything else."

Floyd's arms had dropped to the table during this speech, and he was turning his highball glass around and around in a puddle of water. Now he picked up the glass and without a trace of warning drew back his arm and crashed it against the wall behind The General.

The General did not move. "I know you weren't aiming at me," he said, "but you might have hit me." He brushed absent-mindedly at his shoulders and shook fragments of glass from his hair. "Suppose a piece got in my eye," he said. He raised his voice. "Kilroy, come clean up this mess."

Floyd stood up and pounded the table with his fist. "I — could — turn — this — place — to kindling," he said. He reached across the table, picked up the empty chair next to The General, and held it high in the air.

"Look out there, boy," The General said. "Ain't I telling you I want to help you? What the hell you trying to tear up my place for? That ain't right. That just plain ain't *right*."

Floyd stood wavering above him, huge and furious, his face even more withdrawn in anger than in repose, only the muscles of his body contorted for an act of destruction. Sunk deep in the bruiselike circles that shadowed them, his eyes were closed, as if inside his head some action, which it was necessary for him to consult from time to time, were playing itself out jerkily on a defective screen. Then he tossed aside the chair he had been holding and subsided into his place again.

"You've got a temper," Pruitt said. "You ought to try to take it easy." He walked around the table, picked up the overturned chair, and put it against the wall. "All I was doing was trying to figure out how to make things work," he said. "You got to sneak up on that situation. *Subtle.* You got to be subtle to get around your difficulties in this world. Brute force ain't going to get you anywhere."

Floyd did not answer. He put his head on his arms and in a few minutes began to snore. Glass tinkled faintly as Kilroy brushed it onto a piece of folded newspaper.

For a long time The General sat looking at Floyd. At last he spoke aloud. "There are certain factors in this situation that need further exploration," he said. And then, to Kilroy, "Hurry up, boy. Let's get out of here."

9

THE MONDAY following Nat's party at Sarelli's, Aubrey Hunter came home to lunch in a mood even more abstracted than his usual one. He walked briskly, hurrying along the sidewalk with quick birdlike steps and nodding his head as if he might be looking for a worm. He was still erect and wiry and spry, looking, in his middle seventies, not much older than he had looked twenty years earlier. His face had none of the marks one sees in the faces of old men one loves, marks made by sorrow or laughter or pain or exhaustion, but was uniformly crosshatched with tiny almost invisible wrinkles. Ten feet away from him, it would have been as difficult to guess his age as to guess the age of the pigeons nodding and strolling in the gutter at his feet. His steps and gestures had become jerkier and more mechanical as the years had passed, as if the machine needed oiling, but this was the only evidence that he was old.

Today, however, twice in the three-block walk, he stumbled over slabs of pavement tilted by the roots of the huge water oaks that overhung the street — slabs he had automatically and easily avoided four times every day for forty years. And he walked past his own house to the corner, where he stood for several minutes staring at a blinking traffic signal before he appeared to come to himself and realize where he was.

Inside the house, he put his hat on the lyre-shaped hat tree in the hall and looked at his reflection in the cloudy oval of mirror from which the arms of the hat tree extended. Soundlessly he spoke to himself, shaking his head and frowning. Then he walked into the dining room and sat down at the polished mahogany dining table.

His wife was talking to Anne Farish. Without interrupting herself to speak to him, she rang the silver bell beside her plate and gestured to Clakey to serve him. "If God had intended the bluebirds and the redbirds to mingle, he would not have made them different colors," she said. Delicately she wiped her lips with her snowy napkin. "That's what *I* say," she said decidedly, "and that's what Bishop Kerr says. *This* young man — this curate we have now — certainly isn't going to last long in our church."

"Hello, Uncle Aubrey," Nat said.

"Eh?" he said, and then nodded. "Hello. Hello."

"*Father* Thomas, he calls himself. Father! Next thing you know we'll all be going to confession. You won't catch me — although some people . . . I hate to say it, but Marigold Shotwell has begun to genuflect and cross herself. And Puddin' Carson. You'd never know she was raised a Baptist and didn't join the Episcopal Church until after her husband got the Ford Agency. But that's not what I'm really concerned about, Anne Farish. I don't suppose it can hurt any of them to genuflect and all that (although goodness knows, Mama would turn over in her grave if she could see what passes for Episcopalianism among some people these days). It's the colored people I'm concerned about. The *good* colored people. When members of the clergy *encourage* the troublemakers — why, I've heard he says *openly* that he approved of the faculty walkout over integration at Sewanee last year."

Clakey was serving Aubrey's plate from the silver serving dishes and platters on the sideboard. Nat had stopped eating and was smoking and swinging her foot. Anne Farish frowned at Miss Louise and made a shushing gesture. When Clakey had gone back to the kitchen, she spoke in a stage whisper. "Aunt Louise, you really must *not* talk about the darkies when they can hear you. I'm surprised at you!"

"Clakey's not interested in race relations," Miss Louise said. "And that's what I *mean*. It's people like this young man — stirring up darkies who don't know there is such a thing as race relations. Just you wait until they begin talking about integrating the schools in Moss Ridge, Anne Farish. You don't realize what you're going to have to face. What are you going to say when Anne wants to bring some little brown girl home to play one afternoon? You're going to have to tell her *why* she can't. And do you know what that means? It means you're going to have to *teach* her to be prejudiced — a thing I certainly never had to do to you and Nat. That's the kind of thing this — this *curate* is fomenting. It's a horrible complication of life that neither you nor I nor Clakey has ever had to contend with."

"I think Clakey's kind of like me," Nat said in a dreamy voice. "She's not always sure she's present."

"Really, Nat, you say the strangest things. Sometimes I think you just do it to be mysterious."

"Well, I mean, how can you be sure you're present if you're apparently in a room and the people in it don't seem to realize you're there?" She raised her voice. "Isn't that true, Clakey?"

Clakey opened the door to the kitchen and poked her head into the dining room. "Don't worry, Miss Nat," she said. "I know when I'm present and I know when I'm absent. And Miss Louise ain't going to hurt my feelings, Miss Anne Farish. We use to each other's ways. Can't teach an old dog new tricks, you know."

"Clakey," Miss Louise said, "I don't like being compared to a dog — old or young. But it's true, isn't it? You don't want to come to my church any more than I want to go to yours."

"No'm," Clakey said. "I don't want to be no Episcopalian. I'm a Christian." She grinned at Nat and vanished into the kitchen.

Aubrey was eating his way rapidly through a plateful of black-eyed peas, mustard greens, pork chops, candied sweet potatoes, and corn bread. After a few bites, he stopped, gazed out the window for a few minutes, and then took a small notebook from his jacket pocket and scribbled in it before beginning to eat again.

"Did I tell you all about the Carnival parade on Saint Thomas the year I was there?" Nat said. "You know, Mardi Gras? It was kind of interesting. I mean, the natives have some interesting customs and all. You know in the Islands they call the colored people 'natives.' Did you know that, Aunt Louise? And, of course, they're not natives at all, are they? Isn't that strange? Well, of course, practically everybody down there is *part* native. I mean they don't have much of a color line."

"You mean among the lower classes," Anne Farish said.

"And everybody gets along — or so it seemed to me at the time. They didn't ostracize me because of my being from Mississippi — I mean the natives didn't."

"Nat, I'm sure you didn't *associate* — " Miss Louise said. "You *are* a southern gentlewoman, after all."

"I was going to tell you about the parade," Nat said. "Two floats especially. One of them had a vaudeville team — you know, like Al Jolson and a straight man, and a little jazz band playing Dixieland; and they were all natives — *colored* — but they were in black face — cork, with big red mouths painted on; and they sang 'Swanee River' and 'Ol Black Joe' in southern dialect. And the other float had the Episcopal rector, who was white, in a great big iron pot, and all the natives were dressed up like cannibals getting ready to cook him."

"Well! They evidently haven't much respect for the cloth," Miss Louise said.

Clakey came in and began to clear away the plates.

"I reckon you don't think that's funny," Nat said. "Clakey thought it was a scream, didn't you, Clakey? About the missionary and the cannibals?"

Clakey allowed herself a smile. "Miss Nat's a sight, Miss Louise," she said. "Don't pay her no mind."

"Would you like a piece of chess pie, Aubrey?" Miss Louise said.

He shook his head.

"Are you sick, dear? I've never known you to refuse chess pie."

"I was thinking about the machine," he said.

"You're always thinking about the machine," Louise said. "You've been thinking about it for two years. Have a piece of pie."

As Clakey left the room again, Anne Farish turned to Nat. "Really," she said, "you encourage Clakey to be impudent. It's on your own head if she gets entirely out of control. And mind you, she's the one who'll suffer for it, not you."

"The model is finished and everything works," Aubrey said.

"My, isn't that wonderful!" Anne Farish said. "Aunt Louise says we're going to make lots of money on it."

"I thought you told us three weeks ago that it worked," Miss Louise said.

"Yes, it did. I knew then that it was going to be a success. But

I had a couple of bugs to iron out. Now everything is done." He spoke in an expressionless monotonous way, as if he might have been saying, "We're out of toothpaste."

"Aren't you pleased, Uncle Aubrey?" Nat said. "You sound as if something's wrong."

"I don't see why you don't bring it home and install it right here at the house," Miss Louise said. "You know I need a new washing machine."

"Louise, I've got a lot on my mind," Aubrey said irritably. He was almost never irritable, being far too deeply absorbed in his own ruminations to be annoyed by other people.

Louise's china-blue eyes filled with tears. "Your Uncle Aubrey must have indigestion," she said to Nat and Anne Farish. She looked down at the table, and her hand, the veins standing like blue cords under the wrinkled skin, moved with trembling uncertainty as she readjusted her napkin in its silver ring, touched the pepper grinder, and picked up the bell to ring for Clakey.

Nat stared at the clawlike hand as it stumbled about the table. *She's old,* she thought. *Soon dead.* She shuddered. "We had a good time last night," she said. "I mean last weekend. At Sarelli's. Did I tell you? Didn't we, Anne Farish?"

Aubrey pushed his chair back from the table and stood up. "Come down to the store," he said. "I want to show it to you. Also, I have some family business to discuss with all of you."

"It's my nap time, dear," Miss Louise said. "We'll come later."

"Come on, Aunt Louise, you can skip your nap," Anne Farish said. "I want to see the machine."

．　．　．

The day was cold for mid-October, and the brick walls of the Mid-South Hardware Company breathed a damp and mortary chill. The store had not been open that day. No lights burned in the display cases or in the windows. One bank of fluorescent tubes hanging from long pipes above the center aisle partly dispelled the dusty gloom of the echoing, high-ceilinged room. On either side of the aisle, behind battered oak and glass display cases, rolling ladders stretched up into the semidarkness. Behind them, the brick walls were lined from floor to ceiling with ranks of green pigeonholes and small drawers filled with nuts, bolts, screws, washers, tacks, nails, and small machine parts. The store itself was a jumble of every kind of hardware from cowbells, peaveys, middlebusters, and pitch pumps to aluminum skillets, portable radios, leaf brooms, and dry flies — everything covered with a haze of dust.

A moth-eaten stuffed bobcat as big as an Airedale stood, one foot raised, a fixed snarl on its face, on top of the tall bookcase next to Aubrey's desk. With its disproportionately long legs, small fierce head and stumpy tail, it looked like some prehistoric failure at animal-making. Above the door which opened from the store into Aubrey's workshop hung a huge moose head, its branching antlers thick with dust, a fragile spider web stretched from three of the points to a ragged brown ear.

Miss Louise looked at the animals and shivered. Trophies brought back in the distant past by Aubrey's long-dead partner, they had occupied the same places in the store for fifty years. But she never failed in some way to express her disapproval of them. "Aubrey, this place is a disgrace," she said, the piping voice echoing in the deserted store. "Why don't you have that colored boy sweep in here? And get the dust off that moose's eyeballs, if you *have* to keep him hanging there. Not to mention the spider web on his horns."

"I fired him," Aubrey muttered. "I don't want anybody snooping around in here."

"You *fired* him! Are you planning to keep this place clean yourself? And who's going to keep the store open while you're at lunch?"

"Never mind, never mind," he said. "It's not important, Louise. Come on to the back."

"But who's helping you?" she said.

"I said it's not important. We can talk about it later."

Grinding chips of fallen plaster underfoot, the three women picked their way through a confusion of stock — bushel baskets of dead onion sets and cabbage plants, five-gallon jars holding only a handful each of seeds or beans, stacks of churns and buckets piled on top of old-fashioned black iron cookstoves. From time to time, they had to stoop to avoid the coils of rope, horse collars, popcorn poppers, bullwhips, kerosene lanterns, and casting rods that hung from hooks fixed in crossbars above their heads.

Anne Farish put her hand on Nat's arm and drew her aside by a stack of galvanized zinc washtubs nested inside each other. "Nat, I'm shocked," she said in a low voice. "Uncle Aubrey has let this place go down terribly in the past year. Maybe he ought to sell the business and retire."

Nat shrugged and gently thumped a tub which gave out a hollow ringing sound.

"Look at these tubs," Anne Farish said. "Who in the world buys tin washtubs these days? Charles says a good stock man would make all the difference in the world in here. If Uncle Aubrey would modernize! This could be a going concern."

"Some country people probably buy tubs," Nat said. "Negroes."

"Not when the store is closed," Anne Farish said.

"No wonder he closes it," Nat said. "Think how dull it must be — I'd close up, too."

"After all, it's going to be our responsibility and our headache one of these days," Anne Farish said. "We ought to give it serious thought."

"Yours, maybe," Nat said. "You won't catch me sticking around Philippi to run Uncle Aubrey's hardware store. Not if I can lay my hands on some money."

"Nat, you're *hard*," Anne Farish said. "You don't care about anybody."

"Yes — well, it's a cold cruel world, dear," Nat said.

"Come on," Aubrey said. "Come on." His round eyes were wide in the twilight, and the moment they had unlocked the store and entered it, his body had seemed to quiver with excitement. He paused under the moose head and unlocked another door, this one into his workshop. Inside, in a cleared space, surrounded by old radios and record players, torn-up motors, broken power mowers, and tools of all kinds, stood the washing machine.

Aubrey walked all around it. "Mind you," he said, "it hasn't any fancy case to make it look good. We can worry about that later. This is a working model." He took an armload of towels that Anne Farish had brought for the demonstration and threw them into the machine. "You see that little boomerang-shaped piece in the side of the tub there?" he said. "That's *it*. When the tub has filled and the motor starts up, that little piece vibrates the water at a terrific speed. It's all in the shape of the piece, the way it moves, and, of course, in the speed of the motor. The clothes don't turn over the way they do in an ordinary washer. They just shake. So they don't get all twisted together. No tearing, no getting the buttons ripped off, no ruining the zippers, no trouble untangling the load to hang it out or put it in the dryer. The vibration of the water — you can scarcely even see it — is so rapid, it literally shakes the dirt out of the clothes." He started the machine. "Then," he said speaking more rapidly, as if afraid of an interruption, "when they've had time to get clean (This model doesn't have a timer, but the manufactured one will, of course.), the boomerang retracts into the side of the machine like this" — he turned the switch. "The tub drains, and then (See, it's made of a very tough but flexible rubber.) it collapses on the clothes and squeezes the water out of them. Vacuum-operated. See?"

"But Aubrey," Miss Louise said, "it's so ugly and dirty-looking. Why, it's even rusty in spots."

"I explained to you," he said. "If you'd *listen.*"

"It'll have a case on the outside like a regular washing machine," Anne Farish said. "It won't look like that, Aunt Louise."

Nat, leaning against an old-fashioned radio cabinet, heavily carved in the style of the Spanish renaissance, began to look about her at the piles of abandoned radios and record players stacked on every side of the shop. She lit a cigarette, snapped the switch on the radio, and appeared to be listening to ghostly music. "Uncle Aubrey," she said, "have you ever read that every sound that has ever been made is still traveling through space somewhere in the universe?"

"Really, Nat, don't be ridiculous!" Anne Farish said. "*Sound* is what you *hear.*"

"Now, listen," Aubrey said. "The advantages are obvious. It cuts down wear and tear on the clothes and eliminates a large number of moving parts in the machine. No need for the heavy construction used in a spin-type machine. Cheap to manufacture and cheap to service. The motor and the vibrator. The pump. That's it." Aubrey's voice quivered and creaked with excitement and his face was transformed by awe at his own accomplishment. "This machine is the most important thing that has ever happened to me, Louise," he said. "It's my . . . my . . . It's the greatest thing I've ever done. We can build a plant and manufacture them ourselves. Just *think.*"

Anne Farish shook her head skeptically. "I don't know very

much about business, Uncle Aubrey," she said, "but that doesn't sound practical to me." She spoke briskly and objectively in her high-pitched twittering voice, like a parakeet at a board of directors' meeting. "None of us has the *know-how*," she said, giving the word all the weight of technical slang correctly used. "And to build a plant! We'd have to have an enormous amount of capital. Have you thought about selling the machine to one of the big manufacturing companies? General Electric or Frigidaire or Westinghouse? If it's as good as you say it is, they would bid for rights. And then we could sit back and collect royalties, while they worry about the manufacturing part of it."

"No!" Aubrey said. "This is my opportunity. This is the chance that comes once in a lifetime. That's why I brought Morris Shotwell in on it in the first place, don't you see? I thought he was the one man in the county who could produce the capital and make it possible for us to build the plant right here. I could be in charge of the manufacturing end and he could run the business end. But it's not going to work out that way. We've got to figure out something else." He had said more in ten minutes than he usually did in a day, and now he sat down abruptly on a stool in front of the washing machine, put his elbows on the lid, and rested his head in his hands. "I mustn't allow myself to get overexcited," he muttered. He drew himself erect, got his watch out of his pocket, snapped open the lid, looked at it, started to wind it, found it already wound tight, and put it into his pocket again. "It's not going to work that way," he repeated. "Shotwell . . ." He broke off, got up and walked rapidly all around the machine again. "Nobody knows about the model, see?" he said. "*Nobody*. I took the precaution — at least I had that much sense — of telling Morris that I had torn it down — that I needed the parts for something new I was working on. But he's so stupid about making things, he probably wouldn't even have realized you have to *have* a model. And, of course, I never showed it to anybody else. I was careful about that from the beginning — I mean the people who made parts for me, the machine shops here and in Memphis. Naturally I'd never have let any of them know what I was doing. Somebody might have stolen the idea."

"What difference does it make whether Morris knows about the model or not?" Nat said.

Aubrey began to pace the narrow space around the machine, nodding and moving his lips. He said jerkily, as if someone were pulling the words out of him with a piece of string, "I — haven't — any money. I've got — to get hold of — some money."

"I thought Morris was going to put up the money," Miss Louise said. "That's the lovely thing about this invention — your association with Morris Shotwell."

"If any of you would pay any attention," Aubrey said, "I'm trying to tell you what's happened. He . . . He . . . I trusted him! Trusted him!" He stopped in front of his wife. "He thinks he's got me where he wants me," he said. "He thinks I'm an impractical old man — just because the business is failing, because I'm an inventor, he thinks he can hoodwink me. I know it. But he can't. I'll . . ."

"No," Miss Louise said. "I'm sure you must be mistaken Why, the Shotwells are one of the oldest families in the county, dear. Morris wouldn't . . . You ought to rely on his advice instead of bringing us down here and saying ugly things about him."

"I don't understand what you're talking about, Uncle Aubrey," Nat said. "What did Morris do?"

"Rely on his advice!" Aubrey said. "Yes, he gave me some advice all right. I went down there this morning — to his office — to talk about arrangements — about the future, and we — we — had a quarrel. It all started over whether we are going to put up a plant and manufacture the machine ourselves or — or *sell* it. And I'm *not*. I'm not going to sell. Did Henry Ford sell his automobile? Or Chrysler or Du Pont? Did they turn around and sell their ideas? And when I *refused* — well, he told me that *he* has the patent. It was simpler, he said, and he didn't want to bother me with details. *He patented the machine in his own name.* Then he said he'd showed the plans to a friend of his. (You know him, Louise; it's Calvin Green, that fellow that retired here a couple of years ago — engineer — who used to work for — I forget, but one of the big companies.) Anyhow he did show the plans to this fellow, and he says that it's common knowledge among the big companies that everybody turned down a design like this about three years ago. Too good, he said. Like the light bulb that never burns out. They want a machine designed so that it'll wear out in five to seven years. Planned obsolescence, they call it. So Morris and Green say the way to make money on it is to *threaten* to build the plant and then to sell the rights to the highest bidder for the purpose of *not* producing it. They've already started negotiations with a couple of companies."

"But couldn't you make this one so it *would* wear out?" Anne Farish said.

"That's the *point* of the machine," Aubrey said. "It won't wear out and it won't wear out your clothes. That's what makes it so good."

Miss Louise's attention had begun to wander during this conversation. "I'm sure Morris . . ." she said in a vague voice, and then, in a whispered aside, "Look here, Anne Farish. Here's one of those funny old carved radio cabinets like people used to have in the thirties. What style is it — Spanish? I'll bet I could get it stripped and rubbed down and turn it into a kind of cellarette for the dining room. Wouldn't that be unusual?"

"Louise, listen to me," Aubrey said. "Have you understood anything I've been saying? He patented *my* machine in *his* name."

"But what were you saying about the model?" Nat said.

"*I've* got the model. The proof. And I have the bills from every machine shop that made a part for it. It won't matter that none of the shops knew what the parts were for, that they all thought I was a crazy old man puttering around with another worthless idea. Every one of those shops will identify the parts they made for me. There's no way for Shotwell to prove he invented the machine. He can sit back and gloat now, but I'm going to figure out some way to fix his wagon, so he'll never . . ."

"Oh," Nat said. "But I told . . ."

"Don't interrupt me, Nat. When I got so furious with Morris this morning (The idea! Sell it to somebody who will never do anything with it!), when I said, *Never,* he turns as cool as a cucumber. It doesn't matter what I want, he says. He's in control. He was just trying to do me a favor, and he's still willing — he'll swap me the mortgages on the store and the house — although, of course, the patent is already in his name and he doesn't *have* to do anything for me. And if I want to contest the rights, I'll have to hire a lawyer and take it through the courts, and I haven't got the money even to start. He didn't *say* that, but it's obvious, isn't it, to a moron?"

"Mortgages!" Louise said. "What mortgages?"

"And he knows I'm thinking about something new, too. I had mentioned that to him. A refinement on . . . But that's not important right now. The thing is, he's smart enough to bargain with the promise of enough leeway so that I can finance the beginning of this new project. He thought by doing that he'd get me off the track. Well, I said, *no!* No! He's not going to do that to me. I told him I was going to take a chance on manufacturing the machine myself — that I'd fight him for the rights — that if GE or anybody else had turned down a machine like this one, they had made a big mistake. There would be a tremendous market, if we went into it on our own. He laughed in my face. Told me I was a damn fool. So . . . So . . ." Aubrey was breathing rapidly, his eyes round and wide. He snatched his watch out of his pocket, put it down on top of the machine and began to count his pulse. "I get too excited," he said. "Not well." Then, "What am I going to do? That's the question. What am I going to do about Shotwell and the patent? And the machine? Can we find someone else here to finance it? Or should I sell after all? No. I *won't* sell. And Shotwell! He'll regret the day he tried to cheat me."

"What mortgages?" Miss Louise said again.

"Louise, the Shotwells have held paper on the store and the house off and on for years. You sign the notes yourself when I get them renewed. How do you think I get the money to buy stock for the store? You know the bank turned us down five years ago, and we refinanced through Morris."

Miss Louise shook her head. "I really don't understand things like that," she said. "Papa always said to keep away from mortgages. 'Neither a borrower nor a lender be.' That was what he said. And you're talking about notes, not mortgages."

"Exactly. Notes. Mortgages. Paper. It's all the same thing."

"Morris is a canny businessman," Miss Louise said. "You'd do well to listen to what he says. That's my advice to you. Besides, Aubrey, there's something very important involved here." She glanced at Nat. "We don't want to offend the Shotwells in any way," she said. "Think how nice Floyd has been to Nat this fall. And all those lovely tomatoes and that delicious sweet corn Morris brought you last summer. Why, they're old friends of the family."

"Woman, listen to me," Aubrey said. His hands were trembling and his voice hoarse and weak. "I'm trying to tell you something very important. He's got me by the throat. Do you understand that? He's holding paper on everything I possess. But he doesn't know I have the model. I can make him squirm. I can show him up for the crook he is. And I'm going to."

Miss Louise sat down on a nail keg. It was damp and chilly in the shop, and she had begun to shiver. "I'm cold," she said. "You shouldn't have brought us down here without turning the heat on." And then, "Just look at this place, Anne Farish. Look at this awful, filthy place. Nobody working for him except a good-for-nothing, stupid, dirty, colored boy, and now he's fired *him*." For the second time that day her eyes filled with tears. "We're going to be ruined!" she said in her high genteel voice. "That's what you're saying, isn't it, Aubrey? All your life you've wasted your time on this — this *dirty* — *greasy* — *common* . . . You're no better than a — a mechanic in a service station — a grease monkey. And all the time, if you'd tried, you could have been a planter like anybody else. And *now* — you're broke and you're trying to blame it on Morris Shotwell, and — and ruin things between Floyd and Nat."

Nat heard her name spoken, but she was not thinking so much of the connection between herself and Aubrey's troubles as of the two old people themselves. Where, throughout the luncheon table conversation between Miss Louise and Anne Farish, she had been almost unable to take in what was said — had, in fact, heard it in a garbled way, the words jumbled together, almost as if they spoke a foreign language — she had begun while Aubrey was talking about his machine to listen. And when he had said that no one knew of the existence of the model, she had realized that this was not strictly true. Someone else did know, for she had discussed it with Floyd. But she knew, too, without a word's having been spoken regarding Morris, that Floyd would never give anything to his father — not a word, not a gesture, not a thought; and so she was not concerned that he might have mentioned the model in conversation — she could not, in fact, imagine such a thing as a conversation between Floyd and Morris. She had started to tell Aubrey that Floyd knew about the model, but then had changed her mind. No use, she thought, to complicate the matter needlessly. But, as Aubrey went on talking and her aunt's responses continued to go wide of the mark, Nat began to watch them. Again she felt, at the sight of Miss Louise's mottled ancient hands, a chill — a cold earthy dampness that came not from the walls of the store, but from her very pores. She watched Aubrey's frantic, jerky demonstration and listened to her aunt's muddleheaded admonitions, and a queer new sensation gripped her, foreign to anything her life with the Hunters had yet produced. I've got a bellyache, she thought. Getting the curse? No. She forced herself into ordinary familiar pathways of thought. There's going to be a lot of money involved. Maybe. How can anybody know if this is a real invention, or *nothing?* Aloud she said, "I think you need to get a good patent lawyer first thing, Uncle Aubrey, and get control of the patent. Then you can begin to decide about whether to sell or manufacture."

"No money," he said. "No money. If I'm going to fix that — that scoundrel's wagon, I've got to get hold of some money. I haven't got the cash in the bank for Louise's household allowance next month — to pay Clakey — to *eat.*" He looked at his wife who was wiping the tears from her face and sniffling miserably. Again he got out his watch, snapped the lid, and put it back into his pocket.

"For goodness' sake, stop looking at your watch," Miss Louise said. She blew her nose. "I suppose we'll have to live on our social security," she said. "Like nigras — and — and laboring people."

Anne Farish drew her coat about her and buttoned it. "It seems to me you should have consulted with Charles while he was here," she said. "He *is* a member of the family."

"He hasn't gone far," Nat said. "You can call him tonight in Moss Ridge if you want to."

"It's time for me to be back in Moss Ridge myself," Anne Farish said. "You forget I have two children to look after. I'll discuss it with him when I get there."

"What we need to ask him is if he'll lend Uncle Aubrey some money," Nat said.

"It's a bad time of the year for that," Anne Farish said. "You know we won't settle up and get our land bank money until January."

"Get the patent lawyer, Uncle Aubrey," Nat said. "If he thinks the machine is a good gamble, he'll be willing to worry about the money part later. And it's ridiculous not to have money for food. People don't starve to death. I'm going to borrow some money from Wilburn."

10

Driving to Jackson for the football game the following weekend, Floyd and Nat traveled east and then south through farm and pasture and forest lands, the blue Cadillac racing at seventy and eighty miles an hour through the dead November Delta. Fall — frost — had come early that year. The cane was yellow and the locust thickets along the drainage ditches bare. Stretches of frost-bronzed woodland were misted over with dust, for it had been a dry fall. The road ran straight as a ruler-drawn diameter bisecting the vast flat circle of fields. Sometimes for miles no house or town would be visible — only the fields, bare cotton plants hung with the last trash of this year's crop, squares of greening winter wheat, and occasionally the deep gash of a drainage ditch stretching away to the horizon. And then, from the flatness and emptiness would rise, like the strange excrescences of a Martian landscape, clusters of towering grain silos, like pods in which embryonic monsters might be sleeping; or vibrating metal-sided gins, their long proboscises hanging toward the unloading ramps and extending outward to the trash houses. Here and there, huddled in upon themselves, as if avoiding the eye of a savage god in this naked world, little towns rose out of the emptiness: Pentecost, Belzoni, Sunflower, and Midnight; Nitta Yuma, Rolling Fork, Panther Burn, Anguilla, and Louise. Now and then they passed empty tenant cabins standing in the middle of the bare fields — doors banging in the wind, roofs sagging inward or sliding crazily off to one side or the other, while over the fields the great pickers and combines crept, browsing, half-obscured by clouds of dust, on old stalks and dry grass. They might have been monstrous insects; one could imagine that they had reached through the windows and probed the fragile cabins with discs and scoops, consuming or overturning and obliterating their contents, as they consumed the cotton and overturned and obliterated the dead plants in the fields.

Once, as the car approached a bridge crossing one of the wide black bayous that creep with a sluggish, almost invisible motion through that part of the Delta, a long steel neck appeared, hesitant and then swooping, above the banked earth and low thickets. It swung out gaping jaws and took a bite from the earth, swung back and dumped it on a mound beside the road.

"Look," Nat said. "A brontosaurus! I thought they were *extinct!*"

"They're building a spillway here," Floyd said. "Flood control." In a moment he added shyly. "I can run one of those."

"My!" Nat said.

"Spent one whole summer moving dirt to fill in a garbage dump and shift a levee," he said. "I'm good." He pressed down on the accelerator and the car leaped forward. "It was better than what I'm doing now," he added.

When the car roared through Yazoo City and into the hills rising abruptly from the last banks of the Yazoo River, the landscape changed. The road wound through the hills and it was necessary to travel more slowly. In the pastures along the way, sleek black cattle grazed the dry yellowish grass and gathered at long wooden feeding and watering troughs. There were cedar trees, cones of darkness among the bare cottonwoods and sycamores; dogwood and sumac foliage flamed against the green pines and black cedars. And then, where the hills had been washed to gullies and ravines, and neither fields nor pastures were possible, the kudzu vines covered everything, smothering trees and hills. Green as a poisonous jungle in summer, they were gray and withered now, after the first frosts, hanging like shrouds of witches' hair on the dead trees. The trees, no longer tree-shaped, wholly shrouded with gray vines, rose out of the gullies like dead volcanoes or gigantic anthills. And the vine-covered hills were gray, too, like great heaps of slag. There was no dwelling place anywhere among these vines and no animal, except now and then on the road the body of a skunk or possum or armadillo that had been struck by a passing car.

This was the landscape Nat saw — when she looked. But mostly she did not look. She smoked, drank a can or two of beer from the small icebox they had brought along, and, sitting with one leg under her and her arm along the back of the seat, chattered to Floyd. The queer, shining, blue-black color of her hair, like the color of a grackle's back, flickered with greenish lights in the rapidly shifting sunshine, as the car rushed through the bright cold morning. The smooth tan skin of her arms and her green eyes were beautiful, the haggard arrogant face softened by a gauzy blue-green scarf at the throat of her russet-colored wool dress. When she had come out of her aunt's house that morning to get into the car, she had so dazzled Floyd that the tears had sprung to his eyes. He had opened the door for her without speaking and, going around to his side, had climbed in and set off, with the accelerator pressed convulsively to the floor.

"Slow down a little bit," she had said to him. "The Delta may be dull, but I'd like to live long enough to get into the hills."

"I hate the Delta," he said, "but I was driving fast because . . . because you look so good."

"You like my dress?" she said. She ran her hand over the skirt and seemed to inventory her assets dispassionately. "This color goes with me," she said. And then, "I don't like the Delta either. Especially in winter. You're supposed to, I reckon, if you grow up in it; and it's all right in the spring. But *now* . . ." She shivered. "I always like to be someplace where I can keep a tan," she said. "I look like hell pale."

Floyd glanced at her and nodded, his face as open and unguarded as it ever was. He even seemed to open his eyes wider than ordinarily, as if to see her better.

"The beach is best," she said. "That's one reason I married Jeff. We lived in Concordia, Georgia, you know, and that's only an hour or so from the ocean. Do you like the beach?"

Again he nodded. ". . . to take *you* to the beach," he said.

"Well," she said, "Saint Simon's is nice, and Sea Island. The Cloisters is awfully expensive, but when Jeff was in a mood to throw away money we went there. Tybee is crowded and jukey now, and the others are probably getting that way, all except The Cloisters, but they used to be grand. Anyhow, that's not my worry anymore; I won't be going back to Georgia — except to see Hunter once in a while."

He looked directly at her. "Didn't work," he said tentatively. "Did it?"

"No," she said. She was silent for a moment. "There were lots of things involved," she said. "For one thing, I hated him. I never knew *that* was going to happen. I don't usually — hate people, I mean. It's so much trouble. It's easier to go away. But with him I couldn't. And there was something so . . . I think I hated him mainly because he was stupid. He let me make a fool of him. In fact, he *made* me make a fool of him. I didn't want to." She shrugged. "You don't want to hear about all that," she said.

"Yes, I do."

"He made himself out of a *Ladies' Home Journal* serial," she said. "Or 'As the World Turns.' It must have been the *Ladies' Home Journal,* because he made himself up before TV was invented. And then he expected me to keep telling him the story — to keep helping him make himself up. Dull! My God! And besides, I can't afford to do that. I might get to believing it myself." Then she shook her head. "No, I wouldn't," she said. "That's not the kind of story I like. But anyhow, he was nutty on the subject of love. Love!" She swung her free foot and looked down at it, turning her leg this way and that. "How do you like my shoes?" she said. "Aren't they becoming?"

"Love?" he said.

"That's one reason I like fags," she said. "They never pretend to love each other. When they're having an affair or 'married,' I mean. Funny how different they are from the dikes. With women it's just the opposite. All the paraphernalia has to be there — tender glances, loving consideration, undying faith — to say nothing of anniversary remembrances and things like that. That's another *story* — like Jeff's. But at least it isn't out of the *Ladies' Home Journal.* The men, though," she said, "the fags — they're different. They don't kid themselves. They've left the straight world because they hate it, and they don't try to make it up all over again."

"What do you know about fags?" he said.

"Didn't I tell you I was a kind of a fag moll when I was in Mexico? I mean, I went down there with one I liked very much. That was after I finally made up my mind to leave Jeff, and I was scared — I couldn't have screwed up the nerve to go anywhere by myself. So I went with him, and he had some friends in Taxco. I kept house for four of them that first winter." She laughed. "Of course, somebody from Philippi passed through Taxco on a vacation and went straight home and told Aunt Louise I was living with four men. I explained to her that queers were perfectly all right for a lady to live with, but she still plays like that particular winter didn't happen. She still maintains that I can't cook, for example, just because I couldn't when I was married to Jeff and learned how that winter in Mexico. But I'm really quite a good cook. Eloise — the one I went down there with — taught me how. He had been to a *cordon bleu* cooking school."

"Did you like them?"

"Yes," she said. "They were gay — that's not what I mean — of *course* they were gay. But they were lively, too. Good company. One of them was a gangster — that was why he was in Mexico. He was the most interesting to talk to. For one thing he was honest. But then I reckon most fags are more honest than 'straight' people. Sometime or other maybe they've had to look at their circumstances and learn to live with them. You can hardly pretend you're not a fag and still *be* one. Where if you're straight, you never have to *think* unless you just absolutely want to of your own accord. Like Wilburn or somebody. I mean Anne Farish doesn't have to think, does she — even about what she *is?* If I were a *moralist,*" she said, "I might even say they were courageous (although Eloise was absolutely terrified of mice). Other people — straight people — stay where they are and do what's expected of them and call it being courageous. But really they're just not brave or honest enough, or resourceful enough to do what they'd like to do. I just know that's true, don't you?"

"I don't know," he said. "I try not to do anything I don't want to."

"You're different," she said. And then, "The main reason I liked them was because they liked me."

"What kind of people were they?" he asked. He seemed curiously absorbed in what she was saying — as interested as if she had been talking about gambling.

"Oh, I don't know. They weren't any one kind of people. Some were sweet and some were bastards. The gangster was an intellectual. He was always telling me what to read. And I remember one time he told me that some philosopher — William James? — said that intelligence is the successful coordination of means and ends. That was a straight definition, he said. A fag knows there's no such thing as successful coordination of means and ends, because nobody's ends are ever what they seem, or even what they believe them to be. (You might think he was just being vulgar, but he meant it.) All that makes a fag more tolerable to live with. But, after all, Pete (the gangster) turned out to be a bastard. At the end he went off and left the others to pay all the bills — and I just know he had some money or *jewels* or something — maybe buried somewhere. But Ken and Eloise (Louis, he said his name had been, and he was a transvestite, which is kind of silly, if you ask me. The prettiest boy doesn't look very attractive in drag.) were very *moral*. They used to be shocked because I wasn't shocked at them." She paused thoughtfully. "And then, let's see, they used to like to dress me up. They would think of new ways to do my hair and makeup, and sometimes, if they had any extra money, they would buy way-out clothes for me. So you see they were very thoughtful and considerate. And it wasn't that they wanted me to pimp for them, either — to attract virile men, like some fag molls do. They never asked me to do that, although I wouldn't have minded if they had. As it turned out I did turn up one or two by accident. But usually they didn't have any trouble attracting their own.

"But the main thing about them," she said, "was that they didn't want me to go to bed with them." She drew a deep breath and said soberly, "You see, that was one reason I didn't do so well with being married. It's kind of hard to make anybody believe it, because of this . . ." She ran her hands over her bosom down to the slim waist and patted her hips. "But I don't really like going to bed with anybody." She was silent for perhaps thirty seconds while the car continued to rush through the broad flat fields. "Usually," she added.

"I would never marry," he said. And then, "If you don't want a man to think you're sexy, why do you get yourself up like you do?"

"I didn't mean I didn't like *myself*," she said. "I couldn't bear it if I didn't look attractive. You know, when I was in college I used to say I'd kill myself if my waist ever got bigger than twenty-three inches."

"I don't care about clothes and makeup," he said. "You'd look good to me if you never fixed yourself up."

"You may think that," she said, "but I wouldn't. I'd disappear. I can't even see myself before I put on mascara and eye shadow."

"What did Pruitt say to you about me?" he asked abruptly.

"I don't pay any attention to anything The General says," she said.

"But what did he say?"

"We got off the track," she said. "I didn't finish telling you about Jeff and me. What I was going to say was that *that* was not really why we didn't stay married. I suppose I could have put up with *that* indefinitely, if I had had a reason. I mean, after all, I did marry him for his money. I didn't go into it blindfolded. But he wanted to spend more and more of it on things like furniture — and furniture-store furniture, at that. And he got worse and worse. The more I tried to make him see that you could have a good marriage without furniture and three meals a day at the same boring table, and — *love,* the more he talked like 'As the World Turns.' "

"I like to listen to you talk," he said. "Tell me some more."

"You'd get tired of it after a while," she said. "I mean, me talking. And it wouldn't take all that long. I get tired of it myself, goodness knows. That's why a weekend like this is fun. We . . ." She glanced at him as if trying to gauge his reaction before she spoke. "We'll meet lots of people," she said. "It'll be a change for both of us. Philippi and Aunt Louise — not to mention Morris and the appliance business — aren't as stimulating as they might be."

"People?" Floyd said. "What people?" His rosy little mouth seemed to get smaller and he gripped the wheel so that his knuckles were white.

"A friend of mine — you know, from Ole Miss days — is having open house for everybody before the game. Wilburn told me he and Sunny got an invitation. And somebody else I know is having everybody for drinks and supper afterwards."

"We're not invited to either one of them," he said.

"They're old friends," Nat said. "People I've known very well for a long time and haven't seen for years. They'll be glad to see us."

He shook his head. "I hate parties and strange people," he said.

"Come on," Nat said. "We're supposed to have fun this weekend. Do it my way, won't you? It won't be all strange people, after all. You'll know some of them. And Wilburn and Sunny will be there."

"I don't like Wilburn," he said. "He's probably in love with you."

Nat ignored this. "They came down Wednesday for some tests," she said. "Wilburn says Sunny needs an operation and she's afraid of the knife (not that I blame her), and she keeps looking for a doctor who will cure her without cutting on her. They finished all the tests yesterday, but Wilburn said if she was feeling up to it, they'd probably stay over for the game."

"We don't have to see them," he said sullenly. "I want to be with you."

"You are with me. I'm not going anywhere."

A quarter of a mile ahead of them a combination country store and service station loomed up out of the fields. "This car uses a lot of gas," Floyd said. "I don't get ten miles to the gallon." Abruptly he braked the car and with tires screaming, turned into the graveled area in front of the store and stopped. He got out without saying any more to Nat and went into the store, moving stiffly, his arms held slightly away from his sides.

Dust swirled in little eddies above the gravel; scraps of torn candy wrappers and crumpled snow-cone cups, crushed beer cans, empty cigarette packs, and soft drink bottles littered the porch that ran the length of the store and the area around the gas pumps directly in front of it. In a small cage by one of the pumps, a mangy raccoon paced back and forth, pausing at each side to rub his head and neck against the confining wire. Three white men sat on the edge of the porch, as still as if they had grown there. One, with a long yellow face, his mouth full of greenish teeth, smiled at Nat with a peculiarly horrifying intensity. A Negro came out of the store and began to service the Cadillac. The car trembled and throbbed like a captured bird. Inside, Nat shivered. Nothing in that scene would have persuaded a sane man that the shining car and the woman could occupy the same world as the filthy store and the coon and the four men.

"Turn off-a switch, please, m'am," the Negro said to Nat.

She reached out to the paneled dashboard and turned the key. One of the white men said something in a low voice.

"Nahsuh." The Negro smiled like a performer in a minstrel show.

The white man spoke again.

"Yassuh."

Nat pressed the button to close the window, but the power was off and nothing happened. "I hate places like this," she muttered. "He just stopped here to spite me." She got a compact out of her purse and studied her face in the tiny round of mirror.

The yellow man got up, walked over to the car, and leaned his arms on the window. "My, ain't this a pretty car," he said.

On the other side the Negro froze, his body a thin forked stick, his face blank, his hand moving in a circle, polishing one spot on the windshield with a pink paper towel.

"Yes," Nat said in her ordinary, soft, friendly voice. "Do you live around here?" she asked politely. And when he did not answer but continued to stare at her with moss-green teeth shining wetly, "That's a silly question, isn't it? I reckon you must, of course."

"Did you know you can drive straight to hell in a car like this?" he said. "Ain't that right, nigger?"

"Yassuh."

"We're going to Jackson to the ball game," Nat said.

"I'm a preacher," the man said. "I know. Evil down there. Gambling. Drinking. Fornication. Wash that paint off your face, woman, and come to God."

Floyd came out of the store and got into the car.

"Hell!" the man said.

"How much?" Floyd said.

The yellow man looked at the figures on the pump. "Six-sixty," he said. "You nelly empty." He pulled a small testament out of his back pocket and handed it through the window to Nat. "I give one to ever'body stops here," he said. "Read it."

Floyd reached for his wallet.

Two Negro men approached the store, walking along the dusty shoulder of the highway. They paused not far from the pumps.

"Yeah, yestiddy," one of them said.

"And you hadda pickup?"

"Yeah," the other one said, "but then I seeda white man, so I homp on off down the road."

"He never see you?"

"Nah."

The wind blew and a loose Coca-Cola sign banged against the store front.

"Git on in here, boy," the yellow man said to one of the two Negroes who had paused by the pump. "You already half hour late."

"Hurry up," Nat said. "Hurry up, let's go."

On the road she lit a cigarette with trembling fingers and said nothing. Floyd resumed the conversation as if they had never mentioned going to a party. "You didn't tell me what The General said about me," he said.

"He said you were crazy about me."

"Like in the *Ladies' Home Journal?*"

"I told you I don't pay any attention to what The General says."

"Love," he said in an inquiring voice, as if he had never used the word before. "You don't like to talk about love?"

She shrugged. "I like to *talk* about it," she said. "Love — sex — whatever. But neither one of us needs to worry about that. You don't want to any more than I do."

"No," he said. "I never think about — love. And I don't want to." And then, still in a dispassionate, inquiring way, "Do you think the reason you're not any good at being married is because you don't like to go to bed?"

"No," she said. "I told you I could put up with that. It's not understanding — or wanting — what they want, not knowing why they say the things they say or expect the things they expect or even eat the things they eat. And so *dull!* Like Mr. McGregor and the ice cream."

"What?"

"Anne Farish's husband. Like, if I'm visiting over there, every night it's the same thing. At nine — or nine-thirty, depending on where the break comes on TV that night, he — Charles — says, just as if he'd thought of it for the very first time in his life and was delighted with himself, 'Anne Farish, I'm hungry! You wouldn't think we just had supper a couple of hours ago, would you?' And she says, 'I'll fix you something real special, honey.' And he says, 'Not too much, dear. I'm watching my weight.'

"I reckon it sounds silly," Nat said, "but it's all so *vulgar*. Anyhow she goes to the kitchen and she always has all kinds of awful things back there: a bought angel food cake or pecan pie, two or three kinds of ice cream, marshmallow sauce, and boxes of bought cookies. And she'll concoct something unbelievable — something awful, like maybe pecan pie with Neapolitan ice cream on top and chocolate sauce on top of that; and he sits there and eats every bite of it, and then he says, 'My! That was *nice,* honey.' Always the same thing in exactly the same way: 'My! That was *nice,* honey.' That's a happy marriage! I'd rather never see another human face than watch Mr. McGregor eat ice cream every night."

He made no reply to this and said nothing for some miles while Nat chattered on. Then abruptly he spoke again. It was as if he gathered all his strength to reveal himself to her and perhaps expected as a result some miracle of understanding between them. He even called her by name.

"Nat?" he said. "Listen. I want to tell you something. We're alike. *Alike.* Aren't we?"

"I hadn't thought about whether we are or not," she said.

"We can be — friends," he said, "because . . . because we're both — cold. We can understand each other. All that you said today — about the *Ladies' Home Journal*, you know. I would never ask you to pretend for me like that, would I?"

"No," she said.

"I am — separate — from everything like that. I *hate* — love." He broke off. Then he began again, articulating with difficulty. "I've never tried to tell the truth before," he said. "I mean, I've never tried to *talk* to a woman. I never thought I would find one that I could talk to. And I didn't care."

Nat shifted her position in the car, crossed her legs, and swung her foot nervously. "You don't have to," she said. "Don't worry about it."

"No. Listen. I want us to be — *friends*," he repeated. "I won't bother you. All right? You can relax around me. All right?" He took his foot off the accelerator and as the car coasted to a reasonable speed, he turned to her, his small eyes full of dread and hope, his mouth a painful grimace that might have been meant for a smile. "It would be different from anything that ever happened in my life," he said. "We can be alone all we want to. You don't have to drag me into a crowd to keep me from making a pass at you. You can *relax.* Do you hear me? We can eat together and go to the game, and then afterwards, I'll . . . I'll even take you dancing, if you want me to. Just the two of us. And I'll buy you champagne and . . . and flowers, if you like them — whatever you like. And we'll talk and . . ." He broke off. Sweat stood on his forehead, as if he had been heaving and struggling a long time to move a huge weight, straining every muscle in his powerful body and long, heavily muscled arms.

"You're *sweet*," Nat said.

He glanced at her again, then back at the highway. They were in the outskirts of Jackson now. "All right, then?" he said.

"We can do all that and have *that* kind of good time," she said, "and go to parties, too. Just wait and see. You'll have fun."

11

AND THEY WENT that day from party to game to party, Nat coaxing and cozening him along with her. The houses they wandered through were set among rolling pine hills; pine straw was fragrant underfoot. The gardens, cultivated as religiously as if each one harbored the tree of life and the tree of the knowledge of good and evil, were bare and trim and weedless, banked at their borders with mounds of evergreen azaleas that in the spring would burn with cerise and fuchsia and scarlet and lavender flames. Now, in November, the worn, wooded hills were brown and green, crowned with the somber beauty of pines and cedars and magnolias. Under the tall trees the houses were new, built since the end of the Second World War in modified colonial or ranch style, faced with clapboard or old brick. There were swimming pools in the backyards, and the carports were cluttered with toys: discarded dolls, bicycles, tricycles, scooters, and footballs. In the ranch-style houses there would often be a foyer divided from the living room by a low brick or stone-faced wall topped with a planter box full of philodendron and mother-in-law's tongue.

And there would be appropriately early modern reproductions on the walls — Dufy or Braque or the Picasso blue period. There was even one house, copied from a plan in *House Beautiful*, in which the dining room table was set on a little island in the middle of an indoor pool and connected on one side with the kitchen and on the other with the living room by curving concrete ramps, floored with flagstones.

"You can throw your bones and all in the pool," Nat explained to Floyd, and he peered into the water as if expecting to see orange peels — or perhaps a body — floating there. They were standing on the island. Across the water a crowd of bright-faced chattering drinkers milled through the house, performing the rituals of autumn reunion.

"Nat Hunter! I haven't seen you for *years*. Where'd you *spring* from?" It was their hostess, approaching across a ramp. "Dalton told me you were coming, Nat, honey. And then I saw Wilburn yesterday down at the hospital — I'm a Gray Lady — and he said you were coming to my party. I was *tickled*. Now, I want to hear all about your family and how many children you have and — didn't somebody tell me you were living in Georgia?" A smiling dish-faced woman with eyes set flat in a face without the planes of cheekbones, she was a sorority sister from Ole Miss days. Her eyes crinkled with the genuine pleasure of welcome. She wore a short red chiffon cocktail dress, belted low on her hips in the style of the twenties; her body was thick through the middle and flat-chested, and her bowed legs stuck out below the uneven hem of the dress like bent sticks, too fragile, it seemed, to support her weight. She embraced Nat warmly and left a smudge of lipstick on her cheek. "I'm not wearing this to the *game*," she said, holding out her skirt with both hands. "Don't think I'm crazy. But I just couldn't resist putting it on this morning for the luncheon. Red is so festive." She looked around. "I bet you've never met my husband," she said. "I'm going to find him for you. You know, ugly and bowlegged as I am, I caught the best-looking man you ever laid your eyes on. Can you believe it? I reckon it was because of the war and all." She broke off, looked around, and then leaned toward Nat with a conspiratorial air and, taking her arm, said in a low voice, "Alice is here somewhere, Nat, and I want to talk to you before you see her, so you won't mention . . ."

"Alice who?" Nat said.

"Alice *Warren*. Have you forgotten your own big sister?"

"Oh, of course," Nat said. "I just haven't seen her in a long time."

"But a Tri Omega never forgets her big sister, honey. That's a precious bond, isn't it? Anyhow, she is here, and I wanted to warn you before you saw her, so you won't mention it. Did you know her daughter pledged Delta Gamma at Ole Miss last year?"

"No!"

"It almost broke Alice's heart, and it's better just not to talk about it. When I *think* how wonderful she was, and how we all looked *up* to her that year we were freshmen — when she was president of the chapter and Miss Ole Miss and all, and *now* . . . Well, she's had a *series* of tragedies. The Tri Omegas didn't give the child a bid. That's children for you nowadays. Imagine us not giving a daughter a bid! I mean, unless she was *afflicted* or something. But the older girl had pledged two years ago, and then had gotten pregnant in the middle of her freshman year — *right after she was initiated*. (Or maybe, even worse, it was before and she didn't tell them — went through that *sacred* rite in spite of it. Nobody is quite sure.) And so I suppose, in a way, you can't blame the girls for not being enthusiastic about the younger sister, although from what I've heard, it wasn't that at all, but her teeth, which certainly are a little bit bucked. I don't see why Alice never had that child's teeth straightened. And now everybody says Alice is drinking too much, but I must say I think she deserves all the sympathy in the world." She drew a deep breath and glanced around the room. "Look, Nat," she said, "there's Hermit Crabbe. I haven't seen him for ten years, have you? He's been with North American Aircraft, I think, somewhere — Long Island? Who would have thought when he was an All Southern fullback that he had sense enough to build airplanes? Did he marry a Yankee? Why he's as bald as . . . I would never have recognized him except for those big ears. Would you?"

Here Nat interrupted her to introduce Floyd. He gave them a distracted look and, turning away, peered again into the depths of the pool.

"Any friend of Nat's . . ." the hostess said, and then, "How do y'all like my pool? Isn't it the cutest thing you ever saw in your *lives*? I got the idea from *House Beautiful*, only the one in there was kind of a lily pond, not a real swimming pool. We just love it. We don't eat in the dining room much, anyhow, and we decided to throw caution to the winds and *do* it." She broke off to wave to someone across the room. " 'Scuse me, honey, there's . . ." She looked around with the businesslike glance of a hostess attending to the welfare of her guests and noticed a man standing alone at the other end of the dining room table, staring into the water and disconsolately nibbling a beaten biscuit. "By the way, Nat," she said, "do you know my brother-in-law? You know, Mary Mimms married a doctor from California and they're here on a visit. Jay," she beckoned to him, "this is an old friend, Nat Hunter, and Mister uhh . . ."

"Shotwell," Nat said.

"Will y'all 'scuse me now, honey? I'd better go speak to those folks coming in." She tripped across the ramp toward the living room in a kind of happy dance, waving both arms at a crowd of new arrivals. "Hoddy toddy," she called gaily. "Gosh amighty! Who the hell are we?"

"Rim-ram!" someone called back. "Bim-bam! Ole Miss, by damn!"

"Let's go," Floyd muttered into Nat's ear. "If we want to get a parking space, it's time to go to the game."

"We just got here, Floyd," Nat said. "It's an hour and a half until game time." Her voice, a fourth above its ordinary pitch, had taken on a brittle cocktail-party quality. "So you're Mary Mimms's husband," she said to the man standing beside her. He was finishing another beaten biscuit and ham sandwich. "Jay . . . ?"

The stranger, a small handsome man in his late thirties with features of a slightly Semitic cast, nodded at Nat, held out his hand to Floyd, and smiled. "Stanley," he said. "And you're Dr. Livingstone, I presume?" He gave a sudden surprising guffaw of laughter.

Nat giggled and Floyd stared at the hand as if it were a reptile. "This is Floyd Shotwell," Nat said. "Aren't you a character!"

"Not really," he said. "I'm just nervous among strangers and that's my party joke."

"Did Esther say you were from California?" Nat said. "I reckon you don't know anybody here except Mary Mimms. And where is she?"

"No," he said. "Not *from* California. I live there, but I'm a Rebel — an unreconstructed southern Jew, transplanted to the wilds of Orange County, Cal., scion of a long line of slave beaters."

"My," Nat said. "I didn't know Jews *had* slaves."

"Yes, indeed," he said. "They never had them after the Civil War, but I'm a pre-Civil War Jew. The old-southern-mansion type. From Greensboro, Alabama."

"Oh," Nat said.

"Sephardic," he said. "That's the best kind. Did you know that only two percent of the Jews in the United States are Sephardic?"

"I'm descended from Jane Grey, the nine-day queen of England," Nat said.

"I thought they cut off her head before she got married," he said.

"It's a *collateral* line," Nat said. "Where did you go to school?"

"Alabama," he said. "And Vanderbilt Med. School. And then I took my bride and my covered wagon and went west to seek my fortune. And now I live in a grove of avocado trees and practice geriatrics among the wealthy aged. What's your racket?" he said to Floyd.

Nat laughed. "Racket!" she said in her soft drawling voice. "Honestly!"

"Appliances," Floyd said.

"And what'd Esther say your name was?" Dr. Stanley said to Nat. "I didn't catch it."

"Nat Stonebridge. Hunter was my maiden name. I must have been at Ole Miss when you were at Alabama. Did you know . . ."

"Nat Hunter! Child, I know you like a sister. I roomed one year with Richard Duane from Columbus. Many a night I've had to sit and listen to your praises sung. Weren't you pinned to him once? Engaged, even?"

"Yes," Nat said, "but it's been so long ago, I'd almost forgotten about it. It was because of the fishing being so good. He came over to Philippi to see me one summer and we kept catching all these fish, and Aunt Louise kept cooking them, and he stayed and stayed . . . And one night he asked Aunt Louise for my hand and she *gave* it to him. He was very formal when it came to the proprieties. I reckon she thought she had latched on to a permanent fish market. I just didn't have the heart to explain to them that it was my hand and I hadn't given it to him. So we were engaged until the fish stopped biting. And then I broke it off. But I don't remember his rooming with anybody named Jay Stanley."

"Jacob Stanley Rosenthal," he said. "They called me Rosie. I dropped the Rosenthal when I moved to California. People are so prejudiced out there, it's a nuisance. Not like Alabama."

"Oh."

"Let's see," he said, "didn't you marry Jeff Stonebridge from Concordia, Georgia? I knew him, too, years ago. How is he?"

"I haven't seen him lately," Nat said. "We're divorced."

"At last!" He opened his arms in a gesture of mock welcome. "I didn't know anybody *got* divorces in Mississippi, Alabama, Georgia or Arkansas — not to mention Louisiana, where half the population is Catholic. I come south after being gone for four or five years, and everybody is still married to the same mate he had on my last trip. This is what I'd call a stagnant society. In California, folks tend to swap around."

"You're still married to Mary Mimms," Nat said.

"But she's not the original bride I started out with," he said.

Floyd opened his mouth to speak and then closed it. Nat glanced at him. "Why don't you get me a drink, Floyd?" she said. "I'm dry. Just one and then we'll go. OK?" When he had gone, she turned back to the doctor. "Greensboro," she said. "Is that where you said you were from? Seems as if I've been there sometime."

"The county seat of Catalpa County," he said. "Chief industry is catalpa worms. You shake the catalpa trees and, when the worms fall on the ground, you pick them up and sell them for bait."

"Of course!" she said. "Why that's where I was in jail this summer and the sheriff was so nice to me. My goodness, if I'd known you were from there, I'd have mentioned your name."

"Jail? Now what's a pretty girl like you doing in jail?"

"Well, it's a long story," Nat said. "It all started because of one little can of beer . . ."

"The sheriff,' he said, when she had finished her tale, "Jo Sam Ventura. He has a great raw-boned giant of a wife named Johnnie who used to be principal of the high school in Greensboro. I remember one time when she'd called some of us into her office and was getting ready to take us apart, one little tow-headed country girl kept saying, 'Oh, Lord *Jesus*, Miss Johnnie, Lord *Jesus*. I didn't have nothing to do with it.' And Miss Johnnie says, 'No use calling on Jesus, girl. *I'm* in charge here.'" He looked at Nat appraisingly. She was smiling at him as gaily as a child and her slender body was taut with excitement. "Jo Sam must have thought he'd snared a bird of paradise in his speed trap when you walked into his office," he said. "It's a good thing Miss Johnnie didn't come downtown to check up on him and find you playing blackjack in the jail."

In a few minutes Floyd came up with drinks. "We were talking about last summer when I was in jail in Alabama," she told him. "Remember? I told you about it."

He nodded.

"And those murals," she said. "Do you remember my telling you about the murals in the courthouse?"

"Do I remember them!" Dr. Stanley interrupted. "My greatgrandfather *painted* them."

"The giant Roman lady on the stairs," Nat said. "She gave me the shivers."

"Cornelia. That was his masterpiece. He studied in Paris, my grandmother told me."

"Such eyeballs! As big as footballs."

"Football! We're gonna win today!" A huge heavily-muscled man strode toward them along the flagstone ramp. "Ain't this ole

Nat?" he said. "I hadn't seen you since the Ole Miss-Tulane game in — le's see, I hate to think how long ago it was — forty-seven? Forty-eight?"

"Hi, Hermit," Nat said, holding her cheek for a sister-and-brotherly kiss. "This is Jay Stanley, Mary Mimms's husband, and this is Floyd Shotwell."

The three men shook hands, but Hermit kept his eyes on Nat. "Ten years," he said. "Ten *years*, honey, but you're *still* stacked."

Floyd took a step backward and looked around him, but there was nowhere for him to go. He was surrounded by water.

"Tell me about yourself, Hermit," Nat said. "Esther was saying that you live in New York now."

Dr. Stanley turned to Floyd and the two men looked at each other for a few seconds before either spoke. "Did I understand you to say you were from Philippi?" Dr. Stanley said. "Floyd Shotwell? You don't mind if I call you Floyd, do you? It seems to me I knew a Shotwell girl at Vanderbilt — from somewhere in the Delta. Mary Virginia Shotwell. Is she your sister?"

Floyd shook his head. "I haven't any sisters," he said.

"Where are you two staying?" Dr. Stanley said. "I hear there are several parties tonight. Maybe we can get together again."

Floyd did not answer, but Dr. Stanley went on as if he had. "The Dockerys are giving one," he said. "Do you know Mary Mimms's cousin, Jo Courtwright? Married Jack Dockery? Well, I reckon you wouldn't. She's older than we are, and he was from the other side of the tracks, you might say. But he's crossed over. Made a pile of money on the coast in motels and whiskey. They say he started his own carnival crewe in New Orleans — Parnassus or something like that — for his daughter to be queen of. Tried to buy one of the old crewes first. Of course, that's not possible — yet. Can you make a rough guess what something like that would cost — starting your own crewe? From laying the groundwork, getting some halfway respectable people to join, right on up through staging the parades and the balls?" He waited for Floyd to speak. "Well, it's not like joining the Delta Debutante Club," he said.

Still Floyd said nothing.

"You and Nat ought to come, anyhow," Dr. Stanley said. "That was what I was going to tell you. They — the Dockerys, I mean, have a couple of suites at the Southerner. You know that new motel on Highway fifty-one north?"

"Party?" Nat said. "We're supposed to go to the Carters' for drinks after the game."

"I was telling Floyd, the Dockerys — you know, Jo Courtwright — are having a big one at the Southerner. Mary Mimms and Esther are supposed to invite anyone they like, so why don't you two come as our guests?"

Floyd shook his head like a great bear in a swarm of bees. His huge hands opened and closed convulsively. "Come on, Nat," he said. "We've got to go."

"I'm coming," Nat said.

"I'm going," Hermit said. "To the party, I mean. I'll be there, honey. Come on, don't miss it. We'll have a *ball*."

12

"THE STAR-SPANGLED BANNER" boomed out across the stadium; hundreds of Confederate flags flickering in the hands of the crowd were still for a moment; hats came off, hands went to hearts, and thirty thousand voices burst into song. Afterwards, the loudspeakers crackled with a broken roaring thunder and a voice was lifted in prayer.

"Forty-seven years, oh, Lord, I've watched these fine young Christians on the playing fields of Mississippi, and once again I call down Thy blessing on them. Let them give their best out here on the field this afternoon in this glorious game of football. Keep them clean in thought and deed, oh, Lord. Keep their bodies pure and their lips from the temptations of alcohol. And, Lord, this afternoon in this great stadium, may we all set an example to these boys. Keep us from temptation. Let not our lusts destroy us.

"Dear Father, bless these coaches who are devoting their lives to the guidance of these boys. Bless the referee and the linesmen, Lord. Bless . . . Bless . . . Bless . . ."

At last it was over, the players jogged out onto the field, the cheerleaders ran to meet them, the Confederate flags waved, and a roar like the sound of a tornado went up from the crowd. The hotdog and cold drink vendors shouted their wares. All over the stadium men began to pull out bottles and pocket flasks and to mix drinks. The game had begun.

Most of the men in the stadium followed the game tensely, shouting advice to the players and coaches, roaring encouragement to their favorites, and explaining to one another what should have been done instead of what *was* done. They were like characters in a war movie — cavalrymen or flyers or submariners: the same private jokes and private jargon, the same hostility toward the enemy, the same rough camaraderie and queer sentimentality in the face of an imaginary defeat or death. The women waved their little flags, looked at each other's clothes, and gossiped.

There were some exceptions. Floyd watched with what appeared to be indifference. He had bet a hundred dollars, not on Ole Miss, but on the opposing team. Jay Stanley paid almost no attention to the game; he was a man who liked to talk with women, and coincidence had placed him and his wife on the row below Nat and Floyd.

At half-time the Ole Miss Band and students put on their most famous spectacle — they gradually rolled out the largest flag in the world — Confederate. The flag measured thirty by sixty yards, and the students marched along under it and along its edges holding it up, while the band followed behind, playing Dixie.

. . .

At the Dockerys' cocktail supper after the game, as at similar parties all over Jackson, crowds gathered again. For their party, the Dockerys had rented two suites and an adjoining conference room at the Southerner. The long table in the conference room had been converted into a bar behind which three or four white-jacketed Negro waiters were mixing drinks. On the glassy surfaces of every chest and table were huge arrangements of flowers — great fringed bronze chrysanthemums and yellow gladioli, baskets of talisman roses with yellow petals deepening to peach-colored hearts, daisies and carnations and gardenias and tuberoses and every other kind of flower that florists could furnish.

Wide French doors at the back of each suite opened onto a terrace, but no one went out. The wind was cold and the party inside too gay to miss.

". . . Little Rock, and . . ."

". . . I'm convinced that nullification is the only *practical* . . ."

"Did you hear the one about the niggers skiing up on Grenada Lake? Seems these niggers had never been on water skis before, see? So . . ."

White-jacketed Negro waiters circulated unobtrusively through the crowd offering trays of drinks and canapés, picking up empty glasses, taking orders for refills, and now and then replying to greetings from old acquaintances.

"Henry! Ain't seen you since you used to be at the Greenwood Country Club. What you doing in Jackson?"

"Well, suh, my wife — well, she's going to Jackson State, so I came on down and . . ."

"Fine. *Fine.* In college! That's great."

". . . but federal marshals would have made a difference, I say. I'm moderate, now. I admit it. Maybe I don't want to see my kids in school with niggers any more than the next fellow, but we've got to face the future, and I say if he'd sent marshals in there *quietly*, in their civilian suits, instead of the guard, it would never have raised the resistance. Faubus would never have . . ."

". . . new variety of late-blooming hemerocallis, the most

heavenly peach color — ten dollars a bulb, but I couldn't resist . . ."

"So he's on the ramp here by the lake, see, with his skis on . . ."

The women's voices were light and soft and they talked of flowers and children and food. The men's, as they exchanged with one another a year's accumulation of experience and bolstered one another against the uncertainties of the year to come, took on the peculiar intonation and accent that a certain kind of southern man uses when he talks with his peers or with Negroes. He thickens his natural drawl, and uses a kind of deliberate mock Negro dialect, as if to say: I'm a country boy and proud of it. He may be a doctor or a lawyer, a graduate of an eastern university or of Mississippi State; but he knows how to use this way of talking — this second language — to reassure himself and his associates: "We all know one another; we know what to expect of one another. Or to the Negro: "We're not strangers, after all. Remember the time I helped you get the mule out of the ditch?"

"Gret Gawd, man, the fish are bitin' on Ol' River," he'll say. "You never *seen* the like," although at home or in Sunday school or at the bridge table he speaks, except for his drawl, standard grammatical American, and corrects his sons for a misuse of *seen*.

"So he puts on these skis, like I said, *while he's still standin' on the ramp.* And he waves one arm and hollers, 'Come on, sky king, le's go!' Man, that was a busted-up nigger."

The air in the suites grew heavier, weighted with the fragrance of gardenias and tuberoses, of perfumed women, and with the rich sweet smell of bourbon.

"Drinks, sir? Scotch on the left, bourbon on the right."

Hermit Crabbe had drifted away from the group listening to the story about the Negro water skier and was standing near an hors d'oeuvre table eating a ham sandwich, when a thin, hatchet-faced Irishman with a shock of reddish hair, said to him in a low voice, "Here comes Nat. I wonder what she's done with her spooky friend."

"She's got two," Hermit said. "Have you met the suave little doc from California?"

"Ain't he a pansy?"

"Nat likes pansies — or so she says."

"Huh? Come on now, man. How can that *be*?"

"That's a twosome for you," Hermit said. "Her two pals, I mean. Like Lennie and George."

"Lennie?"

"Don't you remember the book about the big fella that kept mice in his pocket and the little fella that took care of him?"

"Say, what are you, anyhow, Hermit, some kind of intellectual?"

Hermit clapped the Irishman on the shoulder. "I'm a reader, man, a *reader*."

"This doc. How come he's following around after Nat? Where's his wife?"

"Maybe she's . . ."

"Hi, y'all," Nat said. "What are you talking about?"

"Uhhhh . . ."

"Niggers," Hermit said. "What would anybody around here talk about if they didn't have the niggers? That's what I always wonder when I come home."

"Maybe about sex?" Nat said. "Or the Meaning of Life?"

"You folks can joke if you want to," the Irishman said, "but the fact is the foundations of our society are being destroyed. We'd *better* talk about them, and do something about them, too. They're turning our world upside down, that's what's happening. You know what the Bible says: 'Cursed be Canaan, a servant of servants to his brethren.' There was a time when everybody knew that meant the niggers. But *now* . . ." He shook his head.

"My goodness," Nat said. "Is that in the *Bible?*"

"Ham, the son of Noah. That's right. His son was cursed because he looked on his father's nakedness."

"And Noah was *colored?*" Nat said. She shook her head. "The
Bible is so confusing," she said. "All these years I thought Noah
was a Jew."

"No, no," the Irishman said. "You've got it all wrong. It's this
way — before the tower of Babel was built there weren't any Jews
or anything. See?"

"Episcopalians are just naturally ignorant about the Bible," Nat
said. "That's me. I'm a sort of fallen-away Episcopalian. I mean,
I don't know if I fell away from them or they fell away from me,
but somehow we drifted apart."

"I didn't mean to say that Noah was colored. What I
meant . . ."

"But the Bible is full of so many confusing things," Nat said,
"especially if you don't know enough to argue about it. I remember one time Sarah Henry (She's a colored person who used to
work for me, and she reads the Bible and goes to church all the
time.), anyhow, she got into the most terrible argument with my
Aunt Louise who is an ignorant sort of Episcopalian like me, but
not fallen away. *Sarah* said that *Jesus* was colored. And, I mean,
maybe if Noah was colored, then — isn't *everybody* descended
from Noah? But that wasn't what Sarah was talking about. She
was talking about where it says in the Bible, 'I am black but
comely . . .' and she says that that's a prophecy and it's talking
about the Virgin Mary. Well, Aunt Louise got just terribly upset,
and she telephoned Miss Caroline Clayton right away (almost
crying. She couldn't *believe* it.) and said, 'Caroline, Sarah Henry
says that Jesus Christ was a *darky.* And I don't know what to say
back to her.' And Miss Caroline is *very* intellectual, so she explained to Aunt Louise that it's all figurative. It's the church that's

black, see? And the black stands for sin in the church. Nobody's perfect, after all, not even the church. And I went and read the part they were arguing about, and it didn't sound at all like the church to me or the Virgin Mary either. It sounded like sex. But you couldn't convince Sarah. She still says Jesus was black, and Aunt Louise just waves her arms in the air and says, 'I won't listen.' Don't you think that's all kind of confusing?" Nat smiled. "I wish you'd explain it to me," she said to Hermit.

"Not me, honey. Theology is not my forte. But I'll get you a drink. Looks like you need a refill."

"That'll do just as well," Nat said. "Maybe even better."

.   .   .

"You don't look well, Sunny," Wilburn Griffith said to his wife, as they left the Carters' party that evening and got into the car to drive to the Southerner. "We don't have to go to this party, you know."

"I'm fine," Sunny said shortly. She had been silent and remote ever since she had left the doctor's office that morning.

There, in a cold little cubicle painted the queer lime green that doctors' offices are always painted, she had sat, surrounded by the incontrovertible evidence of the malfunctioning of her body — shadowy gray pictures of her intestines, neatly typed reports on the analysis of her urine and blood and the fluoroscoped workings of her stomach and liver and gallbladder and kidneys — and listened while the doctor, speaking with the remote authority of an oracle, insisted that she must have an operation. "You may as well face it, Mrs. Griffith," he had said. "Your husband has told me that I'm not the first doctor you've been to and that he thinks you're looking for someone to tell you he can cure you without surgery. But you're not going to find a responsible man who will say that. The stones are there — *there* and *there*." He pointed to two shadows on the lighted X-ray plate. "They're not going to go away, and one of these days, when one of them moves — there's nothing pleasant about that kind of attack," he said. "Believe me."

Sunny had said nothing and Wilburn had concluded the interview by saying they would talk it over and let him know what they decided.

Now, in the car, Sunny broke a long silence. "I'm *not* going to do it," she said. "They're a bunch of quacks. None of them know what they're doing. Oh, it makes me so — so *furious* when they sit behind their desks and act superior and understanding. I may become a Christian Scientist."

"It's the truth," Wilburn said. "What he told you. The stones are there. You saw them."

"You'd be sorry if I died under the knife," she said. "Then you'd realize I was right."

Wilburn drove on without saying anything for a few minutes. The birthmark that dyed his left cheek a faintly darker brown than the rest of his face had flushed a dull red, when she said, "I might die," and his mouth had tightened to a thin line. But all he said when he did speak was, "You're not being reasonable. Try to think sensibly about it."

"I might," she said. "*I just might die.* There's nothing silly about that."

"Yes," he said evenly. "You might. And I would be sorry. But I wouldn't think it was my fault, so you may as well get off that tack."

"I won't do it," she said.

"I know it's rough," he said. "I really do. I understand how you feel. But it won't be so bad, darling. Not any worse than having a baby, for instance."

"That's different," she said. "I didn't have any say-so about that. And once it gets started, you can't change your mind."

"You didn't have any say-so!" Wilburn broke off and gripped the wheel tightly, his mind seething with hatred for his wife and outrage at her stupidity and cowardice.

"You know very well what I mean, Wilburn. You might think it's all a very good idea to begin with, *theoretically*, but once you get pregnant you certainly can't change your mind and decide not to, because you're scared. I'm *afraid*," she said. "You know how I feel about doctors and knives. And I don't have to do it if I don't want to."

Wilburn answered her calmly. "You know you can't live any kind of life when you're sick all the time. Even if you're afraid, you've got to go ahead with it. I'll try to help you sweat out being afraid." He took one hand from the wheel and laid it over hers. "Why don't we stay on and get it over with? You could go back into the hospital tomorrow and have it done Monday. Mama will keep the children as long as we need her to."

She shook her head.

"If you won't think about yourself, think about the children. What kind of household is it for them with you half sick all the time?"

Still she did not reply.

"And me," he said in a low tentative voice, determined to be honest with her.

"Men!" she said. "I'm worrying about dying on the operating table, and all *you're* thinking about is sex."

"I didn't mean only that, Sunny," he said, "although that's important." Then, "Yes, that *is* what I mean. We have to think about that and talk about it." He continued to speak calmly, although he was in a fury of unreasoning outrage. God knows, I don't want to sleep with her, he thought, glancing at the long face, puffy and unnaturally white, and the thick corseted body. I don't give a damn if I never touch her again. "Try to act like a grown person," he said. And then, "We ought not to be talking about all this now, on the way to this damned party. We'll be more sensible in the morning, both of us." She did not reply and without saying any more to each other they drove out North State Street and the highway to the cocktail supper.

"I don't know why in the world we had to come to this production, anyhow," he said, as they walked through the motel lobby.

"We accepted weeks ago," she said, "and besides, *I'm* going to have a good time. What do you think we should do — go back to our motel and shut ourselves up and glare at each other? *Hello,* Jo. I'm so glad to *see* you," she said as their hostess opened the door and beckoned them in.

Wilburn went to the bar to mix himself a drink. Some doctor, he said to himself (Where did I read it?) made a survey on the relationship between gallbladder trouble and frigidity in women past thirty-five. He stared gloomily at Sunny standing on the other side of the room talking to a woman he had never seen. Her fat freckled arms bulged out below the cap sleeves of her dress, and her belly, in spite of being severely girdled, swelled against the tight silk skirt. Belly full of rocks, he thought. And she doesn't want to get rid of them. She'd rather carry them around the rest of her life, if she can use them against me. He had a moment's horrifying vision of those slimy stones built into a moss-covered wall against which he spent and bruised and ruined himself in a frantic effort to consummate the act of love. But maybe I want her that way, he thought. Is it possible that I married her just because she *is* that kind of woman? Has anyone made a survey on that? Yes, he answered himself. There are surveys proving all sides of everything.

Love! he thought. Jesus! It was as if he held in his conscious mind, wholly open to his own understanding, all the miserable and contemptible devices by which he and all men lived and persuaded themselves that their lives were tolerable; and as if, at the same time, he sensed with awful intensity the coming of death, a great engine bearing down on him and his confusions. He turned to the bar and, ignoring the waiters, poured himself an old-fashioned-glass half full of whiskey and drank it, his mind a dark burden of misery. Then he refilled his glass, walked across the room to where long French windows opened onto a terrace, and stepped outside.

The sun had set and left a clear, cold, gradually darkening, blue-green sky, light pouring out of unimaginable depths of darkness, as if it were the first day of time and God had said, *Let there be light.* As he stood there, the first stars appeared, light out of light, and he watched them, feeling an obscure comfort that they were there, still, as always, in precisely the same relation to one another as one expected them to be: First to the south, a brilliant white one; then to the east, another; and, as the constellations began to emerge and form themselves, there was Pegasus wheeling along high overhead and, lower down, above the treetops, Piscis Austrinus, the southern fish; far away in the east, Perseus and Auriga and Taurus; to the west, high in the sky, the Northern Cross and, lower down, Aquilla and Sagittarius. He named to himself from the positions of the constellations the bright stars that he had first seen: Capella and Fomalhaut and Vega, feeling still a curious pleasure at having located himself in the universe. He gazed a long time at the heavens; he had a trick of opening his eyes wide when he was looking intently, as if to take in as much as possible, and he did this now, staring up above the dark pines that had begun to bend and sough quietly in a chilly night wind. There was no moon and the sky was very dark by now. He thought of his children and said to himself that at home it would be a good night for taking out his little telescope and setting it up for them. They might get a good look at the Great Nebula in Andromeda.

His anger had died and he was as calm and happy as if none of the week's traumas had happened. A formless, almost wordless emotion, an inexpressible joy, filled him like clear water pouring into a deep pool. Just to see it, he thought, to be alive and conscious . . .

Behind him the noise of the party rose and fell.

After a time, when Capella was high in the eastern sky and Pegasus had moved westward past the zenith, he turned his back on the now invisible pine trees, that still gave out their fragrance and the soft whoosh of their motion, and on the jeweled and wheeling sky, and began to watch through the long French windows that opened onto the terrace the people inside the house. The windows were made of small panes framed with heavy mullions like bars — as if, he thought to himself contentedly, the people inside were imprisoned and he free in the cold wide winter evening; or maybe as if he were a visitor to an aquarium peering into a huge, lighted tank. He felt a revulsion against going into the house, as strong as if he were an air-breathing creature about to be held forcibly under water; and he stayed for a little while longer outside, watching. Lips moved, hands gestured, and heads nodded, but he could hear only a confused murmur of voices.

He saw his wife cross in front of the window and could tell that she had had too much to drink. She was clinging to the arm of a man he did not know and gazing flirtatiously up at him. She's not supposed to be drinking, he thought. She'll be sick tonight.

Across the room from the windows onto the terrace a group of men stood talking and gesticulating. One, tall and emaciated, with thin black hair brushed to cover his balding skull and the alert controlled face of a successful lawyer, squatted like a quarterback in a football formation, pivoted, and threw an imaginary pass. Then he stood up and began to demonstrate in detail some particular technique of holding and throwing the ball.

What does it all mean? Wilburn thought vaguely. They're bound to have reasons for such strange obsessions.

Nat drifted in front of the glass, followed by Floyd and, a moment later, by the small handsome Jewish doctor to whom Wilburn had been introduced that morning. She glanced through the French windows, saw him standing with the light on his pale, serious face, hesitated, as if about to come out, smiled, waved, and turned away. She began to talk, first to the doctor and then to Floyd, who was hovering behind her, drifting rather than walking, and wavering with changing currents. He opened and closed his mouth, as if he, too, were unable to breathe under water. Nat held out her hand to him, her arm and wrist brown and slender and graceful as a mermaid's. Then the doctor swam between them, a Negro waiter drifted up with a tray of drinks, and Floyd seemed to float away, back against a wall where he stayed motionless, looking at her.

She's on a party kick tonight, Wilburn thought — some sort of make-believe — and that California fellow knows how to play. She doesn't want to talk to me. I might break up the game. She was dressed in an emerald green sheath of raw silk, and Wilburn saw that there was a frayed seam on the shoulder. I suppose Nat's the only woman who has ever worn out a cocktail dress, he thought. He looked again at her face, turned in profile now, its expression as uncertain as an actor's who has forgotten his lines. She's sorry she saw me. Probably just being aware that I am looking at her is like an electric shock to a sleeping man. He groped after the tail end of a memory that would not quite come to him and, watching her more closely, saw a queer jewel-like glint from the greenish skin by the corner of her eye. She's got on that crazy eye shadow with sequins in it, he thought happily. My God! And again he pursued the elusive memory, lapsing into the kind of reverie that sometimes came on him like intoxication and could produce an insight, a sudden falling into place of multiple confusions, that was more exciting to him than a beautiful woman or his own fields white with cotton under the September sun.

Something to do with disguises. Yes. It was a tale that he had heard his Cousin Louise tell about Nat half a dozen times; how, when she was a little thing, during the first year or two after she had come to live with them, she would never go out of the house without a disguise. One day Louise had said to her, "Come on, dear, you'll have to go to church with me; it's brass-polishing day, and Clakey's off; I can't leave you here by yourself."

"Wait," Nat had said. "I have to put on my disguise. I'll be an Indian girl today."

Louise had said, "I haven't time to wait, dear. Come on."

"Well," Nat had said, "I suppose, if you haven't time for me to change, I can go as a plain woman from New York."

"Nat, dear," Louise had said, "you know it isn't proper for a little girl to go around all the time in disguises. You're old enough to be a little lady like other girls." Nat hadn't appeared to hear. Her lips had moved soundlessly, as if she were telling herself a story. "Your little friends are going to think you're queer," Louise had said. "And first thing you know, you'll be growing up, and if you're an Indian girl or something like that, they won't ask you to join their clubs. And if you're not careful, you'll get to college and they won't ask you to join their sorority."

"You've got on your Christian disguise," Nat had said.

"Nat!" Louise's eyes had filled with tears. "Do you think God wants to hear you say a naughty thing like that?"

"Well, you do. You always wear a special outfit on Thursday for the brass and another special one on Sunday. Aren't those your Christian disguises?"

"What a *bad* little girl you were," Louise would always say at this point in her story. "It's a wonder you weren't the death of me."

But Nat *knew* when she was playing — even then, Wilburn thought. Didn't she? And what about Floyd. He looked at Floyd standing with his back pressed against the wall as if against a last solid vertical in a vertiginous universe. His white, hairless hands were knotted in fists at the ends of his long arms and his eyes were cold and wounded. Wilburn felt again, as he had when Miss Louise had told him that Floyd was courting Nat, a queer twinge of fear, a flash of insight into the seething confusion behind the small wounded eyes, a chaos of hatred and bewilderment verging on psychosis.

He opened the French windows abruptly, went in to the party, and went immediately up to Nat.

"*Ishustvennyi Sputnik Zemli II,*" the doctor was saying. "That's the full name of it. *Artificial Fellow Traveler Around the Earth.*"

"But that poor little dog! Wouldn't you know the Russians would do a terrible thing like that? No telling how many wires and contraptions she is hooked up to. Oh, it's awful! No morals. Those people are without morals. And you don't know where to turn. I would write to the SPCA, but I'm sure they'd be *helpless* against the Russians." An elderly lady with neat white hair and the face of a kindly elementary school teacher had joined the group and was speaking in a low serious voice.

"It's in the interest of science," the doctor said solemnly. "You know, *thousands* of dogs get cut up every year for scientific reasons." He was a little bit drunk.

Nat turned to Wilburn. "I love everybody tonight," she said. "I'm that kind of tight. Isn't that fine?" She spoke more slowly than usual and enunciated her words carefully. "And — I'm going to California." She nodded at the doctor. "Absolutely. Mary Mimms invited me officially. And I'm going to pay them a visit just as soon as — as that bast-a-a-ard, Jeff Steinbrude, sends me — my — money. They live practically right on the beach."

"But they're communists," the old lady who was worried about the dog said to Dr. Stanley. "*Atheists*. And did you know her name was Curly? Just like an American dog. There is certainly something strange about that."

"A friend of my Aunt Louise's," Nat said, " — you know my Aunt Louise Hunter? A friend of hers says that's where the Asiatic flu is coming from. They're orbiting the germs."

Wilburn laughed.

"It's all very well for you young people to laugh," the elderly lady said, "but, mark my words, you'll laugh on the other sides of your faces one of these days when there's a commissar in every block, and you can't breathe without his permission. And as for the Asiatic flu, if they aren't bringing it over here, *who is?* The Chinese, probably. Did you ever think about that?"

"Peck. That's what he is. Do they have pecks in Alabama, Jay? And did I tell you their name used to be Steinbrude? But Stonebridge is so *aristocratic*. I may take back my maiden name."

"Nat!" Floyd called out in an agonized voice.

Everyone stopped talking and turned toward him expectantly. But before he could say any more, Sunny came into the room and joined the group. She took Wilburn's arm and he felt her weight sagging against him. "I feel terrible, Wilburn," she said. "I have this *awful* pain. I think we'd better go." Her face was white, the freckles standing out against its pallor.

"Here," Wilburn said, "sit down a minute." He guided her to a chair, conscious of a ruthless gaiety in himself. One of the stones has moved, he thought. She'll have to do it whether she wants to or not. At least we'll settle that.

Everyone began to talk again in lowered voices, glancing covertly now and then at Sunny, as if deciding whether or not to adopt the useful pretense that she was not there. Only Dr. Stanley looked at her openly, with detached interest. And

Floyd did not look at all, but still gazed at Nat and said again in a queer dreamy way, "Nat . . ."

Sunny sat huddled in the chair for a few minutes, with Wilburn bent over her, and then to everyone's surprise she drew her legs up against her chin, so that her fleshy white thighs were exposed, and screamed.

Since it was now impossible to pretend that Sunny did not exist (and anyhow, such a pretense is more useful when pain is boring than when it is exciting), everyone shifted into the formal pattern of emergency. The doctor took charge. The men became gruff, self-possessed, and solicitous; the women divided themselves into groups — the kind who left the room to keep from fainting or weeping and the kind who administered poised and officious care. Sunny screamed again.

"Wait," Wilburn said. "Wait." His gaiety was gone and now he was conscious of nothing except his wife's agony. He knelt beside her and put his arms around her. "Wait a minute, now," he said.

There was muttered conversation around them and two of the men left the room. Nat backed slowly away from Sunny and stood against the wall near Floyd. "Let's go," Floyd said in her ear. She shook her head and said nothing.

Wilburn looked up at Dr. Stanley who had bent over Sunny and was looking at her more closely. "Well," Wilburn said. "Let's get her out of here." His ears were cottony and deaf and his face felt numb.

"They're bringing your car into the carport," one of the women said.

"Let's get her into a bedroom where I can examine her before we do anything else," Dr. Stanley said. He reached into his pocket and pulled out his keys. "My bag is in my car, over by . . ."

"No," Wilburn said. "It's a gallstone. It's moved. We just got it diagnosed this morning. No use to waste time."

"All right, men," Dr. Stanley said. "Let's put her in the car. I'll drive to the hospital with them. Somebody call emergency admitting. What hospital and who's your doctor? All right. Somebody call him, too, and tell him to meet us there."

"Nat?" Wilburn said.

Nat, who neither fainted nor wept nor brought ice packs and hot-water bottles in emergencies, but who looked at everyone with a guarded and closed face, alert, ready for flight, did not reply.

"Come on, Nat," Wilburn said. "We need you."

Nat gulped down the highball she was holding. "I'm not very good at this kind of thing," she said softly to Floyd. "Maybe you'd better get another drink to take along."

He stared at her. "I've got a bottle in the car," he said, "but we're not going."

"Just for a few minutes, Floyd. I have to. Wilburn will be mad at me if I don't play like old friends. Get the car, hear? We don't want to get stranded down there."

He shook his head.

"I can't *help* it," she said. "Come on."

13

AT THE HOSPITAL they lifted Sunny out of the car and onto a rolling stretcher. She was moaning continuously now, and shivering, and she lay on the stretcher with her legs drawn up against her belly, a lump of pain, her black cocktail dress hiked up so that a broad expanse of soft white thigh was visible. She still had on a hat, a wisp of veil and black velvet. It had been knocked askew and was hanging by combs, half on and half off her head. She began to retch, and someone took the hat and laid it on the end of the stretcher. Wilburn covered her legs with his overcoat.

Inside the low tunnel-like hall of the hospital, the air vibrated almost visibly, as it seemed to Nat, to the hum of air-conditioning units, generators, and fluorescent lights. The lights were very bright and so placed that there seemed to be no shadows. A nurse and a young man in a green jacket walked by with blank faces and got into an elevator. The stretcher was pushed against a wall in the open hallway and the ambulance attendants and Dr. Stanley disappeared. The hall was empty. Nat and Wilburn stood beside the stretcher, staring at the floor and furtively at each other, like strangers waiting to be introduced. No one seemed to hear Sunny's moans and occasional screams or her agonized retching.

At last someone came out of a door marked *Keep Out* — a woman in a wrinkled dirty uniform who moved her lips carefully when she spoke, as if she had a mouthful of tobacco and was afraid it might dribble out.

Wilburn stopped her. "Do something," he said. "Get something to stop the pain. Can't you people see she's in agony? Where is everybody?"

"I'm just an aide," the woman said. "Here's a pan for her to vomit into. Move so I can clean up this mess."

Dr. Stanley and a nurse appeared now. "We can take her into number three," the nurse said. "This way." She pushed the stretcher off down the hall and into a tiny room crowded with all sorts of machinery and equipment.

"No sedation," the doctor said to Wilburn. "Not until her doctor gets here and decides what course to take."

Sunny sat up on the low stretcher, screamed, then stood up and, bending down so that her head was below her knees, staggered across the room. Her long pinkish hair came loose from its pins and tumbled down, dragging the floor. In a corner she squatted, moaning.

"Now that won't do, Mrs. Griffith," the nurse said. "Naughty, naughty. Come on, let's lie back down and be quiet like a brave girl."

"Don't touch her!" Wilburn said. "What are you talking about, *brave girl!* Come on, darling, we'll help you. Scream as loud as you want to. Just a minute now. We're going to help you. Goddamn these people, anyway." He was muttering in her ear half-incoherently as he drew her into his arms and half-carried her across the room to the stretcher. Then, to Stanley, "*Do* something, damn it. She's *suffering.* Those stones are tearing her to pieces."

"Now, Mr. Griffith . . ."

"Here. Nat. *Nat!*" She was standing outside in the hall and came in when he called. "Stay with her," he said. "I'm going to find out why her doctor hasn't gotten here." He put Sunny's hand in Nat's.

"There's no point in your calling Dr. Case, Mr. Griffith," the nurse said. "He has been reached and he will be here shortly. However, if you will go to the front office and enter Mrs. Griffith as a patient, we'll be ready to go right into surgery, if that's what Dr. Case decides to do. Do you have the number of your Blue Cross policy with you? Just come with me, please, and I'll direct you . . ."

"My *God*," Wilburn said. "My policy number! Are you crazy?"

"Calm yourself, Mr. Griffith," Dr. Stanley said. "These attacks are *like* this. And we cannot use any sedation right now. It would mask the symptoms and it might get in the way of the anesthesiologist later."

From the stretcher Sunny spoke for the first time. "Go on, Wilburn," she said. "Maybe it'll hurry things up. I think I may be a little bit better. It's not hurting so much now."

Nat held Sunny's hand; Wilburn and the nurse went out. Dr. Stanley stood looking dispassionately down at Sunny. "Classic," he said to Nat. "She has all the symptoms." He recited, as if reading from a medical book: "In general, the attacks are severe, causing the patient to writhe, roll or double up, to walk about in anguish, or to shout and cry because of acute distress. Vomiting is usual. In many cases these symptoms are accompanied by profound sweating. Pain located in upper right quadrant of abdomen, radiates through to the back, usually beneath the right scapula — right there, Mrs. Griffith. Does that hurt?" He palpated the area around the scapula. Sunny moaned. "You see?" he said to Nat. "Patient is commonly female, middle-aged, often fair in complexion. That's a strange thing, isn't it? The fair, fat, and forty disease, we call it in the trade. It would be interesting to follow that up." He looked thoughtful. "Ah, the mysteries locked up in the genes and chromosomes," he said. Then, "Take it easy, Mrs. Griffith. I'll be back." He nodded to Nat and walked out.

Nat held Sunny's hand, alone with her now and frightened. She felt the relaxed and then suddenly convulsive grip of Sunny's fingers on hers. She trembled, clenched her teeth against a rising wave of nausea. "Could you pretend it's not you?" she said. "I did that when I was having Hunter, and after a while it helped. You put the pain in one place — like in a box over in the corner of the room, and put yourself someplace else. It got like it really wasn't — wasn't me, I mean. And it kept me from making a fuss. I mean, don't you think it's kind of common to yell when you're having a baby?" She shuddered. "Although I could have yelled for joy to get that little squirming thing outside of me instead of inside."

Sunny shook her head. "Ahh-h-h-h," she moaned.

"Not that it's like this," Nat said. "I mean I know this hurts a lot worse than having a baby, but . . ." She continued to speak in a quiet ordinary voice. She resisted the temptation to raise her voice in a shout, although she felt as if she were at the entrance to a huge wind tunnel, leaning backwards against the suction of the air through the tunnel that threatened to drag her in. The roar of the wind, the circular distances of the bright shadowless tunnel, the vision of herself tumbling away, cartwheeling through its diminishing distances, spinning like a coin at the vanishing point of its perspective — all this had passed through her mind as she had come into the hospital, down the long low corridor with its white, shadowless, throbbing lights and its expressionless wanderers in their stiff uniforms. Now the roar and the suction of the air were in her ears even more strongly. Sunny on her stretcher seemed about to be snatched away into the roar. Nat gripped the metal side of the stretcher with one hand and held onto Sunny's hand with the other.

"Hang on," she muttered. And then, in another effort at exorcism, "What does it feel like, Sunny? Maybe if you can tell me exactly what it feels like, if you talk about it calmly, it will begin to go away." I am calm, she said to herself. I am actually here in this place, *awake*, not dreaming. I know that. But I'm afraid, *afraid*. I want to run away. I'm afraid of getting sucked into the tunnel. No. That's not real. No tunnel. All the same it would be better for me to leave. If I go away quickly, I will be all right. I'll stay sure I'm awake. Wilburn will understand, if I go. I'll get Floyd and we'll go. I can get drunk. Drunker. Then I'll be sure to be able to go to sleep really. No dreams. She looked at Sunny who was quiet now, lying on her side on the stretcher, her eyes wide open, her hands held lightly against her belly, as if waiting for the first ripple of a labor pain. Then she opened her mouth and shrieked like a rabbit broken in a hound's jaws.

I'll go. Or — trapped! The wind howled in the tunnel and Nat felt her hair lifted, ripped at by the wind, her face burned by the wind.

A strange doctor came into the room, followed by a nurse, an orderly, and Dr. Stanley. Without seeming to see Nat, they gathered around the stretcher. The doctor poked and looked briefly, there was a muttered conversation and, still as if there were no one in the room but Sunny (and she a dead body), they rolled the stretcher away.

Dr. Stanley followed, then stuck his head back in the door.

"Nat," he said, "I'll be getting back to the party. See you later, OK?"

Nat nodded, but she had not heard what he said. *Now. I'll go,* she thought. *Get Floyd and go.*

Wilburn came into the room and Nat got up. "Wilburn," she said, "I can't . . ." But at the sight of his drawn face, the brown smear of birthmark dark against a greenish pallor, a pang of sisterly love struck through her, as strange to her as the first sight of the sea to a desert wanderer. "Don't look so sick, Wilburn," she said. "Here. Sit down. Floyd will get you a drink."

He shook his head.

A nurse looked into the room. "Mrs. Griffith has been assigned to four-twelve," she said. "That's on the north wing. You may wait there, if you like, or you may go up to the waiting room outside surgery on the third floor."

All this while Floyd had been standing, flattened against the wall as if he too felt the pull of the wind tunnel, outside the door of the emergency admitting room. Like the nurses and doctors, he seemed not to hear Sunny's screams. He kept his eyes closed and his chin drawn down against his breast. Now, Nat took him by the hand and, following the nurse's directions, led him to an elevator which mounted with them through layers of sleeping and waking sufferers to a small waiting room outside the surgery section of the hospital. There Floyd sat down, bent forward, and stared at the floor, his shoulders hunched, his hands hanging between his knees.

Wilburn walked across the room and stood looking out the window across the roof of the utility wing of the hospital opposite them, a low windowless block with a huge round chimney towering up beside it, from which black smoke poured out, darkening the starlit sky. After a while he said, "Over there, where that chimney is — see? That's where they burn up people's cut off legs and arms."

"Wilburn!" Nat said.

"Abortions," he said.

"Sunny's going to be all right," Nat said. "Settle down."

"I think it used to be when you were sick, people you knew took care of you," he said. "Do you remember that? The doctors were people you knew. They might even be your cousins. Even the nurses. I can remember when they used to come to your house . . . But it must have been too much trouble, too personal — too painful. Do you suppose?" He was talking in a low thoughtful voice, almost as if to himself. "Did you know that nowadays doctors always keep an aide in the office with them when they examine a woman, so they'll have a witness in case she accuses them of trying to rape her? Imagine! Even someone as old as my mother. They don't mind insulting her." He sighed. "And now they've got Sunny," he said. "She's nothing but a body they're carting from one spot to another, doing this and that to it. No wonder she was scared to come and do this. You put yourself in their hands and you're like a side of beef in a slaughterhouse. You might as well be hanging from a pulley with a meat hook in the muscle of your leg, getting shoved from one cold room to another."

"Wilburn," Nat said, "you can't operate on anybody for gallstones at *home*. I suppose what used to happen was that people died of gallstones."

"Ugly women in plaster of Paris uniforms, and smooth-faced men in green plaster hospital gowns. Have you noticed how the faces of doctors are smooth? As if years of scrubbing — sterility — had included washing away every line of expression in their faces. And the ones who are not that way — who *react* — I suppose the wear and tear kills them young. That's why you don't see many of them. The others — they're in a dream — a dream of impersonality and professional efficiency where they're the heroes, and unknown women in dirty uniforms clean up the vomit and the feces. It might be better to die than to get involved with those people."

"You *have* to stop talking like that," Nat said. "You know very well I can't put up with that kind of talk. I'm a very suggestible person. And you're not doing Sunny one bit of good, or yourself either, talking about it would be better to die if you can't have kindly old Dr. Mugwump operate on you on the kitchen table without any anesthetic. That's not my idea of homey. Floyd, go and get some ice someplace and get your bottle out of the car. Wilburn has to have a drink whether he wants one or not.

"Besides," she said, "you know very well Ben Casey is not like that, or Dr. Kildare, or Dr. Zorba; and even Dr. Gillespie has a heart of gold beneath a crusty exterior. And these days all good doctors study under Ben Casey or Dr. Kildare."

"All right," Wilburn said. "I didn't mean to scare you, Nat. I'll behave. It's just that when I went down to the office to register Sunny, I passed an open emergency room door, and there was blood all over the floor, and some doctor was sewing up a young boy on the table, and another one was standing by the table watching him, eating a hamburger. I hadn't realized they served supper in surgery."

Floyd went out to his car and got his bottle and brought it in. Nat got a pitcher of ice from a nurse on the nearest patients' wing, found a paper-cup dispenser, and in the bathroom fixed three drinks of bourbon and water. Wilburn put his beside him on a table and, after one tentative sip, drank no more of it.

"I don't need to get fuzzy-headed," he told Nat. "I'd better stay sober. Besides," he added, "I can't drink it anyhow."

During the long wait that followed — an hour and a half or more — Nat drank her drink and his and part of Floyd's. Floyd fell asleep on the sofa, lying on his side, his long legs drawn up against his chest. Even in sleep his face was closed, and his breathing, as it seemed, was not deep and relaxed like the breathing of a sleeper, but silent, shallow, invisible. His eyelids quivered now and then and a shudder ran across his body, as it does over the body of a dog that dreams of chasing rabbits. But he may not have been asleep at all. He may have been pretending.

"This fellow, Case," Wilburn said in the middle of a long silence, "the doctor. He told me when they were getting ready to take her in that from his examination it looked as if the gallbladder had perforated. That's one reason she was in so much pain."

"What does that mean?" Nat asked.

"Peritonitis," Wilburn said.

Nat's control was beginning to waver. She was getting drunker. For a long time the word, *peritonitis*, kept repeating itself inside her head like the clackity-clack of a moving train: *peritonitis, peritonitis, peritonitis.* But she said nothing. She did not even begin to talk too much, as she usually did when she was drunk; but occasionally when Wilburn was not looking at her, she gently knocked her fist against her forehead. Under ordinary circumstances, she would have thought of some very good reason for leaving and would, at the same time, out of the peculiar convictions by which she lived, have made it clear to Wilburn that she was leaving because she wanted to and not for the thought-up reason she gave. Wilburn would have known what she was doing and would have been willing, even immersed as he was in his wife's agony, to furnish her with whatever opportunity she needed to protect herself and, at the same time, to expose herself. It was the habit of his friendship with Nat and would not have been surprising to him. Tonight, however, something stayed her. She knocked her fist against her forehead and did not go. Perhaps — yes, certainly — it was that unfamiliar pang of love she had felt when Wilburn had come into the emergency room downstairs — a piercing wound that out of a stirred depth in herself of which she had known nothing, she had been forced to receive and acknowledge. She stayed and, because of this unfamiliar feeling (realizing, perhaps, that sometimes people have no other tools), used the conventions of solicitation that she would ordinarily have shuddered to touch. What could one do for Wilburn here, under these circumstances, except to stay and be conventionally solicitous?

Finally the doctor came into the room. The operation had gone off as well as it could under the circumstances, he said. As he had expected, he had found the gallbladder perforated and the beginnings of peritonitis. But he believed they had gotten to her soon enough. She was in the intensive care room and would be there for at least forty-eight hours. She would be unconscious for several hours and under heavy sedation for a day or two. It would be best for Mr. Griffith to go back to his motel and get a few hours sleep. Things looked pretty good, but, of course, with peritonitis an honest doctor must not minimize the fact that the patient was in a serious condition. No, Mr. Griffith could not see his wife. Members of a patient's family were admitted to the intensive care room only at specified times and for brief visits. Tomorrow, perhaps, for a very few minutes.

14

AFTERWARDS the three of them left the hospital, down the humming elevator shaft in the chrome-trimmed cage, along the throbbing bright corridors and out into the hospital parking lot.

In the middle of the expanse of grayish slag that stretched out a block or more from the side of the hospital, a half-dead sycamore tree marked the place where their cars were parked. Its slanting trunk and heaviest limbs were cut brutally back so that it was a twenty-foot stump with three or four small crooked branches. The white trunk glimmered in the changing brilliance of flashing neon signboards along the edge of the lot. The wind stirred a scattering of leaves and litter underfoot. Across the lot, the dark bulk of the hospital chimney loomed against the sky, pouring out a pall of black smoke that drifted sluggishly over the sleeping city.

Nat used a last shred of wavering sobriety and self-control to say a quiet good night to Wilburn, and he got into his car and drove away.

Sitting in the front seat of the blue Cadillac, she began to shake uncontrollably. "M-m-mostly I shake instead of crying," she said to Floyd. "I think I must be d-d-dry inside. I hardly ever cry, you know." Her teeth were chattering so that she could hardly talk. She laughed. "M-m-maybe that's why I like to d-drink," she said. "Yes, that's why — because I'm dry inside." She continued to laugh, the edge of hysteria in her voice masking its soft irony. "How dry I am!" she said.

Floyd said nothing.

"That's a joke, Floyd," she said. "You s'posed to laugh." Then, "Come on, let's go back to the party."

"I'm going to take you to the motel," he said. "We're not going to any more parties." He looked at her coldly and spoke with a cold and dreamlike slowness, as if rage and frustration had thickened his blood and weighed down his limbs like the gravity of a heavier planet. He took the key from his pocket and started his car, moving slowly and awkwardly. Yellow leaves dropped from the mutilated sycamore tree onto the hood of the car and the littered parking lot.

"Jay said they'd see us later," Nat said.

"The hell with Jay."

Nat seemed not to hear him. "Did you hear what Wilburn said about burning up people's cut-off legs?" She half-retched, half-coughed and began fumbling clumsily through her purse for a cigarette.

"So?" Floyd said. "What are you supposed to do with cut-off legs — have a funeral for them and buy them a lot in the cemetery?"

"Don't be mad at me, Floyd," she said. "I couldn't help any of it tonight, could I? It — it wasn't my fault Sunny got so sick. And then, I — we — couldn't go off and leave him up there waiting by himself, when she might die. Could we? I'm sorry. Hear?"

He turned the car around and pulled out of the parking lot.

The streets were deserted. No cars passed them, but once they bore down in the darkness on a cluster of gleaming, shifting eyes, three dogs that stared at the car and then vanished as the headlights flashed over them.

"I said I'm sorry, Floyd."

Without taking his eyes from the street, he reached across and patted her once or twice on the shoulder as one might pat a sick animal — cautiously, to avoid getting snapped at, and with the distant sympathy of another species. "It's over, anyway," he said. "We may as well forget it."

Nat lay back against the seat with a sigh and her shaking began to subside as they drove through the silent city toward their motel. She had been moved to terror and hysteria as much by the prospect of facing Floyd's anger and then of spending the night sleepless and alone in her motel room as by the events of the past few hours. She knew that she would do almost anything rather than close the door of her motel room and be alone. She had had nights before when sleeplessness or nightmare had driven her out of small rooms and into bars and the company of bartenders or of wandering strangers like herself, who fled the night. One of the reasons she lived mostly in resorts was that bars were always open and bartenders, as long as one didn't make a nuisance of oneself and could pay for one's drinks, were friendly.

She did not wonder about her sleeplessness, any more than someone else would wonder that, miraculously, he *did* sleep, that no gray swamps of anxiety sucked him to breathless terror and no moving walls closed in on him. She accepted her nights as the ordinary climate of the world and used whatever resources she could find to live through them.

But here, in this dry town, there were no bars. There was no place to go at three o'clock in the morning. There was only Floyd between her and the solitude that slipped, easily, sickeningly, into nightmare — and *this* night into a nightmare of pain and knives, of dying trees and chimneys pouring out fat black smoke.

Now, after his pat of tentative forgiveness, she was sure she had Floyd under control again. She would not have to spend the night alone. She would follow her old and always successful expedient of telling him the truth. And, as men always were, he would be astonished at the truth from a woman, and he would be docile and helpful. He would come into her motel room and sit down in the armchair beside her bed and watch her patiently and listen to her talk, until her abraded consciousness drowned itself in whiskey and she slept.

"Come in," she said to him at the door of her room.

He shook his head. "It's late." He moved his lips carefully, as if afraid that his face might crack.

"I'm scared, Floyd," she said. "I've got to get drunker before I can go to sleep. And I don't want to be by myself. I *can't* be by myself. Come in. You can put up with me a little while longer, hmmmm?"

"Scared?" He was sober, watchful.

"You know I don't like to be by myself," she said. "And that was all so gruesome tonight, it makes it worse."

He looked at her standing in the cold light of the motel corridor, her black hair tangled, her mascara and lipstick smeared, the frayed seam at the shoulder of her dress torn open now so that the sleeve had slipped down and exposed her shoulder and upper arm. He could see the delicate line of her collarbone, the rounded muscle of her upper arm, the beautiful articulation of bone and joint and muscle, the smooth brown skin, and the shadow at the hollow of her throat. "You're drunk already," he said, grinding his teeth. But he followed her into the room.

She sat down on the edge of the bed, picked up a cigarette from a pack on the table, waited expectantly for him to light it and, when he did not, lit it herself and smoked as if the smoke could induce oblivion. Then she got up and walked restlessly around the room while he fixed their drinks. Her walk, her movements, were wavering, as if a cog had slipped slightly, so that her timing was off.

"Make mine stiff," she said. "I want to hurry up and pass out." She smiled a silly smile at him when he brought her drink, as if the will to be drunk had made her already drunker. "You're a *friend*, Floyd," she said in a sudden access of sentimentality. "Good friend. You don't mind keeping me company, even if I get drunk and boring, hmm? I'm very boring when I get drunk. Worse than most people because I don't go to sleep as soon as most people, so it lasts longer. And I talk. I talk and talk and talk. What shall we talk about, hmmm?"

"Nat?" he said.

"Did I ever tell you about the time I stayed all winter on Saint Croix with . . . with . . . well, she was *very* rich, and her name was, hmmm . . . let's see . . . Helen Mitchell, and she had been the mistress of somebody like John D. Rockefeller or Guggenheim or one of those *foundations* — or maybe it was King Carol of Rumania. And when they broke up, he settled quite a lot of money on her — like, I mean, you know, several *million* dollars, so she was kind of a foundation herself. And she liked having me around, because she thought I was funny, so she awarded me a fellowship. I visited her all one winter on the beach — a cozy little *family* setup. There was her current lover who was, naturally, colored. (That's stylish now, you know.) And then there was her ex-lover who was staying in a little beach house on the *estate* with *his* current lover who was a boy — fifteen. And then there was her little boy — her *child* — by her husband, who was an English sea captain, and the little boy's nurse — am I boring you? — and me, to make things jell. My, the conversation was intellectual."

"I don't care about all that," he said. "I know people live like that. But I don't care."

"I didn't believe they existed," she said, "even though I was living with them. But the little boy — her son — that's who I was going to tell you about. He was an *alcoholic*. No one ever paid any attention to him, see? Like once, while I was there, the nurse took him off to her place about ten miles down the road and kept him there for nearly a week and nobody missed him. And I reckon he got hooked on whiskey just going around at parties and drinking the dregs of drinks. By the time I knew him he stayed drunk almost all the time. He was six."

Floyd said nothing.

"Fix me one more drink, Floyd," she said, and gave him her glass. "He was a cute little boy," she said. "He used to come and get in bed with me nearly every morning — since I was just about the only person around there who wasn't sleeping with somebody — usually two or three somebodies. He'd be sober then, and he was a very gentle, sweet child. He kind of reminded me of Hunter. That's . . . that's . . ." She glanced up. "Did I tell you I had a son named Hunter?"

He nodded.

"He stayed with Jeff," she said. "That was natural, wasn't it? But never mind all that tiresome business. This little boy, as I was saying — I'd have really been crazy about him if he hadn't had such an awful temper. But if you crossed him, he threw things and tore down the curtains. I was kind of scared of him when he got mad. And one time . . . let's see . . . one time . . ."

"What would you do when you were scared of him?" he asked.

"I don't know," she said drowsily. "Just don't cross him, that's all, I guess. Go . . . out on the beach . . . or something. One time. Let's see, what was I going to say?"

She was sitting on the edge of the bed again, and he was standing over her, holding her refilled glass in his hand. She looked up at him standing there, his heavy body blocking out the light from the lamp on the table across the room, and shivered. Something about him is a little bit scary, she thought fleetingly, but she was too drunk to know exactly what it was. Pretty soon I'm going to be able to go to sleep, she thought. He stood there and held out the glass until she took it. She could not see his face very clearly because the light was behind him. He was like a gigantic dark marionette leaning slumped in his strings, his hand held out woodenly toward her, his other arm dangling.

"But I don't know whether I can work you," she muttered.

"What?" he said.

She reached out, took his hand, and pulled him down beside her. "I like you, Floyd," she said in a childlike placating voice. She leaned her head against his shoulder. "I'm getting drunker," she said. But she was still trembling like a captive wild creature. "Dreams," she said. "Dreams. If we keep on talking, you see, we don't have to . . . Did you hear what he said? They burn up arms and legs . . . Abortions."

"You didn't have to stay up there with Wilburn," he said. "Or even go in the first place. Why didn't you leave?"

She opened her eyes wide and looked directly at him, and something flickered in her face — a wholeness of response that she instantly masked. She had been about to say, Because Wilburn is my friend. "I'm naturally friendly and self-sacrificing when drunk," she said. "My true self comes out."

"I'm going," he said.

"Let me finish talking," she said. "I haven't finished telling you . . . Let's see . . . Oh, yes, you can't go until I tell you how — how *sorry* I am I was bad to you today." Her voice began to slur slightly now, although she had been talking clearly with her ordinary soft, slow intonation. "Bad to you all day," she said.

"And . . . Devil made me act that way. I . . . I get at a party and the devil gets in me. Hmmmm? And you were so *good*. Put up with me all day. You never said a mean word. Let me flirt with that . . . And tonight. Went to the hospital like a *soldier*. That's what I wanted to tell you about. You're a friend, Floyd. So now . . . Now you can't get mad and ruin our friendship. Can you?" Hopefully, as a child takes the hand of his partner, in "Thimble, Thimble," she took his clenched fist in hers.

A shiver went over him, but he got up. "I'm going," he said again.

"No. *Please*."

"*Nat!*" Her name was a kind of roar of anguish.

"Shhh," she said, putting her finger to her lips.

"What the hell are you *doing* to me?" he said. "Do you think . . . ?"

"Don't you remember what you said this morning?" she said, "about how we . . . we could be friends and all?" She was still shivering, shoulders bent, black hair falling over her face.

He put his arm around her. She put her head on his shoulder again, continuing to shiver. He pulled her to her feet and, jerking the spread off the bed, draped it around her; then he sat her down. "I'll warm you up," he said and took her in his arms and held her quietly for some minutes.

"Nat?" he said in a low hoarse voice. "Nat?"

"Ummm? Friends. Like you said. This morning. 'Member?"

He disengaged himself from her and laid her on the bed. Then he took off her shoes and stockings. He pulled a chair up close beside the bed and sat down in it and stared at her for a few minutes. She was not asleep but in a kind of half-waking dream. She moved restlessly, murmuring unintelligible words. He got up from the chair and, going around to the other side of the bed, lay down beside her.

"We're good friends," she said clearly. "Wilburn?" Her eyes were closed. She turned toward him, reached out, stroked his cheek, drew him closer to her. "Wilburn?" she said again, softly. "I do love you, you know."

He heaved himself up in the bed, throwing aside her arm and the soft hand that rested on his cheek. *"Wilburn!"* he said in a strangled voice.

She opened her eyes and stared at him, saw his face, dark and hard, cold as stone, raging. She rolled out of bed and stood up. "No," she said. She shook her head. "No."

Without a word he rolled across the bed and stood up in front of her, the heavy sloping shoulders slumped toward her, the wooden hands reaching.

"It's all right," she said. "I . . . I can sleep now."

"You're beautiful," he said. "I hate all women in the world but you." The huge white hands gripped her upper arms and he drew her to him.

"No," she said. "We were *playing* . . . just talking and playing, but now . . . time to go to sleep now." A confusion of images whirled through her mind, rising out of interior darkness: the hospital chimney reared up and poured out its sluggish fat smoke; she heard Sunny's screams, as if, at a distance, that scene were playing itself out again for someone else; Wilburn's tired face appeared and vanished. But she felt the pain in her arms where Floyd was gripping her and knew that he was shaking her gently, as a cat might shake a captive bird that quivered against its jaws.

"We won't talk about Wilburn anymore, will we?" he said. He stopped shaking her and lifted her off the floor so that her face was opposite his, her eyes looking into his small cold eyes. He put her down and pulled her against his chest.

She was enclosed in his arms, the walls of the room drawing in around them, the illusion of his looming body taller and taller in a space grown smaller. She felt the terrible panic of claustrophobia. Her mouth was full of the taste of iron, her chest bound with strips of iron. She fought for breath as if the space of the room were a vacuum. I've gone to sleep after all, she thought. This is bound to be one of those dreams. And to make it true, she slumped against him in a pretense of sleep. She could feel the power and tension of his body, but she closed her eyes. "Won't be afraid," she murmured. "I'm asleep . . . asleep. Both . . . dreaming. Can't *really* . . . hurt . . . anybody . . . dreaming."

He shook her again. "I'm not dreaming," he said, "and neither are you." She was limp in his hands and he shook her harder. She heard the grating of his teeth.

"Wake up," he said. "You *will* wake up. See *me*."

She jerked herself free from him and backed off. Standing in the middle of the room, she saw them both in the mirror behind him. First his face — his *real* face — directly in front of her, looking at her, full of that awful cold passion, then, beyond him, in the mirror, her own figure, draped in the motel room bedspread, insubstantial, wavering, and, between her and her own ghostly reflection at the back of the mirror, the reflection of his powerful, brooding, slumped back, the back of his small, round, rocklike head and the taut muscles of his neck.

"I'm going to scream," she said, speaking firmly, as if to an unreasonable child. "Go away, you hear, or I'm going to scream. Go out the door and shut it. If you don't — if you touch me again — I'll scream so loud, everybody in the motel will hear me. Do you understand?" She paused. "After all," she said in a low voice, "I reckon I'll just have to stay by myself tonight."

He took one long step toward her, put his arm around her neck, and covered her mouth with his hand. The crook of his elbow gripped the back of her neck; his thumb was against her cheekbone, and his fingers gripped her jaw, clamping it shut, so that she could neither speak nor bite. He laughed quietly. She had never heard him laugh before.

"You won't have to stay by yourself," he said, his mouth against her ear. "And you're not going to scream. Understand? If you scream, I may kill you. You hear me? Did you know I get very angry sometimes? Very angry?"

She began to make a loud, humming, moaning noise against his hand.

"No," he said. "Quietly. Quietly." He spoke quietly himself, almost absently, and he held her as easily as if she were a baby. "I'm going to tear you to pieces," he said. "Are you still cold? Be cold." He dragged her across the room to the bed, laid her down on it, and put a pillow over her head.

Nat twisted her body against his hands and, as the pillow came down, butted her head frantically against its soft enveloping bulk. She knew, with one piece of her mind, that his hands were still on her arms, unmoved by her struggles. But at the same time, in another part of her, she felt herself to be inside a drum that turned with a sickening roar, over and over, separating her very inmost self from all reference points in the universe, so that there was no pain, no light, no room, no Floyd, no gravity even, but only a terrible flying darkness. But still she bucked, like a headless chicken flapping in the barnyard dust, against his hands.

He raised one side of the pillow, so that she could see him — his dark face, his rosy mouth and cold eyes, the dome of his shining forehead. Holding his hand over her mouth, he leaned down to her and spoke again. "Lie very still," he said. "If you don't lie still, I may smother you — by mistake." He flopped the pillow back down, covering her head completely, and held it there with one hand while with the other he ripped away her clothes.

I'm going to die, she thought. He's going to kill me. And without warning, out of pain and nightmare, a wild, joyous intoxication swept over her, a kind of exultation. Die! I'm going to die! Shut of it all — all awful nights and poisonous dead days. *That* was what I was looking for. Quick, now! Quick! Sleep!

Her limbs, heavy with desire, her eyes weighted with soft darkness, she would have stretched out her arms to him, if she could.

But she opened her mouth, and the dry starchy pillowcase crushed against her tongue like a dusty gag; she felt the weight of his body on hers, and again, suffocation, the soft, resistless, airless wall of feathers around her face. Out of some last reservoir of intelligence and strength and will, she forced herself to lie still. Carefully, she turned her head sideways so that her nose was in a pocket of air between pillow and mattress. She breathed lightly, carefully, spread her legs wide, and willed herself to relax to him. Out of the feather-muffled darkness she heard his hoarse voice against the pillow.

"I love you, Nat," he said. "I love you."

She held herself as still as a dancer, as a poised diver, held her still mind in her cupped hands as if it were made of crystal.

He says, he loves me, she thought. My God. And then: I'll think of something funny, she said to her mind. Lightly she breathed, in and out. Raped! Who would ever think a girl would get raped at the Colonel Rebel Motel after the Ole Miss-Tulane game? Aunt Louise would certainly not believe it, if anybody told her about it. After all, he's from such a lovely family.

15

THE FLUORESCENT TUBE over the mirror in the motel bathroom pulsed, flickered, dimmed, and swelled to brilliance. In the next room Nat lay in darkness, the pillow pressing like earth on her eyelids. She breathed carefully into the pocket between pillow and mattress. The weight of Floyd's body pressed down on her like a stone, her breasts shriveled and she felt the dry tearing pain of violation. Below the control that held her as still as a corpse, that made her try and yet fail to imagine herself insensate, dead, the terror of suffocation, of being shut into the earth, the grave, beat like the clang of a monstrous bell.

Outside her darkness, where *he* was, the room was bright. They lay together on a rose-colored bedspread, surrounded by the metallic motel-room colors of curtains, rug, and calendar landscapes. His eyes were open, staring.

After it was over, she felt him rooting with his hand under the pillow. He found her mouth, put his hand over it, and threw the pillow aside. His face was not two inches from hers. She saw the narrow forehead, curving back into baldness, shiny with sweat and dark with pulsing blood, the small, wounded, deeply-circled eyes, and the rosy mouth with a queer expression on it of astonishment, triumph, and fear. She thought, swallowing and grinding her teeth, I'm going to vomit.

"If you won't scream, I'll let you go," he said.

She nodded.

He took away his hand and drew back a few inches. They looked at each other, wary and fearful, as dead men might, discovering in the final lapse of decay that after all the dead are conscious, capable of action, and able to destroy each other.

Nat's face was smeared and bruised with mascara. Her skin had a greenish pallor and the puckered look of age under its broken mask of pancake and tan. Her body shook with a scarcely visible tremor. She rolled away from him and sat up on the far side of the bed, her back to him. She groped at her slip and drew it down over her trembling legs.

He got up, pulled on his clothes, and left the room without another word.

Nat sat for a long time on the edge of the bed. Every now and then she would pull at her slip and with both hands draw it downward and press her legs together. She looked at her watch. It was ten minutes past four. She stood up and, gazing at the wall in front of her, did not move for another long time. Then she picked up her cocktail dress from the floor. It was ripped from neck to hem. She sat down again with the dress on her lap and stared at it, turning it over in her hands and finally spreading it out on the bed and fitting the torn edges of the material together. Her heart, her very limbs, were filled with unspeakable sorrow and bewilderment. At the center of her flesh had been uncovered a stone — or a seed — on which was written: *The world is both real and evil.*

"I'm not dreaming," she said.

At last she got up, went into the bathroom, and looked into the mirror.

The motel room hummed with emptiness. The light over the bathroom mirror continued to flicker and fade, ready to burn out.

It needs a starter, she thought.

She shuddered.

Moving with jerky, hurried rigidity, she went back to the bedroom, put on the suit she had worn to the football game and her topcoat, stuffed everything else into her suitcase, and started to leave the room. At the door she hesitated. Then she came back, sat down on the bed and looked for a long time at the telephone. At last she picked up the directory, looked up a number, and dialed. "Ring Mr. Griffith's room," she said. She waited a long time before anyone answered.

"Wilburn? Something . . . Something has happened . . . No, to me, not to Sunny. No, no. Sunny's OK. It's just me. I need to come over there. OK? I know it's the middle of the night, but I have to come. And you have to promise — before I come — that you won't do anything I ask you not to do . . . I know it sounds queer, but that's what you have to do . . . Wilburn, listen. I mean it." Her voice was dry and blank. "All right? I'm going to call a taxi and I'm coming right now." She drew a deep breath. "I'm sorry," she said. "I know how tired you are. But I have to. There isn't anybody but you."

. . .

She spent the next two days in Wilburn's motel room. Sometimes, while he was at the hospital, she would lie for hours staring at the ceiling. Sometimes she sat and looked at the television screen. She did not bother to change stations. During this time she said to him only that he must say nothing and do nothing about what had happened.

It seemed to Wilburn, when he came into the room after hours at the hospital, first waiting for Sunny to be moved from the intensive care room, and then sitting by her side in her room, that he always found Nat in the same position he had left her in. Only there would be the illusion that she had sunk deeper into the bed, drawing sheet after sheet of immobility over her body. It was as if she sank through layers of pain toward a center of darkness of which he had no knowledge. He was helpless before her silence and immobility. He would leave and go back to the hospital, wandering the corridors, sitting in the drugstore, standing in front of the book rack beside the newsstand, or sitting by his half-conscious wife, listening to her occasional moans and mumbled words. She, too, wrapped in a cocoon of drugs, was shut away from him.

A dull rage lay like a clot of mud in his belly. Sometimes it turned over there and a wave of nausea went through him. "I'm supposed to be a man," he would mutter to the book rack. "I ought to kill him. When I get back to Philippi, I'll kill him."

But he had accustomed himself too well in his life to the discipline of examining his bare thoughts, and he knew, at the moment of imagining he would kill Floyd, that he would not. His intelligence said as clearly as if he were reading the page of a book, *No!*

After that unequivocal, instinctive *No*, he would find himself fighting through a thicket of confused emotions. His children — Sunny — Nat — were caught in all the fragrant and painful reality of their flesh in that thicket. And Floyd, too, with vines as thick as snakes growing over him, standing like the zombi that he himself had evoked as an image of himself.

Wilburn would sit down in the hospital lobby and light a cigarette. All right, he would say to himself. First, it wouldn't do anybody any good to kill him — not Nat, and certainly not Sunny or the children. Second, the main reason for your frustration, old buddy, is that you're afraid you may have to think yourself a coward. You're afraid that the real reason you won't do it is because you haven't the guts or the spirit for it. And even more contemptible, maybe you're wanting to cut a figure in the eyes of the world. (Charles Taliaferro, for example? Would you like him to admire you, to say to his friends, "Yes, Wilburn shot the bastard. Any man would have done the same thing. He won't have any trouble getting off."?) That's what makes you sick at your stomach — *not cutting a figure.* And third . . . His attention wavered, but he forced himself to go on thinking these miserable thoughts. Third, what you thought in the second place — you know it's partly true. You're partly a coward. The muscles in his neck and shoulders tensed and he clenched his fists. For a moment, in his mind, he saw Floyd forcing Nat down, ripping at her dress with his huge hairless hands, heard her whisper to herself, admonish herself, "Lie still. Just a few minutes longer." He clenched his fist and made an inarticulate sound.

From behind a protective pane of glass the receptionist peered at him and then looked away. Doubtless she was accustomed to displays of anguish.

Wilburn got up and again began his wanderings through the hospital corridors. And still he ran again into that final immovable *No!* Kill a man? (Or is he less than a man?) No!

As for Nat, she lay on the bed and looked at the ceiling. She shook her head stubbornly in response to his pleas that she see a doctor. Once, when he had gone so far as to say he would call one, no matter what she said, she raised herself on her elbow and spoke.

"Listen, Wilburn," she said, "it's true he hurt me. But it's not bad. I'm going to be all right. And what do you think I'd tell a doctor? That I've been *raped?* At my age? By a man I was spending the weekend with? Or maybe by you?" She shook her head and lay down again. "Besides," she said reflectively after a while, "I've been thinking about it, you know. It's not much more than Jeff Stonebridge has done to me plenty of times — only I would be more or less expecting it, and I wouldn't be afraid he was going to kill me." She hesitated. "And I would be pretending it wasn't happening," she added. She looked at him with the opaque and impenetrable face of an insane person. "All women get raped one time or another in their lives, Wilburn. Didn't you know that?"

"No," he said angrily. "I didn't know it and I don't know it." He turned away with a shrug of frustration. "What's the *matter* with you, Nat?" Then he drew a chair up to the bed where she was lying and took her hand, feeling it tremble under his with a faint fearful tremor. "Listen. Haven't you ever had . . . had a lover you cared for?"

"For God's sake," she said, "I don't want to talk about sex."

He persisted. "People do care about each other, Nat," he said sadly. "They do." He took hold of her shoulder and gave her a gentle shake. "After all, you're *here*," he said. "You didn't go someplace else."

"Is that what you want, too?" she said in a lifeless voice.

He got up. "Damn it, Nat," he said, "use your brain. Wake up! I don't want to go to bed with you. I haven't got a shred of lust left in me — you know that." (But that's not true, he thought, even while he was saying it.) "And stop feeling sorry for yourself. What did you expect from that poor bastard?" He broke off. Then, "I'm leaving," he said. "I'll see you later." He slammed out of the room.

It was late Monday night. He stomped out into the motel parking area and stood under the cold November sky, already wondering what he was going to do with himself next. He had nowhere to go, no one he cared to see in this strange city. And thinking, too: Yes, she's right. Lots of women get raped every day. But Sunny? Does she feel that way?

He looked up and automatically began to orient himself under the heavens. "Which way . . . ? Let's see — north — there's Cassiopeia and so, yes, there's the North Star and the Little Dipper and . . . East over there, with the twins rising and, up high, the Pleiades. He craned his neck and stared up at Orion directly above his head. There's the old hunter, he thought, the old, blind rapist.

The weather had turned colder. A sluggish wind, wet and sharp, smelling of snow, blew on his face. Heavy clouds hung low on the northern horizon. Far off, tracking a contemptuous cat in some patch of backyard shrubs, a dog yapped steadily. Wilburn turned and went back into the motel to Nat.

"I only meant that I wanted you to try to live and be . . ." He had started to say, "be happy," but he did not. "To *be*." He repeated. "That's all. Are you awake?"

She nodded and opened her eyes. "Conscious," he said. "Loving . . . something . . . someone. Our lives'll be gone, Nat, and you'll have spent yours in some kind of trance."

"Oh, Wilburn," she said, "you're nothing but a — an — optimist. While I — *now* . . ." She seemed to be trying to think exactly what she wanted to say. "I want — *now* . . . Maybe I want to tear everything to pieces. And I hardly know why. But I won't," she added in a low voice. "I'll find something better to do."

"An optimist!" he said. "That's not true."

"And it's not true that I'm in a trance."

"Anyhow," he said, "we'll forget it. OK? We'll just try to get you put back together."

She nodded. "All right," she said. She slept.

And he, lying on his bed in the same room composed speeches that he would never make to anyone: "To spring out of time and nothing into life — isn't that miracle enough? Even enough religion? Isn't there some way to be content with that — some way to smell one's own death in the air and still to whistle and swing on the wire like a field lark in the spring; to follow the stars across the night and mark their places in the sky, isn't that enough for anyone?"

Nat turned and moaned in her sleep, and warded off dreams of evil with an outflung arm.

16

On Friday afternoon of the weekend that Nat and Floyd spent in Jackson, General Pershing Pruitt went downtown to the Mid-South Hardware Store to call on Aubrey. He had dressed carefully for the occasion in a new shiny blue shantung suit, shot with iridescent greenish threads, and a wide-brimmed, western-style hat of a slightly darker shade of blue. He had a green handkerchief in his pocket and his shoes shone like patent leather. His 1957 Oldsmobile had just been washed and waxed. The paint gleamed and the upholstery was spotless under its transparent vinyl seat covers. Altogether The General looked like an exceedingly prosperous gambler.

Parking his car in front of the shabby old store, he sat for a few moments without moving. A sign on the door said "Closed," but in the dimly-lighted interior someone was moving about. He got out of the car and tried the door of the store, but it was locked.

General Pershing was not a man to be discouraged by small obstacles. He stood patiently in front of the dusty show window, his hands behind his back, and examined the display of washtubs and dead tomato plants. Before very many minutes had passed and before it was necessary for him to invent a plausible excuse to get in, the door opened and two Negro men came out, carrying cardboard cartons full of trash. He nodded affably and, waving his hand in a "That's all right, I'm expected" gesture, stepped in.

The store was empty except for Miss Louise Hunter who was sitting on a high stool behind the old-fashioned bookkeeper's desk at the back. The bobcat stood on top of the display case behind her. The moose head hung on the wall above. Miss Louise, swathed in a print cotton duster with a scarf around her head and a gauze mask tied over her nose and mouth, was looking up at the moose.

The General clicked his keys several times on a counter top and cleared his throat.

"Young man," Miss Louise called in a muffled voice, "this store is not open for business today. You'll have to come back tomorrow."

The General took off his hat, strode toward the back, and made Miss Louise a sweeping bow. "I was — hmmm — looking — ah — for Mr. Aubrey Hunter, the distinguished inventor," he said.

"Mr. Hunter is out of town," she said. "He's in Memphis on business. He'll be back tonight, if you'd like to come in tomorrow." The General made no motion to leave. She stared at him from above the mask, the blank expression in her round pale blue eyes indicating that she was concentrating on the job at hand. He cleared his throat again. "If you want to leave a message or something," she said absently after a moment, "I'm Mrs. Hunter."

The General put his blue cowboy hat on the counter and began to remove his gloves. His eyes had not stopped moving since he had come into the store, darting from shelf to shelf, counter to counter, and door to door. "May I introduce myself?" he said. "I am General Pershing Pruitt — a great admirer of Mr. Hunter's."

Miss Louise had an old-fashioned feather duster in her hand, and now, waving it like a conductor's baton, she spoke to the two Negroes who had come back into the store and stood waiting for orders. "Lee," she said, "start on those counters over there, please. There are some rags and a bottle of Windex in the cabinet up front. I want everything on those shelves dusted and the counters shining. And Ernest," she pointed her duster toward the back, "go through that pile of boxes. Practically everything in there must be trash. Throw away those dried-up onions and to-mato plants and those weevily-looking peas and beans. And when you finish that, take everything out of the windows and clean the glass inside and out." Then, "I'm sorry," she said. "There's so much to do down here . . . What did you say?"

The General raised his voice. "So you're Miss Louise Hunter," he said. "I've heard my father speak of you so often. And I've met your charming niece. In fact, you might say she's a dear friend."

"My niece? Anne Farish?"

"Yes m'am, I've met Mrs. Taliaferro, too. But I was speaking of Miss Nat. Those two lovely ladies! I had the privilege of attend-ing a party with them not long ago. Got acquainted with them through my good friend Floyd Shotwell. And I've long looked forward to meeting you, Miss Louise — if I might call you Miss Louise. Like I said, I've heard my father speak of you so often by that name. And I like the old-fashioned way of addressing the ladies."

"Isn't that nice," Miss Louise said. She took off the gauze mask and for the first time looked directly at him. "It's not often these days that I meet a young man who appreciates the old-fashioned courtesies. Did you say you were a friend of Floyd Shotwell's?"

"Yes, m'am, I . . ."

"You must think I'm a lunatic," she said, "sitting down here in this filthy place — and in this getup." She waved the mask. "I . . ."

"The truth is," she said, "I've made up my mind to clean this place up and I had to protect myself. It's *dangerously* dirty. And the only time I can get it done is when Aubrey is out of town. He doesn't like me to come down here. I had the greatest difficulty persuading him to give me the keys. But it's for his own good. He shouldn't be *breathing* this air . . . So you're a friend of Floyd Shotwell's?" She nodded kindly at him. "Did you want to leave a message for Aubrey?" she said. And then, "Do sit down."

The General sat down on a stool across the counter from Miss Louise. "Yes m'am, Floyd and I are buddies," he said. "And then, too, we're involved off and on in business ventures together. And, uh, Floyd has been telling me what a remarkable man your husband is. Matter of fact, Floyd spends most of his time talking about the Hunter family. All he thinks about these days is Miss Nat." He cleared his throat and gave a dry chuckle, then took his green handkerchief from his pocket and began to roll it into a neat ball, touching it lightly with long fingers like the tarsal claws of an insect. "But *Mr. Hunter!*" he said. "I had no idea we had a brilliant inventor right here in Philippi. Just think of it! And you say he's away for the day? I *would* miss him."

"He's a dear boy," Miss Louise said. "Floyd, I mean. We're devoted to him. He and Nat make a charming couple, don't they? So often a man is too short for a tall girl like Nat. But not Floyd. Did you say you were from Philippi, Mr. . . . ?"

"Pruitt. The family is originally from Carrollton," he said. "My grandfather settled in the Delta some sixty years ago."

"Pruitt? I didn't know there were any Pruitts in Okatukla County. The only ones I know of used to live in Issaquena County."

"Yes, m'am, Issaquena. That's right. My grandfather had a big place down there."

"Oh," Miss Louise said. "That must be the Mayersville Pruitts. We're distantly related to them. But I thought that whole family had died out."

"That's right," The General said. "I'm the sole surviving bearer of that name." He shook his head sadly. "Gone. All those old folks gone. Hard to believe, ain't it? The South ain't what it used to be."

"You're so right," Miss Louise said. "Sometimes it seems to me as if we're living on the surface of *quicksand*. I wouldn't be surprised to feel myself *sinking* — you just don't know what you can count on these days. Like this." She waved her feather duster at the store. "When you think that this is actually the oldest continuously operated hardware store in the state of Mississippi . . . Did you know that? Who would have believed that Aubrey would let it get so filthy. I had no *idea* . . . If I hadn't come down here with him the other day to see that . . . that . . . and when I *realized* the condition of this place, I was horrified! So that's what I'm doing here with Lee and Ernest while it's closed up."

The General leaned forward on his stool, as if ready, out of pure solicitude, to soothe away with his long slender fingers the lines of perplexity in Miss Louise's troubled face. "Yes, m'am," he said, "times have changed. *You* see it here. I see it in my work. Now you take the function of the old-fashioned commissary. The country store. That's something that's vanishing from the Delta. From the *South*." He paused. Miss Louise nodded sadly. "Used to be," The General said, "and not so many years ago, either, you'd find all the men of the neighborhood, any afternoon you were looking for them, gathered around the table in the back of the commissary — er — conferring — exchanging views. That's how I used to conduct my business. But now! Half the time they're gone. They're throwing their money away on the horses in Hot Springs. Or they're in Memphis or New Orleans or New York City. Why I've even seen some of 'em buy airplanes and fly to Las Vegas! The hands are gone off the places. Tractors do everything. And tractors don't need commissaries. Or diversion. How can you get up a game when . . . ? And where are all those fine solid old country people used to run the commissaries? Moved to Little Rock. Or Birmingham." He shook his head. "I don't like it," he said. "I liked the olden days when folks who lived in the country stayed in the country and you knew exactly where you could find them on a rainy January afternoon. Tradition! Continuity! That's what gives a man's life dignity."

"The South needs more young men like you, Mr. — er — Pruitt," Miss Louise said.

"Call me Pershing," The General said. "Why, let's see, if you're related to the Mayersville Pruitts, we must be cousins. Ain't that right?"

"I suppose we are," Miss Louise said. "Yes, and I'm certainly glad to hear you're a friend of Floyd's and Nat's," Miss Louise said. "Sometimes I think Nat doesn't have the respect for tradition and family ties that she might have. What did you say your business was?"

"Broadly speaking — " The General chuckled, "you might say I'm a money man. Always willing to take a chance on a fellow's making a good crop."

"Oh. Are you with the Staple Cotton Association?"

"I'm an independent operator," The General said. "But I don't want to talk about *me*, when I can hear about that remarkable husband of yours. Floyd tells me he's one of the most brilliant men in this part of the country and . . ." He paused, rolling and palpating the ball of handkerchief between his long fingers, eyes alert. "I'll be honest with you. Although you might think it's a little bit presumptuous of me. I'm a student of human nature. That's my interest — my hobby, you might say — in life. And that's why I came to call on Mr. Hunter. There's nothing in the world that fascinates me like an unusual type personality — a man with ideas. Somebody *different*. And when Floyd told me about your husband and his machine, right here in Philippi! — which, incidentally, I understand Floyd and his father are interested in financing for your husband (And, may I add, you couldn't find a better pair to work with — willing to take a chance on something good — yes. But knowledgeable. Conservative in the best sense of the word.), I said to myself . . ."

"That's what I've been telling Aubrey," Miss Louise said. "*Exactly*. You have no idea . . ." She broke off and shook her head. "I'm sure you know," she said, "that Morris Shotwell is a member of one of the oldest families in the county. And even if Marigold was . . . But actually, Marigold has nothing to do with it. What does it matter what people say about Marigold? She is a splendid person — the backbone of the Guild. And what it is that has gotten into Aubrey about Morris Shotwell I do not understand. As a matter of fact that's the real reason I'm down here cleaning up this dreadful place this afternoon. Because of Aubrey's quarrel with Morris. *Somebody* has got to take hold and keep this place going until Aubrey comes to his senses and sees that Morris . . ."

The General appeared to be listening with intense concentration to all this. His nostrils flared, as if he were trying to take in from the atmosphere the sense data that would tell him what to do next. He cocked his head to one side and stared unblinkingly about him. "I did understand from Floyd that his father and Mr. Hunter had had a misunderstanding," he said. "You know, Floyd confides in me. I've been able to help him in one or two financial ventures and he relies on me for advice."

"Well, heaven knows I wish *I* had someone to rely on for advice in all this confusion," Miss Louise said. "Did you say your grandfather was old Winston Pruitt?"

"That's right," The General said. "That's my family. But, as you said, they're all gone now. I reckon you may be — uh — the only cousins I've got left around here. But you're more fortunate, Miss Louise. You have your nieces, and Charles Taliaferro, too. I'm sure you're not lacking for good advisers."

"Well," Miss Louise said, "Anne Farish — she's always been the one of those two girls with the common sense — is *trying* to help me make some practical decisions. She says we simply have to modernize this place. Suppose nothing ever comes of the machine? That wouldn't surprise *me* in the least. Nothing ever came of the plowpoint. Or the record machine. I suppose you've heard about that?"

The General nodded.

"And if nothing comes of this, who's going to pay the grocery bill? Besides which, we have an obligation to the community. Did I tell you this is the oldest continuously operated hardware store in the state of Mississippi?"

"I know it," The General said. "My father used to say . . ."

"We have an established — a long-established reputation. And if we use our brains — Anne Farish says — we can make a profitable concern of it again." She drew a deep breath. "And the first thing that ought to go," she said, "is that moose. That *dreadful*, filthy . . . !"

"Moose?"

Miss Louise pointed at the moose head on the wall above her and shuddered with revulsion.

"Would you like me to help you take it down?" The General said.

"Young man — Pershing — I believe the good Lord must have sent you here to help me this afternoon," Miss Louise said. She hesitated. Then, "Aubrey would never notice it was gone, would he?" she said. "No, he wouldn't. He's so wrapped up in his — *ideas,* he doesn't even *see* the store anymore."

"That's the way it is with a theoretical type personality," The General said. "I've observed it many times among my business associates. A man like Mr. Hunter becomes absorbed in his calculations, wrapped up in the — uh — processes of his — mind, and he pays very little attention to practical considerations. While people like you and me are practical people. We create the atmosphere that makes it possible for these — uh — dreamers to work. We're observant. We're improvisers. We seize the opportunity of the moment."

"What I really like to do," Miss Louise said, "is cook. And then — the Church. Flowers, for the altar. Brass. My religion is my life. But here I am — seventy-two years old — confronted with *this.* And I have to make the best of it." She looked up at the moose head again and sneezed. "We *could* take it down, couldn't we?" she said. "I don't believe he would know the difference. Especially right now, being so absorbed in the machine and everything." She picked up the keys from the counter. "I think there's a tall ladder in the back," she said. "Would you really help me?" She waved her feather duster at Lee and Ernest. "There's enough cleaning to do down here to keep them busy for a week, and I do want to get as much accomplished as I can before Aubrey comes back and gets in my way."

"Miss Louise, I would be honored," The General said.

"I hate for anybody to see this workshop," she said as she unlocked the door. "It's an absolute disgrace. But I don't dare touch a thing. Aubrey would notice *that* all right. He doesn't allow a soul in here."

Inside The General drew a deep breath. "So this is where the great man works," he said. "May I ask you a question or two?"

"Here's the ladder over here," Miss Louise said. "I really can't answer any questions about how Aubrey works. It's all a mystery to me. In fact, I hadn't been back here for years until last week when Aubrey brought us all down here to show us . . ." She broke off. "Well," she said, "he had a lot of things down here he wanted to show us and talk about. I don't understand half of it. My father always used to protect me from sordid business affairs. And Aubrey has been so secretive. But I know why. It's because deep down in his heart he knows he's wrong. Here," she indicated the ladder with her duster, "this is what we're looking for. And don't bump into that — *thing* — there in the middle of the floor. Aubrey would certainly know if anything happened to it — if a screw was out of place. He loves it better than — chess pie."

The General took his time. He looked at the "thing." Then he looked all around the room at the dismantled motors and empty radio cabinets and boxes of tools.

"Here's the ladder," Miss Louise said again. "It's getting late. If we're going to take that moose down, we ought to do it right now."

The General picked up the ladder and she followed him out of the room. "The truth is," she went on, half to herself, "he's getting old. He's slipping. That's the only explanation. No use to lock the door. We have to put the ladder back when we've finished. Now. Put the ladder against the wall right here behind the desk. And, let's see, you're going to have to have a screwdriver, aren't you? Here's one in the desk." She shuddered. "I don't see how anyone can bear to *touch* it. When I think of the *years* it's been up there accumulating dirt — ugh!"

The General climbed the ladder and carefully loosened the screws holding the moose head to the wall. A cloud of dust sifted down around him as he worked and Miss Louise retreated to a safe distance and put on her mask. "I don't see why the bobcat can't go, too, while we're at it. Here, Lee," she called. "Come help us with this creature, please."

The General handed the head down to Lee who set it carefully on the bookkeeper's desk, balanced on its mounting — staring with dusty glass eyes at the ceiling, the long antlers spread behind it. Dust sifted down and settled on the head and on the desk and newly polished counter. The General came down off the ladder.

"It's pretty big," he said. "What are you going to do with it?"

"Throw it away," she said. "Send Lee out to the city dump with it. And I'm going to send the bobcat, too, while I'm about it. Right now. Get them out of here, Lee." She poked at the moose head with her duster. The head tilted, rocked, toppled on the slanting surface of the desk, fell sideways, and dropped with a crash onto the counter next to the desk, shattering the glass in the counter top and breaking off one of the antlers. Long shards of glass crashed down inside the showcase and broke two or three earthenware pots that were displayed inside. Small fragments flew in every direction, showering the floor, Miss Louise, and The General. One struck Miss Louise on the wrist and a drop of blood appeared and trickled down her hand.

"Oh," Miss Louise said. "Oh, oh, oh." She began to cry, the tears rolling out of her round blue eyes and soaking into the gauze mask.

"Here," The General said. "Here, here. Don't upset yourself, dear lady. It's just the counter top. You can get it fixed."

"I've c-cut myself," she said.

He held out his green handkerchief.

"No," she said. "That green dye might be poisonous." She took her own white, lace-bordered handkerchief from the pocket

of her duster and mopped away the blood, continuing to sob bro-
kenheartedly.

"Now, now," he said. "Now, now." He clicked his tongue
nervously.

"It's just that it's all so *h-h-hard*," she said. "Here we are getting *old* and we're going to have to live on our Social Security like
— like *colored* people, and I don't understand it. Did you know
that Nat actually had to get Wilburn Griffith to lend us some
money? And even if he is a c-c-cousin, it doesn't seem right.
Aubrey's just losing his mind like his father did. That's the only
explanation I can think of. The next thing you know, he'll be running around with loose women. And . . . and Anne Farish has
gone home to Moss Ridge and left me here to cope with it all by myself." She pulled off the mask and mopped her eyes, smearing her
cheeks with dirt and tears. "Because Nat certainly hasn't any practical grasp of things," she said. "I don't suppose she'd *care* if
Aubrey began running around with loose women. She borrowed
that money from Wilburn, and now she acts as if that's all she
needs to do — when if she would just go ahead and marry that
nice boy, it would solve all our problems."

"But . . ."

"And now Aubrey's gone traipsing off to Memphis to see a lawyer that somebody told him knows all about patents, when he
hasn't the faintest notion what he can use to pay him with. And
what he *needs* to do is to clean up this dreadful, filthy place. And
patch things up with Morris. That's what any sensible person
would do. Because after all, it's more important to see that Floyd
and Nat have a *chance* — if she'll just take it. The truth is,
nothing is ever going to come of that horrible rusty old machine
back there anyhow. No woman in her right mind would have it
in her house." She gestured toward the workshop in the back.

"Back there!" The General muttered. He edged toward the half-open door of the workshop and peered in. Then he scurried in and began to examine the machine, lifting the lid and looking into the tub, walking around to the back to look at the works.

"Yes," Miss Louise called out hysterically. "That's it! That's the great secret! That's what's going to spoil the chance of Floyd and Nat's marriage. Because I happen to know that Floyd is right under his father's thumb — and who would think for even a moment that Morris will consent to his marrying Nat when Aubrey is going around as much as telling people that Morris is a — a — *crook*."

The General was crawling over the machine like a roach looking for crumbs, touching the surface here and there with his long fingers. "So this is it," he muttered. "She's right. It don't look like much." Then, on noiseless feet he hurried back toward the counter by the desk where Miss Louise, still weeping, was trying to sweep up the broken glass. He picked up the moose head out of the broken case and dropped it into an empty cardboard carton. "Here, boy," he said to Lee who was standing against a wall watching them but saying nothing. "Get this thing out of here, will you? And tell the other boy to come back here and clean up this mess."

"Ohhhh!" Miss Louise wailed. "When I think how hard we've been working to get everything nice! (Lee, take that bobcat with you too. To the city dump, mind you, not just outside.) And I arranged all those pretty little pots — the nicest I could find — so the garden club girls will begin to come in here and shop. And then that — *damn* moose falls on them. Ohhhhhh." And she wept again.

"Please," The General said. "Please. You mustn't upset yourself like this. Why, you shouldn't have to worry your head about such things for a minute — a lady like you. It's . . . It's all going to be straightened out. I — I — er, happen to — uh — know. In fact, I've discussed this matter with Morris and — uh — Floyd. They asked my advice, you see, as an — uh — objective outsider and . . . I . . . Well, the truth of the matter is I agreed to try to discuss this affair with Mr. Hunter, and I'm confident that we can patch things up. That's what I'm doing here this afternoon. You and I know a man like Morris Shotwell is going to do the right thing by Mr. Hunter. Now, you just stop crying and tell me all about Mr. Hunter's side of it, so that I will be in a better position to work things out when he comes back." He patted her encouragingly on the shoulder. "Come on, now," he said. "Sit down over here and let the niggers clean up this mess."

She sat down on a stool behind another counter. "I don't know what got into me," she said, "breaking down like that. But it's all so . . . confusing."

And she told him as much of Aubrey's story as she could remember — how Aubrey had brought them all down to the store that Sunday afternoon and demonstrated his model ("So it really works," The General muttered.) and how he had talked to them about suing Morris for the rights. But she didn't remember much of what he had said. She had been interested, at the time he had been talking of his troubles, chiefly in the carved radio cabinet which she wanted to make into a cellarette for her dining room, and she had missed a considerable part of the story. The General managed to learn from her, however, first, that the model was crucial to the legality of the patents; second, that Morris had had the machine patented in his own name; third, that Morris did not know the model still existed; and last, that Aubrey and Morris had quarreled when Aubrey had refused to consent to a sale of the rights.

The General listened, keeping perfectly still, his eyes intent and bright. When she had finished telling him everything she could think of, he went back to the workroom again, this time on the pretext of putting away the ladder. One glance around the room showed him that the back entrance was a heavy double door secured by an iron bar which dropped down across the doors and rested in two massive angle irons. He scuttled across the room, talking at the same time in a loud voice to Miss Louise, and shoved the bar back so that he could enter from the outside. Then he came out and closed the door behind him.

"Now, give me the key, Miss Louise," he said, "and let's lock this workroom. Good. I'm just going to keep you company until your nigger comes back from the city dump. You sit down right here and don't do another thing. You've overtaxed yourself. And I'll help this boy finish cleaning up the mess here. Sit down! Don't give it another thought. It's a pleasure. And you're not to worry about this counter. It can be replaced for very little. Or you could shift these counters over here and it would never be missed. Especially by a man like your husband. Would you like us to do that?"

"Don't bother about it," she said listlessly. "It's not going to make any difference to Aubrey, anyhow."

"Just one word of advice," he said to her after they had finished clearing away the broken glass. ("Put this stuff out on the street, boy.") It would be better for you not to mention our conversation to Mr. Hunter. Please. All right? That way, I can approach him in my own way and I'll be able to have a more objective type conversation with him. You can comfort yourself that you've been a great help to him this afternoon. My understanding of the situation has been infinitely deepened."

When Ernest came back with the car, the four of them left the store together. The General stood on the curb bowing and sweeping his blue hat through wide circles in the air until Miss Louise had driven away. Then he, too, left.

That night late, timing his visit to miss the policeman's hourly walk past the Mid-South Hardware Store, Pruitt drove a pickup truck down the black-topped alley behind the store. He was alone. Pulling open the heavy doors, he walked in, and lighting his work with a flashlight, disconnected the machine, picked it up as easily as if it were an empty carton, carried it out into the alley, and put it in his truck. Then, going back into the workshop, he took from his pocket a small, thin angle iron with a piece of strong fishing line attached to it. He pulled shut one of the double doors, raised the heavy bar that secured the doors, hooked the iron under the bar, and ran the cord over the top of the closed door and down the outside. Holding the cord taut, he stepped out into the alley, closed the other door, paid out the cord until the bar dropped into its slot, worked the cord across the top of the door and down the crack between the two doors to the ground, and carefully drew out his iron under the door. Then he got into his truck and drove away.

17

SUNDAY NIGHT when he had called home, Wilburn had told his mother that Nat was staying over to help him with Sunny — that nurses were hard to find and Sunny needed someone with her constantly. Mrs. Griffith had relayed the message to Miss Louise Hunter. Tuesday, Nat went home on the bus.

In Philippi she found Miss Louise and Aubrey in a chaotic situation. Aubrey had stayed away overnight on Friday instead of coming home as he had expected to do. He had rushed off to Memphis to see the patent lawyer without bothering to make an appointment; and he had had to wait until Saturday morning to confer with him. He had come home Saturday night and, when he went down to the hardware store the next morning — as he always did, even on Sunday — had found the model gone. He had immediately concluded that Morris had somehow got wind of the existence of the model and stolen it.

"Nat told that boy about it," he said to his wife. "That's what happened. I never should have let any of you see it or know about it."

"Aubrey," Miss Louise said, "Nat and Floyd are not even in town. And they haven't got your machine in the backs of their heads. Now you settle down and try to be sensible."

She was sure that he must have hidden the model away somewhere himself. Who else could possibly have done it? He's losing his mind, she thought, just as I feared. If only he doesn't start running around with loose women like his father did.

"I'm going to call the police," Aubrey said.

"The police! You're not going to get us involved with the police, Aubrey Hunter."

But he did call them. On Sunday afternoon he took two officers to the store and unlocked the back workshop. They looked around briefly, listened to what the old man had to say about looking for fingerprints and other evidence, and went away.

Monday morning he called them again. He had not told them on Sunday whom he suspected of stealing his machine, but now he accused Morris Shotwell. Miss Louise stood behind him sobbing.

After this call, the chief of police came out to see Miss Louise. He explained that there was no evidence that anyone had broken into the store — no broken windows or skylights and no jimmied locks — that everything appeared to be untouched except for the dusty square on the floor where Aubrey said the machine had stood, and that it was, in fact, unlikely that anyone had entered the building unless he had a set of keys.

"Mr. Hunter is getting old, Miss Louise," he added hesitantly. "I just want to be sure there really *is* a machine and that you are both sure it really has been stolen."

"Oh, yes, it exists," she said. "I've seen it. But you're right, he's getting old. He's a good deal older than I am." And she poured out her fears that he might be getting senile.

After this admission, the conversation was entirely amicable.

They agreed that it would be unwise, even insulting, to question the prominent and well-to-do Mr. Morris Shotwell regarding his knowledge of what had happened and decided that Miss Louise's first explanation of the disappearance must be true: Aubrey had somehow spirited away and hidden the machine himself.

"Maybe he doesn't even know he did it," the chief said politely.

"But somebody is bound to have helped him," Miss Louise said. "He couldn't have gotten it out of there by himself. Lee and Ernest, maybe."

"Who?"

"The two colored men who help us in the yard and at the store sometimes."

"Well, m'am, we'll question the niggers, if you'll give me their names, and we'll keep an eye on them and an eye on Mr. Hunter. We may be able to find out where he's put it."

"An eye on Aubrey!" she said. "You sound like he's a criminal. I'll keep an eye on him myself. And I'll talk to Lee and Ernest. You'll just scare them and they won't tell you anything."

"All right, Miss Louise," the chief said. "Any way you want us to handle it. And you just try not to worry about him, m'am. You'd be surprised how many old folks there are right here in Philippi who keep us busy with notions that somebody has broken into their houses and stolen their things. I reckon you just ought to be glad he doesn't think *you* stole it."

It did not occur for a moment to Miss Louise that it might be The General who had stolen Aubrey's model. It's true she did not mention his visit to Aubrey, but, if anyone had asked her, she could hardly have given a reason for concealing it, except perhaps that he might still be used as a mediator between Aubrey and Morris. The machine was gone — whoever had taken it and whatever the method — but Morris was still a central fact in

the Hunters' lives, and Floyd and Nat were still to be considered.

Tuesday morning, Aubrey popped out of bed, put on his clothes,
ate his breakfast and, after another fruitless call to the police, began to rummage through drawers and closets with furious concentration.

Miss Louise followed him around the house, asking over and
over in her ladylike little voice, "What are you looking for, Aubrey, dear? Let me help you." Then, "You don't know where
things are in that closet, dear, and I can put my hand on anything you want in thirty seconds." She had not yet had time to
dress. She had on a flannel nightgown and wrapper, and her
hair hung down her back in two skimpy white braids.

Aubrey shook his head, said nothing, and continued his search.
At last, stumbling over her as he rushed from room to room, he
turned on her. "It's *my* house, ain't it? I *live* here. I bought every
stick of furniture in it. If I want to turn every drawer upside-
down and set fire to the place, I can do it. So get out of my way."

"You did not," she said. "My mother left me that desk you're
looking in right now, to say nothing of the walnut sideboard in the
dining room and every piece of furniture in the parlor except the
marble-topped table."

He pushed her aside, snatched open a drawer in the desk, an
old, broken one that had been shoved years earlier into the back
hall, and found what he was searching for — a pearl-handled
.32 caliber pistol that Miss Louise's father had bought for her to
protect herself with as a young girl. He took it into his bedroom,
got a small tool kit from his closet shelf, and drawing up a chair
to his desk, sat down and began to break it down.

She had followed him into the room. "What are you going to
do with that gun, Aubrey?" Her voice was hardly more than a
whisper.

"I'm going to clean it and oil it," he said. "Then I'm going to see Morris Shotwell, and if he doesn't give me back my model, I'm going to kill him."

"My God," Miss Louise said. "My God." She had shed so many tears by this time, she hadn't a drop left.

He didn't say a word.

"The police will find out who took it," she said. "You haven't given them a chance."

He shook his head and pushed an oily rag through the barrel of the pistol.

"Listen to me, Aubrey," she said. "*Listen* to me. Morris hasn't got your machine. I know who took it. It was *you*. You took it yourself and hid it away someplace and you don't even know it, because you're crazy. You're losing your mind just like your father did."

"What?" he said. "*What?*"

"Think! Where did you put it? Who helped you move it?"

"Woman," he said, "you're the one who's crazy. Do you think if I knew where it was, I'd be getting ready to shoot Morris?" He began to put the gun back together.

"Oh-h-h-h," she said. "You don't care about anybody. You don't care what happens to me — not one bit. What do you think will become of me if you shoot Morris and end up being sent to Parchman? Who's going to take care of me? Or even associate with me?" She gave a kind of moaning shriek. "You might even get sent to the gas chamber," she said. She had been moving closer to him as she talked, and now she reached over his shoulder, snatched up the cylinder of the little gun, and, thrusting her hand into the pocket of her robe, retreated toward the bathroom. "It's not even your gun," she said. "It belongs to me. My father gave it to me to protect myself with, and you're going to use it to *ruin* me."

"Give me that cylinder, Louise," Aubrey said. "Nobody is going to steal my machine and get away with it. Do you understand?" He got up and advanced on her, holding out his hand. His face was red and he spoke as if the blood in his veins had stiffened his tongue. "Dobody," he said. "Dobody."

"Ohhhhh, he's lost his mind, lost his mind," she moaned and, turning, fled into the bathroom, dropped the cylinder into the toilet, and flushed it.

Aubrey, standing in the doorway, gave a queer kind of hiccup and, sliding down against the lintel, subsided slowly to the floor. "You . . ." he said. "You . . ." hardly seeming to notice that he was sitting down instead of standing up. "My m-m-m-machin-n-ne," he said. His head dropped forward onto his chest, and he toppled sideways.

She had to step over him to get out of the bathroom, calling out quaveringly, "Clakey! Clakey! He's dead. Call the doctor. He's dead."

Clakey came hurrying in from the kitchen, picked him up as easily as if he were a child, and laid him on his bed. Miss Louise sat down in a rocking chair and hung her head between her knees to keep from fainting, while Clakey called the doctor.

Aubrey revived almost immediately. He was already conscious by the time the doctor arrived ten minutes later to examine him and to hold a long conference with Miss Louise about slight cerebral accidents, blood pressure medicine, anticoagulants, bed rest, a quiet life, and tranquillizers.

"He had a fit," Clakey said. "That's all."

After the doctor left, Miss Louise had Clakey fish the pistol cylinder out of the toilet with a pair of fire tongs. (It had been too large to go down.) Then she wrapped all the parts in waterproof plastic, put them in a small metal box and hid them under the house. "After all," she said to Clakey, "it was given to me by my father, and in spite of this dreadful occurrence, it still has a sentimental value to me."

By afternoon, when Nat got home from Jackson, Aubrey was sitting up in bed calling for his clothes. He had not wavered in his determination to kill Morris. But his legs would not hold him up.

Nat sat down in the bedroom with the two old people and listened carefully to Miss Louise's account of what had happened. Occasionally she interrupted with a question. "Shouldn't Uncle Aubrey be in the hospital?"

"No," Miss Louise said. "Dr. Burroughs said he would be all right at home. Besides," she added, "he won't listen to a word of reason about anything. We'd have to carry him out kicking and screaming to get him there. And what would the neighbors say about that?"

Farther along in the conversation Nat turned to Aubrey and asked what the patent lawyer in Memphis had advised him to do. To this Aubrey gave a coherent and reasonable reply. The lawyer had assured him that his possession of the model would be adequate to protect his right to the invention. He had suggested that he (the lawyer) write to Morris, inform him of the existence of the model, and outline the legal steps that would be taken against him, if he did not restore control to Aubrey. This step, however, Aubrey had decided to postpone. He had determined to come back to Philippi and talk to Morris himself.

"I wanted to send him to jail," Aubrey said, "but the lawyer said I probably wouldn't be able to — that he would get off with a fine. So I decided to see how much money I could get out of him. I figured if I threatened to expose him, it would force him to agree to my plan to build a plant and manufacture the machines myself."

"But he would be putting up the money," Nat said. "How could you keep him out?"

"I . . . I hadn't worked that out in my mind, yet," Aubrey said. "And now — now you've gone and told that boy about it all, and he's stolen it, and . . ."

"Floyd didn't take it, I don't think, Uncle Aubrey," Nat said. "But anyhow you ought to have left it all for the lawyer to handle. You'll get a better deal that way."

While Aubrey talked, Miss Louise was standing at the head of his bed slightly behind him. She made signals to Nat over his shoulder, shaking her head, rolling her eyes, and indicating by sign language that Aubrey was crazy.

Aubrey leaned forward and shook his finger at Nat. "Who broke the counter?" he said. "That's what I want to know. And who carried off my moose and my bobcat? It's all very well for the police . . ."

"Now, wait a minute," Nat said. "Don't get excited. Tell me again, *quietly*, what you found when you went down to the store."

"It's all very well for the police to say nobody's been in there," he said in a calmer voice, "but somebody broke the counter and carried off my animals. Louise, get out from behind me. I know very well you're trying to signal to Nat that I'm crazy."

"Aubrey, I've already explained to you that Lee dropped that horrible moose on the counter and broke it. I was there when it happened."

In the middle of this conversation — in the middle of a sentence — Aubrey dozed off, and Miss Louise began to explain to Nat as rapidly as possible what she thought had happened. ". . . stole it himself . . . senile . . . lost his mind like his father did and . . . murder . . . *murder* . . . said he was going to *kill* . . . Whitfield . . . gas chamber . . . poverty . . . disgrace." These were the walls she crashed into and fled first in one direction and then in another, like a feeble and terrified old white mouse in a strange, electrified maze.

Nat got up and made the old lady sit down and drink a glass of sherry. "He's not crazy, Aunt Louise," she said. "And we won't let him kill anybody. Calm down and put all that out of your mind. He made perfectly good sense. He may be right about Morris having the machine — although I hate even to think about it. But whoever has it, it's not Uncle Aubrey. I don't believe he could have taken it off without knowing he'd done it."

"Maybe he did it in a fit. Maybe he had a fit down there at the store Sunday, and we don't know about it."

"Somebody took it," Nat said. "Could it have been Morris? How would he have found out about it? No." She answered herself. "The only way he could know would be if . . ." She broke off, got up abruptly and went to the window, where she stood with her back to Miss Louise, rubbing her hands slowly up and down her thighs. She sighed and, seeming to straighten and brace herself against her own fears, turned and went on. ". . . would be if Floyd had told him. And I don't think Floyd did. He hates him too much."

"Floyd? Hates his father? What a thing to say, Nat. You shouldn't . . ." Miss Louise paused and then went on. "Floyd could help us, Nat, if you asked him to. I know he could. I've been thinking about it. And, oh, yes, I want to tell you, too, about the nice young man, the friend of Floyd's who came down to the store when I was cleaning it up Friday afternoon. I keep thinking, if we can get him, too, if they would both help us, maybe we could talk some sense into Aubrey."

"Where could it be?" Nat said. "Who could have taken it?"

"Listen to me, dear. He was a most impressive young man, so old-fashioned, and . . ." She told Nat about The General's visit,

how he had said he was going to negotiate an agreement between Morris and Aubrey, and how he had helped her to take down
the moose.

"Did he see the model?"

". . . one of the Mayersville Pruitts. I didn't realize there was
anyone left alive bearing that name. I thought old Winston Pruitt died without children, but . . ."

"The Mayersville Pruitts," Nat muttered. "Now I've heard everything. Did he see the model?" she said again.

"Yes, I showed it to him."

"Aunt Louise!"

Miss Louise put her face down in her hands and rocked her
plump body backward and forward. Then she looked up at Nat
with anguish in her round blue eyes. Her soft face was drawn
and white. The little vertical lines around her mouth had grown
markedly deeper in Nat's absence, almost as if she had had her
teeth pulled. Her small mottled old hands dropped to her lap
and plucked uncertainly at her dress. "Somebody's got to help
us," she said. "And I thought . . . If he isn't a Mayersville
Pruitt, who is he?"

Nat sighed. "Maybe he is, Aunt Louise," she said.

"What are we going to do, Nat? What on earth are we going
to do about *everything?*"

A new expression crossed Nat's face, alert, attentive, bemused,
as if she might be listening with astonishment to the beating of
her own heart. "I'm going to help you," she said. "I reckon you'd
better tell me evey single thing you can remember about The
General's visit. That's the first step."

. . .

Floyd had returned to Philippi on Tuesday morning. Like Nat,
he had left the motel in Jackson in the middle of the night. He

had gathered his clothes, gone to her room with who knows what idea of what he would say to her, found her gone, paid their bills, and left. He did not go directly back to Philippi. Instead he got into his car and drove. He hardly noticed what direction he took, but drove south on Highway 51 until he came up against the seawall in Gulfport. There he fell asleep in his car and slept until the police wakened him and told him to move on. Then he turned eastward and drove, keeping always to the roads that were within sight and sound of the green water of the Gulf. Sometimes he ate, or he slept for an hour or two. Monday at noon, somewhere in southern Florida, he turned his car around and started back to Philippi and Nat. Cities dropped behind him under a brilliant summer sun — Tampa, Panama City, Pensacola, Mobile. Then, moving northward into winter, the ugly little towns of Mississippi: Hattiesburg, Jackson again, Yazoo City. There he stopped briefly under a cold morning sky and then plunged downward out of the hills into the river-smoked bowl of the Delta, through misted woods and fields, roaring blindly across the flat bottom of the bowl. He turned off the highway before he got to Philippi and drove to The General's gambling club. He had a key and he let himself in, built a fire, and, lying down on the floor in front of it, slept until the middle of the afternoon. But the fire died, the room grew cold, and he roused to build it up again. Afterwards he sat for a long time in front of it. That was Tuesday.

Toward evening The General came in, followed by the thin dark handyman and bartender whom he called Kilroy. Kilroy went back to the makeshift kitchen and began to arrange bottles and setups for the evening card game. The General, who seemed almost to be crackling with excitement, stood over the fire, rubbed his long slender hands together, and immediately began to chatter.

"Boy, I been waitin' for your *return!* Got all kinds of things to talk about. All kinds of things, fella." He slapped Floyd lightly on the shoulder. Floyd flinched and shoved his chair back from the fire. "I been looking after our interests while you've been down in Jackson having a ball. Trust The General, boy. He'll keep the pot boiling." He chuckled happily.

Floyd stared into the fire and said nothing.

"Why didn't you call and say you were out here, fella? I'd a been out earlier."

"I wanted to think," Floyd said. "That's why I came out here."

"Don't do it," The General said. "It's bad for you. Especially thinking about women — and I'll bet it's Miss Nat that's on your mind. But follow my advice and don't think about her. Action, boy. That's what women like. And, I might add, in the general conduct of my affairs, I've found that a bare minimum of thought followed by immediate action is usually successful. While the other fellow is sitting around ruminating, you're . . . Did you have a good time in Jackson? How'd the trip go? Great time, hmm? That's a *woman* for you, Miss Nat. Eh?"

Floyd sat and looked at The General and said nothing. On his face that had been still as a mask for three days was a faint expression of amusement.

"Why didn't you call and say you were back, fella?" The General said again. "I'd a been out here sooner. You know what I been doing this afternoon? Visiting the sick. You can smile, but that's something I'm always conscientious about. It pays off. People don't forget it. And old Horseshoe Calloway had a hernia operation yesterday, so I went out and took him a beautiful little pot of African violets. Picked 'em out myself. But I don't want to bore you talking about my obligations. I've got plenty on my mind, boy, plenty that concerns me — and *you*." He drew a deep breath. "You remember what we were talking about out here two, three weeks ago — old man Hunter's invention and all?"

Floyd nodded.

"Well, now, pay attention, Floyd, and stop mooning, because I got some interesting news for you. I made a discovery while you were gone."

"What are you talking about?" Floyd said.

"Well, you were pretty drunk when you told me about that machine, and how your daddy must be figuring to get control of it. You might not remember. But I've been thinking about it."

"I remember telling you about it," Floyd said.

"All right, now, listen. The grass ain't growing under my feet. I found out what your daddy's plans are and I found out where his weak spot is, and I took action. Boy, I mean I took action!"

"Oh?"

The General explained to Floyd exactly what he had found out from Miss Louise about Morris's control of the patent, how he had, almost by accident, but at the same time as a result of his own alertness and sharp observations, found out about the existence of the model, and how he had stolen it. "I've got the model!" he said. "I've actually got it!" He had been moving excitedly about the little room as he talked, rubbing his hands together, taking the handkerchief from his pocket, and rolling and unrolling it in a neat ball; now he stood directly in front of Floyd and rolled the ball rapidly back and forth between his palms, rocking forward on his toes and then back, as if he were gathering momentum to spread his wings and buzz off around the ceiling.

"Now," he said. "The next thing to do is to confer and make up our minds exactly how we can put our good fortune to the best use."

"Where is it?" Floyd said.

"Huh?"

"Where did you put the model? Is it in a safe place?"

"Oh, it's safe, all right," The General said. "Don't worry about that. But this is what I want to talk to you about. I've been re-flecting on the whole problem and it seems to me that we're in a great strategic position with both sides. And you're the key to it. See? You're the one who can go to your dad and explain what we've got. Why the old bastard may — probably *will* be tickled to death when he finds out what we've done to him. We've out-maneuvered him. Don't a daddy want his boy to be a chip off the old block? So there's every chance, see, that he'll be will-ing to be reasonable. He'll realize he's got a son with a future in the business, see?" He chuckled happily. "We've got him!" he said. "We're in."

"Where did you say the machine is?" Floyd said.

"Wait a minute. Let's pursue this a little bit further. What are you going to say to him? This is how it strikes me. Explain to him that we're ready to sell the model to the highest bidder — either to him or to Old Man Hunter. And we don't necessarily want money either — he'll know Hunter can't offer us any money. Of course, you can get a little money out of your daddy if you want to — maybe enough for you to pay me off. And if you want to push for a better setup in his business — shares and salary raise and so forth — that's up to you. But for me — all I want is a little piece of the machine. Just an opportunity to gamble on it. Not too much, now. I'm a reasonable fellow. And if we ask too much, we might louse up the deal. He might figure it won't be worth it to him to buy it. You got that straight?"

"What about Mr. Hunter?" Floyd said. There was a pecul-iarly bemused and absent expression on his face. He spoke slowly, as if his thoughts were far away. "Maybe . . ." he said, "maybe it would be to our advantage to deal with him instead of with my father."

"Let's see," The General said. "OK. Let's be fair and square. Offer it to Old Man Hunter, too. What would happen in that case?

Would it work out better? If we offered it to Hunter and he gave us a share in it, we'd have to have a larger share, because everything would be more uncertain. He'd still have to get the patent rights back from Morris. It'd be more of a gamble. But, on the other hand, we might be able to get complete control. Old Hunter, from what I can gather, hasn't got much sense. He'd be a hell of a lot easier to control than your father. We could give each of them a chance to make us an offer and then see which one was most to our advantage. And here's this. If we offered it to the old man, we could get Nat on our side. Say! I've just thought of something. Couldn't we tell her I'd gotten wind of the fact that Morris was getting ready to steal it and I took it to protect it from him? That way, they'd all be so filled with gratitude, they'd be eating out of our hands." He nodded happily. "I'm a man who likes people to get along," he said. "I don't like unpleasantness. I want folks to like each other and be happy."

"Nat . . ." Floyd said in the same dreamy voice.

"Boy, you're gonna be flying high! You can take that beautiful little doll to Las Vegas, if you want to — to Monte Carlo, even!"

"Nat . . ."

"That's right. Or anybody else you want." He rocked forward on his toes. "I did it! I did it! A beautiful, beautiful stroke."

"Where did you say it was?" Floyd said.

"That's one of the smartest things I've done," The General said. "Aside from using the angle iron and string to lock the doors from the outside. Nobody would find it in a million years — not even if they suspected me of taking it. You know that storage house back of the old jail? It just happens that I have a key to it. Used to be, when a particularly good friend of mine was sheriff, we ran a little game back there; and I happened not to give him back the key when he went out of office. Well, they've got it full of old office equipment and files from the courthouse now. Nobody ever goes in there and, if they did, they wouldn't see the machine. I stuck it back in a corner in there and just turned a big cardboard carton upside down on top of it. You might say it's under police protection."

"And what is it you think we should say to Nat?" Floyd said.

"She's the one who can make the old people behave," The General said. "Although I *will* say I had the old lady eating out of my hand the other afternoon. She likes an old-fashioned gentleman — and she trusts me already. In fact, she thinks I'm her cousin. But Nat can put it to the old people so they'll see the right thing to do is to give us our share — in return for us saving the model. And while she's dickering around with them, you can approach your father, and we'll see who makes the best offer."

"Pruitt," Floyd said, "approaching my father with a double cross is like approaching a buzz saw."

"It's not a double cross," The General said. "Don't *talk* like that. We're giving him an opportunity to protect himself from a double cross by Hunter."

At this point the telephone rang in the kitchen. The Negro, Kilroy, answered, brought the phone into the front room, and without saying anything handed it to Pruitt.

"Hello. General Pershing Pruitt here," he sang out in a lilting voice. And then, "Why, Miss Nat!"

Floyd settled into his chair like a mound of earth sliding into a chasm, moving and collapsing into himself, his very limbs, as it seemed, losing their shape and tension. Kilroy looked curiously at him. "Would you like a drink, Mr. Shotwell?" he said. Floyd shook his head and Kilroy drifted silently back to the kitchen.

"We were just talking about you, as a matter of fact," The General said to the telephone. "Floyd and me." There was a silence. Then, "You still there, Miss Nat?"

For the convenience of card players the telephone was on a

long coiled line, and now he moved closer to Floyd, dragging a chair with him, sat down beside him and held the instrument slightly away from his ear and close to Floyd's so that they could both hear what she said. Floyd did not move.

"I said, you still there? You faint or something?"

"No. I'm here."

"Well, now, did y'all have a big weekend in Jackson, honey?"

"General," Nat said, "you've got Uncle Aubrey's washing machine, haven't you? How did you get it?"

"Wait a minute, now, Miss Nat. Slow down. I ain't got it. Not on me, you might say. Ha, ha. I heard downtown yesterday (Cop who's a good friend of mine told me.) that your uncle was claiming somebody stole some invention of his." He covered the mouthpiece with his hand. "We don't want to admit anything on the telephone," he said. "She might have somebody listening in. We've got to see her in person."

"Aunt Louise told me you were in the store Friday afternoon, and that you saw the model and she told you about the patent fight," Nat said.

"Yeah, yeah, I had the pleasure of meeting . . . I mean, honey, she's a lady of the old school, ain't she? We got along just great."

"Let's talk about the machine," Nat said.

"Did you have a good time in Jackson, honey? Win any money on the game? Did I tell you Floyd's sitting right here beside me? But I ain't had a chance to talk about the weekend with him yet. I just got here."

Floyd buried his face in his hands.

"I'm going to call the police and tell them you're the one who stole Uncle Aubrey's model," Nat said. "I know it's bound to have been you."

"Now, look here, honey, you're being too hasty. First place, I didn't take it. Second place, if I had, there's not a way in the world anybody could prove I did — or find it. And if I get in trouble, you know, I wouldn't be able to help you find who actually did take it. You follow me?"

"No, I don't," Nat said.

"Well, I'm exactly the fellow who may be able to help you," The General said. "I've got all kinds of contacts in the county. I'll tell you right now, it's hard to pinch a pack of gum in the Arcola dime store without me finding out who did it and who fenced it — if I want to. So — I could put out some lines — see? I could drop a word here and there, and it wouldn't be long before I turned up some information. Who knows? Maybe some kid took it for a joke. Maybe Morris has got it — or knows where it is and who took it. Had you thought about that possibility? If he don't have it already, we sure wouldn't want him to get his hands on it, would we?"

"You did take it, didn't you?" Nat said.

"I'm gonna help you in spite of yourself," The General said. "I'll pretend like I didn't hear that. I know you're upset, honey. But listen. We can't talk so good over the telephone. We're going to have to confer, y'hear me? I've got some good suggestions. Listen, this is what you've got to take into account, regardless, honey. Your uncle is too old to be in control of that thing. It's gonna take some intelligence and drive to get the most out of it. You know that? Why, when I sit down here and think about what that machine could mean to the future of the Delta, it staggers me. We've got the welfare of the entire state to consider, you hear me? And your aunt says the old man is going crazy. Hell, he's old. Suppose you get the model back. What are you going to do about all that, huh? Now, don't say a word.

I just want you to think about it all. No, don't say a word. We'll talk again — right away. I'll be back in touch with you tonight. OK?"

"All right," Nat said. "I can wait until tonight."

"Did I tell you Floyd's here? You want to talk to him?"

"No," Nat said. "I don't believe so. Not now." Then she was silent.

"You hung up, honey?"

"No."

"Well, that's all. Just keep your shirt on."

"All right," Nat said and hung up.

Floyd stirred and his body seemed to recreate itself out of dust. Abruptly he stood up, his long arms held slightly away from his sides and his hands tense. He studied The General for a moment.

"Now, let's see," The General began.

"Don't say anything," Floyd said. "I'm thinking." He walked over to the window and stood looking out into the darkening sky.

The General turned on the electric light hanging above the card table, scurried lightly into the kitchen, scrabbled around in the icebox, and came back with a piece of cheese and a handful of crackers. "Get on out here and get these rooms swept up, Kilroy," he called over his shoulder. "We got a game starting in less than an hour." To Floyd he said, "You hungry?"

Floyd shook his head.

Kilroy came in and began to push a mop slowly around the room. The two men continued to talk, as if he were not present.

"Well? Well?" The General said. "What do you think? What's the next step?"

Floyd turned away from the window and faced him. "You'd better sit tight and not do anything for a few days," he said. "Nobody will connect me with the model, because I was gone when it was stolen. So I'm the one to begin the negotiations."

"That's the boy."

"You don't do anything, understand? Not anything. Keep your card games going as usual. Everything as usual."

"All right. Who you going to first?"

"It doesn't matter," Floyd said. "I'm going to both sides. I'll probably see Nat tonight and him tomorrow. But you stay away from Nat. Stay off the phone and away from her. That's the safest thing you can do."

"Right. Right."

"It may be that my father will be the man to deal with," Floyd said. "All Aubrey Hunter has is a pipe dream. Morris has money and power."

"But you can't let him intimidate you," The General said.

Floyd laughed. "I'm leaving," he said. "I'll be talking with you."

But he did not go near his father that day or the next. He stopped by the appliance store and got one of the pickups and, as soon as it was dark, he went to the old storage house behind the abandoned jail, jimmied the lock, and got the washing machine. Then he drove out into the country along one of the routes he took every week when he was collecting for his father and dropped it off in an empty cotton house. He came straight back to Philippi, stopped at a service station, and telephoned Nat.

She answered the phone and he spoke quickly, without preamble, so that she would not hang up. "I know where your uncle's model is," he said. "And I can get it back for him — if *you* want me to."

At the other end of the line there was a silence. Then Nat said, "Floyd?"

"You understand what I said?"

"Yes."

"I'll come by and pick you up and we'll talk about it," he said. "Be on the front porch waiting for me."

. . .

He stopped the pickup truck in front of the Hunter house and sat hunched over the steering wheel looking down at his hands where they rested heavily on the wheel. He did not blow the horn or look to see if Nat was coming. The night was very dark. There was no moon. The two huge water oaks that overhung the sidewalk and street in front of the cottage still held their leaves, as water oaks do in a southern climate until December or January; and their shade blocked out the light from the streetlamp at the corner. Nat came down from the lighted porch and cautiously along the dark walk. A little way from the truck she stopped. "Floyd?" she said.

"Yes."

"It's so dark, I can't see you. Is that your truck?"

"It's Morris's," he said. "Get in."

"I'm afraid of you, Floyd," she said. "I don't want to get into a car with you."

He spoke out of the darkness without intonation. "Afraid?" It was as if he had forgotten all that had happened.

"You might kill me," she said. "And I think, after all, I want to stay alive for a while."

"I'm sorry about that," he said in a low voice.

"Thanks," she said shortly. "If you want to talk to me, why don't we meet tomorrow someplace — like on the corner of Main and Persimmon in front of the post office — at noon."

"Do you understand what it is that I want to talk to you about?" he said.

"Yes. But I'm afraid of you."

"You'd better talk to me *now*, whether you're afraid or not. It's important to you. A lot of money is involved. And I'm the only person who can help you."

"The General seems to think he is the man who has things under control."

"He thinks he is, but he isn't. I am."

"All right," she said. "Tell me what it is you're in control of."

"Get in the car, Nat. It's cold and I can't see you."

She stood in the darkness for a moment. Then she walked jerkily to the truck, opened the door, and holding herself meticulously erect, got in. She hesitated a minute and then slammed the door.

"I'm going to take you to The Coffee Cup," he said. "We can talk there, and you won't have to be afraid of me."

She nodded in the darkness.

"Did you hear me?"

"Yes. That'll be all right."

There was only one restaurant in Philippi that stayed open past nine o'clock at night. They drove there, went in, sat down at a long vinyl-covered counter, and ordered coffee. They were the only two customers in the restaurant. The waitress brought their coffee and went back to her chair behind the cash register, where she sat and drowsed.

The two cups of coffee steamed and grew cold in front of them while Floyd explained to her exactly what had happened. "So I have it now," he finished. "I have it hidden where neither he nor anybody else is going to find it. He's going to have a jumping up and down fit when he finds out."

"Are you going to give it back to us?" she said.

"Not exactly," he said in a low voice.

"You mean you want to sell it to us? You want a share in it?"

"No! I don't want any money. And I don't give a damn about the machine except for two things. One, I don't want Morris to get it, and the other . . ."

"Well? What?"

He looked at her and said nothing.

"What's the other thing?" she said.

"Nat?"

She looked at him and shook her head. "No," she said. "Please. No."

"All I want in the world is you," he said.

"No."

"I would be good to you. *That* . . . that wouldn't happen again."

"I've got to go home," she said. "I'll walk." She looked out at the dark street. "No. I'll . . . I'll call a taxi."

"Nat," he said, hurriedly, "listen to me for just a minute. If you will sleep with me for a while — just for a little while (We can set a limit to the time. . . . I know you couldn't — wouldn't want to — indefinitely.), but if you will, I'll bring it back."

"No. I can't."

"If I brought it back to you, you would have control of it. And it's going to make just as much money as your uncle thinks it is. You wouldn't ever have to think about money again. Do you realize that?"

She shook her head. "No," she said. "*No.*"

"All right," he said. "Listen. What are you going to do if I don't bring it back? All of you. You know Morris is going to take the house and the store. The General told me this afternoon that that's what he is going to do. Who's going to take care of your aunt and uncle? And now your uncle is sick. Have you thought about all that?"

"Yes," she said. "I've been thinking about them."

"Give me six weeks," he said. "Just six weeks out of your life. That's not much." He reached out toward her as if to take her hand and then drew quickly back. "That's all I'll ask for," he said. "Then I'll give it back to you."

She sat for a long time looking down at the counter. At last she said in a low voice, "How do I know you would give it back to us at the end of the six weeks?"

"You'd just have to believe me," he said. "But you know, if I say I will, I will, don't you?"

She looked at him. "I suppose so," she said.

"I would do anything for you you wanted," he said. "You . . . you might get to like me better."

"My God, Floyd!" she said. "Do you know what you're saying?"

He paid no attention. "Well?" he said. "Will you?"

A shudder, like the sob of a child who has been weeping for a long time, went over her body. She had not taken off her coat, and now she drew it closely around her and stood up. "I'll think about it," she said. "Give me a day to think about it."

18

In spite of the confusion and misery in her household during the weeks that followed Aubrey's attack, Miss Louise continued to follow her ordinary routine. She went to market on Monday and Friday, attended the meetings of the Blue Stockings and of her Episcopal Guild, paid her regular Tuesday afternoon visit to the King's Daughters' Old Peoples' Home, and on Thurdsay went to church to polish the chancel brass.

"We have to hold our heads up and go on as if everything were all right," she said to Clakey. She was dressing for her Thursday morning at the church, and Clakey, as was her habit, was helping her.

"You think Mr. Aubrey's going to be all right with nobody here but me?" Clakey said. "You know, he don't pay me any mind, and he ain't been up but two days. I didn't have no trouble with him long as he couldn't stand up. And you was here yesterday. But this morning he's up already, back there in his room staggering around on his own two legs. Suppose he takes a notion to go after Mr. Shotwell again? How I'm going to stop him?"

"He didn't take a notion to go after Morris yesterday, and he probably won't today. And if he does, you can call Nat. Big as she is, she ought to be able to control him." Miss Louise pulled the edges of her girdle down over her hips, imprisoning mounds of flesh like crepey dough. "Here," she said. "Get this hook under my arm. You missed it."

"I'll call her," Clakey said, "but I ain't guaranteeing she'll answer." She handed Miss Louise a slip and helped her pull it over her head.

"I don't believe Aubrey has Morris in the back of his head," Miss Louise said. "He hasn't mentioned him for days. And he's been sitting at his desk back there talking to himself and doodling ever since right after you left here yesterday. I had the greatest difficulty getting him to go to bed last night. He's working on some new . . ."

"Louise! Clakey!" Aubrey put his head in at the door. "Somebody's been meddling with the papers on my desk. Things are out of order," he said. "And I found this in the trash basket." He waved a scrap of paper with scribbling all over it. "Don't touch anything back there. You understand? Not anything! If you see a piece of paper on the floor, leave it there. I'm right at the *point* . . . I've got an idea for a modification on the ret bars of a cotton picker, and if I can work out a few bugs in it, it's going to raise the quality of machine-picked cotton a hundred percent. Think of that, Louise. Just think of it!" His sparse white hair stuck out in odd directions, as if he hadn't combed it for days, and his beaky alert face was alive with joy.

"Sit down, Aubrey dear," Miss Louise said. "There are some things — now that you're feeling stronger — there are some things we need to talk over, you know, about the store and money and . . . and . . ." She broke off. "I'm worried," she said.

"Right at the point!" he said. "I absolutely cannot afford to

think about anything else. Ask Nat. Nat's taking care of everything. Don't worry, Louise. Sell it. I don't care. Anything!" He
waved his paper, stumbled over the threshold and staggered off
toward his room. "Don't touch anything. Not a pin," he shouted.

"You see?" Miss Louise said. "He's forgotten all about Morris.
I suppose we should thank the Lord he's got something new to
think about. He's not going to shoot anybody as long as he's got
a new invention on his mind."

"Yes'm." Clakey picked up Miss Louise's brass-polishing smock
from the bed and handed it to her.

"Oh, *Clakey!* Why can't he be like other people? *Why?*" She
sat down in a taffeta-upholstered slipper chair and wordlessly
stuck out her plump feet. Clakey squatted in front of her and tightened and tied her shoelaces.

"I hadn't ever known nobody that was like other people,"
Clakey said. "You always talking about it, but I don't know nothing about it."

"You're just sniping, Clakey. You know what I mean. Why
couldn't he have been a planter? Or, if he had to have a hardware
store, why couldn't he run it in the ordinary way and make money
out of it? Why couldn't he be a businessman? If my father had
known I would come to this in my old age, he would have reached
out of his grave and snatched me back from the altar."

"Miss Louise," Clakey said, standing up, "I'm worried about
Nat. She ain't herself."

"*Miss* Nat," Miss Louise said absently. "Get me that orange
stick, please." She began pushing back the cuticle of her nails
to expose the half moons that are a mark of beauty in a woman's
hands. "And another thing," she said, "not a soul around here is
worrying about that model. Just because Wilburn has lent us a little money, they go along as happy as crickets on the hearth — not
a thought for tomorrow. Aubrey's hidden it. Yes, he has. No one

can convince me he hasn't. We've got to find it and . . . Morris
. . . we've got to . . ."

"Nat ain't herself," Clakey said, speaking a little bit louder.
"You taken a look at her lately?"

"She's herself, all right," Miss Louise said. "Selfish. You'd think
in a time of crisis like this she would think of *me*. But instead,
she moons around the house all day and stays out all night at parties. Although I will say, at least she's going out with Floyd Shotwell. Sometimes I think that boy is our only hope. That's why I
don't say any more to Nat than I do. Waiting. I don't want to scare
her away from him — she's so contrary, I might, if I said a word.
But when I think, when I *consider* that she could crook her little
finger at him and solve all our problems . . ."

"How she's going to solve our problems if Mr. Aubrey hid that
machine?"

"They could *persuade* . . ."

"She ain't hardly been out of her room for a week or more,"
Clakey said. "Not while I'm here, anyhow. She don't touch her
food. She's sick."

"She's had an engagement with him nearly every night this past
week," Miss Louise said. "Why doesn't she go on and marry him?"

"Miss Louise, don't you know that's a bad man?"

"No, I don't! I know Nat needs a husband and we need the
Shotwells. And I know we have to figure out some way to extricate
ourselves from this *dreadful* situation and find the model, and,
and sell the invention; and nobody — neither Nat nor Aubrey
nor anybody else — is trying to do a thing about any of it. Here."
She thrust the orange stick at Clakey and got laboriously to her
feet.

There was a padding sound of bare feet in the hall and Nat
stopped in the open doorway. Her black hair hung tangled to her
shoulders. She wore a long-sleeved cotton nightshirt, cut off above

the knees. Her slender wrists had a fragile look below the cuffed sleeves. "You don't need to worry about all that, Aunt Louise," she said. "We're going to get it straightened out. It just takes some time and patience."

"How? *How?* Don't you realize, Nat, that the money Wilburn lent us is going to run out? Then what are we going to do?"

"Floyd is going to get the machine back for Uncle Aubrey," Nat said. "And then Morris will have to go ahead with the plans like Uncle Aubrey wants him to — or else we can sell to the highest bidder." She spoke matter-of-factly. "You can see how *he* is," she said. "Uncle Aubrey. He doesn't care anymore. We can work it out so that you and Uncle Aubrey will get the money you need. In the long run, it'll be better if we sell it."

"Well! It seems to me, knowing that I'm in a state bordering on nervous collapse, you might have told me all this a little earlier," Miss Louise said.

"I was going to," Nat said. There was an expression of intense and intelligent concern in her eyes, and she reached out, as if she were about to say, "This is what's going on." But then she came into the room and stood looking around — at the spotless white organdy curtains drawn back from the windows, the white Marseilles bedspread, the ruffled green taffeta chair, the profusion of flowers on every surface, on the wallpaper, on the rug, and on the draped dressing table: great bouquets of full-blown roses, daisies, and ragged robins ("I've always been a lover of nature," Miss Louise would say.) — and instead of speaking she crossed the room and stood for a few minutes leaning one arm on the mantel above the coal grate that was never used, now that the cottage had central heating. Absently she reached out and touched the Dresden shepherdess that stood, crook in hand, gazing with empty china eyes at her male counterpart who leaned against a china stump at the other end of the mantel. "I haven't been feeling very well," she said.

"No wonder. Going barefoot in November! To say nothing of bare-legged."

"I wrote to the patent lawyer for Uncle Aubrey," Nat said. "We are getting things straight."

"And Floyd is going to bring the machine back! You see, Clakey? I knew we could depend on him to help us. When is he going to bring it? And where has it been?"

"It's too long and complicated to explain, Aunt Louise. And there are some technicalities involved. Just don't worry. He'll get it back soon — within a few weeks at the longest."

"He's a dear boy. Do you hear that, Clakey? He's a *splendid* person."

. . .

At the church that morning, sitting at the long table in the sacristy, Miss Louise opened her prayer book and, as she was accustomed to do each week before she began to polish, read to herself in a whisper the collect on the page she first looked at. Today it was: "Grant, we beseech thee, Almighty God, that we, who for our evil deeds do worthily deserve to be punished, by the comfort of thy grace may mercifully be relieved; through our Lord and Saviour Jesus Christ. Amen." It may be that this collect seemed to her today a vaguely unsatisfactory one. At any rate she leafed through the prayer book and in a few moments found another: "We beseech thee, Almighty God, look upon the hearty desires of thy humble servants and stretch forth the right hand of thy Majesty, to be our defense against all our enemies. Through Jesus Christ our Lord. Amen."

She put on her rubber gloves and set reverently to work.

In a few minutes, Miss Caroline Clayton came in and sat down beside her. A childless widow of so many years standing that most people no longer realized she had ever had a husband, she was, although younger than Miss Louise by ten years, her closest friend. "I've always preferred to associate with young people," Miss Louise would say. "It keeps me in touch with the world."

Miss Caroline had a reputation in the church and in the Blue Stockings Club for having been a beauty and a belle in her youth, but now, each year, there were fewer people to pass along the tradition of her youthful successes, and certainly no one would have guessed them from looking at her. She had been slender once; now she had the dry, papery look of one to whom the flesh — food, sex, or sunshine, perhaps even sound sleep — had lost all but distasteful meanings. Her mouth was thin; even her bones looked thin; and her head shook continuously with the tremor of incipient Parkinsonism, so that as she spoke she appeared to be denying every word she said, or making a mute comment on the stupidity and immorality of whomever she happened to be discussing. There was, however, a certain obsessive intelligence in her face. "She's exceedingly interesting company, you know," Miss Louise would say. "She knows more about hemerocallis — just to mention one subject she's an authority on — than anyone else in the state. And I don't argue with her. That way we get along."

Today, however, Miss Louise was forced to get into an argument. She had intended to devote herself with pure concentration to her work — to raise herself by this dedication above the difficulties of her life. "Things are going to be better," she had added in a whisper to God after her prayer. "I must put Aubrey and Nat and money out of my mind."

But Miss Caroline plunged into conversation as soon as she sat down at the long oak table, taking the precaution only of glancing about the room to see that they would not be overheard and observing that the three younger women seated at the other end of the table were chattering about their own affairs.

"Louise," she said in a low voice, "I knew you'd be here this morning. I've been wanting to talk to you for several days — that is, not wanting to, putting it off, really, because it's an unpleasant subject. But I felt I *had* to — just had to, in spite of my own feelings. And I said to myself, I'll put it off until Thursday, and we can talk at Altar Guild, and that will give me time to be absolutely sure I'm right, and . . ."

"Don't talk to me about anything unpleasant, if you can avoid it, dear," Miss Louise said. She rubbed briskly at the base of a candlestick. "I've been *bowed down* with family troubles lately. It's all too complicated to talk about, and in fact, I don't really understand a great deal of it, myself; but I am not exaggerating, Caroline, when I say it involves treachery, violence, and *money!* Aubrey's attack last week is just the latest in a series of misfortunes and, although I am hopeful that things may take a turn for the better, it's possible we haven't seen the worst of it yet."

"Well, I'm sorry, Louise, but I simply cannot avoid telling you about this. My conscience would give me no peace." Miss Caroline's head shook like a cottonwood leaf in the wind.

Miss Louise's blue eyes opened wider. She picked up a toothbrush and, dipping it in polish, began to scrub at the raised design on the shank of the candlestick. "I'd rather do anything than these candlesticks," she muttered. "Too ornate." She drew a deep breath and added, "May the Lord be my witness, Caroline, I don't want to hear about any more trouble today."

"Louise, Dr. Parsons has seen your niece — *Natalie* — coming out of the Family Rest Motel twice *at night,* or rather, in the morning, because it was broad open daylight, six A.M." Miss Caroline spoke in a sibilant whisper, fairly whistling the "s" in "twice."

"You know he goes every week to read X-rays at the clinic in Moss Ridge, and he stops there for coffee on his way out of town. He saw her and a man — he thinks it was Floyd Shotwell — come out of a cabin in the back and get into a car and drive away."

"These young people," Miss Louise said. "Nat *will* stay up all night partying and having a good time. I know it's not good for her, but she will go . . ."

"That is not the conclusion Dr. Parsons drew when he saw her," Miss Caroline said. "And it was not her health he was concerned about. She had an overnight bag."

"Really, Caroline! Are you inferring that *Nat* — that a *Hunter*, whose great-great grandmother was a Griffith . . !" She scrubbed furiously at her candlestick. "I don't care to hear any more about it," she said. "I told you to begin with not to talk to me about trouble."

"Implying," Miss Caroline said. "Dr. Parsons *inferred* from the bag and *implied* to me, and I'm telling you."

"And you needn't correct my grammar, either," Miss Louise said.

"Really, Louise, you're living in the past. Young people are not what they were when you were growing up or, for that matter, when I was. In fact, it is the conviction of a great many well-informed people that our society has become exceedingly decadent. How else can we explain the fact that the very fabric of our national life is saturated through and through with communism, atheism, and flagrant sexual immorality?"

"Well, Nat is certainly not a communist," Miss Louise said. "And my blood pressure is going up so fast I can feel it in the top of my head. You had better hush, or I may faint right here in the sacristy."

"It's your duty to listen to me, if you have a shred of family feeling left," Miss Caroline said. "After all, this is as painful to me as it is to you. But it is a matter about which measures will have to be taken." She paused, but Miss Louise said no more. She had taken off her rubber gloves and was sitting with her elbows on the table and both hands on top of her head, as if to keep it from blowing off. "I did my best to scotch it," Miss Caroline said. "'No!' I told him. 'You're bound to be mistaken.' But *he* said, 'I'd know Nat Hunter anywhere. That figure is unmistakable.'

"Well, all I could say was, 'That's a tale you do *not* have to repeat, Francis Parsons, if you have a drop of Christian charity in your veins. You could file it under the Hippocratic oath or something. Because the blow would be too much for Louise Hunter at her age — with her high moral standards.' That was *all* I could do. And so I felt I had to come straight to you — because, of course, he *will* repeat it — to anyone who'll listen. He's a gossip just like his father was before him. Do you remember how old Dr. Parsons used to go out to the courthouse and read all the wills and then spread the contents of them over three counties? So, in my opinion, you had better have it out with Nat right away. It seems to me it would be a good thing for her to leave Philippi for a while. 'Time heals all wounds,' and people will eventually forget. But right *now* — you know yourself, Louise, that Philippi — *our* Philippi, *Old* Philippi — is not going to countenance flagrant immorality. Are you listening to me, Louise?"

"I simply do not believe it," Miss Louise said. "He's a vicious gossip. Besides," she added weakly, "they're engaged . . . I *think*."

.   .   .

"So that's the story she tells me," Clakey Morrison said to Sarah Henry later on the same day. "She says, 'Miss Caroline told me so and so, Clakey, and I says to her, well, it's *not* true, Caroline Clayton, and besides, they're en-gaged.' " Clakey mimicked Miss Louise's delicate, ladylike way of speaking. "Ain't that the limit, Sarah? 'I'm going to speak to Nat,' she says, and gets that kind of blank look in her eyes that she gets when she's thinking about one thing and pretending it's another. 'It's no use for Caroline Clayton to say Nat ought to leave town,' she says, 'right now when . . .' But she don't finish that. Instead she says again, 'I'm going to speak to Nat and caution her to be, more, more, uh, *circumspeck* in her behavior.' " Clakey laughed drily.

" 'You going to tell her to quit what she's doing?' I say, 'Or you going to tell her to quit letting people see her?'

" 'She's not *doing* anything,' she says, 'but a young woman has to guard her reputation.' "

Clakey and Sarah were sitting with their chairs drawn up to the butane heater in the front room of Sarah's tiny house. The room — half bedroom, half living room — was crowded with furniture: a double bed in one corner, a small heater against the back wall, a sofa and several chairs around the heater. Two double beds took up most of the space in the back room of the house. Sarah had a daughter and several grandchildren living with her.

Today, however, the children were at school and the daughter out. Sarah and Clakey were alone. Clakey had taken off her shoes and, with one ankle cocked on the other knee, was rubbing absently at a bunion on her foot. "My Jesus," she said. "This foot's going to be the death of me."

"Try soaking it in epsom salts," Sarah said.

"I ought to try retiring and getting off of it," Clakey said. "I'm due for my Social Security next year."

Sarah, leaning back in her rocker, picked up a piece of quilting and began to run a delicate line of featherstitching down the side.

"My, that's pretty," Clakey said. "I believe you are about the only person left in this part of the country can make a pretty quilt."

"Thank you," Sarah said. She glanced up. "So anyhow," she said, "go on. Then what happened?"

"Well, I told you last week I was worried about Nat, and by today I knew what was going on. So I say, 'For Lord's sake, Miss Louise, let Nat alone. That's my advice. She's got troubles, and she's dealing with 'em the best way she can.'

" 'Troubles!' she says. 'We've all got troubles. If it wasn't for Wilburn Griffith, I wouldn't have the money to pay your salary,' she says, 'and that's the truth.'

"But I wasn't going to let her get away with it. I thought to myself, this is one time I'm going to bring her up to the lick law. She's going to look facts straight in the head. 'Her troubles is your troubles, Miss Louise,' I say. '*He* — I mean that Shotwell man — he's got that machine someplace, and she's trying to get it back from him. And the fact is, I *know* it, because she told me.' But Sarah, I didn't tell her the full entire truth. I actually couldn't make myself say to her: He's making Nat sleep with him.

"So she says, 'I don't believe *that* for a minute.'

" 'Don't you see she ain't herself?' I say.

" 'I see she don't eat a bite. She'll end up with ulcers and galloping consumption, if she don't stop starving that precious figure of hers.'

" 'He's the one causing it,' I say. 'Comes around here to get her. Bangs up onto the porch, don't no more speak to me than if I was a post. So I don't speak to him. I don't say good morning or nothing. I just look at him. Finally, like he can barely get it out, he says, "Where is she? Tell her I'm here." And when I call her, she gets up and goes out to him, and he takes her on off like a old rag doll drug on a piece of string.'

" 'It's not your place to talk about Miss Nat's friends in that disrespectful way,' she says. 'Didn't I tell you she's going to marry him? Didn't she say herself this morning he's the one going to get the machine back? And how did we get off on this, anyway?' she says. 'All I'm talking about is what Caroline Clayton told me at church today. And I'm going to caution Nat about considering the appearance of things. That's all I'm talking about,' she says, 'and that's all I want to hear about.'

" '*I'm* telling you,' I said, 'old as you is, you better open your eyes and look at the world and you better look at Nat.' (I still couldn't come out and say it. Too many years I got the habit of saying to white people — even her, stupid as she is — what they want to hear.) 'Something queer is going on with her, something turrible,' I say, 'And that man is behind it.'

" 'Cook, mind your kitchen,' she says and switches on off, mad as can be."

Clakey's dark pockmarked face was grim. "Well, I'm used to that," she said. "Her idea of winning a argument is to leave before you can answer the last thing she says. Usually she goes out still talking and mutters the last of it (which is probably something about *darkies*) under her breath. But I never have let nothing she says bother me." A brief smile touched the wide stern mouth. "I got two things to consider," she said. "Me and Nat. You know I've loved Nat from the day she walked into my kitchen the first time. I always have been partial to a spunky child — and one with no put-on about her. As for *me*, with my reputation, I could quit the Hunters tomorrow and take my pick of jobs cooking for the best people in Philippi. Maybe even making more money than they pay me, although God knows it's not likely anybody in Philippi is going to pay a good cook what she's worth. The truth is, I would've left them after Nat grew up, but there were things that kept me there. One thing about Miss Louise, she is naturally the kind of woman a good cook likes to work for. She takes pleasure in my work and that's the truth. She likes the old-fashioned way I run my kitchen and she don't stint ingredients. If a recipe says butter, she ain't going to say, 'Use margarine.' In fact, she wouldn't have a stick of margarine in her icebox. Also, I'm not young. It's too late for me to change — I'm used to her ways and she's used to mine. So there you are: It's a poor substitute for love, but it's the best we got.

"But the fact of the matter, Sarah: If I'm going to stay on there another day, somebody's got to take a hand in this mess. I can't look at Nat no longer. And I'm afraid the rest of 'em are going to land in the poor house — or Whitfield. So, soon as I finished up the dishes today, I come on out here. Caught a ride with my nephew who was going down to Greenville and will pick me up on his way back. Because I figure I need some advice, and you might be the one to give it to me."

Sarah continued to run her needle deftly in and out of the piece of quilting for some moments without saying anything. Then, "Let me study awhile," she said.

Clakey nodded and the two women, one dark and squat and muscular, the other gaunt, with a skin as tawny as a tiger's, sat over the fire like two carved figures, their faces lapsing into the practiced stillness of bearers of secrets.

After a while Sarah said, "Mr. Griffith would do something, if we could figure what to tell him. Don't necessarily want him to get all fired up and kill Floyd Shotwell, though, do we?" At the thought of this possibility, however, a suppressed tension made the muscles in her arms and shoulders quiver, and an expression came into her eyes like that in a boy's who is watching a good fight.

"It's probably a fact that Mr. Griffith is the only one can help us," Clakey said. "That's the main reason I come to see *you*."

"Well, we got to figure out what to tell him and what we want him to do," Sarah said again.

"I wouldn't care if he did kill him," Clakey said.

"What makes you so sure *he* — Shotwell — is making her go to bed with him?"

"She told me. I asked her this morning why she was drooping around the house like a chicken with the pip; and she said she'd agreed to do it, and in return he was going to give 'em back the machine. But who could believe that's what he's really going to do?"

"I slept with more than one man out of necessity," Sarah said, "and so have you."

Clakey did not answer.

Sarah smiled. "They in a mess," she said, "and that's the truth." She continued to stitch and smile.

"I'm talking about helping Nat," Clakey said.

"All right. All right. I'm studying. And this is what I think. First we got to find out where that machine is. You can't do nothing without that. Now let's sit here and figure out who might give us a lead on it."

"Well, there's Mr. Lee Gillespie and Mr. Ernest Goldsmith," Clakey said. "They was working at the store the weekend it got carried off. They might've seen something I don't know about."

"We'll call 'em," Sarah said. "Also, I know Mrs. Burton — the Shotwells' cook. She might've heard something around there. That's a turrible lot of people, them Shotwells, she says. Stay shut up in their own rooms and don't hardly even look at each other, much less talk."

"Let's start with them, then," Clakey said. "Lee and Ernest and Mrs. Burton. See what we can find out from them and then decide what to do next."

After her first telephone conversation — with Lee Gillespie — she turned thoughtfully to Sarah. "He says that man, Pruitt, the gambler, was in the hardware store all afternoon the day before they missed the machine, talking crazy to Miss Louise. You know who I'm talking about? That's the only thing happened out of the ordinary. But Pruitt got Miss Louise to open up the back of the store, and he saw it back there. You suppose . . . ?"

Sarah slapped her hands together. "Mr. Royal," she said. "Deacon Royal of the New White Stone Church. He works nights at that gambling club. If Pruitt is mixed up in it, he'll know about it."

They telephoned Mr. Royal and made an appointment, and when Clakey's nephew came back from Greenville, the two of them rode into town with him. "I can't resist," Sarah said. "I got to hear the rest of this tale. I can catch a ride to the country in the morning with that peckerwood, Doy Moore, works at the commissary — that is, if you'll let me spend the night at your house."

. . .

Mr. Royal — Kilroy — heard Clakey out silently as they sat together in the comfortable living room of his brick bungalow in Philippi. Mr. Royal owned and lived in one of the most impressive Negro houses in the town; it had three bedrooms, a full bath, hardwood floors, and a paneled den. Only doctors and undertakers were housed as well as he. He was a man of considerable prestige among his associates — among all the people of the Negro community. He had five children: a son now working on his M.A. degree at Purdue University, two sons at the University of Illinois, and two daughters in high school. He had been at one time (and his wife still was) a teacher at the Carver High School in Philippi; but the exigencies of raising and educating his children had forced him into other fields. He had bought a cab and had begun to drive after school every day. Then he had bought another, and now he owned a fleet of five taxis, one of which he still drove for a six-hour shift before he went on duty at the gambling club in the evening. He also owned sixty acres of farmland, thirty more than the small piece that had been left him by his father, who had been an independent farmer and professional hunter all his life.

In his own living room, Mr. Royal no longer seemed the wisp of a man that he appeared to be when he was effacing himself at The General's club. He was thin, but his thinness was tense and wiry and his long, dark face was alert and ascetic. On the wall behind him was a gun rack with his father's guns on it, and on either side of the rack, pictures of his father, one with a bear he had trapped and let loose at the right place and time for it to be shot by the president of the Southern Railroad who had come down from Washington, D.C., to shoot a bear; the other with a mule team of which he had been particularly proud. Above the mantel was a bad oil painting of his wife done by one of his daughters and on the opposite wall photographs of all his children. He sat among the possessions and accomplishments of his family, his beautiful dark eyes intent and interested, while Clakey told her story.

"We thought maybe you could help us," Clakey said when she had finished. "That you might've heard something out there . . ."

He nodded. "I know some things," he said. His voice was deep, his manner detached. "I can probably help you — or rather I can tell you what I know. Whether I would really be helping you is another matter." He lapsed into silence.

"Well . . ." Clakey said. She broke off.

"I'm considered a silent man — stupid, I suppose," Mr. Royal said. "That is, among white people. You know my reputation. Pruitt is mainly responsible for that. And, of course, I never say a word to that son of a bitch, if I can avoid it. But, as *you* know very well, Mrs. Henry, from our work together in the church, I'm a speaker when the occasion calls for it. True, I speak slowly. I used to have a stammer and I cured myself of it. Did you know that? Also, I have an excellent memory for conversation — you might say I have trained myself to stay silent and to remember anything that might be useful to me. Out *there* — at the club — I seldom hear anything useful, anything but filth and stupidity; but I continue to listen. Once in a while somebody reasonably intelligent is in the game, and once in a while he'll . . . Well, it was out there, for example, that I learned that seven acres of land along Okatukla Creek were going on the market — the best land on my place. But none of that's relevant to what you ladies are talking about." He turned his thin dark face thoughtfully from one to the other of the two women. "So you want to know what's been going on between Shotwell and The General," he said, and, lapsing into a kind of mock Negro dialect, "Y'all wants to he'p yo' white folks. Ain't that *fine!*" He paused. "It's none of my business what kind of relations you *darkies* have with white people," he said, "but there's one thing I have to say. You'll be better off if you stay clear of that mess. Let 'em stew in that pot they're brewing up for themselves."

"They ain't none of my white folks," Sarah said. "Mrs. Morrison come to me chiefly because I work for Mr. Griffith and I could get his ear for her, if we need to. I got no interest in it but curiosity."

"You might as well come down off that high horse, Mr. Royal," Clakey said. "We know you're an educated man and we have respect for you. But I don't hate these people. And Nat! Well, Nat might as well be black, as far as I'm concerned."

"Mrs. Morrison, you can't help being sentimental, can you?"

"You keep that hate coiled up inside you like a rattlesnake long enough," Clakey said, "and it's going to strike out one of these days at a white man and hit your own instead."

"Clakey, we asking a favor of Mr. Royal, and you gonna offend him," Sarah said.

"No, no," he said. "I'm not offended. You ladies can white-folks yourselves into the grave, as far as I'm concerned." He sat back in his easy chair and took a cigar from a box on the table beside him.

"I got to live in God's world," Clakey said. "I don't waste myself. So you just tell me what you know and I'll use it the best I can."

Mr. Royal spent some moments lighting his cigar. "But mind you, when you do (die, that is)," he finally said, "pay attention to who comes to your funeral. If any of those Griffiths and Hunters condescend to show up, you can sit up there with Marse Jesus afterwards and listen to 'em describe to their *friends* how quaint and amusing it all was."

"Have your say," Clakey said.

"My name is Kilroy," he said. "Hadn't you heard? I been there." But he told them, after all, first of the conversation between Floyd and The General the night Pruitt learned about the machine, then of the conversation after Floyd returned from Jackson, and finally of something that had happened just a few days earlier.

"We were driving out to the club as usual," he said "(Pruitt picks me up at the taxi stand at about six o'clock on the nights he's got a game going.), and we started on out to the country. Well, we turned the corner there by the Gulf station on Muscadine and Highway sixty-one, and there's Shotwell sitting in the station getting that Cadillac gassed up. Pruitt sees him, slams on the brakes, turns in there, and hops out of the car.

" 'Say,' he says, 'I was expecting you at the club last night and the night before last. I been expecting you for several days, called your house three, four times and never could get you. Where you been?'

"Shotwell is standing by his car, rubbing at a little piece of dirt on the hood and he doesn't even look up. 'I've been busy,' he says.

" 'How about that deal we were talking about?' Pruitt says. 'You made any progress?'

" 'We're not going to do that after all,' Shotwell says.

" 'What do you mean, we're not going to do it?'

" 'We're just not, that's all. I made other arrangements.'

"Well, Pruitt pulls that handkerchief out of his pocket and starts rolling it around like a crawfish with a mudball. 'Maybe you're not,' he says, 'but that don't stop me. If you ain't got the nerve to negotiate, just leave it to me.'

" 'You haven't got the machine anymore,' Shotwell says, just as calm as if he was saying, 'It looks like rain.' He's satisfied with the looks of his hood now, and he opens the door of his car, to get in, not paying any attention to Pruitt, so Pruitt has to jump out of the way to keep from getting hit by the door. 'I went down to the jail where you said it was and picked it up. And I've made my own arrangements.' He looks straight at Pruitt with those cold black eyes. 'This is not a good deal for you to be in on,' he says. 'Maybe we can work out something for you later.'

"I wish you could have seen him." Mr. Royal laughed reminiscently. "I don't know when I've seen anything that's given me so much pleasure. Pruitt — he turned a kind of dark purple. He looked like a plum just starting to shrivel into a prune; and he began to tremble all over. But still I could see his eyes darting. He was figuring, figuring — looking for a hole to scuttle through. But the poor bastard is not very smart, you know. He's just found a way to make a lot of money out of people who have the same nutty obsessions he has.

"The tears actually came into his eyes when he realized that that big deal was slipping away from him. 'I can't understand it,

Floyd,' he says. 'I did it all for you. I treated you like a brother, and now you're going to double-cross me out of it. That ain't *right*,' he says. 'It's immoral! I *trusted* you.'

" 'That's where you made your mistake,' Shotwell says. 'I told you I didn't care about anything but Nat. Didn't I?' And he hands the gas station fellow some money and starts up the car.

" 'Wait,' Pruitt says, 'Wait. We got to talk this over.' He reaches in through the window and puts his hand on Shotwell's arm.

"Shotwell sits there a minute gripping the wheel and then he says, not even looking up, *'There's nothing to talk about.'*

" 'What about the money you owe me?' Pruitt says. 'What about that?'

" 'Don't worry,' he says. 'I'll pay you one of these days. But I haven't got time to think about it now.'

" 'Haven't got time!' Pruitt yells and kind of shakes him by the arm. 'What do you mean, you haven't got time?'

" 'Take your hand off my arm,' Shotwell says. And then, without waiting to see if he will, Shotwell guns the motor and whips out of there. Pruitt's arm slams against the side of the window frame, the car brushes against him — that big tail fin, I reckon — and the next thing you know, he's sitting on the ground yelling.

" 'You'll never get in a decent game in this county again,' Pruitt hollers. He's actually crying. 'In this state!' he hollers. 'Never! You hear me?'

"But of course Shotwell didn't. He was gone. He never looked back. And he hasn't *been* back."

"But where is the machine?" Sarah said. "That's what we want to know."

"Oh, I forgot to tell you. That's the greatest part of all. He told him where it is! 'It's in my house,' he says. 'I had it stored out in the country, but I decided I'd better put it where I could keep an eye on it. It's locked up in my room. Nobody goes in there but me.

And that's where it's going to stay until I'm ready to move it. And if you think you're going to break in over there and take it, think again. Also,' he says, 'I wouldn't advise you to tell my father or anybody else anything about its being there, because if you get in my way, I'll kill you.'"

Mr. Royal turned his long, sensitive, arrogant face from one to the other of the two women. Clakey looked back at him thoughtfully and said nothing. Sarah was smiling.

"I do like to hear a good story," she said. "And this story about these white people getting so stirred up over a washing machine . . ." She shook her head. "And it ain't over yet," she said. "Not by a long shot."

"Well, that's all there is to my part of it," Mr. Royal said. "Use it as you like. But remember what I said about funerals."

Clakey's ordinary austerity relaxed for a moment and a look of compassion crossed her face. "You men!" she said. "You're not tough enough. The best of you will never be tough enough."

"That's an easy thing for a woman to say," Mr. Royal replied. "But it all depends on what kind of tough is needed when."

19

When Wilburn stopped outside his kitchen door at noon
the next day to scrape the mud from his boots before coming in
for lunch, Sarah Henry was striding about the kitchen, clashing
pots together and singing in a strong contralto:

> Redeemed, redeemed, redeemed.
> Oh, I—I—I been washed in the blood
> of the Lamb.

As soon as she saw Wilburn, she broke off to say that she needed
to talk with him.

"Me and Clakey," she said, "(That's Miss Louise Hunter's
cook.) got a kind of complicated story to tell you. Clakey don't
really want to. She's afraid it won't make nothing but trouble.
But I say we got no place else to turn so we got to chance it."

Wilburn felt an immediate revulsion from hearing about anybody else's troubles, particularly troubles he might have to deal
with, but all he said was, "All right, Sarah, tell on."

"We don't want to talk to you here." She jerked her head toward the bedroom. "Don't want Miss Sunny to be bothered with it for one thing, sick as she is and all. And for another, don't want the nurse or nobody to hear it. In fact, Mr. Griffith, it's more your business than it is ours. So, if we could come to your office some time today . . ."

"All right," he said. "What time will you be through here?"

"Around two-thirty. But Clakey's in town and she probably can't make it out here before four."

"That suits me," he said. "You all come over to the commissary around four-thirty and I'll be there."

At four he was already sitting in his commissary office staring out the window. The year's work was almost finished. The gin across the road still clanked and vibrated, but the dozens of waiting cotton wagons had been reduced to two or three. The fields to the north of the gin had been stripped of everything but a few trashy scraps of cotton clinging to the bare stalks, and in those to the south the stalks had already been cut and the land broken out. Wilburn gazed out at his bare fields and at the heavy November sky and, absently, at the surface of his mind, listed to himself the things that needed to be done on the place during the next week or two. Then he turned to his desk and began to look through the stack of seed tickets and due bills that had accumulated on his desk during the time he had been in Jackson. He checked names and numbers and made an occasional note in his ledger.

He worked quickly and accurately, but he was thinking of other things. Below the practical problems that had occupied him during the past two weeks (He had had to travel from Jackson to Philippi and back several times, spending a few hours in Philippi, arranging his children's affairs and his business, riding over the place, writing checks, and making lists of instructions.) his mind had seethed like an anthill kicked open. He had not seen or talked to Nat during this time. He had not had time, or so he told himself; and besides, she needed a breather, a chance to recover and to be quiet. But he had *thought*.

Driving, whistling to himself in the car, going through the motions of eating, in the hospital coffee shop, meals that tasted like sodden newspaper, sitting by Sunny's bed and delivering messages from their children and friends, he would see without warning his vision of the rape: Floyd, his clothes kicked half off, stumbling over his own trousers, his heavy, white body looming in the quivering fluorescent light. Then, Nat, forced down on the bed, the pillow descending. He would see Nat with that huge white hand over her face, the fingers digging into her brown skin, hear the obscene whisper, see her spread her legs obediently. And at this his thoughts would break off with: Suppose she's pregnant? From *that!* He would feel the running of saliva in his mouth, as if he were about to vomit, and a heavy burning stone of frustration in his belly would heave and turn. Then, not likely, he would think. Not very likely. And to control the revulsion of his body, he would try to think about the Hunters' financial situation. As soon as I get things going at home on an even keel — sometimes he spoke aloud, just to hear himself speak — I'll call Nat and we'll try to straighten them out. We'll be able to make something work. He would begin to explore as many alternatives as he could think of — ways to make Louise and Aubrey self-sufficient, if it turned out that, after all, they wouldn't make any money from the washing machine. But he could not occupy himself for long with these practical considerations. His mind kept returning to Floyd, to Nat.

And then, every time, as if there were some tie between the two, he would think of Sunny and of his own life, in an uncontrollable fierce way that he did not recognize in himself and did not know how to deal with. He would feel in himself a sickness of lust and frustration beyond his own knowledge of himself. He wanted a woman, any woman. Not Sunny, he would think, not that fat white slug of a body. But the existence of his lust, after Nat's rape and Sunny's pain, seemed, in the very physical moment of his knowing it, obscene. He would push it violently down and take up again old thoughts of making his marriage work: As soon as she's well enough, we have to confront each other, to be open with each other, to love.

Impossible! his mind would say. And besides, why should we? Why even try it? I've got in my head some sentimental, marriage-counselor's notion that a man and his wife can expose themselves, can love without reservation. Pursuing a silly seductive dream. Never was and never will be.

And he would say to himself, full of contempt and rage, I'm like a woman. Women go over their lives in this obsessive way. A man acts. He gets drunk, or gets a mistress or leaves, or — all three.

During this time it seemed to Wilburn that he began to feel a hatred for himself, a revulsion from the confusions which his own mind held steadily before him, a shattering of his knowledge of himself, that could never be mended. He felt himself staggering like a man in an earthquake. The world shook, and he knew that one more quiver might split apart his stable carefully constructed piece of it. He would beat his hands on the steering wheel of his car or grip the thick handle of his coffee cup as if to crush it.

Who can help me? Who can help me? That was his cry.

In answer, he heard the roar of the wind past the windows of his car, the clatter of the coffee shop china, the silence of the night sky.

And then, without warning or reason, something else would happen. For a moment, in the midst of confusion and sickness, he would feel a surge of vitality and self-confidence, of pure happiness, as if he were a boy. I am intelligent and healthy, he would think, full of life and energy, able to make things work. But the feeling would dissipate, and he would be left stranded on another quivering mudflat of inaction, pursuing fantasies down the tortuous convolutions of his brain, half-convinced that he was insane.

Today, sitting in his commissary office, checking seed tickets while he waited for Sarah and Clakey, Wilburn still felt himself to be a kind of battleground, lying passive under the charging battalions of his dreams and passions. Methodically he added a figure to the neat row in his ledger and framed his thoughts in complete sentences, as if good grammar might produce order and sanity.

My life has been impinged on by a piece of chaos, he said to himself. I have always known, from the very beginning of growing up, that order is fragile, that I have nothing with which to shore it up except the strength and steadiness of my own arms. I constructed this tiny, fragile piece of order — a faithful wife, children, my own fields, work I love — and called it reality, and now something has happened to it. I have put Nat's way of looking at the world over against it and have admitted somewhere inside myself — corruption. She sees and has made me see my reality — that pure, fragile order — as a dream. Good dreams, bad dreams, what difference does it make, when one admits the possibility of waking? It's as if she had fired a shell into the wall of my reality, a jagged piece of chaos into my gut. I'm like a soldier with a live shell in his gut. In a war, doctors would build a wall of sandbags around me and put their hands through holes in the wall to operate and cut the shell out.

He got up abruptly, his own words echoing in his head as if someone else had said them aloud, walked out of the commissary, and crossed the road to the gin. There, he climbed up into the trailer where one of his men, standing hip-deep in seed cotton, was guiding the nozzle of the sucker around the bed of the trailer sucking up the cotton as if with a gigantic vacuum cleaner. He tapped the man on the shoulder. "Mote," he shouted, cupping his hands to make his voice heard over the roar, "go get the tarps that Clarence stacked in the tractor shed yesterday and cover those trailers. It looks like it's going to rain. I'll do this."

The Negro man looked at him in astonishment. "James up there in the gin doing nothing, Mr. Wilburn. He'll take over for me. You git on down."

"Go ahead," Wilburn said. "I'll call him."

He spent the next twenty minutes wrestling with the heavy hose, guiding the sucker over the cotton, his brain stunned by the uproar, until he saw Sarah and Clakey strolling down the road toward the commissary. Only then, remembering his appointment with them, did he swing himself down from the trailer, shout for James to come take his place, brush the lint from his khaki work clothes, and walk across the road to the commissary.

After Clakey and Sarah had told him everything they knew, he sent them away. Then he sat for a time in the commissary, the roar of the sucker still beating against his ears. After a while, he got up, got into his pickup truck outside the commissary, went home, went quietly into his house, took down a .22 pistol and some bullets from a high shelf in the closet in his study, and left again, without speaking to anyone. He got into his truck, loaded the gun, put it on the seat beside him, and started toward town.

By the time he had driven half the distance to Philippi, he had thought of half a dozen reasons to turn around and go home. In the first place, he thought, how do I know for sure that what they told me is true? How can I be certain they're not trying to make trouble for reasons of their own or for no reason. He recalled how Sarah had been singing like a bird in the kitchen at noon when he had come in:

Redeemed, redeemed, redeemed.
Oh, I—I—I been washed in the blood
of the Lamb.

And this fellow, Kilroy — Royal — what do I know about him? He pressed his foot down harder on the accelerator. Or Nat may have told Clakey that he was *making* her sleep with him for reasons of *her* own, he thought. Cynical. She's always used people. But what use would a fantastic lie like that be to her? And besides, she never lies. Then: Maybe she doesn't mind, he thought. Maybe she even likes it, or it's worth it to her for the money she thinks they're going to get out of the damn machine. What do I know about her feelings except what she chooses to tell me? And besides, it's none of my business. My responsibility is to Sunny and the children. I don't need to get mixed up in this at all. Sunny's sick. And even Nat — if she'd wanted help, she would have called me, wouldn't she?

He heard the whistle of an approaching freight train on the tracks that paralleled the road and for half a mile he kept ahead of it. At the crossing he thought, if I had had to wait, I would have had time to think. But he did not have to wait.

For a few minutes then, he slowed down, but as he drew nearer to Philippi, the muscles in his legs and arms tensed. He gripped the steering wheel of the truck and pressed gradually harder on the accelerator. At the same time, he was saying aloud to himself, "I'm not going to have anything to do with it!" At the city limits he saw the speed limit sign and slowed down, braking the truck and cursing himself for he was not sure what reasons.

A goddamned washing machine, he thought, and laughed aloud. All this craziness over a washing machine. It's not possible! I'm going to turn around and go home. But instead he drove straight through the town without hesitation and out into the suburb where the Shotwells lived. I'll call the police, he thought.

No sense in this. Get a search warrant, go into the house, get the machine, and take it back to Nat. That's all that needs to be done. But he was quite sure there would be nothing simple about getting a search warrant and persuading the police to go into Morris Shotwell's house.

When he came to the block the house was in, he slowed to ten miles an hour and drove past. It was almost six o'clock now, already getting dark. He could see the shadowy bulk of two cars, one of them Floyd's, parked in the carport. He drove to the corner, turned the truck around in a driveway, and came back. This time, as he passed the house, Marigold came out of a side door, followed by a Negro woman. They got into her car, Marigold in the front seat and the woman in the back, and drove away.

For all the world as if Marigold were the chauffeur, Wilburn thought.

At the corner, he turned the truck around again and this time he pulled up in the Shotwells' driveway and stopped. He picked up the pistol and put it in his pocket. I've got to use something to threaten him with, he thought. He could pick me up and break me in half if he wanted to. Then: *A .22 caliber pistol is not going to stop him.* A scene from an old movie began to play itself for him. The zombi approaches the hero — stiff-legged, arms outstretched. Behind the hero a beautiful girl is cowering. The hero fires shot after shot at the zombi, but it continues to approach, unhurt, hands outstretched. *It's going to choke me to death.*

Wilburn walked up the front steps and rang the doorbell. No one answered. The house was dark except for a light in a bedroom on the north side. He walked around to the door Marigold had come out of and knocked. Then he tried the door and, finding it unlocked, opened it and walked into the kitchen.

"Anybody home?" he called, as politely as a neighbor dropping in with flowers or fresh vegetables warm from a summer garden.

There was no answer.

He groped for the wall switch and turned on the kitchen light. The room was neat and empty, the counters bare except for a pile of wax fruit in a wooden bowl, with a row of shining copper molds hanging above it, arranged as if for an illustration in a house magazine. Wilburn sniffed the air, but there was no trace of the smell of food in the house. He opened his eyes wider, as if he might see something he had overlooked, and rubbed his hand against the lump of the pistol in his pocket. "Floyd?" he called.

He opened a door and looked down a long empty hall, its walls bare and painted a pale rose. At the end a crack of light showed under a door. He walked down the hall, running his hand along the wall to orient himself in the semidarkness. Standing in front of the door, he said again, loudly, "Floyd?" No one answered, but inside the room he heard the sound of creaking, as of someone getting up from a bed, and in a moment a key turned in the lock, and the door opened.

"Who is it?" Floyd stood in the lighted doorway, a book in his hand, his finger marking his place.

He was reading, Wilburn thought. *How could that be?* He tried desperately to see the title of the book, as if it might give him a key to Floyd's mind — might change everything. At the same time he felt the blood thudding in his head and the queer tingling surge of adrenaline in his fingertips.

It seemed to Wilburn that everything was happening very slowly. Floyd stood for a long time peering out into the dark hall before he spoke again. He was wearing a pair of khaki pants and a sleeveless undershirt. His sloping shoulders and long powerful arms, the small head that always seemed somehow more solid, the bones made of a heavier, more rocklike substance than an ordinary fragile human skull, were outlined by the light behind him. Wil-

burn could see beyond him pieces of a bare uncarpeted room —
the corner of a bed, a pile of books stacked on the floor against one
wall, and, directly opposite the door, at the far end of the room, a
large cardboard carton. It crossed his mind that Floyd's room
looked like the room of someone who is just moving out.

Wilburn put his hand in his pocket and took hold of the little
pistol. "I want the washing machine, Floyd," he said.

"What? Who is it?" Floyd touched the wall switch beside his
door and a light came on in the hall. "Wilburn?" He smiled and
raised his hand as if in a gesture of welcome. "What are you doing here?" he said.

"I came to get the washing machine. That's all. Just give it to
me." Wilburn felt a pounding and pressure in his ears, as if he
were deep under water.

Floyd still smiled, as if in welcome. But he shook his head
slowly. "Go home," he said. "It's none of your business."

Wilburn took the pistol from his pocket and held it out, lying
flat on his palm. "I have to take it with me," he said apologetically.
"I have to have it." *Is that my voice I hear?* he thought. *Am I
stupid enough to think he's going to give it to me?*

Floyd looked at the gun, shook his head, and said nothing.

"I'm sorry about everything," Wilburn said. "Even sorry for
you."

Floyd reached out slowly, as if to take the gun. "Things may
change," he said. "I mean for Nat and me."

Wilburn drew back and shifted the gun in his hand so that his
finger was on the trigger. "Sorry for all of us," he repeated.
"Sunny . . . what a mess for Sunny, if I have to shoot you. Over
a washing machine. Nobody would believe people could get into
such a mess over a washing machine."

"It's not over a washing machine," Floyd said. "And you don't
think it is. Go home, Wilburn. You don't want to shoot me. You

haven't thought about it, but you don't. You don't want to do me any favors, do you? And I don't really care if you shoot me, see? I might even be glad if you did. You haven't thought about that."

"I have to take it back to Nat, that's all," Wilburn said. "Get out of my way." He could see that Floyd was not going to move, and he knew that he could not move him. He had an instant's vision of himself beating against that rocklike body, and then a memory of himself as a child in a mock sparring match with his father — a battle in which his father, laughing, held him off with a long arm, while he felt his birthmark burn scarlet and flailed away until he wept from rage and frustration.

Floyd spoke in a low peaceful voice, his face open as Wilburn had never seen it, his whole manner gentle and filled with what appeared to be pity. "What a mess you're getting ready to get yourself into," he said. Then, again: "Things may change for Nat and me. That's why you can't have it, see? He moved forward and again reached for the gun, but this time Wilburn backed off, aimed deliberately at the little finger of the reaching hand, and pulled the trigger. The hand began to drip blood on the polished oak floor. The bullet thudded into the wall and a chunk of plaster dropped and shattered on the floor. Floyd flinched, but he continued to move forward.

The second time Wilburn shot, he aimed carefully at a point far out on Floyd's right shoulder. The bullet, fired point-blank from just six feet away, struck Floyd's shoulder, and he staggered and caught himself against the door frame.

"Don't do it, Wilburn," he said, his voice still kind and calm.

Wilburn stepped lightly forward, stretched out his foot, and, jerking quickly, tripped him. Floyd fell. His head struck the edge of the side rail of his bed and he lay still.

Oh, God, I've killed him, Wilburn thought, as bitterly as if he had not been shooting at him. What a goddamned mess. I'll have to get a lawyer. Jail? Will it be over in time to plant cotton? But he did not think at all that he had killed a human being. He put the gun back into his pocket. Marigold has just gone to take the cook home, he thought. She'll be back any minute. His blood was still pumping through his body, and he felt stronger than he had ever felt in his life. He squatted on the floor beside Floyd and, taking his wrist between alert fingers, found a strong regular pulse. Then he shoved Floyd aside and, crossing the room, jerked the cardboard carton open, and saw the machine. Without pausing for a moment, he dragged the carton across the room, down the hall, through the kitchen and out the back door. In the carport he saw a wheelbarrow, tilted the machine onto it, trundled it down the driveway, and hoisted it onto his truck.

Leave him there? he thought. Marigold. Don't want to frighten her. He went back into the house and looked at Floyd again. The wound in his shoulder oozed a little blood but the trickle from his finger was drying. There was a large knot on the side of his head. He remembered now how you should treat a patient in case of shock and he pulled a spread and blanket from the bed and covered Floyd with them. In the kitchen he found a notebook and pencil hanging on a peg by the wall telephone, tore out a page and wrote on it, "Mrs. Shotwell. Don't be alarmed, but Floyd is in his room on the floor unconscious. He is not badly hurt, I don't think. Wilburn Griffith." He put the scrap of paper in the middle of the kitchen table, and put a banana from the arrangement of wax fruit on each side of it, so that Marigold could not miss it when she came in. Then he went out again, got into his truck, and drove through town to the Hunters' cottage on Muscadine Street. I should have called a doctor, he thought. Stupid.

He parked his truck in front of the Hunters' house and got out. It was dark now, and he stumbled as he crossed the blocks of sidewalk that had been tilted by the roots of the great water oaks.

He rang the doorbell and waited a long time, hearing faint sounds from inside the house. He was filled with an overwhelming impatience. "Let's get it over with," he said aloud. "Hurry up. Hurry up." Finally he heard footsteps inside the house and Anne Farish opened the door. He looked at her blankly. "Oh," he said. "I didn't know you were in town."

"I just came this afternoon." There was a suggestion in the set of her bosom, bound tight and carried high, of the severest disapproval, and this was true in spite of the careful smile of welcome she gave him.

Wilburn sniffed the air like a wary dog. What have I done wrong? he thought, taking on without hesitation whatever guilt the air might hold. I'm bound to have done something wrong. But it wasn't wrong to go get the washing machine. He stood shivering in the doorway, feeling the downward drain of his strength, as if it might be running into his shoes, which in a few minutes would overflow and pour the best part of himself into a puddle on Miss Louise's porch.

"Come in," Anne Farish said.

Inside the house they stood and looked at each other as stiffly as strangers. She did not ask him to sit down.

What the hell's going on here, anyhow, he thought. Don't you know I'm the one who lent Aubrey the money to keep going? Then he laughed out loud at himself. I'm bucking for Pruitt's moral category.

"I beg your pardon?" Anne Farish said.

"I'm sorry, Anne Farish. I was thinking about myself. I'm a little bit nutty tonight. Is Nat here?"

"She's lying down."

"Well, I need to see her," he said.

"Wilburn, we are in the middle of a kind of family crisis here," she said. "If you could come back . . ."

"I know you're in the middle of a crisis. I couldn't be more aware of it," he said. "But I need to see Nat now. Is she in her room?"

"As I was saying, I just came in this afternoon, and I found Aunt Louise terribly upset. It seems to me, considering her age, that Nat could be a little bit more considerate of Aunt Louise's feelings." She drew herself up even tighter and nodded her head, cocking her round parakeet eyes at him. "But we'll settle all that," she said. "It would just be better — more convenient — if you came back another day."

He brushed past her and strode down the hall. "Nat?" he called. "Nat? Are you here? It's me, Wilburn." He opened her bedroom door without knocking, walked in, and closed it behind him.

She was standing in the middle of the bedroom, naked, a towel in her hand.

"Nat," he said, "why didn't you *call* me?"

She wrapped the towel around her body, sarong fashion, and retreated into the closet.

"I didn't mean to catch you naked," he said. "I was in a hurry."

She stuck her head out from behind the closet door. "That's all right, Wilburn," she said in her soft slow voice. "*I* don't mind. But you know, if you get a good look at me, you'll throw *rocks* at Sunny."

Wilburn sat down on the edge of her bed, rested his chin on his hands and began to laugh.

"You *would*," she said and came out of the closet with a robe on. She sat on the edge of the bed beside him.

"Why didn't you tell me?" he said again. "I would have done *something*."

She stared at him. Then she grinned. "You're a nosy bastard, Wilburn," she said. "How did you find out what's going on?"

"Never mind that," he said. "Why didn't you tell me?"

"You can't do anything about it, honey," she said. "This way, I'm going to get things straightened out — if Anne Farish will just keep her hat on; and then we'll be rich."

"Rich!" He took her hand in his and bowed his head over it and touched it with his lips.

"It's not so bad," she said. But as she spoke, he saw that every hair on her arm had risen as if an electric current had gone through her body.

"I've got it," he said. "It's outside in the truck."

"*What?*"

He jerked his head toward the street. "The machine," he said. "You don't need to worry anymore, Nat. You don't ever have to put your foot in the room with him again unless you want to. I've brought the damn thing back."

20

THE NEXT MORNING, when Nat arrived at Hunters' Refuge, there was a festive air about the house. It was the end of the third week in November now, and the following Thursday would be Thanksgiving. The children, to celebrate their mother's return from the hospital in Jackson, had gathered armfuls of autumn leaves — gum and red oak and the last of the yellow sassafras — and stuffed them into vases in the living room and study. A fire of cedar kindling and pecan logs was burning on the living room hearth, and Sunny, in a quilted blue robe, was lying propped on the sofa, a pile of magazines on the floor beside her and a piece of handwork in her lap. Nat did not knock, but opened the front door and came into the room, carrying her suitcase in one hand and a hatbox in the other.

"Sunny?" she said in her soft, low, questioning voice. "Hey! You're out of bed! That's great. Wilburn said you'd be kind of expecting me." She closed the front door and stood hesitantly just inside. "I hate to be a nuisance and all," she said.

Sunny dropped her work on her lap and made a gesture of welcome. "Come in, Nat," she said. "Put your things down." She raised her voice. "Sarah? Come show Miss Nat where she's going to stay and take her suitcase back for her." There was no answer from the kitchen. "She must be outside," Sunny said. "She'll be along in a minute or so. Sit down."

"No hurry," Nat said. "I can find my own way after a while." She picked up a battered doll from the wing chair opposite the sofa and, laying it on the coffee table, sat down. "I'm sorry I haven't been out to see you since you got home," she said, "but I reckon Wilburn told you things have been a little bit complicated."

"Yes, I know," Sunny said.

"And now here I am on your doorstep like a poor relation. But I won't have to stay very long, I don't think."

"You can stay as long as you need to, Nat," Sunny said. "It's all right."

"Can you stand it? And has Wilburn told you about what a hero he was and all? I know he has, or I wouldn't mention it, because I don't want to upset you. But there wasn't any way he could keep from telling you, was there? I mean, even though you don't feel so well and all. Suppose they came to take him away to jail and you didn't know a thing about it, that would be a worse shock than hearing about it from him."

Sunny nodded.

"It's all right if we talk about it, isn't it?" Nat said. "It's not going to make you get sick or throw up or anything? I know how that is, because I got so last week, I threw up practically every time the clock struck or a car drove past the house."

"Right along through here," Sunny said, "I feel like you do after you have a baby. I'm so glad it's stopped hurting, I don't believe anything could make me sick." She hesitated. "Maybe you can begin to feel like that, too, pretty soon," she said.

"Maybe," Nat said. She drew a deep breath and, stretching out her legs, cocked them up on the coffee table. "I think I'm doing better already." She got a cigarette from her purse and lit it. "Has — has the sheriff or anybody been out here yet?" she said.

Sunny shook her head. "Not yet."

"I wonder why? You know, it kind of makes me feel as if nothing that we *thought* happened really happened. I mean, between Wilburn and Floyd."

"I don't think they're coming," Sunny said.

"Who?"

"You know — the sheriff or the police or *anybody.*" Sunny picked up her handwork and ran the needle carefully back and forth through the canvas a few times and then laid it down again. "I can't work for very long at a time," she said.

"What do you mean, they're not coming? I've been — my stomach has been in a knot since last night, trying to think — I guess it really was my stomach trying to think! My head doesn't work all that well anymore — what was the best thing to do? First I thought I should talk to Floyd. (I called the hospital and they told me he'd been admitted out there.) I thought I'd go straight out and talk to him. And then, knowing how Floyd is, I decided maybe he wouldn't tell anybody how it had happened — I mean, out of sheer orneriness. He's never going to tell anybody what's happened to him or why, if he can avoid it. And then I remembered the note and that Marigold (Wilburn's note that he left on the kitchen table. Did he tell you about that?) — Marigold would know; and so then I thought maybe if I went to Marigold and told her that I would tell everybody in the world what Floyd had done to me, she'd — she'd get it hushed up somehow. Wilburn wouldn't have to go to jail or anything; and you wouldn't be mad at me, and sicker, and God knows what else you might be — I'd deserve almost anything from you. I thought I'd go to her.

Because, of course, it's *got* to come out that he was shot. That *somebody* shot him. I mean the doctor has to make a report to the police.

"But I didn't do anything. I don't know why. Except I thought, Wilburn doesn't want me to do anything. I know he doesn't and so I won't. But I'll testify. Nothing will keep me from telling the world why Wilburn shot him. Nothing."

"I don't think anything is going to happen, Nat," Sunny said. Her face was pale and considerably thinner than it had been three weeks earlier, but her voice was strong and calm.

"How can it not?" Nat said.

"It's already 'not.' Wilburn went back to the Shotwells' house last night after he left you and, of course, they were all gone. He never did see Morris. Well, when the house was empty, Wilburn assumed that they'd all gone to the hospital, so he went out there. I don't think he knew what he was going to do, Nat. He just went, he said, feeling kind of crazy and that he had to do something. Maybe give himself up or find out if he was supposed to give himself up. He's not all that familiar with what you do after you shoot somebody, I don't suppose.

"He was at the desk when Marigold came down in the elevator. He said she was as white as a clown. You know she wears that white, white makeup (Why, the Lord only knows.) and bright red lipstick. But of course Wilburn didn't think about makeup. I suppose he thought she was getting ready to faint or something. Anyhow, he went right up to her, but he said she just glanced at him and nodded — you know, like you do at acquaintances, if you have somebody in the hospital and are preoccupied and want to go away without talking to anyone — and was going out the front door when he stopped her. Called to her, and she kept right on going, as if she hadn't heard him; then he was sure she needed help, so he chased after her and actually had to grab her by the arm to make her stop. There wasn't a soul with her.

" 'I'm in a hurry, Wilburn,' she said right away before he could say a word. 'I don't mean to be rude, but I'm late — *late*. Excuse me, I'm late,' and she tried to pull away from him, but he wouldn't let go. She had on one of those tall hats she wears and it had got knocked off center, and he said her eyes were all glazed over as if she were looking at something a long way off.

" 'Didn't you get my note?' he said. 'How is Floyd? Is he all right?'

"And she said something about 'bridge' and 'river' and 'I'm late' again, and 'a long drive.' She was still trying to pull away from him and he was actually holding on to her.

"Wilburn said he knew then that she must be planning to kill herself. 'But he's going to be all right,' he told her. 'I'm *sure* he is. Calm down, Mrs. Shotwell. Haven't you talked to the doctors? Didn't they tell you he's going to be all right?' And then it struck him that of course the reason she was going to jump off the bridge was not because of Floyd's getting shot and maybe dying, but because of the *scandal*. 'Where's Mr. Shotwell?' he said. 'Don't you think you owe it to him to talk it over with him? You can't leave him to face it all by himself.'

"By this time she'd been pulling him along, trying to get loose from him, and he'd been following her and trying not to seem to be holding on to her; and they were outside the hospital. It was cold, Wilburn said, and the wind was blowing those old sycamore trees out in front of the hospital so that the branches creaked like rusty hinges. The clouds were moving fast, so that sometimes the moon would jump out and the trees would be as white as bones in the darkness. Then it would go behind a cloud and you couldn't see across the street. Marigold tried again to jerk loose from him.

She's so big — almost as tall as Wilburn, and he's five eleven — and with that hat on, she was towering over him. He said he thought to himself, my God I'm not going to be able to hang on to her, she's out of her mind."

" 'Morris?' she said. 'He's at the movies. He went to see *Anastasia*. He'll go to see anything with Ingrid Bergman in it. Of course, she's a splendid actress, it's true, but I must say I think it's shocking the way the general public has *accepted* . . .' Her voice trailed off almost as if she were talking in her sleep, he said, and then she blinked and said, 'It did win the Academy Award last year. I know it's good.'

"He couldn't think of anything to do except to keep talking," Sunny said. "He told her that she had to keep calm and get control of herself. 'Nothing is as bad as it seems at first,' he said. 'There's no reason to — I mean you mustn't *despair*. Floyd is going to be all right. And things will be different.' (You know, that's Wilburn's theme song: Things will change. Things will get better.) 'In a year or two,' he told her, 'all this will be forgotten.'

"And she looked at him as if she thought he was crazy. 'Let go of my arm, young man,' she said. 'I have a bridge engagement to keep on the other side of Old River, I have two women to pick up, and I'm already late.'

"He couldn't believe he was hearing the same thing she was saying. 'My note,' he said. 'When you got home and found Floyd, didn't you see my note on the kitchen table?'

" 'I haven't the slightest idea what you're talking about,' she said. She was looking at him very cautiously now. He had let go of her arm when she told him to and she was backing away. 'Maybe it'll be in tomorrow's mail,' she said. 'And as for Floyd, I haven't *found* him anywhere.'

"He looked up at the hospital and it was still there, looking as it always looks, like it might be supposed to be a Mediterranean villa or something. 'He *is* up there, isn't he? I mean Floyd *is* in the hospital? The doctor has seen him and everything? Is he all right?' " Sunny laughed weakly and winced. "Absurd," she said. "Absurd. But it hurts my stitches to laugh."

At this point the front door banged open and Wilburn came in, bringing a whirl of crisp November air. He opened his eyes wide at Nat and nodded; and then he threw his heavy parka on a chair and, going over to the fireplace, poked up the fire and threw on a log.

"I was telling Nat about what happened at the hospital last night," Sunny said. "About your meeting Marigold and all. But I'm a little bit tired. You finish." She lay back on the sofa, settling herself into the cushions, and closed her eyes.

Wilburn sat down. "Nothing happened," he said. "*Nothing.* Floyd didn't get shot. I didn't break into the house and take back the washing machine and I didn't leave Marigold a note. That's Marigold's version of the evening. Floyd stumbled over a humped-up corner of the rug in his room and fell and hit his head on the bed. He has a slight concussion, but he was able to drive himself to the hospital. Oh yes, I think he cut his shoulder when he fell and had to have a couple of stitches. And she was *so* surprised that I had heard about it. She just couldn't imagine where I had gotten my garbled account about his being shot. I tried to explain it to her. She's a *fine* actress, Nat. She was inching away from me as if I were a coiled rattlesnake. And she made it very very clear that if I pressed *my* explanation with anybody, they would have to send for the boys in the white suits. A pity. A fine boy like me, with a family to support."

"Oh, Wilburn," Nat said. "They'll get you. Someway, if it takes twenty years, Morris Shotwell will get you."

"I suppose Morris owns one of the doctors. Maybe he owns the whole hospital," Wilburn said. "Anyhow, somebody ate that bullet. Probably broke a tooth on it." He turned to his wife. "How are you feeling, Sunny? Everything all right?"

She nodded without opening her eyes.

"Oh, yes," he added, "Marigold said one thing — gave me one solid hint before she left for her bridge game. 'You were so kind to come and inquire about Floyd,' she said, using that careful voice you use when you think you may be talking to a nut — a dangerous nut. 'Tell *Sunny* how much we appreciate your coming,' she said. 'I hear she's been ill. You must take good care of her, Wilburn. I know you've been under a strain with her illness and everything — and just at cotton-picking time, too. But you must pull yourself together and take good care of her. I've heard that after a serious operation the least physical or emotional shock can give a person a dangerous setback.'"

In the back of the house a door slammed and they heard Sarah's voice in the kitchen singing:

> *Meetin' at the building soon be over, soon*
> *be over, soon be over.*
> *Meetin' at the building soon be over, all*
> *over this world.*
> *All over this world, my Lordy, all over this*
> *world . . .*

"Wilburn," Sunny said, "ask Sarah to show Nat her room and take her suitcase back."

"I'll take it back in a minute," Wilburn said. "No hurry." He turned to Nat. "What about you?" he said. "Are you all right?"

Nat nodded. "Things got interesting after you left last night," she said. "You know, Anne Farish already had the bit in her teeth before you arrived with the washing machine. Aunt Louise had called her yesterday afternoon and explained our *difficulties*, or as much as she could figure out of them from what Miss Caroline

Clayton (and Clakey) told her, and Anne Farish came flying right over. She knew she had to get me out of Philippi someway, and she knew she had to wait until I had gotten the model back to do it, and she knew I was broke, and she was in a quandary. Anyhow, I was expecting — more or less anything. At the time I was mainly trying to figure out how I could stall long enough to get the damn thing back before Anne Farish drove me out into the storm.

"Aunt Louise — well, you know, Wilburn, Aunt Louise is *old*. You — you forget about it, but she is; and something *happened* to me about her and Uncle Aubrey this trip. I couldn't keep myself from feeling sorry for them. I tried — I really did. But somehow they seemed — *real* to me." Her eyes filled with tears. "And helpless — as if they had never known before that the world was a jungle — that they were going to be eaten by tigers — if not today, tomorrow. I hadn't *really* ever been able to know that terrible thing about tigers either, but then, all at once I did know it — about them and myself and everybody, and . . . I suppose you and Sunny think that's ridiculous," she said. "Ridiculous. It is. I know I must be losing my mind or something. I need to go to the beach for a while." She drew a deep breath and was quiet, the tremor in her brown hands that moved Wilburn to love and pity willed into stillness. She blinked once or twice and the tears in her eyes were gone.

"But what I was going to tell you was about Anne Farish," she said. "When she realized you had solved the problem — by a *miracle* — just like that — *blam* — she went back to the kitchen and ate the biggest piece of Boston cream pie you ever saw in your life; and then she came on up to my room and we had a sensible sisterly conversation. We agreed that I would have to leave right away — if not last night then this morning. She even called Charles and got him to promise to lend me some money. You know Mr. Coleman says Jeff absolutely is going to have to come through with the alimony eventually, so this will be enough to last until he does. What she explained to me last night was not only about how embarrassing it would be for Aunt Louise to have me in Philippi now, at least until all the gossip about me and Floyd has died down, but also about her kids — Anne Farish's I mean. You know, little Anne is sixteen now, and she's supposed to make her debut year after next, and as Anne Farish explains it, the least breath of scandal and she won't be *asked.* You can imagine what a tragedy *that* would be! You know Anne Farish wants to climb to the absolute *pinnacle* of Moss Ridge society, and that's an essential stepping-stone. So — I've got to go. Besides, as she said, it's for my own safety. Who knows what Floyd will do next?" She was silent for a moment. "And who *does* know?" she said. "So that was when I called you, Wilburn, and asked if I could come out this morning."

A log broke in the fireplace and sent up a shower of sparks. Wilburn got up, carefully rearranged the remaining logs, and added another.

"The only good thing that's happened this trip," Nat said, "was meeting *The General.* I wouldn't have missed that for anything. Poor fellow, I can't bear to think about how *disappointed* he must be."

"Have you ever seen a skipjack?" Wilburn said.

"A what?"

"It's an odd kind of beetle. When it lands on its back, instead of lying there waving its legs in the air like most other beetles do, it has a little mechanism like a spring that it releases, and it flips right over on its legs and flies off."

Wilburn and Sunny's little boy, Billy, came into the room, wandered over to the fireplace with a pack of cards in his hand, and, sitting down in front of the fire, began to build a card house. In a few minutes it was three stories high. He added card after card with delicate precision.

In the kitchen they could still hear Sarah singing:

> *Moaning at the building soon be over, soon*
>   *be over, soon be over.*
> *Moaning at the building soon be over, all*
>   *over this world.*
> *All over this world, my Lordy, all over this*
>   *world.*
> *All over this world, my Lordy, all over this*
>   *world.*

"Maybe I can come back for a visit after Anne has made her debut," Nat said. "By that time the scandal of my sexual aberrations will have died down. Who knows, maybe Miss Caroline Clayton will have dried up and blown away. Sunny?"

Sunny opened her eyes. "Yes," she said.

"Aunt Louise sent you a caramel cake. It's over there in the hatbox. She cried when we broke the news to her that I was leaving; and when I said I was going to stop by to see you all on the way out of town, she said she would just send it to you. It was still warm — right out of the oven. And Wilburn, Aubrey said for me to tell you to come look at the sketches he's made for something that goes on a cotton picker — a new kind of ret bar. Do you know what he's talking about? Maybe, he says, you'd like to go in on it with him. Your share could pay back what we owe you, if it turns out to be a success. Or, if it doesn't . . ."

"Never mind, never mind," Wilburn said. "We'll work something out."

"There's no hurry, Nat," Sunny said. "You can stay here awhile, and we won't let a single soul know you haven't left. Your Aunt Louise and everybody can think you're gone. I don't want you to rush off without even thinking about what you're going to do or where you're going to settle."

"You mean you'd *conceal* me?" Nat said. "Wouldn't that be exciting? Bring me my meals in secret and all — just like the crazy wife in *Jane Eyre!* You're a wonder, Sunny — loyal to the bone, as Aunt Louise would put it. But Sarah would never let you get away with it. Every colored person in Okatukla County would know I was here within twenty-four hours. And anyhow, I think I already know what I want to do. You know, Mary Mimms and Jay Stanley (Do you remember the party where we met them in Jackson, or were you too sick to take it in?) invited me to come out to California and I'm going to call them long distance tonight and, if they still want me, I'm going out there for a visit. They're right on the beach. And something is sure to turn up in California. You know, something always turns up in California. Maybe I can even put down some *roots* out there. Who knows?" Nat took her feet from the coffee table, sat up straight, turned slightly sideways in her chair, crossed her legs at the ankles, and shook back her shining black hair. Then she grinned at them. "Do you suppose I might break into the movies?" she said.

• • •

Nat has been back to Philippi two or three times since that disastrous visit in 1957. But she waited to come until after Anne Taliaferro had safely made her debut. She spends most of her time on the West Coast now. She's gotten several walk-on parts, in crowd scenes in movies, that have kept her going during the occasional periods when Jeff doesn't come through with her alimony. She has made a great many friends in Hollywood and, when times are particularly rough, somebody will always put her up for a week — or a month. She's always good company — if she keeps the drinking under control and doesn't set fire to the house. But when she does come to Philippi, Nat never stays long. Her visits make Miss Louise nervous and, after a few days, after she sees that everything is under control and spends an evening or two with Wilburn and Sunny, Nat takes off again.

Charles Taliaferro must have realized, after the washing machine disaster, that it was necessary, and might even be profitable, for him to take a hand in his wife's family's affairs, and he did manage in the long run, with the help of the patent lawyer, to get Aubrey some money for the patent rights to the washing machine — not that anybody ever manufactured it. Morris Shotwell's friend, the obsolescence expert, must have been right in his theory on that subject. It was *too* good.

Lately, people in Philippi hear more and more frequently that Anne Farish is planning to put the two old people in a nursing home in Greenwood. Clakey has retired, and every year it is more difficult to get reliable help — particularly the kind of old-fashioned cook who will put up with the Hunters. They're getting more crotchety all the time, and so feeble now that they're a constant source of worry to Anne Farish.

And who knows what kind of trouble Nat will make if Anne Farish does decide to put Louise and Aubrey away? She never has liked to think about being shut up in little bitty places — with no way to get out.

$\mathcal{V}$OICES OF THE $\mathcal{S}$OUTH